The

EVER

AFTER

Amanda Hocking lives in Minnesota, had never sold a book before April 2010 and has now sold her millionth. She is 'the most spectacular example of an author striking gold through ebooks', according to the *Observer*. In her own words, Amanda is an obsessive tweeter, John Hughes mourner, Batman devotee, Muppets activist and unicorn enthusiast. Her books include the Trylle trilogy, the Kanin Chronicles, the Watersong series, the Valkyrie duology and the Omte Origins trilogy.

D1321519

By Amanda Hocking

Freeks

The Trylle trilogy
Switched
Torn
Ascend
Trylle: The Complete Trilogy

The Watersong series
Wake
Lullaby
Tidal
Elegy

The Kanin Chronicles
Frostfire
Ice Kissed
Crystal Kingdom
Kanin: The Complete Chronicles

The Valkyrie duology
Between the Blade and the Heart
From the Earth to the Shadows

The Omte Origins trilogy
The Lost City
The Morning Flower
The Ever After

The
EVER
AFTER

Omte Origins Book Three

Amanda Hocking

PAN BOOKS

First published 2021 by Wednesday Books
an imprint of St. Martin's Publishing Group

First published in the UK 2021 by Pan Books
an imprint of Pan Macmillan
The Smithson, 6 Briset Street, London EC1M 5NR
Associated companies throughout the world
www.panmacmillan.com

ISBN 978-1-5290-0134-1

1 3 5 7 9 8 6 4 2

A CIP catalogue record for this book is available from the British Library.

Printed and bound by CPI Group (UK) Ltd, Croydon, CR0 4YY

Visit **www.panmacmillan.com** to read more about all our books
and to buy them. You will also find features, author interviews and
news of any author events, and you can sign up for e-newsletters
so that you're always first to hear about our new releases.

The
EVER
AFTER

1

✤

in the Air

Every night, I dream of an endless sky the color of a summer grapefruit, luminous and bright thanks to the three suns, and every morning, I wake up in a dank prison cell. I opened my eyes, expecting the same dark stone ceiling barely six feet above me, the same way I had for the past . . . *alai*, how long had it been?

But as I blinked my eyes, adjusting to the bright sunlight, and I saw the rows of people in navy blue seats, confusion and adrenaline surged through me like a nauseating electricity. I wasn't in a prison cell in . . . wherever I'd been.

I reached over the passenger beside me, an old woman who snorted in irritation as I pushed open the tiny window shade. Below us was nothing but the vast blue ocean.

"We don't reach land for another three hours," she said huffily, and I muttered a thanks before closing the shade and leaning back in my seat.

In the back of the seat in front of me, a rumpled plane ticket had been shoved into the pocket, and I pulled it out. The name *Emily Miller* on top was the name I traveled under, with the fake documents that the Mimirin provided. The flight was going to Minneapolis, Minnesota, which was some relief because at least I was going home.

But how the hell had I gotten here?

I closed my eyes and tried to focus on the last thing I remembered. There were flashes of things, foggy images of a prison cell. And a young woman—pale with cobalt and white makeup painted across her eyes in thick lines like war paint—glaring at me with anger darkening her face. And an albino woolly elk, and a haunting choir singing about a morning flower.

Those were all vague and disconnected from each other, more impressions than true memories. I could remember *fear* but not what I had been afraid of.

The last thing I clearly remembered was . . . kissing Pan. In a hotel room, on the island city of Isarna.

So I kissed him, and I felt his restraint crumble. His hand was on my side, pressing into the soft flesh beneath my shirt, and he pushed me against the window. I wrapped my arms around him, kissing him deeply.

And then someone had interrupted. Had it been Dagny? Or was it Noomi?

Noomi. My half-sister.

My stomach rolled. She'd been so angry, but I couldn't remember why.

Everything until Isarna I could still remember clearly. The four of us—my flatmate Dagny Kasten, her professor Elof Dómari, head researcher Pan Soriano, and myself—had gone to Sweden as ambassadors for the Mimirin—a respected troll library and institution of higher learning. We were on a mission to find the First City, my missing amnesiac friend Eliana, and my father. We had gotten so close.

But then it all disappeared into nothing. I couldn't make sense of the glimpses I remembered.

I sat up straighter in my seat and looked around the cabin of the plane. I hadn't gone to Isarna alone. When I tried to stand up, the seat belt pinched at my waist, so I unbuckled it and stood up too fast and banged my head on the overhead bin.

The man in the aisle seat got up, mistakenly thinking I was heading to the bathroom. But since he suggested it, it sounded like a good idea. The plane ticket was still balled up in my hand, and I surveyed the passengers as I walked down the aisle but didn't recognize any of them.

In the tiny mirror above the even tinier sink, I saw my reflection for the first time in . . . in I had no idea how long. Above my left eye, the larger of my eyes, was a fresh bluish splotch of a bruise, but my face was pale and sallow. My tangles of dirty blond hair were pulled up in an especially messy bun.

And I finally looked down at the outfit I had on. A large gray sweater featuring a smiling cartoon moose under the phrase *Glad Älg,* two sizes too big for me, and indigo linen pants that were uncomfortably snug in the thighs and hips. These clothes weren't mine.

I leaned back against the door and uncrumpled the ticket, looking for more clues about what was happening. The destination was the airport in Minnesota, which could explain why Pan, Dagny, and Elof weren't on the same flight as me. They were probably going to Oregon, back to the Mimirin.

But why wasn't I going back to the Mimirin too? Förening in Minnesota was my home, basically, where I'd lived before I left for my internship in June. But I had been renting an apartment in Merellä since then, and all my things were there.

Had I been kicked out of the Mimirin institution, or even the city of Merellä? And if I was, what of everyone else? Had

Pan been sent to Ottawa, Elof to Ondarike, Dagny to Ningrava?

Then I finally noticed the date at the top of the ticket. 8 AUGUST 2019.

That couldn't be right. We flew out of the States on the Fourth of July. I remembered watching the fireworks from the plane, and I could only account for a few days after that. That meant I was missing weeks.

A month of my life was just . . . *gone.*

I put my hand over my mouth to hold back the frightened sob that wanted to escape. I squeezed my eyes—

My mind instantly went to Pan, lying in a dark room, blood all over the floor. He gave me a hazy smile and told me, "I would follow you anywhere, and it's worth whatever risk there is."

—then I opened my eyes and took a deep breath. Freaking out in a cramped airplane bathroom wouldn't help me or anyone else, no matter how badly I wanted to.

I splashed cold water on my face, and when I left the bathroom, I went straight to find a flight attendant.

She was a middle-aged woman with dyed bright red hair and kind eyes, and her name tag said *Kirsten.* She listened politely and answered my questions, even when they bordered on the ridiculous. Like "What day is it?" and "Are you sure that's the correct date?"

When I asked, "Did you see me get on the plane with anyone else?" that's when her expression changed to concern.

"Are you in trouble?" she asked me quietly, her kind eyes studying me. "Did you board the plane against your will?"

Maybe. Probably. I have no idea.

"Um, no." I shook my head and forced a smile. The last thing I needed was a human police force getting involved, especially with their highly sensitive airport security. "Just really jet-lagged." I laughed, a brittle sound that didn't help at all. "Can I get a ginger ale?"

She sent me back to my seat with a plastic cup of soda, and she kept an eye on me the rest of the flight. I sipped the soda, ignoring the queasy feeling it gave me in my stomach. When Kirsten the flight attendant was busy elsewhere, I slid out of the seat and checked my overhead bin for my duffel bag, but it was empty of any recognizable luggage.

I hadn't been able to find anything around the seat, besides the crumpled ticket, and I had my fake "Emily Miller" passport in my pocket. That was all I had on me. I was traveling across the ocean with no cell phone, no money, no one I knew, nothing. And I had no idea what was waiting for me on the other side.

2

hostage

The hyper-surveillance in airports made me uneasy, so I wanted to get out of there as fast as possible. But I couldn't give up on the hope that there was something waiting for me in baggage claim.

As I waited, I chewed my lip and tried to come up with a plan if I was stranded alone in a large human metropolis. Then, as I tried to remember if pay phones were still a thing in the human world, I heard a familiar voice saying my name.

I turned around to see Finn Holmes standing there, and I was so relieved I burst into tears. I ran over to him and threw my arms around his neck, and he hugged me back.

"You're home now, Ulla," he reassured me in his warm, rumbling voice.

"What are you doing here?" I asked when I finally released him, and I wiped at my eyes with the long sleeves of my sweatshirt.

His eyebrows pinched together, and his eyes filled with concerned confusion. "You asked me to pick you up here. We spoke on the phone a few days ago."

"What?" I shook my head in dismay.

"We were negotiating your release for weeks." Finn put his hands on my shoulders, warm and comforting, and he bent slightly so he could look me in the eye. "You were held hostage by the Älvolk."

Fresh tears sprang into my eyes. "I don't—"

—an image flashed in my mind: Noomi glaring down at me, and a tall man looming behind her.

A painful bolt of lightning shot through my brain, and the image dissolved to Eliana. She wore a long white dress and stood in front of a raging waterfall—

"I don't remember," I stammered. "It's only bits and pieces. I don't know where I've been for the past month."

"Okay, it's okay." Finn put his arm around me. "We'll figure this out together. The important thing is that you're home now."

The baggage carousel let out an angry alarm announcing the incoming luggage, and I nearly jumped out of my skin. A moment later, my battered old duffel bag tumbled out on the conveyor belt, and I ran to grab it, as if someone else would run and snatch it before I had the chance.

Even though I really wanted to open my bag and dig through it right then and there, to see what of my possessions I still had, it didn't seem like a good idea around so many humans.

I didn't even really feel comfortable being around them at all, so I grabbed my bag and followed Finn out to his car without really saying much. I sat stoically in the passenger side of the Jeep until we were out of the airport completely, and on an open stretch of highway.

"What about my friends?" I asked finally. "Were they released too?"

"It's my understanding that Dagny Kasten, Elof Dómari,

and Panuk Soriano were released back to the Mimirin at the same time you were released back to Förening," Finn said.

I let out a sigh of relief and rested my head back against the seat rest. "How come I'm here and not in Merellä?"

"It was a condition of your release," he explained. "You were not to return to the Mimirin."

I looked sharply at him. "What? Why not?" I suddenly flashed on Noomi, glowering at me, and Indu, his weathered face and unrelenting smirk. "Who made the demands?"

"Wendy did most of the negotiating," he said, referring to the Trylle Queen and his friend. "Along with the head of the Mimirin, the Korva, Ragnall Jerrick."

I'd met with Ragnall once, shortly before we'd left for Sweden. I had wanted to go to find Eliana and my father, but the Mimirin officials had gotten excited about the potential. I had formed relationships with Eliana, Jem-Kruk, and my father, Indu Mattison, who all had ties to the First City and the Älvolk that resided within. Because of this, Mästare Amalie had appointed us ambassadors to visit the First City and find out all that we could about the secretive kingdom.

Not that I had any place to complain. If Ragnall and Amalie hadn't taken an interest in our trip, we never would've been able to go. The Mimirin funded the entire trip, with Amalie calling it an expedition for our heritage.

"But who did they negotiate with?" I pressed.

Finn had one hand on the steering wheel, and he kept his eyes on the road as he spoke. "I know they were in contact with Patrik Boden. He's the one in direct contact with the Älvolk leaders."

Patrik was the Markis Ansvarig in Isarna, the troll island where we'd been staying while we looked for Áibmoráigi, the First City. We'd only been there a few days when—

—the memories cut to black. I remembered being at the Isarna city hall, admiring their collection of artifacts, and Patrik had been explaining things. But then it was like the world stopped mid-sentence. It was all black, and my head throbbed painfully when I tried to remember more.

"Who were the Älvolk leaders?" I asked Finn, and rubbed my temple in a vain attempt to relieve my growing headache. "Was it Indu? Indu Mattison?"

I could see his face—weathered olive skin, black hair going silver at the temples, dark eyes scrutinizing me, and his constant smirk. And then it was gone.

I could hardly remember the face of my father.

"I don't know," Finn said.

"What about Noomi Indudottir?" I closed my eyes, trying to remember the other name. There had been someone else, another girl with jet-black hair and paint across her eyes. "Tuva? Did you hear anything about Noomi or Tuva?"

He shook his head. "I don't think I heard their names."

"How did you know the Älvolk had me? Like, how did anybody find out we were in trouble?"

"The docent with you, Professor Elof Dómari, set up a dead man's switch," Finn explained. "He'd instructed Patrik to contact the Mimirin if they didn't hear from you within seventy-two hours. When that time passed, Patrik contacted Ragnall, and then Ragnall called Wendy. They began the negotiations, and Wendy let me know what was going on."

"So the negotiations lasted nearly a month?" I asked.

"It is my understanding that the Älvolk were difficult to reach and changed their demands several times, and that really prolonged the process," Finn said. "But we wanted you home as soon as possible."

"I know," I said. "I'm just . . . missing a whole month of my life."

"What's the last thing you remember?" Finn asked carefully.

A series of hazy images ran through my mind—the city hall in Isarna with a jeweled fox skeleton on display, kissing Pan in the hotel room, and Noomi watching me as an all-girls' choir sang a haunting hymn in a language I didn't completely understand.

"The last thing I remember clearly is arriving in Isarna." I shook my head. "Then it's all a blur."

"When we get back to Förening, I'll get in touch with the healers I know," Finn said, keeping his voice hard, to hide the worry underneath. "I already let them know that you might need them today. I wasn't sure what condition you'd be in. There might be a way that they could bring your memories back."

I unbuckled my seat belt so I could reach into the back seat and open my bag. It was too big to haul into the front, not without impacting Finn's ability to drive, so I started rummaging through it.

"Ulla, you can't hang over the seat like that," he told me firmly. "It's not safe."

So naturally, I clambered back, practically falling on my head and kicking the ceiling before I managed to safely right myself.

"That's not what I meant," he muttered, then louder, "Put your seat belt on."

I did, then immediately returned to my search of the bag. It was mostly full of my dirty clothes, and they were actually mine, unlike the ill-fitting outfit I'd woken up in on the plane. Why had I been in that when I had plenty of my own stuff?

And then I felt it. The thin, cold rectangle of my cell phone. I made an excited squawk. It was dead but my charger was tangled in a bralette. Once I got it separated, Finn plugged my phone into the dash to charge.

While I waited for that, I went back to rummaging through my things. At the very bottom of the bag, I found a book. *Jem-Kruk and the Adlrivellir.* I flipped through it, but the book fell open to the last page.

And there, in my own handwriting, I'd scrawled important messages to myself.

Senka is your mother, Indu is your father
Don't Trust Noomi or Illaria
They're Your Sisters but they LIE
Áibmoráigi is on the northwest mountain beyond
  Lake Sodalen
The Lady in the Long White Dress is a waterfall
Find the waterfall, find Eliana
Jem-Kruk might be a liar
You and Pan kissed (and you both liked it)
Johan (Hanna's grandfather) knows the truth about
  Senka & Jem-Kruk

And then below all that, in big angry letters:

IT'S ALL ABOUT THE BLOOD!

3

Return

The Jeep had hardly rolled to a stop, and I heard Hanna scream as she rushed out the front door. The younger kids followed close behind her—seven-year-old Liam, four-and-a-half-year-old Emma, and three-year-old Niko toddling after—all of them running up the grassy embankment to greet me.

As the kids descended upon me—Emma jumped, boldly but correctly assuming I'd catch her—Mia came out of the house more slowly, because she was wrangling the twenty-two-month-old twins. Luna was fussing, pulling at her dark curly pigtails, even with Mia carrying her on her hip, and Lissa held her hand as she took slow, uncertain steps.

Their house was a large peridot green cottage, surrounded by the big full branches of towering oak, maple, and pine trees, along the thick forest of the bluffs along the Mississippi River. I'd nearly forgotten how beautiful it was here, and how good it felt to be home.

"What happened? Where have you been? Did you see Eliana?" Hanna peppered me with questions the second she let me go, and the other kids followed suit, lobbing their own barrage of inquiries at me.

"Were you working? Will you live with us again?" Emma asked, her voice high-pitched and insistent.

"Why do you look weird? Are you sick? I look weird when I'm sick sometimes," Liam said knowingly.

"Ulla, Ulla!" Niko shouted, followed by demanding babble I couldn't understand. He held his pudgy hands to me until I scooped him up.

"Give her space," Mia commanded, and Finn took the twins from her so she could give me a proper hello. She pulled me into a side hug, since my arms were full of Niko. "Welcome home, Ulla."

We all went into the house, and I let the kids interrogate me. They didn't believe me at first when I told them I couldn't remember what happened, but once they were convinced, they grew bored fairly quickly because all my answers were "I don't know."

I sat at the kitchen table, sipping sun tea and hungrily devouring the mulberry tarts Hanna had made. Finn asked his mother to take the younger kids upstairs to play, so it was only Mia, Hanna, and myself sitting around the large farm table.

"What's going on?" Mia asked, eyeing her husband.

Finn came back from helping herd the children up the stairs, and he took the Jem-Kruk book from my bag. "I don't know, but it's definitely odd." He set the book on the table and slid it across, toward Hanna and Mia.

"Why do you have Grandpa Johan's book?" Hanna asked, wrinkling her nose.

Mia looked just as confused, and she touched the cover tentatively. "Where did you get this?"

"From the Mimirin," I said. "I'm borrowing it, technically." So far, I'd just stolen it and defaced it, but that wasn't the kind of example I wanted to set for Hanna, so I modified the truth.

Finn sat down beside me and asked them, "What do you know about this?"

"Not much." Mia flipped through the first few pages absently, her brow furrow deepening, and she shook her head. "Nikolas's—" She stopped, her eyes flitting to me. "Hanna's—" She stumbled again, now looking to Finn.

"Nikolas's father wrote children's books," she started again, and this time it went more smoothly. "He published a few of them, but all of that was when Nikolas was very young. By the time I was dating Nikolas, Johan hadn't written in years and years, and he'd put that all behind him."

She looked at me and Finn. "Why are you asking about it?"

"Because it's just like I said!" Hanna announced excitedly. "This book is about Eliana!"

"Maybe," I allowed. "But there are some things that correlate to real life in unusual ways."

"What do you mean?" Mia asked.

"I think I've met Jem-Kruk," I said, filling her in on all the things I'd told Finn on the car ride home. "And Senka—Jem-Kruk's friend mentioned in the book—may be my mother."

"Wait." Hanna's big brown eyes widened. "Are you saying that your mom is related to my father? Does that make us cousins?"

"No," I told her definitively before she got carried away. "No, I haven't read anything that suggests that. But it does seem like your grandfather might know something."

"What about Eliana? I was reading the book, because there were things that matched up. Like the grapefruit pink sky, the suns called Kyr, Nuk, and Veli, and the dragon reference," Hanna said without taking a breath. "There's probably even more, but she didn't remember much—" She gasped. "Do you think that what happened to you is the same thing that happened to Eliana? Like with her amnesia?"

"I—I don't know," I admitted. "Maybe, but she had forgotten her entire life. I'm only missing the past month."

"I bet it's the same," Hanna said firmly.

All the while Hanna and I had been talking, Mia had been leaning back in the chair, her arms folded over her chest, and her lips pressed into a tight line that only grew tighter.

"I'm sorry, but I'm having a hard time understanding," she said. "Nikolas has been gone for a long time. What could he possibly have to do with—with—" She waved a hand in frustration. "With your imprisonment, and my daughter's elusive pixie friend?"

Mia took a deep breath and the severity of her expression relaxed slightly. "This all seems strange and . . . overwhelming. For me."

Upstairs, Liam let out an angry yell, which was followed by Emma screaming.

"Hanna, why don't you go upstairs and help Grandma Annali with the kids?" Finn suggested. She rolled her eyes, but she complied.

Once Hanna had gone, Finn looked to his wife and apologized. "I'm sorry. I didn't realize this would be upsetting to you. I wasn't thinking."

"No, it's fine." She shook her head. "How is this all connected?"

"I think the place in the book is real, and that Johan has been there," I said. "And I think it's where my mother and Eliana are from."

"He never mentioned anything like that," Mia said. "Johan and Sarina had lived in Eftershom since before Nikolas was

born. They never even talked about living anywhere else."
She paused, thinking. "At an anniversary party once, Sarina
did say something about them moving into their house right
before the big thunder snowstorm.

"Not much happened in Eftershom, so everyone talked
about the big thunder snowstorm that happened two years
before I was born," Mia said. "So that was 1989."

"That was before the book was published," Finn said. "At
least, according to the publication date on the back page."

"He wrote that book *for* Nikolas, when he was still a
baby," Mia explained. "So he had to have published it from
Eftershom. But by the time I started dating Nikolas, we were
teenagers. We didn't want to talk about fairy tales or his father."

She looked out the window, watching pensively as the
branches of a weeping willow swayed in the breeze.

"I just haven't thought about any of this in such a long
time," she said finally, still staring off. "I can reach out to Johan. Obviously, he'll know more about his own life than I do."

Finn got up and went around the table to sit beside her, and
he put his hand on her arm. "Are you okay?"

She nodded and wiped at her eyes. "I don't know why,
thinking of Nikolas just . . ." She managed a sad smile and
pushed her chair back. "I just need a moment."

Mia went into another room, and Finn waited a beat before going after her. I knew that she loved Finn and their
children and their life together, but she had also loved Nikolas. She didn't talk to me about her first marriage much, but I
knew they'd both been young and in love. Mia had only been
nineteen when she became a widow, and Hanna was still in
diapers.

It was nearly ten years ago, when the Trylle and Vittra were
at odds, gearing up for what would be known as the War for

the Princess. It officially kicked off when the Vittra attacked the sleepy Trylle village of Oslinna, where Mia, Nikolas, and Hanna were living at the time. Hobgoblins with supernatural strength snuck in during the middle of the night and completely decimated the town.

Mia said once that it looked like a tornado had gone through afterward, with houses completely flattened. Nikolas was killed trying to protect Mia and Hanna.

While Finn was off comforting Mia, I reached across the table and pulled Johan's book back over to me. I flipped through it, scanning the worn paper, until I spotted a passage underlined in bold ink.

"A bird will fall in love with a magi but where will they hatch their egg?" Senka asked sadly.

I turned through more pages, searching for other underlined passages, and I finally found another, thirty-three pages later.

The suns set in the green sky when the good morning becomes the violent night.

And then another twenty-one pages later, a similar message underlined:

"Remember the words of the *häxdoktor*—the suns will set in the green sky when the good morning becomes the violent night," Jo-Huk warned his brother.

The final lines I found underlined were at the very end of the book, in the unsigned acknowledgments. There were only three sentences, brief but impactful.

Some stories demand to be told, and this was one of them. I thank my family for allowing me the time to take my hand at telling it. All of this was written before, and no doubt it will be again.

Finn's cell phone rang from the other room, a shrill tone loud enough to easily be heard over the sound of screaming children if need be. A few minutes later, he came into the kitchen with a hopeful smile.

"That was my friend, the one that might be able to help you recover your memory," he said. "They can meet you at the palace right now, if you're up for it."

I nodded. "Yeah. I'm ready to remember everything."

4

exchanged

Finn and I waited in the parlor, and I was happy that I'd changed out of my ill-fitting attire into a much more presentable crocheted romper. I had been to a few events at the palace—ancillary invites, thanks to Finn—but those had all been in grand ballrooms crowded with other guests. This was my first time in the smaller, more private but still luxe areas of the Queen's residence.

The Trylle palace was the most modern I had seen, an opulent white mansion near the top of the bluffs with plenty of windows to make the most of the lush view of thick forests and a wide river.

The parlor was in the corner of the palace, with the two outer walls made entirely of glass. The wallpaper was cream colored with a subtle shine accentuating a pale green vine pattern. Books lined the shelves on one wall, and on the other, above a marble fireplace, was a painting of a stunning young woman, sitting in a garden.

We waited, Finn poised and still, one leg crossed over the other as he sat on the settee. I sat across from him, literally on the edge of my seat. I had an irrational fear that the delicately carved legs and embroidered satin would collapse under me, like it was made of matchsticks.

"Who are we meeting?" I asked as I watched the hands tick slowly on the bronze grandfather clock behind Finn. Before we'd left, all he had told me was that it was a mutual friend of the Queen's, and she wanted to meet with us too.

"Tove Kroner," Finn said. "You've met him before."

I had, but only a handful of times, and he'd hardly spoken to me. The few times he came by the house, I was usually busy with the kids, and he generally seemed very soft-spoken. What I knew of him was that he was an advisor to the Queen, and he'd married the Chancellor Bain Ottesen several years ago.

"He can help recover memories?" I asked in surprise.

The kids talked a lot about all the cool telekinetic abilities he had, and I had personally seen him make the kids "fly" by lifting them in the air with his powers at Liam's birthday party last year. But I'd never heard he was capable of something like this.

Many trolls had the ability of persuasion—a telekinetic power to get someone to do something using only their thoughts. Basically, a mild form of mind control.

Finn had attempted to use it on me earlier today, at my request, by thinking *Remember the last twenty-four hours*, but it had been completely ineffective. So I couldn't imagine that he'd brought me here for Tove to try that, but I didn't think that Tove flying me around the room would help either.

"No, he'll be here as support mainly," Finn said. "His younger sister Sunniva has a unique set of abilities. Their mother is a great healer, and Sunniva's inherited some of her skills. Both Tove and Sunniva can see auras, but she can also heal them."

"She can *heal* auras?" I shook my head in confusion.

I didn't understand what that meant or how it could

recover my memories. Admittedly, I didn't know much about auras, just their general definition. Auras were the luminous radiation that surrounded all living beings, emanating from within, and their coloration could give indications about someone's health, mood, even true intentions.

But auras weren't visible to everyone, and since I couldn't see them, I didn't study them.

"Auras appear to be light floating around you, but they're really a part of you," Finn explained. "But they also can work like a road map, darkening in the areas you're hurting or need help. Sunniva's had some success with working on those dark spots to ease psychological trauma and pain."

"I don't think my memory loss is due to trauma, though. I left myself notes in preparation for it, so I knew it was coming. It had to have been a spell or some type of troll ability."

"I presumed as much, so I told Tove the same," Finn said. "He still thinks he and Sunniva might be able to help you."

A minute later, the door to the parlor opened, and the Queen strode in. It was the first time I had seen Wendy without her entourage.

But here she was, on her own and stripped of her usual pageantry. Her long curls hung down her back, free of her crown, and she'd left off most of her jewels. She was in her late twenties, with a stark silver lock of hair contrasting with her otherwise dark brown hair, and she had friendly eyes and a cool, anxious smile.

I got to my feet the moment she opened the door, but Finn still beat me. Wendy went to him first, giving him a cordial hug while offering apologies. "I'm so sorry to keep you waiting. Tove and Sunniva are on their way."

"No apology necessary," he assured her. "You've already done so much. I'm only sorry that I need to keep imposing on you."

"Finn, it's no imposition, and you know that," she said, then turned to me. "Ulla, it's so good to see you after the ordeal you've had." She dismissed my curtsey with a wave of her hand and motioned for me to sit down beside her on the settee.

"I'm all right, all things considered," I said.

"Good." She smiled. "We were all so worried about you here."

"Thank you. I appreciate all you've done to help."

"You are a citizen of the Trylle kingdom, and it's my duty to protect you," she said. "Your family are among my oldest friends. There was no choice between your life and a flowering plant."

". . . what?" I asked.

"That's what we traded," she elaborated. "The mourning flower."

"What?" I repeated. "What are you talking about?"

"I'm not sure how much you remember." She glanced to Finn, and he gave a small shrug before she looked back at me. "We negotiated through Patrik Boden in Isarna, who was talking with the leader of a radicalized tribe called the Älvolk. Most of the time, he only sent lengthy screeds about his beliefs with no real discussion at all.

"But eventually, the only thing they demanded was the *sorgblomma,* more poetically known as the mourning flower," she went on.

"I thought that was just made up," I admitted.

Emma had a book called *Sunny Plants for Funny Kids,* and it had everything from Venus flytraps to Tolkien's fictional Ents. I'd assumed that a globeflower with the Latin name *trollius funus* was a myth like some of the others.

If the illustrations were accurate, it was an arctic bush with large peony-like flowers. The petals were mostly a bold yellow-gold but they became a vivid red near the stem. The stem itself was filled with a viscous, aloe-like substance that "bled" out if the thorns were broken off.

The most notable thing about the flower—and where its name came from—was that it smelled like death. Sickly sweet and musty with floral undertones.

"The mourning flower is real, but the only known plants have been solely in my family's possession for generations," Wendy said.

"What does it do? Why do they want it?" I asked.

"We're not sure," the Queen admitted with a surreptitious glance toward Finn. "We're hoping that your recovered memories could shed some light."

I swallowed hard. "I don't know if I'll be able to help."

"Don't worry." Finn leaned forward and rested his arms on his knees. "You're here, and you're safe, and your only focus is on getting better."

"I'm just trying to wrap my head around the fact that I was exchanged for . . . flowers," I said. "What about the others? Were the flowers ransom enough for all of us, or were they traded for something else?"

"It was a package deal—all of the plants for all four of you." Wendy hesitated slightly before continuing. "That's part of the reason that the negotiations took as long as they did. We needed time to be sure that the *sorgblomma* doesn't have any dangerous applications."

Finn made a sound—a subtle grunt of disagreement—and she frowned.

"We all value your lives, but I had to be sure that I wasn't handing a radical cult a weapon of destruction," she said, then softer, more empathetic: "I'm sorry for any suffering you endured, but it is my duty to keep the kingdom safe."

"So what were the applications of the flower?" I asked.

"The nectar in the stem can be used to flavor tea, but it

leaves a bitter taste and even a spoonful can lead to stomach upset," she said with a sigh. "We couldn't find anything more serious than that. Markis Ansvarig Patrik asked the Älvolk what they wanted the flowers for, but the only answer he got was their insistence that the flowers always belonged to them. Indu claimed—"

"Indu?" I asked, startled to hear her saying his name.

"Indu Mattison, one of the leaders of the Älvolk cult," she said. "You remember him?"

"Sorta. Not really. He's . . . he's my father," I said, but the words felt cold on my tongue.

Her eyes widened. "He never mentioned that." Then she looked to Finn. "Neither did you."

"I only just found out today," he told her.

"It's one of the last things I remember clearly," I said. "We met in Isarna a month ago."

"So he held his daughter hostage in exchange for a flower and tea flavoring." Her brow furrowed, and her lips pressed together, and I realized this was the first time I'd seen the Queen worried.

5

aural

The wood floor felt cold and hard against my back, and a stiff satin pillow was beneath my head. Tove Kroner crouched beside me, carefully laying a damp washcloth across my forehead. His dark hair fell into his eyes, and he brushed it back while glancing up at his sister as she circled us.

Both Tove and Sunniva had said that this would go smoother without unnecessary auras, so Wendy and Finn had left us alone, rather reluctantly on Finn's part. We'd had a brief introduction—Sunniva didn't look much like Tove (she was a small bird of a girl with wide dark eyes and her hair pulled back into a tight braid, he a tall willow with wild hair silvering at the temples and eyes of mossy green), but they were nearly identical in mannerisms.

Their eyes were always darting around, and they took quick, faltering steps, as if they were always changing their minds about where to go. But they stood tall, shoulders back and heads held high, so they came across as confident but distracted, giving them a strange air of being lost and arrogant.

"Are you ready?" Tove asked, but he kept glancing back

and forth between me and his sister, so I wasn't sure who he was asking.

"I think so," I said uncertainly.

Sunniva didn't answer, and instead, she grabbed a nearby end table. It was a circle of green marble, supported by bronze legs shaped like twisting ivy, and she pushed it toward me, unmindful of the legs scraping against the parquet floor.

I craned my head up, watching as she stopped at my feet. She climbed up onto the table, her bare feet on the emerald stone, and looked down at me.

"Her halo is so dark," she said, and exhaled roughly through her teeth. "Like there's a storm just above her head."

Outside, thunder clapped, as if she had summoned it, and honestly, I couldn't say for sure that she hadn't.

"What does that mean?" I asked.

"Usually, your aura is lemon yellow, clear and bright," Tove answered carefully. "Right now it's . . . it's flickering between murky gray and dark orange, with a black cloud around your head and dark particles floating around you."

"And that means I have my work cut out for me," Sunniva simplified. "Lie back, stay still. You'll feel better if you close your eyes. This shouldn't hurt too much, but if it does, tell Tove."

My mouth had gone dry, but I managed to say, "Okay."

She pushed the sleeves of her mint-colored blouse up to her elbows, and when she held her hands toward me, her gold bangles clinked together.

"Close your eyes," she commanded tersely, so I did, and thunder rumbled loud enough to shake the room. "What's the last thing you remember?"

"I was in Isarna–"

"You don't need to say it," she said, cutting me off. "Just hold it in your mind."

Riding in the carriage, pulled by Tralla horses on the island of Isarna, the museum in Öhaus with the bedazzled fox skull, kissing Pan in my hotel room, the lined face of Indu as he told me that he was my father—

—and then it was pain cracking through my skull, and I cried out. I flinched, unable to stop myself, and the pain subsided.

"I told you to lie still," Sunniva said flatly.

Tove scoffed. "Sunniva, she's in pain."

"The process can hurt," she said, sounding only slightly sympathetic. "But it's the only way I know how to do this."

I opened my eyes, only for a moment, and Sunniva's dark brown eyes were glowing silver as she scowled down at me.

"I need you to go back to the memory, the one you were on when it started to hurt," she commanded.

I took a fortifying breath and pushed through the fog of my mind. Indu's face smirking at me shifted to a young woman with his blue eyes under thick eyebrows. My sister Noomi.

The pain flared again, a crackling expanding inside my skull, but I gritted my teeth and focused on Noomi. She was glaring at me through the iron bars, and her mouth was moving, but the words came out slightly delayed, sounding far away and warbled.

"*You will go, but you will not remember any of this,*" Noomi promised me. "*The* inovotto muitit *is absolute agony as the memories are ripped from your mind.*"

"*Why do you hate me so much?*" I asked her emptily.

"*I hate you because you exist,*" she said coldly.

My head felt like it was going to explode, and I groaned in pain.

"Stay with it," Sunniva said firmly. "I know it hurts, but I need you to stay in it."

Noomi's face appeared before me again, but it was different, from another day. Bold stripes of cobalt blue across her eyes and bloodred on her narrow lips. Her hair was plaited tight to her scalp, woven with strips of leather.

"Is it time to go?" I asked.

"There's been a change of plans," she said with a wicked smile.

"You can't just take her!" Dagny said, and despite her conviction, her words were soft and far away, like they were being carried on the wind.

But then cuffs were on my wrists, made of a strange oxidized metal that left it more jade than copper. They were heavy, far heavier than they'd looked in Noomi's hands, and the metal burned my skin.

"Where are you taking her?" That was Pan in the prison cell across from mine, his face pressed against the bars, an arm outstretched through the narrow gap between them.

Noomi didn't answer him and instead led me down the long narrow hall, out of the dungeon and into the darkness.

And then a doorway appeared, glowing a pale orange, and Noomi pulled on my shackles, dragging me along. Through the door was a small, sparse room with a large apothecary table by the far wall. Half-melted marigold candle pillars burned dimly on top of that, the wax pooling on the warped wood.

In the center of the room, four men were standing around an empty bed.

And then another memory overlapped it—Pan lying on the same bed, his blood pooling on the floor around him.

I must've been squirming because I heard Sunniva tell Tove to keep me still, and I was only dimly aware of an ambient pressure around my body, pressing me to the floor.

But I was barely cognizant of that, and even the burning pain inside my skull didn't affect me much. It hurt like hell, but it was more like it was happening to someone else, in another room.

I was in the medica as Noomi led me to the narrow cot surrounded by four men. Indu Mattison stood at the head. To his left was a hunched-over older man, hidden by the hood of his crimson robe. He was the häxdoktor, and his name—Lemak Axelson—appeared in my mind.

The two men to my father's left were young—the older of the two was maybe my age, but the other had a doughy face and looked fifteen or sixteen. They wore gray kaftans, plain compared to Indu's with the runic designs.

"What do you want with me?" I asked as Lemak, the häxdoktor, began unwinding a long rubbery tube.

"Everything will be okay, Violetta." Indu's voice was like syrup as he used the name my mother had given me, and he patted the cot with his meaty hand. "Lie down and it will be over soon."

I told him I didn't want to but then I was on the cot anyway, and the younger men were holding me down. Indu held my left arm away from my body, his fingers digging painfully into the soft flesh of my forearm.

"It will only hurt for a moment, Violetta," Indu tried to assure me as the häxdoktor screwed a long metal syringe needle onto the end of the tube.

"My name is Ulla," I said through gritted teeth, and I felt the burning stab as Lemak jabbed the needle into my arm.

From the corner of my eye, I could see the blood, dark and red, as it flowed through the semi-opaque tubing.

"Why are you taking my blood?" I asked.

As I turned my head to get a better look, a dozen images flashed before my eyes. In the same place, the pale skin of my inner arm facing up toward the pale orange light.

My unmarred skin flashed to swollen, bloody track marks

to the needle into my arm to an inky black spider crawling down my elbow. And then, for a split second, the cuff was gone, replaced by a friendship bracelet made with bright string and plastic beads.

Somewhere, far away, my body was on fire, the flames eating through my skull, and I faintly heard Sunniva telling me to hang on just a bit longer. But I couldn't do it. It all hurt too much.

I opened my eyes, and I was staring at the dark stone bricks of my prison cell. The wood bunk was hard and cold against my back, and Dagny wiped a cold rag against my face.

"What's going on?" I asked her weakly. "Why are you doing that?"

"You're sick, Ulla," she said, but her voice cut out. Dagny's mouth was moving, but it was Sunniva's voice that came through. "I don't think you can take much more of this."

I tried to shake my head, but it wouldn't move. "I can't stop."

"Is she awake?" Pan asked, shouting from across the way. But I could hardly hear him, his voice was fading away.

"I'm losing you," I whispered as I closed my eyes.

"Ulla, you need to come out of it." Tove was shouting, but I could hardly hear him over the crackling flames burning through the fog in my brain.

I was moving—not consciously, but I felt the ground pull away from me, and the wind moving over my skin only fanned the burning pain. Someone was shouting but I couldn't understand what they were saying.

And then, abruptly, cold water washed over me, and I sat up, gasping for breath in a porcelain tub in the gilded palace bathroom.

"Are you okay?" Tove asked as I wiped the water from my eyes.

My heart raced, my head throbbed, and my skin felt sunburnt all over. But I was breathing, and I was alive, so I nodded.

6

recovery

Four hours later, I still couldn't fully shake the heat. Finn and Mia had set up an air mattress for me in the twins' room, and I sat on it with a fan on me while I sipped iced tea.

I had on a tank top, and I kept checking my left arm for the infected needle marks I'd seen. But my arms were fine. There were a few faint pink dots, like fading scars, and a purplish bruise on my wrist. But nothing like what I'd remembered with Sunniva.

Sunniva had apologized, when I'd still been in the Queen's bathroom, with the showerhead raining cold water down on me. She'd stood in the doorway, her arms folded over her chest, and her tone was impassive when she said, "Whatever is blocking your memories is stronger than anything I've encountered."

"But I did remember something," I said. "And I need to remember the rest of it."

Sunniva exchanged a look with Tove, and the worry in her dark eyes belied her aloof exterior. "I'll do what I can."

Tove reached behind me and turned off the showerhead.

"Let's get you back to feeling normal before we worry about what to do next."

If I hadn't felt so exhausted and achy all over, I would've pushed it more, but the truth was that I did need a bit of time to recover, even if I didn't want to. So I let him help me out of the tub and wrap me in a plush towel.

Finn took me home—after chastising Tove for letting things go too far, even with me insisting that I was okay. Once I got to Finn and Mia's house, I changed out of my wet clothes into cool, dry pajamas, and they wrangled the kids away from me so I could crash for a long, dreamless nap.

When I woke up, I was still warm, despite all my efforts to cool off, but I didn't feel quite so run-down anymore. Mia had brought me an iced tea and offered to keep the kids at bay for a little longer, although she warned me that eventually Niko or Hanna would sneak through.

I wanted to make the most of my solitude, and I pulled out my phone. This morning, I'd tried calling Pan and Dagny, both her cell and the landline at our apartment, but there'd been no answer. Though it had given me time to wonder dourly if it was still "our" apartment, since I didn't know if I'd ever be allowed back to Merellä.

But this was the first time I'd checked my phone in hours and I had a slew of text messages, all from Pan.

Are you okay? Where are you?

Call me when you can.

I don't know what's going on, but I just wanted you to know that I'm with Dagny & Elof. I can't wait to hear from you.

And then finally, a long multi-text essay:

I'm back in Merellä and the reception is spotty, so I don't know when we'll talk. I'm in Dagny's room using the signal booster. We just got back from a meeting with Amalie and half a dozen Mästares. Dagny thinks they were the Information Styrelse, even though they specifically denied it.

Amalie told us about the negotiations, and that the Vittra exchanged some weird flower for us. They said that they'd decided to end your internship. It technically ended while we were gone, I guess, and Sylvi and Calder thought it would be better if you waited until things were more sorted out before you tried coming back.

They told me they sent you back to stay with Hanna's family in Förening. I hope that's true, and Dagny thinks it is, but it's hard to feel reassured when I can't remember the past month. Can you remember anything?

For me, it's like a terrifying black hole where my memory should be.

One of the last things I remember clearly is kissing you in Isarna. And I hate that I don't know if we kissed again, or if it was the last time, or if I did anything stupid to mess things up.

I don't know if I should've said that. I don't know if you even remember that. I hope you do.

The meeting with the Mästares turned into an interrogation, which all got very frustrating, very fast. I don't think Amalie believed us that we couldn't remember anything. Someone finally had to tell her to knock it off after she asked me if I could remember anything about Áibmoráigi for the ninth time in a row.

Elof started pressing about the Ögonen, and he was talking to Dagny about some charm or concoction they can work up in the lab. He's determined to recover our memories.

He's been running all kinds of tests. He took so much blood from me I nearly passed out. He believes that the Älvolk did something to us, that they must've wanted something from us to hold us for so long.

Did they tell you the Älvolk were the ones that held us hostage? That your father, Indu, was the one behind it? I'm sorry if they didn't.

I'm sorry if they did. This must be so tough for you.

I know you want answers, but I don't think you should try to contact Indu. They're calling him a terrorist, and he's banned from all five kingdoms. If he returns to Isarna, he'll be arrested on sight. He's not somebody you want to be involved with.

I wish I could talk to you. I have to head out to get Brueger from the dog sitter, and Dagny is heading back to the Mimirin to work on something with Elof. I'll be in and out for a while, but I'd still like if you could call me when you have the chance.

I called him, and then Dagny. When neither of them answered, I decided to try any number I could remember. Fortunately, I'd called Dagny down at the lab enough that I knew the number by heart.

"Troglecology Department, Docent Elof Dómari's lab, this is Dagny Kasten speaking," she answered in her formal, clipped way.

"Dag, it's me, Ulla."

"Oh, Ulla, it's so good to hear your voice," she said. "I have no idea how long it's been since I talked to you. I'd swear it was yesterday, but it also feels like it's been ages."

"Yeah, I know exactly how you feel," I agreed.

"Are you in Förening? Are you safe?" she asked.

I filled her in on the situation as I understood it, but I just barely touched on Sunniva's recovery attempts—"Finn's put me in touch with an aura healer to try to restore memories"—

and Dagny explained that Elof hoped for something similar with the Ögonen.

As I suspected, she didn't remember anything at all, and she wasn't surprised by my vague recollection of a prison cell.

"And I think they were stealing my blood," I confessed.

"Stealing your blood?" she echoed. "Like vampires?"

"No, they weren't drinking it." I paused, thinking. "I don't know what they're doing with it. Maybe drinking it, I guess. But they took it with a syringe. I don't know if they took yours or not, but I have some scars on my left forearm."

"I had no new marks on my arms, but I did have a three-quarter-inch scar on my right temple, a two-day-old bruise on my ribs, and a three-inch diagonal healing cut across my lower back," she replied matter-of-factly.

"You sound awfully certain," I commented.

"Elof and I did full-body exams for any new marks. It was the only way we could discern any abuse or violations."

"And you didn't see anything that could be a needle mark?" I asked.

"No, and we specifically checked for that. But Elof did find a pair of odd dots he thought might be from a psionic stun gun's prong."

"Sorry you guys went through that," I said.

"You went through it too," Dagny reminded me gently. "I'll talk to Elof and see if he has theories about why they wanted your blood. I'm sure he'll have questions. Is it okay if he calls you later?"

"Yeah, of course."

"What are you going to do now?" Dagny asked. "Are you staying in Förening?"

"For the immediate future, I think so."

Truth was that I didn't know where else to go. With my internship gone, I was out of work, and I didn't have a place to live. Most of my possessions—other than the boxes stored in the Holmes's basement and what I still had in my duffel bag—were in the apartment. I'd have to go to Merellä to get my things soon, not just because I wanted my stuff but to free up the space so Dagny could find a new flatmate.

I told her as much, and I promised to square up the back rent as soon as I could.

"No need," Dagny said. "Amalie and the board took care of it. Our apartment is paid through the end of September. She said we shouldn't be punished for a crime committed against us."

"That was very generous of them," I said.

"Amalie has been quite magnanimous," Dagny admitted. "Far more than other Mästares."

"Why do you think she's being so nice?"

"She wants to find out what she can about the First City. The other Mästares seemed more concerned with following the rules." She sighed then. "So it goes."

In the background, I heard a loud clatter, and Elof calling Dagny's name.

"I have to go help Elof with something," she said. "I'll talk to you soon, though, Ulla. Stay safe."

"You too," I told her, and ended the call.

Then I lay back on the air mattress, and I stared up at the fluffy white clouds on the pale blue ceiling of the twins' room, and I tried to figure out what I was going to do from here.

7

BINRASSI

Niko had been the first one to sneak into the room, but I was ready for a reprieve from my growing anxiety. Everything felt so up in the air, and I was so untethered.

Not to mention the near boundless hospitality that Finn and his family had shown me. But I couldn't possibly expect that to last forever. They had six children and Finn's mother to worry about, plus Finn's high-stress job as the minister of defense of the entire Trylle kingdom.

I allowed myself a few more minutes alone with Niko, reading him a passage from *Sunny Plants for Funny Kids*. It didn't say much of interest. *With petals of gold and nectar of red, this big flower smells of the dead.* When I finished, I put it back on the shelf and scooped Niko up in my arms before heading downstairs.

I found Mia and Hanna in the kitchen, trying to make sweet-and-sour red cabbage with mushroom and quinoa sausage for supper with the twins crawling around. I managed to entertain the littler kids, keeping them out from underfoot while Mia sautéed and boiled in pots and pans at the stove, and while Hanna cut and prepped nearby and made quite the sous chef to her mother.

Hanna used the time to ask me a thousand questions, but she grew increasingly disappointed with my constant refrain of "I don't know" and "I don't remember."

"How long are you going to be here?" Hanna asked finally.

"Um, I'm not sure." I sat cross-legged on the floor, with Lissa on my lap, leaning forward and using her pudgy hands to help her sister stack perilous towers of plastic cups.

Mia was sautéing the mushrooms with her back to me, and she looked over her shoulder at me. "You know you can stay here as long as you want."

"I could kick Emma out, and you could stay in my room," Hanna offered.

"Hanna, no," Mia admonished her before Hanna got too carried away with fantasies of evicting her little sister. "Finn and I were talking, and we could empty out all the things we put in your room after you moved out. We hadn't meant to turn it into storage like that, but my summer cleaning got away from me."

"No, I don't want you guys going to any trouble. I'll be fine on the air mattress until I can figure out what I'm going to do next."

"Well, there's no rush. You've been through a lot, and you need time to sort things out. We all understand, and we just want you to be okay."

"Thanks, that—" I was going to finish with *means a lot to me,* but at that exact moment, Luna decided to clock Niko in the head as hard as she could.

He immediately screamed, so Lissa started to cry, and within seconds, all the kids were having a meltdown. Hanna finished cooking while Mia and I dealt with consoling everyone else.

They calmed down in time for supper, but then everyone was talking, and the conversation never went back to me or my future plans. Which was fine by me, because I didn't want to talk about it anyway.

The great thing about having ten of us in the house—five of them under the age of eight—was there was always so much commotion going on, and it was easy to get lost in it if you wanted to.

Despite my lengthy midday nap, I was exhausted by bedtime. Unfortunately, the twins weren't nearly as ready for sleep as I was at nine-thirty P.M. After three rounds of their favorite lullaby, Luna finally went down, but Lissa was still fussing.

I'd tried everything I could think of, so I took Lissa from her crib, and I held her in my arms. I can't say for certain that it worked for her, but within minutes, I was out.

And the next time I opened my eyes, *I was in the dungeon again.*

Not the prison cell, but the corridor outside of it. It looked the same as it had last time. Narrow and dark, although the stones seemed more rust colored. Or maybe it was just because it was brighter. All the lamps were lit, with one on either side every few feet.

The hallway ended in an almost blindingly bright light, and I shielded my face with my arm as I walked into the atrium. It was a tall silo of a room, with a stone staircase that wound up to the glass roof letting all the sunlight pour in.

A woman was standing on the stairs, a few steps up from the bottom, and she smiled serenely. Her long dark hair floated ethereally around her, and her pale gown adorned with flowers of goldenrod and poppy red seemed to be one with her luminous bronze skin.

"You need to hurry," she said in a voice that was deeper than I would've thought. It was throaty and almost seductive.

"Why?" I asked as I walked toward her, and she started running up the stairs, so her floral train billowed out behind her.

"Hrudda, binrassi." Her sultry baritone was urgent but her lyrical drawl made it sound almost playful.

She ran faster, and I didn't want to lose her when she went through the doors at the top of the stairs, so I chased after her.

I followed her outside, where the air felt crisp but strangely warm. I found myself in a beautiful city built into the side of the mountain. Tall stone buildings straight out of the fairy-tale picture books I read to the children, with vine-covered turrets. Around me were houses, a stable, a garden with wilted flowers.

Despite all the buildings, all the carts unattended in the dirt roads, all these signs of life, even a fire crackling in a pit, I didn't see a single living thing. The eerie stillness was broken when the wind picked up, bringing with it a rustling and a rattling of metal, like broken bells.

I spun around slowly, but I couldn't see the woman I'd been following. Dark clouds were rolling in, blocking out the sun. A dense fog was sweeping over the town.

The harsh air burned my throat, making me cough, and I realized it wasn't fog but smoke.

I couldn't see through it, but I heard the rumble of stones collapsing into each other. The ground was shaking, and I started running, as if I could outrun the smoke and stone avalanche.

"Help!" I shouted. "Help me!"

"Hurry, hurry, binrassi," she said, her voice booming through me even though I couldn't see her.

I tried to run faster, but I tripped on the unstable ground. There was a flash of bright green, cutting through the billowing smoke. And then the building behind me began to *collapse, and I had no time to react as the heavy stones tumbled down on me.*

I opened my eyes, gasping for air as I stared up at the clouds painted on the ceiling. Lissa babbled softly beside me, quiet toddler ramblings of comfort.

"Thanks, Lissa," I said, but my voice was hoarse, and my throat still burned the way it had in the dream.

I put Lissa back in the crib, and then I went down the hall to get a drink of water and clear my head of the intense, vivid nightmare.

8

Familiarity

Hanna had been on the phone with her grandfather, Johan, while Mia and I set up Hanna's laptop in a quiet corner of the house. After quite a bit of back and forth, Hanna thought she'd finally gotten Johan to understand how to video chat.

The three of us sat on the couch, with Hanna's laptop across from us, propped up on some wooden blocks on top of the coffee table. The laptop screen was black, except for the lime green phone icon in the center, and the only sound was the electronic *da-da-da* of the ringing.

"He hasn't answered yet," I said.

"I told him to answer when it rings," Hanna said wearily.

"Maybe you should call him on the phone," Mia suggested.

"No, Mom, he's got it. Give him a minute."

Finally, the ringing stopped, and an old man squinted at the screen through his small oval spectacles that sat on the end of his nose. The salt-and-pepper hair on his head was slightly darker and thinner than his bushy beard.

"Oh, hello," he said. "I can see you all. Can you see me?"

"Yes, we can." Mia smiled. "It's nice to see you again, Johan."

"Hi, Grandpa," Hanna said with a lackluster wave.

His smile deepened. "It's so nice to be able to see your face when we talk."

"I thought you'd enjoy video chatting," Mia said.

"Yes, it seems like a wonderful invention," he agreed. "Now, I don't think I quite understand what you were asking about earlier. Something about a book?"

"I had some questions about the book you wrote," I said. "The one you showed me when I tried to drop Hanna off back in June, about Jem-Kruk."

"Why?" he asked in surprise. "You can ask me anything you want, of course, but I can't imagine that old fairy stories are of that much interest to you."

"But is that all they are?" I asked.

"What do you mean?" Johan asked.

"Is any of it true?" I asked.

He laughed, a warm chuckle, and readjusted his glasses. "No. They're only stories."

"Were you inspired by anything from your life?" Mia tried.

"Well, I'm sure I was, the way I imagine most authors are," he said. "But I feel like you're trying to find out about something in particular. Perhaps it'd be easier if you just asked straight out."

"She met Jem-Kruk," Hanna blurted out.

He shook his head. "What?"

"I met someone named Jem-Kruk," I clarified. "And he seemed to match the description in your books."

"It's an unusual name, to be sure," Johan said. "But I taught at a tracker school, and I had students named Iago,

Artemis, and Dartha. Naming a child after a character from a children's book is a fairly common occurrence."

"But there was other stuff," Hanna persisted. "My friend Eliana came from a land of three suns and pink skies."

"I'm afraid I don't know anything about a place like that," he said. "Truth be told, I don't even really remember writing the book. My wife and I were little more than newlyweds still, and Nikolas was only a baby. I was having my go at tracking, so I'd be gone for long stretches of time. The stories were something I wrote to ease my boredom and to feel close to my family.

"But I was miserable, and sleep-deprived for most of it," Johan went on. "I know I wrote the book, but I have no recollection of it."

Hanna frowned and her brow pinched up, and she'd gotten that look, like she was about to start arguing. Mia leaned in and put a hand on her daughter's back, curbing Hanna before she got going.

"Nikolas always spoke fondly of his childhood," Mia said. "I don't think he was ever aware of any hardships in the family."

"I've always thought it's such a blessing that children never know everything about their parents," he said, but he sounded morose.

"As I've been talking about these things with Hanna, I realized that I know very little of your life before Nikolas was born," Mia said.

"I grew up in a small village, and I doubt that it was that much different than yours." Johan leaned back in his chair slightly. "I am happy to talk to you about Nikolas or your lives or yes, the fantasy world I told my son as a bedtime story thirty years ago. But I am rather perplexed about your interest in this."

"It's sort of hard to explain, but I've been trying to find my parents," I began uncertainly. "And somehow, the paths keep leading back to this book. My mother's name is Senka, and she's from another kingdom, called Alfheim."

"Alfheim?" His bushy eyebrows raised high. "No, that's not a troll myth. That's the humans and their Norse myths."

"They've based other stories on us too," Hanna interjected. "Grandma Annali always says that even a broken clock is right twice a day."

Johan chuckled, but it wasn't as warm as it had been before. Even his smile changed, his lips pressed together in a thin line nearly hidden by his beard. "She sounds like a smart woman."

"So you don't know anything more about Jem-Kruk or Senka than what's in your book?" I asked, giving it one last attempt.

"No, I'm saying that I don't even know that much," he corrected me. "All of that was made up, and I don't even remember making it up anymore."

"If you don't want to talk about the book, Johan, that's fine, and completely understandable," Mia said. "But we'd still like to talk to you about your life and about your childhood and Nikolas's."

He was silent for a moment, staring off at some spot beyond the computer. Behind him, I could see the rows of books filling the curved shelves that surrounded him in his towering study. He was sitting in the room where I'd chatted with him at the beginning of the summer. It had smelled of earthy sandalwood, and we'd sat near the fireplace, him sipping wine while telling me how the tales of Jem-Kruk were his favorites.

And now he didn't seem to want to talk about it at all. Maybe he was put off by the intrusion, or maybe he was hurt that Hanna's interest wasn't more motivated by love. Or maybe it was something else entirely, but I didn't know what was going on.

Finally, he asked, "Is that true, Hanna?"

"Yeah," she said. "I'm ready to know about Nikolas."

"Well, I'll have plenty to tell you, but I'd like some time to collect my thoughts before we get into that," he said. "Maybe we can set up another one of these video chats later on with Grandma Sarina? I know she has a lot she wants to talk to you about."

Hanna smiled. "Yeah, I'd like that."

"Sarina did have a . . . friend named Senka," Johan said. "Years ago, and I don't really remember her anymore, but I can talk to her. It's likely not the same Senka you're looking for, but Sarina will most likely be happy to speak with you."

"Yeah, that would be really great," I said.

He smiled in a way that didn't quite reach his eyes and said, "I'm always happy to help."

9

plans

The conversation veered after that, with both Mia and Johan getting teary-eyed, and I felt like I was encroaching on a private moment. I excused myself, and they talked for a while longer, just long enough for me to make a pot of tea on the stove.

Mia tried to apologize about the conversation not being more fruitful for me, but I told her that she'd already been more helpful than she needed to be. The call seemed to have left her sad and tired, so I offered to make lunch for the kids while she lay down.

She took me up on it, and soon I was boiling carrots I'd plucked fresh from the family garden. And as I stood over the stove, it occurred to me how seamlessly I slid back into the life I had before.

When Finn and Mia took me in five and a half years ago, I'd known that I couldn't stay here forever. I'm nineteen years old. I have to make my way in the world eventually.

The problem was that the options in the Trylle kingdom—or any of the kingdoms—were so limited. I'd been homeschooled since I got to Förening. (Finn had initially hired a private tutor to catch me up because my Iskyla education had been severely lacking.) But I had still made a few friends around my age, and I saw the choices they made with the hands they'd been dealt.

Sybilla Janssen and Alva Lund had become trackers, the same as their older siblings and parents had before them. But those jobs were drying up, both because the royal families weren't having children at the rates they once were and because the Queen was trying to stop the reliance on the changelings. Fewer changelings meant fewer trackers.

There were still plenty of spots open on the Queen's guard, which served as the military and the police. My friend Isak Vinstock had joined, hoping to get on the detective track, but the competition was so steep, he'd been languishing in Oslinna for years, working on the recovery, rebuilding homes and facilities.

Isak wasn't the only one who went to Oslinna either. I knew of several other kids who had gone there for the construction work.

But most of the trolls I'd been friends with stuck around Förening, with many still living with their parents. A few were going to Förening Tertiary Educational Center, getting education degrees to work in the grade school, and another was apprenticing at his mother's organic specialty bakery.

And there were the others that got married right out of high school and were already starting families. Even in 2019, it wasn't uncommon for Trylle to marry young, sometimes even as young as sixteen or seventeen. Non-royalty were faring better with fertility, but Finn and Mia's well-populated home was an outlier these days.

That basically covered all the options for someone like me in Förening—soldier, teacher, baker, wife. There was nothing wrong with any of them, of course, and they were all fine pursuits in their own right. But I wasn't sure that any of them were what I wanted to do. I mean, marriage someday, ideally, but I wanted to figure out who I was and what I wanted to do with my life first.

My reason for going to the Mimirin institution was that I had hoped to find out where I came from. If I knew where I came from, I'd know where to go, right? Besides, I had to put all of Finn's linguistic lessons to good use.

But the more I learned, the more questions I had, and the more uncertain I felt about myself, my future, and my place in the world. And I had the big black hole of the Lost Month hanging over me.

The kids were fussing for lunch, and I didn't have time to worry about all the existential questions weighing on me when preparing food for the family.

It worked so well, I spent the afternoon busying myself with the kids—feeding them, cleaning up after them, entertaining them. They made it a lot easier to ignore the dread at the pit of my stomach.

Eventually, I ended up outside in the warm sun. Behind the house was a small barn and a decent-sized pasture—an angled grassy clearing, surrounded by a stone wall to prevent errant children or animals from tumbling off the sheer bluff face at the edge of the artificially leveled field.

About two dozen animals occupied the small farm. A few angora goats, a pair of potbellied pigs, five chickens, several fat Gotland rabbits, and an adorable grump of a pony named Calvin. I'd gone out to the barn with Liam and Emma, so we could visit the animals and take care of them. One of Liam's chores was feeding the chickens, and Emma attempted to help by mostly dumping feed all over the ground.

"Ulla!" Hanna shouted, and she walked into the barn,

holding a cordless phone outstretched toward me. Flour dusted the ends of her dark ringlets, and her apron was stained with dark purple plums from the pies she'd been stress-baking.

Since her grandfather hadn't revealed all the secrets of the universe (or confirmed Hanna's pet theory that she was the princess of some far-off land), Hanna had been in a rather sour mood.

"Who is it?" I stepped out of the chicken pen, and I hoped it was Pan. We'd been playing phone tag all morning, with my sleeping through his calls and him not answering mine.

Hanna shrugged. "Dunno. Grandma answered and she thought they sounded important."

"Thanks." As I took the phone from her, I heard more feed spilling on the floor, immediately followed by Emma and the chickens squawking excitedly. "Can you watch the kids for a second?"

"Fine." She sighed and walked into the chicken pen while I slipped out to the pasture to take the phone call in privacy.

"Hello?" I answered.

"Hello, Ulla," Elof said. I was happy to hear his voice, but my heart sank a little because it wasn't Pan. "How are you doing?"

"Good," I said, too earnestly. "I mean, considering everything. How are you?"

"Oh, I've been better," he admitted with a weary sigh. "Although I am riding the little ego boost after being declared a very important troll by that lovely woman who answered the phone. It sounds like you and Hanna have a winsome family."

"They are fantastic," I agreed. "Did you need something?"

"I only wanted to give you an update. Or a warning, as it were," he said, sounding rather ominous. "We've been trying to recover memories."

I walked across the field and leaned against the stone wall,

and I stared down the hillside. "Have you made any progress?"

"Well, yes, in that we learned that aural healing is too
volatile and dangerous for memory recovery," he said with
forced optimism. "We hadn't known that before, and we do
now."

"What are you talking about? I tried aural healing, and I
was fine," I said, but even I knew I was downplaying overheating so much I needed an ice bath. I wanted a day or two
of rest before doing more healing with Sunniva, but I did plan
on doing it again.

"We tried it this morning, with one of the Ögonen attempting to heal Dagny's aura," he explained. "It was under
my supervision, with Mästare Amalie instructing the Ögonen
through their psychic communication. Before you worry, Dagny is all right. A bit singed and worn out, but she's recovering fine."

"Recovering? What happened?" I asked.

"We knew overheating would be an issue, so we had taken
precautions," he went on. "But ten minutes in, Dagny . . . well,
she was basically cooking."

"*Alai.*" I gasped. "Are you kidding me?"

"Her eyebrows actually had embers burning, and we immediately stopped and got her in the ice bath. Amalie brought
in a healer, and they were able to reverse most of the internal
damage. Her left eyebrow will take a bit to fully grow back,
but she's otherwise fine."

I exhaled. "That sounds horrifying. I'm glad she's okay."

"Me too," he agreed heartily. "But it also means that aural
healing with the Ögonen isn't a viable option for us. Dagny
was lucky she made it without any permanent damage, and
she was only under for a matter of minutes. Unfortunately,
that wasn't enough time to make much headway into the

memories. She only remembered something about a boulder on a mountain and following an elk through it."

"What about me?" I asked. "I had some memories come back when Sunniva Kroner tried it with me."

"You overheated when she tried it, and the Ögonen are more powerful," Elof reminded me grimly. "I don't want to risk cooking you alive to recover a few memories."

"So then, what's the plan?" I asked. "If aural healing is too dangerous right now. What are you trying next?"

"I don't really know yet," he admitted. "I have been working on an infused serum, but it hasn't proven effective yet. Dagny's looking into incantations, trying to reverse the spell they used on us."

"What can I do?" I asked.

"I'm afraid I don't really have much of a way of direction for you," Elof said. "If you find something worth pursuing, you ought to do it, but you need to be safe."

"Yeah. Of course."

"I'm sorry that I don't have better news for you," he said. "But I wanted to warn you about the issues with aural healing before you got hurt."

"I understand, and thank you," I said.

"I don't know how much help I can be so far away from you, but if there's anything I can do, let me know."

"Do you know anything about why the Älvolk wanted the *sorgblomma*?"

"I don't know much about the plant," he said. "We Vittra consider it to be sacred, and all scientific testing on it has been banned for fear of damaging it. So all I can really say is that the kingdom was not happy about surrendering it."

10

sisterly

Hanna was in her room, lying on her bed reading *Jem-Kruk and the Adlrivellir.*

She'd been hiding in her room since supper, which was unlike her. When she needed space from her younger siblings, she would escape outside, playing in the woods that surrounded her house. But even then, she wasn't ever gone for long. She got bored and lonely fast.

"How are you doing?" I asked as I poked my head in the doorway.

"I'm okay." She dog-eared the page she was reading, and set her book aside.

I went into the room and sat on Emma's bed, across from her. "Are you sure? You've seemed kinda down since the video chat."

"I'm not *down*." Hanna stared up at the ceiling and frowned. "I've just been reading the Jem-Kruk book because I was so sure that it would somehow help us find Eliana, and when you came back, I was certain you'd bring the key to all of it."

She fell quiet for a moment, chewing her lip. "You know I was worried about you when you were gone."

"I do know that, and I'm sorry. I never meant to worry you or anyone else."

"Duh, Ulla." She smiled weakly at me. "I'm not trying to make you feel bad or anything. I'm saying it was scary when you were gone. Mom and Dad tried telling us that everything was fine, but I could see how worried they were. And for Dad to look *that* upset, I knew things had to be bad.

"But I never gave up," she went on. "I always knew you'd come home safe. But I also knew that you'd come back with answers, and we'd be able to get Eliana."

I swallowed hard. "I wish I had more answers. And I haven't given up on finding Eliana either."

"How? Where are you looking?" Hanna's voice grew more anxious as she spoke, and she sat up on her bed. "You can't go back to where you came from, even if you remembered where it was. It's way too dangerous."

"I'm not going back anytime soon," I replied carefully. "Right now I'm just trying to remember what happened when I was gone."

"So then where are you going?" she asked.

"Who says I'm going anywhere?" I countered.

"I heard Mom and Grandma talking. Mom said she was going to put a real bed in the playroom for you. But you told her no, not to bother."

"I don't know what I'm doing yet," I admitted. "And you do have a pretty full house here. I don't think me sacking out in the playroom forever is the best plan for any of us."

She snorted. "So you're biding your time until you can go find your real family?"

"Hanna." I got up and went over to sit next to her. "You and your family *are* my family. But I'm nineteen, and I want to find out what happened to my birth family. That doesn't mean I don't care about you, or that I'm going to cut you out of my life."

She stared down at the floor, chewing the inside of her cheek as she worked things over in her head. "Not even for your real sisters?"

"Why would you ask that?"

"Because this fell out of the book." She opened it and pulled out a napkin that had been pressed between the pages.

Indu had given it to me when Pan and I first met him in Isarna, back before he stole my blood, back when he was still trying to get me to trust him. On a napkin at the tea shop, he'd written the names of four of my sisters.

In my efforts to find him, I'd discovered records that he'd fathered children with the Omte, Trylle, and Skojare. But all of them had died in infancy. I hadn't had a chance to talk to Indu about that—at least not that I remembered—but he'd been happy to tell me about his four daughters who were still alive.

The names had been written on the napkin for me:

Noomi Indudottir (her mother was Skojare)
Bryn Aven (her mother Runa Aven is Skojare)
Minoux Moen (with Asta Moen, also Skojare)
Juno Indudottir (due in August with Bekk)

Noomi had been my prison guard, if my recovered memories were correct, and she lived in Áibmoráigi with Indu, so I didn't plan on catching up with her anytime soon.

Minoux Moen and Asta I'd never heard of before and didn't know where to find them, but the Skojare had a rather small kingdom. They most likely lived in Isarna in Sweden or in the capital city of Storvatten in Canada.

But Bryn Aven and Bekk Vallin I knew. Bryn had been the one to get me out of Iskyla five and a half years ago, and we'd kept in touch since then. I had met her parents once—her Skojare mother and her Kanin father—but Indu was claiming that he was really her father.

Bekk had been the one to help me find Indu in the first place, but she'd also been the one to give Indu a forewarning that I was on his trail. To top it off, she was pregnant with his child, something she'd done on purpose for reasons I didn't fully understand.

But considering the average life expectancy of Indu's children and that he had held me hostage and stolen my blood, I had plenty of reason to believe his other daughters could be in danger.

"Those are your sisters, right?" Hanna asked.

"They might be," I allowed.

"You should talk to them."

I looked over at her. "I'm surprised to hear you saying that."

"No, I know I'm just being silly." She suddenly sounded tired. "And you're right. We're family now, no matter what, so if you have more sisters, that just means I have more sisters too." She smirked. "Not that I need more sisters."

I laughed.

"But is that Bryn your friend Bryn?" Hanna asked, and I nodded. "Did you know she was your sister before?"

"I still don't *know* that she is," I corrected her. "But I never thought she might be until Indu mentioned it."

"When are you going to tell her?" Hanna pressed.

I sighed. "I don't know."

"I'm always happy to tag along, and I think I've proven myself a worthy sidekick."

"Really?" I raised an eyebrow. "That's how you describe your time in Merellä?"

"I helped you and kept you fed. I'm basically the Alfred to your Batman."

I laughed again. "I do not think that's an accurate description of us at all." I smiled down at her. "I missed you, kid."

"I missed you too."

11

missed

I couldn't sleep, even though I was exhausted. I'd spent the day chasing kids and the evening planning my next move. The twins slept soundly in their cribs, while I tossed and turned on the air mattress.

I didn't want to disturb them, so I grabbed my cell phone and crept down the stairs. Everyone was asleep, so I could've just hung out in the living room without bothering anyone, but it was a beautiful night.

I went outside and sat on the front steps. The air was strangely still but with a slight chill, and the moon was nearly full, bathing the secluded yard in cool light. The house was at the edge of Förening on a gravel road that wound down the hillside. It was still a hundred feet above the river that cut through the tall bluffs, but most of the town was built up higher, closer to the peak and surrounding the royal palace.

The town in general was quiet, but out here, with everyone sleeping, it was only the far-off sound of the river and a nearby owl hooting in the trees. I took my phone out and pulled up the voicemail Pan had left me earlier that evening.

I'd been in the shower after a diaper blowout incident with Luna, and I had missed his call, *again*.

Twice already, I'd listened to his message, but I hit Play again.

"Hey, Ulla," Pan said, his deep voice sounding disappointed. "I was hoping to talk to you, but our epic game of phone tag continues. At least I got to hear your voice on the outgoing message."

After a brief pause, he said, "I probably shouldn't have said that." His audible embarrassment made me smile and tears formed in my eyes. "I didn't mean it in a creepy way. I just . . . I miss you."

For a moment, it was only the sound of him breathing. I stared up at the moon. Clouds moved rapidly across it, despite a total lack of wind. They were thin—altostratus clouds if I remembered correctly from Liam's *Big Book of Weather*—so I could easily see the moon through them, but they gave the night sky an eerie chartreuse glow.

"It's all so frustrating." Pan's recorded voice cut through the night. "I'm trying to get back into the swing of things. Me and Brueger are working tonight, herding the woollies around. But first I'm going to stop by and bring Dagny something to eat.

"I don't know how much you know," he went on. "Dagny said that Elof warned you about the aura dangers. She's okay, but she's super grumpy because Elof made her take the rest of the day off. But I thought I'd check on her anyway. Plus, Brueger's been pretty fond of her since she dog-sat him back in June.

"What I'm trying to say is that I'll be in and out most of the night, so I don't know when you'll be able to reach me," he said with a sigh. "But just give me a call when you can."

He went silent for a second, then, "I hope everything is going well for you. Stay safe. Bye, Ulla."

The voicemail ended, and even though it was late, I decided to give it a shot. I dialed the number for Pan's apartment, willing him to pick up the phone.

"Hey, this is Pan Soriano. I can't get to the phone, so leave a message, and I'll get back to you when I can."

"Hi, Pan." I cleared my throat to rid it of the painful lump. "It's Ulla. Obviously. I don't know if you're working or sleeping, and if you're sleeping, I'm sorry if I disturbed you. I probably shouldn't have called so late. I just couldn't sleep, and I thought maybe . . .

"I just wanted to tell you that I've decided what I'm going to do next," I confessed to his voicemail. "I want to get back to Merellä, but I don't know how that will work since my internship is over. There's a bunch of stuff I need to sort out.

"So I decided to check with someone I trust," I went on. "Indu says that my friend Bryn is my sister, and I've known her way longer than I've known him. I called her up today, and she still lives in Doldastam. I asked if it would be okay if I came up for a visit for a few days, and she said sure.

"It's the kind of conversation that's better in person, and she said she had a couple days off coming, so it all works out really. So. Tomorrow I'm heading up to Doldastam."

I sighed and stared up at the eerie sky and the rapidly shifting clouds. "It's good. I'm looking forward to it, honestly. But . . . I know it'll be longer before I see you again. I don't even know when I'll talk to you. I'll be on the road or on a train, moving slowly across the Canadian wilderness, so I have a feeling that this game of phone tag is only going to get more epic.

"I can't complain too much," I said sullenly. "But I want to anyway. Everything feels so up in the air.

"But I am okay. Better than Dagny, it sounds like. Since you'll probably talk to her before I do, tell her I'm thinking of her, and I hope she feels better soon. I hope you're doing good—that all of you in Merellä are good—and I can't wait until we actually talk."

I took a deep breath. "Bye, Pan." My voice caught in my throat and I hung up so I could let out the sob I'd barely been holding back.

I missed him so badly. I had a constant dull ache of longing in my chest, and I knew it would remain until I could hold him in my arms again. For the first time, I wondered if all of this was worth it. If maybe it would be better to give up my hunt for the past so I could actually have a present.

The owl nearby had been hooting the whole time I left the message, but it fell silent. The temperature dropped suddenly, and goose bumps sprang up on my arms. I waited for a minute for wind or rain to follow, but it never did. The air remained perfectly still, and the clouds moved in, finally blotting out the moon. It was dark and cold, so I went back inside the house.

12

studious

The worst part of leaving was mostly behind me—telling the kids I was leaving again. Surprisingly, Hanna took it the best, but she understood that I'd be back. Emma started wailing, and then Niko and Lissa joined in.

It had been a rough morning, and it wasn't even eight-thirty A.M. We'd thought it would be better to do it before Finn left for work. By the time I went up to the room to finish getting ready to go, everyone had stopped crying, except for Emma, but she spent twenty percent of her days crying.

I was doing one last sweep around the room to make sure I wasn't leaving anything behind, and someone knocked on the bedroom door.

"Come in," I said, assuming it was Mia or Finn, because none of the others would've knocked.

Instead, it was Sunniva Kroner, smiling thinly at me. She was more casually dressed than when I had seen her last—a striped crop top and skinny jeans, with her long curly hair pulled up into a messy bun. Gold hoop earrings hung in her ears and bangles sparkled on her wrists.

"Oh, *alai*!" I said in surprise, and then remembered in

dismay that she was a high-ranking Marksinna, and I wasn't, so I attempted a hasty bow.

Sunniva waved her hand quickly to stop me. "No, no. Don't do that." She surveyed the room from under her thick lashes, and her eyes landed on my bag. "Are you going somewhere?"

"Yeah, I'm visiting a friend for a few days, maybe a week. But I'll be back."

"Good." She admired the handcrafted Dala horse on the twins' dresser. "Are these handmade?"

"Yeah, at the Trylle Toy Shoppe, the owner makes them. Every kid in town has one."

"Oh." She set it back on the dresser. "I didn't grow up here, so I never had one. I'm a changeling."

"I never had one either," I said, unsure of how else to respond.

Most of the Marksinna and Markis around her age had been changelings, meaning they had been switched at birth with children from wealthy human families and raised far away from Förening in human cities. Because of that, and the class differences, I didn't interact with any of them very often, so I didn't really know how any of them felt about the process.

"Anyway." Sunniva looked back at me, her dark eyes studying me. "I didn't come here to talk to you about toys."

"What did you come here to talk about?" I asked.

She went back to looking around the room, and she paced slowly between the cribs as she spoke. "I've been training with my mother. Aurora. I don't know if you know her."

"I know *of* her," I clarified. The Kroners were a powerful and wealthy family with strong ties to the royal family. Everyone knew of them.

Sunniva shook her head. "It doesn't matter. Aurora's a

great healer. *Was*." She paused. "*Is*. The powerful abilities run in my family—Tove moves things with his mind, Aurora can heal even deadly wounds, Noah has flashes of precognition. They're all very draining and dangerous. They *age* you."

"If you don't want to do this, I understand," I replied carefully.

"No, it's not that. It's the opposite of that, really." She faced me. "It's taking longer to get the hang of because of the amount of energy it takes. But I know I can do it. I will be able to. And I wanted to make sure you understood that you don't have to do this. Aural healing is a volatile thing—auras don't like being manipulated by outside sources."

"Most things don't," I said.

She smiled faintly. "You should be aware of the risks."

I considered what she was saying and then asked, "If I say that I don't want to do this again, would you keep training and practicing your aural healing?"

"Yes, I would," she answered without hesitation.

"Why?"

"When I found out I was a changeling, I didn't want to come here," she explained. "But what changed my mind was that I wanted to get a handle on the intense, superhuman things my body can do, and the only way I could find out my full potential was to come to a place where everyone understood what I am.

"That's why I'm here. That's why I'm learning this," Sunniva said. "And if I can help you or others along the way, even better."

"I can respect that," I said. "And I'm up for it if you are."

Sunniva smiled, deeply this time. "Excellent. I'll keep working with Aurora and Tove while you're gone, and when you get back, hopefully, we can meet up."

I nodded. "I'll see you then."

13

Dreams

The train was trying to rock me to sleep, but it wasn't helping. I lay in the narrow bed, watching out the long window as the boreal forest slowly passed by under the moonlit sky.

Doldastam—the capital of the Kanin kingdom—was located in the Canadian subarctic, nestled along the Hudson Bay. It was so far north, it was only accessible by train or plane, and train was the far cheaper option. It also took a lot longer. It was only my first night "riding the rails," and I had one more night to go.

It wasn't so bad, though. I had gotten an upper-berth bed, the upper window gave me a beautiful view of the Canadian wilderness in full summer bloom, and now I had plenty of time to worry about everything.

The last time I'd been this far north had been five and a half years ago, after the Invasion of Doldastam. Finn's younger sister Ember had fought beside Bryn during the war, and she'd been killed during combat. After the war ended and the new Kanin King, Linus Berling, was crowned, he held a ceremony in remembrance of all the lives lost.

I had gone there with Finn and Mia, and we had stayed

with Finn's parents—who had lived in Doldastam then—for a few days. Most of the time had been spent grieving and helping the Holmeses, but I had snuck in a quick visit with Bryn.

That was the only time I had ever been to Doldastam. The handful of times I had seen Bryn since then had been when she came south to Förening, working as the King's personal guard.

The village I grew up in, Iskyla, was even farther north and more isolated. The only road out of town went to a neighboring Inuit village, and it went no farther. They did trading with the humans by boat and plane—that's how my foster father got his art books and travel magazines, and when I was older, that's where I'd go to buy old paperbacks and movies from their meager store.

I had never been farther south than Iskyla, not since I'd been left as a baby. Not until Bryn rolled up in the middle of winter. My foster family—Oskar and Hilde Tulin—owned a small inn. In the winter, there were hardly any guests, and the few guests we did have were almost always townsfolk that needed a night away from their own home for one reason or another.

In the summer, we got the occasional lost tourist or adventurist hikers—I found no fewer than four different battered copies of *Into the Wild* forgotten in the rooms after they checked out of the inn—but most of the guests were workers passing through, from the southern cities to the mines and the lakes.

Bryn had come looking for the truth behind the dynasty controlling her kingdom, and she'd found the answer, with my help because I knew everybody in town. I was only fourteen then, but I knew the options in Iskyla—for work, for love, for friendship, for finding my parents—were very slim, and I saw a chance to escape, so I took it.

Mr. Tulin tried to give me a good life, but life in Iskyla is hard, and Mrs. Tulin never saw me as anything more than a burden. After I left, I kept in touch with Mr. Tulin, mostly through letters, but last winter, he stopped replying. A month later, Mrs. Tulin sent me a small package and a letter, telling me he'd passed away.

The package contained what little memorabilia she still had from my childhood. A few medical and school records, a few photographs, and a small painting that Mr. Tulin had done.

And now I was riding right back into my history, and it left me feeling sick and anxious. Lying in bed, staring out at the darkness, reminded me of the cold nights alone in the inn, listening to the wind howling at the feeble windows, with frost so thick over the panes, I couldn't see outside.

On the train by myself, I felt sad and alone. I missed my friends, my family—both the ones I had and the ones I never had the chance to really know.

But the exhaustion of the travel wore me down. My ear-buds played the Carpenters, and I cried softly into my pillow as I finally drifted off to sleep.

The sound of the ocean woke me up—the crashing waves and far-off gulls calling to one another, but faintly behind that, I still heard Karen Carpenter singing, demanding to know if a superstar still remembered her. I opened my eyes, and I was on the beach in Oregon, just beyond the city walls of Merellä, and the sharp drop-off around them. I looked back at the citadel, towering above me, and the only gap in the stone wall was the crescent-shaped arch that let the Forsa River flow easily underneath.

I'd gone through that once, walking along the narrow banks, out to where the dirt and mud became pebbles and sand. That's where Hanna and I had found Eliana, hiding from a Shadow and a Dragon—Illaria and Sumi.

But now I was alone, with frothy waves crashing onto the rocky beach. A sharp pebble stung the bottom of my bare foot, and I felt the cool spray from the ocean. All the while, the Carpenters' mournful melody played on, somewhere nearby.

"Ulla!" Pan's voice was behind me, and I whirled around to see him standing there.

An unsure smile played on his full lips, and his warm, dark eyes were full of longing. He wore an amethyst button-up shirt, with the top few buttons undone. With the wind sweeping through his wavy black hair, he looked like a fashion model.

His hair was longer than I remembered it, curling just below his ears, and I had the strongest urge to run my fingers through it.

"Pan." I threw my arms around him, and he held me to him and lifted me up off the ground.

When he set me back down, I pulled back so I could look him fully in the face. I wanted to study every part of it—his deep-set eyes behind thick lashes, his high cheekbones, and the subtle crooked smile on his lips that never completely went away. At least not when we were together.

"This is a dream, isn't it?" I asked him sadly.

"Sort of, but I am really here," he said with a wink.

"What?"

"It's a lysa," he explained. "I've only done this once before. Dagny had to walk me through the whole process, and I'm not very good at it so I had to wait until you fell asleep. There's a way that you can pull someone into a lysa even when they're awake, but it's a lot harder."

A lysa was similar to a persuasion, in that almost all trolls could do it and almost no humans could. I'd never had one before, but I had learned about them in school. They weren't very common, since it was far more tiring to astral project somewhere than it was to use a cell phone.

It was sort of like a dream, if the dream was really happening on the astral field. Our bodies remained in the physical world but our essence could meet together in a psychic link. Meaning I could feel his touch and smell his skin as if he were right here with me.

"Cell phones are usually easier than a lysa, except with you and me it seems."

"How long has it been since I've seen you in person?" I asked, staring up into his eyes.

He licked his lips. "I don't know."

I touched his arms and chest, and the feel of him—so strong and warm and *here*—made me flush with heat. "I've been worried about you. And Dagny and Eliana."

"Well, you don't need to worry about me. I'm fine. Dagny's mostly fine, and she's in good hands with Elof, and I've been checking on her."

I smiled. "Good."

"Where are you right now?"

"On a train in the middle of Manitoba. I'll be in Doldastam the day after tomorrow."

The wind picked up, turning icy, and the blue sky darkened—not with clouds, but like the sun was setting in a matter of a seconds. Not that there was even a sun in the sky. I shivered from the cold, and the seagull calls came out warbled and screeching.

"What's happening?" I asked.

"The lysa's breaking. I'm sorry. I'm not very good at it." He rubbed his hands on my bare arms, warming me.

"No, don't be sorry. I'm just happy I got to see you."

The song that'd been playing changed to something haunting and strangely familiar. It was a language I didn't know—Nordic but more guttural with elongated vowels—but somehow . . . I knew exactly what it meant.

ennlindanna fjeur seern densolla
den orn av gullat svoavva ennung
on i ennsommora morgana guovssahas
doai fulla i vallihanna

the linden flower watched the sun
the bird of gold soared over the meadow
and in the summer morning light
the two fell in love

"Where's that coming from?" I asked Pan.

His brow furrowed. "I thought the Carpenters were something you were listening to?"

"That is. But what's the other one? About the flower and the bird?"

He shook his head. "I don't hear anything else."

The ground was shaking and the waves receded, leaving us floating on an island in the middle of nothing. The starless indigo sky engulfed us, and I grabbed Pan, holding him close to me while I still could.

Everything was rumbling, but still the song bled through—*junggar enns morgda visavilla / singing his mourning song*—I kissed Pan, fully, deeply, mouth on his and my fingers in his hair, holding him to me.

And then I felt him evaporate from my arms, his warmth replaced with cold air. I was alone in the darkness, with only the final words of the song hanging in the air—*enn morgana fjeurn on ennsommora orn / the morning flower and the summer bird.*

I sat up, alone in my bunk on the train, gasping for air. My foot still stung, and I pulled back the blankets to see it bleeding—exactly where the rock had pierced it in the lysa.

14

north

As the train slowly crept toward the station, I watched from the window, and lyrics from the song in the lysa repeated in my head. When I'd woken up, I'd written it all down in a hurry so I wouldn't forget. But the song lingered in my mind, and when I closed my eyes, the words hung in the air, like the fading aftermath of fireworks in the night sky.

grotta insa ihkku
anda cieri insa saddjavvi
on fjeurn kvavarrid enn orn vandavar

And even though I didn't know the language—it had an Old Germanic flair, not that dissimilar from Norse, but it was much more guttural and distant enough that I shouldn't be able to understand it—it all made perfect sense somehow.

she wept all through the night
until her tears became a lake
and the flower drowned awaiting the bird's return

It was a strange thing to have an ancient-sounding, bluesy a capella song stuck in my head, but here we were.

The train ended at the station in the human town of Churchill—the Polar Bear Capital of the World, if the sign was to be believed. Doldastam was nearly an hour-long drive away, so Bryn was supposed to be waiting for me with one of the Kanin's vehicles.

I grabbed my duffel bag and kept my head down when I walked through the station, not that any of the humans seemed to notice me. I don't know what kind of deal the Kanin made with the Churchillians or if it was part of their cloaking spell, but they didn't bother me and that was good.

Outside, I squinted into the bright morning sun, and I spotted a guy leaning against a white Range Rover. His chestnut curls were cropped short, and he looked at me over the top of his sunglasses. When he smiled and waved at me, I finally recognized him as Ridley Dresden, Bryn's boyfriend. They had been together for years, but I had only met him once, when I visited Doldastam.

"How are you doing, Ulla?" he asked as he stepped toward me. "Do you need help with your bag?"

"No, I'm good," I said, and he opened the trunk so I could toss my bag inside. "How are you?"

"Good, good," he replied. "Bryn's busy with a work thing. She has the rest of the day off, but she had some meeting with the Högdragen she couldn't get out of. So she asked me to give you a ride."

"Well, thank you, I really appreciate it." I offered him an apologetic smile.

"No problem," Ridley said cheerily, and he opened the passenger-side door for me. He jogged around and got in. As he turned the car on, he asked, "Is Avicii okay?"

Upbeat electronica came out of the speakers, and honestly,

I was happy for the reprieve from the haunting choir in my head—*grotta insa ihkku / anda cieri insa saddjavvi.*

"Yeah, it's great," I said, and settled into the seat. "It sounds like Bryn has been busy."

Ridley chuckled. "That's an understatement."

He pulled out of the parking lot, and within minutes, we'd taken the main street past the shops and inns, and we were out of the town. On either side of the narrow road, the summer tundra of tall grass and wildflowers surrounded us.

"She's the guard to the King," Ridley went on, drumming his ringed fingers on the steering wheel in time with the music. "And the last few Kanin monarchs were murdered, or at the very least died under mysterious circumstances, and Bryn really does not want to continue with the precedent."

"Her career's always been important to her," I said.

"That's true. She's passionate about her work, and she's great at it. That's one of the first things that drew me to her. I just wish she'd take more time for herself . . . and for us." He shook his head, as if clearing it, then grinned over at me. "That's why I'm so glad you're here. Bryn's cashing in some of her vacation time she's stocked up, and she can kick back and relax for once."

The smile I managed felt tight and sick, and I swallowed back my guilt and doubt. "I hope we can have a nice time."

"I'm sure you will," he said confidently.

As we drove—the flat landscape increasingly broken up with tall, slender pine trees—Ridley and I chatted about his life with Bryn in the Kanin capital. He'd worked for the kingdom, training trackers, but after the war, he retired and floundered for a while, like many of his fellow soldiers and citizens. Eventually, he'd landed on his feet, and he got a job working at a greenhouse.

"Fortunately, Bryn was so supportive of such a dramatic

career shift," he explained. "But I really love it. It's so much more satisfying knowing that I'm helping feed our kingdom instead of working an elaborate grift."

He was talking about changelings, the troll practice that involved kidnapping human babies and stealing their money. Ridley—as a tracker and teacher—had never been a changeling, but he'd helped bring dozens of changelings—and their stolen inheritances—back to the kingdom.

A decade of that work had really worn on him, and now he excitedly talked about the hydroponics they'd installed. They'd had such a great season last year, the food treasury had made a neat profit exporting pickled beets to the Skojare.

We had at least another fifteen minutes to go, and we'd run through all the small talk—he'd even talked to me about Bryn's Tralla horse, Bloom, and suggested I go for a ride while I was here. Everything around us was completely overgrown with the looming evergreen hybrids the Kanin cultivated, with long weeping willow–like branches, helping to conceal the road and the city.

Ridley wasn't talking, and the current song on his playlist was a quiet ballad. As I looked out the window at the leering trees, the lysa song grew louder in my head.

anda varrid ins om ennung / lindanna fjeura blommid anyo / enndast efdar deen orn varrid torrid was the latest refrain—*until he bled on the meadows / linden flowers bloomed anew / only after the bird bled dry.*

Finally, through the hungry branches scraping against the hood of the car, I saw the iron gate and the tall stone wall that surrounded the city. As we rolled toward it, the music in my head fell silent.

Ridley talked to the guard at the gate, who waved us through. The main road was narrow, winding through the rows of small cottages buried in overgrown bushes. Making matters even more slow going, the streets were lined with pedestrians—mostly trolls, but plenty of chickens, rabbits, goats, and several fat donkeys.

We turned in front of the palace—a large, stocky building of gray stone. The castle's cold façade was broken up with stained-glass windows depicting various events in the Kanin history. The palace was on the far south side of the city, along the wall, and Ridley drove us around it, past a trio of modern apartment buildings.

He parked in front of one closest to the wall, and led me up the three flights of stairs. As he opened the door, he announced cheekily, "Welcome to the penthouse suite."

Their apartment was small, but the ceilings were high and the sparse, light décor made it feel cool and open. White walls with clean lines, blond wooden floors, and potted plants were everywhere.

"We don't really have a 'guest room,' but there's a futon in the office." He motioned to the open door off the living room. "The bathroom's next to it if you wanna freshen up."

"Thanks," I told him, and I took him up on the offer. After I finished in the bathroom, I went to the office to drop my bag on the futon.

It was a small room with pale smoky gray walls, a narrow bookcase, and a sleek blond desk with a laptop, a succulent in a jar, and a notepad. On the walls, photos had been hung in copper frames—an older picture of Bryn with Ember, another of Bryn with a pudgy little boy, a silver Tralla horse, a few others with folks I didn't recognize—but it was the ones of her family that gave me pause.

Bryn smiling brightly with her mother, Runa—blond, blue-eyed, a softer, older version of Bryn—and her father, Iver—black hair, dark eyes, olive skin, a quiet intellectual with little in common with the athletic, strong-willed Bryn. But no matter their obvious similarities—or lack thereof—one thing was abundantly clear as I looked at their picture with three smiling faces, their arms around each other: that they cared about each other.

From the office, I heard the apartment door open, and Bryn asking Ridley if I was there.

"Hi, Bryn," I said as I came out.

She smiled at me, her hands on her hips and her blond curls pulled back into a slick ponytail. "Hey, Ulla. Sorry I couldn't be there to pick you up. I hope your trip was okay."

"Yeah, yeah, it was," I said.

"So." She glanced over to the kitchen. "I don't know how you're feeling or what you—"

"I think you're my sister," I blurted out.

15

confessions

Bryn stood in the living room, her eyes wide and confused. She still wore the crisp white pants of her guard uniform, but the blazer hung on the back of the chair, so she just wore a tank top that showed off her scarred, muscular arms.

"What are you talking about?" she asked after a tense silence.

"I know it'll sound far-fetched, and I'm sure it doesn't help that I'm just saying it like that," I said quickly, and I knew I was talking too fast, but I felt nervous and couldn't slow down. "I wanted to wait for the right time, but then I saw you, and I just wanted to talk to you about it, and so I'm just telling you, we might be sisters."

"Okay," she said cautiously, and glanced over at Ridley. He was standing near the sliding glass doors that led out to a small balcony, his arms folded over his chest, and he only shook his head.

"You're clearly upset. Why don't we sit down and talk about it?" She motioned to the couch, so I took a deep breath and sat down, and she perched on the arm of the couch.

"Are you thirsty? I'll get you some water," Ridley said, and went into the kitchen.

"So, Ulla, why do you think we're sisters?" Bryn asked gently.

"You know how I was left as a baby in Iskyla?" I asked her, speaking more at my regular speed.

She nodded, and I launched into the whole thing, from the few things I knew from Mr. Tulin to finding out about Indu from Bryn's friend Bekk to my journey to Isarna to meet Indu myself.

"So you're saying that this Indu is going around impregnating all those women?" Bryn asked skeptically. "Why?"

"I don't know exactly," I admitted. "Most of them don't seem to survive."

"Why not?"

I shrugged grimly. "I don't know, actually."

Bryn stared straight ahead, out the glass doors, the sunlight shining across the balcony and the city wall beyond. Her face was impassive, and her posture was rigid and still—no doubt from her guard training—except for her right hand, where she twisted the rings on her fingers.

"This Indu doesn't sound like a reputable guy," she said at last.

Our water sat on the mirror-top coffee table, ice cubes slowly melting in the glasses, and Ridley sat on the ottoman nearby, his fingers tented together.

"He held me hostage for a month and erased my memory," I said flatly. "I would not call him trustworthy, no."

Bryn looked over at me. "Then why do you trust him on this?"

I handed her the napkin, the one with the names written on it. "Bekk confirmed he is the father of the child she's carrying, and I met Noomi in Sweden. I haven't looked into Asta or Minoux yet."

"The mothers are all Skojare and Omte," she said, almost to herself.

"He seems to target those two tribes. There's a Skojare and Trylle population in Isarna, but instead of 'dating' there, he made multiple trips across the ocean to find prospective mothers in the Omte capital," I explained.

She stared down, her jaw tensing subtly under her pale skin. "Strong women," Bryn said with a sigh. "He's looking for strong women to carry his child. Physically, the Omte and Vittra are the strongest, but the Vittra are nearly infertile. The Skojare are surprisingly resilient, with high tolerances to cold, pain, and lack of oxygen."

"The Kanin and Trylle got things going for them too," Ridley chimed in, and his skin rippled, shifting its usual olive to eggshell to match the walls around us. He—like many of the Kanin—had the ability to blend in with the surroundings, like a chameleon.

"Those are something beyond biology," Bryn said. "Magical and powerful, yes. But not the main concern if you're on the hunt for a womb to help you make a big, strong baby." Her eyes landed on me.

"There's only one place to go from here," Bryn said, and stood up. "We have to talk to my mom."

"We?" I asked in surprise.

"You're the one who knows about this. She'll want to talk to you." She went toward the bedroom. "I need to change, and then we can go."

I gulped down some water, and Bryn returned a moment later in jeans and a striped tank top. She said a quick goodbye to Ridley and kissed him on the cheek, then we were out the door.

"Don't say anything you'll regret!" Ridley called after us as the door swung shut.

As we went down the stairs, I asked Bryn if now was the best time to have this conversation with her mom. In her matter-of-fact way, she informed me that her dad was at work, her mother was a teacher with summers off, and she should just be getting back from her morning swim in the nearby lake.

They had moved to Storvatten, the Skojare capital, for some time after the Kanin Civil War, but they had found life there too stifling, and they returned to Doldastam. Bryn had briefly lived in the family home while they were gone, so they were able to move right back into the house she'd grown up in.

I followed Bryn down the cobblestone roads, occasionally falling behind her long, purposeful strides. Doldastam resembled Merellä more than it did Förening, but it was strangely greener here, with plenty of bushes and tall evergreens, tangles of vines growing over the houses, gardens bursting with vegetables in the narrow strips between them.

Bryn stopped at a cottage near the center of town, and she opened the front door without knocking. The house smelled of seawater with a faint undertone of waterlilies, and the walls were pale blue. Old antiques and Kanin artifacts crowded the shelves, but the rest of the space felt airy and open.

"Mom?" Bryn shouted.

"Bryn?" her mother yelled from upstairs, and a moment later, she was jogging down the steps. Her short, pale blond hair was damp and wild, and she wore a long sundress with bright teal flowers that brought out the color of her eyes. Runa Aven was a tall, beautiful woman, looking even more radiant than when I had seen her five years ago.

"What's wrong?" Runa asked her, then glanced over at me. "Did something happen?"

"No, we just need to talk," Bryn said.

"Yeah, of course." Runa motioned to the living room. As I walked by her, she asked, "You're Bryn's friend, Ella?"

"Ulla," I corrected her.

"Ulla, right." She smiled thinly and sat on the chair across from us. "I didn't know that you were visiting."

"It was a spur-of-the-moment thing," I said.

"Ulla thinks she's my sister," Bryn said, apparently having decided that my "blurt it out" method was the best way to go.

"Wh-wh . . ." Runa looked between the two of us, her mouth agape. *"What?"*

And then Bryn launched into an abridged version of Indu's story, skipping over my rambling personal bits for the condensed facts. Runa didn't say anything while Bryn talked, just stared ahead with her lips pressed together.

Runa hardly reacted at all, until Bryn handed her the napkin with the names. Then she made a small gasp, and put her hand to her mouth as tears formed in her eyes.

"It's true, isn't it?" Bryn asked.

Runa's hands trembled as she wiped at her eyes. "I eloped with Iver when I was only sixteen, and our families were furious because we were from different tribes. We were disowned, disinherited, stripped of our titles."

"I know what you and Dad went through to be together," Bryn said icily. "Because the two of you were so in love."

"We were," Runa sobbed, then took a deep breath so she could speak more calmly. "I loved Iver then, and I still love him now."

"You've been married to Dad—to *Iver*—for twenty-six years, and I'm twenty-four years old," Bryn told her mother harshly. "The math says that if Iver isn't my father, then you must've cheated on him."

"I'm not trying to defend what happened," Runa said, speaking slowly and carefully. "I'm merely explaining. After we were married, we moved here to Doldastam, away from my friends, my family, my lake. I was shunned, and Iver worked long hours to support us. The winter was so dark and cold, and I was alone, very, very alone.

"I went out to the bar one night, and Indu was there," Runa went on. "No one else would even talk to me, because I was Skojare. But he did. He bought me a drink, and then another. We talked for hours and then . . . we spent the night together. And I never saw him again."

"Does Dad know?" Bryn asked.

Runa sniffled and nodded. "After you were born. You were a few weeks old, and I thought he should know the truth. Iver already loved you so much, and he never stopped, he never thought about leaving you. With time, he forgave me, and we moved past it."

"But I didn't deserve to know the truth?" Bryn asked sharply.

Tears streamed down her mother's cheeks. "I told you the only truth that mattered—that Iver and I love you more than anything. You're our daughter, Bryn."

16

Birthright

The visit with Bryn's mom had been mercifully short, and Bryn didn't say much on the walk back to the apartment. I took a long shower—both because I needed to wash the stress and grime away, and to give Bryn the privacy to talk to her boyfriend and process what she'd learned today.

When I came out of the bathroom, Bryn apologized for the awkwardness, and she forced a smile as she suggested we still try to have a good time.

"You're never in Doldastam, and I never take time off, so we ought to make the most of it," she announced.

And she had a point, so I agreed, and we spent the afternoon doing things around town while we pretended that Bryn wasn't internally reeling. We saw the Tralla horses, and we rode her horse, Bloom, around the edge of the city. For supper, she took me to Juni's Jubilant Confectionery, and I had the most delicious *semla* ever.

After that, Bryn took me on an after-hours tour of the palace. She explained all the battles depicted in the giant stained-glass windows, and when we went around the corridor with all the kings' portraits, she knew facts about every one.

I took a picture of Elliot Konrad Strinne, the sixth monarch in the Strinne Dynasty and the twenty-eighth monarch of the Kanin kingdom. Nearly twenty years ago, he'd fallen ill with an infection of the blood, and he'd died when he was only twenty-six years old. According to Pan's mother, she'd worked as a human trade liaison to the King, and she and Elliot had fallen in love and they had Pan together.

Since he was half-human and a technical claimant to the throne, the Kanin kingdom refused to acknowledge Pan's request for a paternity test against Elliot's blood. The Inhemsk Project worked hard to discover the proper lineages of trolls of mixed blood and find their place in the kingdoms, but they only had limited power within the Mimirin. Pan would likely never get confirmation one way or the other that Elliot was his father.

But looking at the portrait of Elliot on his coronation, painted when he was younger even than Pan was now, I could see the resemblance was undeniable—the same dark eyes, full lips with the subtle smile at the corners of the mouth, thick sharp eyebrows, and strong shape of the jaw.

When Bryn had shown me everything of interest—including the new chandelier with a bajillion crystals that had to be replaced after the Invasion of Doldastam—we went back to her apartment. We sat on the balcony, our feet propped up on the railing, sipping wine and watching the late-evening sun setting slowly over the boreal forest that surrounded the city.

"Thank you for showing me around today," I told her. "I've had kind of a rough summer, and it was nice to have a vacation from that."

"Yeah, I know what you mean." She took a big gulp of her drink. "Sorry for being distant today."

"No, I'm sorry for dropping a big downer like that on you."

"It's definitely not a fun way to start the day, but I'm glad you told me. It's just a surreal thing to think that my entire life has been based around the fact that I was born half-Kanin, and it turns out that might not even be true."

"I can only imagine."

"You met Indu, right?" she asked.

I nodded. "Yeah. I think I spent about a month with him, but I don't remember most of it."

"He erased your memory so you wouldn't remember what he'd done." Her voice was hard and flat. "He's a real bastard, isn't he?"

"Yeah, I think he is."

"You don't know what he wants? Why he's going out, knocking up ladies, building up an army of daughters, and stealing your blood?" she asked.

"He's also collecting rare flowers from the Vittra," I added.

"So he's an eccentric bastard," she said wryly.

"I'm working with a Trylle healer, and I'm hoping that if I get my memories back, I'll know what's really going on," I said.

"I know some of them. Which healer?"

"Sunniva Kroner. Her brother Tove is helping too."

"Mmm." She took another drink. "The Kroners are powerful. If anyone can do it, they can."

"I hope so."

Bryn was silent, and in the fading light, her jaw tensed as she stared up at the sky. "I have to know."

"What?" I asked.

"I have to know for sure if Indu is my father or not," she said, her voice low. "There's still a chance that my dad is . . .

my dad." She looked over at me. "The Inhemsk Project does DNA testing, right?"

"Uh, yeah." I pulled my feet off the railing so I could sit up straighter. "But we don't have his DNA."

"No, but we have yours," she countered. "We can check if we're sisters."

"Yeah." I nodded. "I mean, I think so."

"Good." She smiled thinly, then downed her drink in one long gulp.

Bryn offered me another drink, but the length of the day—the last few days, honestly—hit me all at once. I declined and changed into my pajamas just before sacking out on the futon.

I woke up from a nightmare I couldn't remember, but I was gasping and sweating, and it took a minute to shake the feeling that spiders were crawling all over me.

But when I realized I was safe in Bryn's office, bathed in morning light, I took a deep breath, and I got up to open the window. I pulled over the desk chair so I could sit right in front of it and let the cool summer breeze blow over me. It also let in the stench of the city, mostly the horse manure this close to the palace stables, but the air felt good, cooling the drying sweat on my skin.

The thing about Bryn's apartment was that the walls were very thin, but that wasn't surprising. The complex was king-dom housing, similar to the tacky addition on the Mimirin, made for government employees. The biggest difference was that this was new and modern, because the old one had been destroyed in the war. At the Mimirin it was mostly docents and intellects, but here it was all guards and trackers.

From the other room, I heard Bryn and Ridley talking—her quieter but firm and calm, him a bit louder, anxious, un-certain.

"I'm not telling you not to do this," Ridley was saying. "But you are talking about using part of your savings on something really spur of the moment."

"I know, but this is important to me," Bryn replied evenly. "I have to know who I really am."

"But Bryn, you *do* know who you are," he argued. "You've always known. You're the most bullheaded troll I've ever met, and that's not changing if you're Kanin or Trylle or human, for Odin's sake."

"Really? You really believe it wouldn't change anything if I was human?"

He was silent, then mumbled something I couldn't hear, then louder, ". . . but that's not okay. You shouldn't lose your job."

"But I would, and we both know it," Bryn said.

"Do you think Indu is human?"

"Ulla doesn't know for sure. She thought maybe Omte or *álfar.*"

"So he could still be Kanin? Or human?" Ridley asked, and Bryn didn't make an audible response. "Then maybe it's better you don't know. Right now everyone believes you are Skojare and Kanin—and you really might be. You've worked so hard to be accepted as you are. Why change that perception?"

"Because it's not the truth. I won't live a lie, even a beneficial one."

"But I don't know why it has to have any bearing on you," he persisted. "Iver still raised you. You still grew up completely enmeshed in the Doldastam culture. Hell, you led the rebellion that saved the damn kingdom. You *are* Kanin, no matter what your blood says."

Her voice was thick when she said, "It's not about that."

"Then what is it?" Ridley asked.

"Our abilities are passed through our blood," she reminded him gently. "You can change the color of your skin because your father could, and I'm drawn to the water because of my mother. Indu has been going around impregnating as many women as he can because he thought it was important to pass something along. If he is my father, I need to know what's in the blood he gave me."

17

By the sea

Over breakfast, Bryn told me her plan, which she'd apparently been working on throughout the night instead of sleeping. She'd gotten time off from work, arranged for fake passports from the Kanin rectory, and bought plane tickets for the two of us.

I protested about the expense, because it was a lot more than a train, and I couldn't afford to pay her back right now. She just shook her head and told me she did it for herself.

"We can get the train in two days and waste the next four to five days traveling, *or* we can fly out of Churchill in a few hours, and with a couple stops, we can be in Merellä by the morning," she explained.

After we finished eating, I got dressed and packed up my stuff. Ridley had been around during breakfast, sipping tea and not saying much, but things didn't seem tense exactly. When I came out of the office, they were kissing and talking softly to each other.

He helped carry our bags down to the vehicle, and drove us to the airport. He and Bryn held hands. Watching the two of them together like that made me miss Pan, and a rush of excitement washed over me.

It didn't really hit me until just then. Within twenty-four hours, I'd be back in Merellä, back within arm's reach of Pan. I still had no idea what the future might hold for us, or where my feet were going to land. But I knew that I really liked Pan, and I couldn't wait to see him again.

The realization did not help with the travel. Hours sitting on a tiny plane didn't ease my anticipation. Being around so many humans always made me anxious. They always wore too much cologne—I don't know why they were so hung up on dumping alcohol and oils over themselves, but it always made me sneeze.

That was annoying, but it wasn't the source of my anxiety. Humans could be so quick to turn on each other, but I'd read enough history to know that they had a tendency to use violence when they encountered something new and strange. On top of that, airports had become sort of battlegrounds for humans, with security everywhere, looking for anything that didn't belong.

And I didn't belong.

Bryn had been a tracker before she joined the guard, so she was far more used to moving seamlessly among the humans. It also helped that she was more ordinary-looking than me. She was prettier, really, but I meant that her eyes matched each other.

As we made our way through the airport in Winnipeg to catch the next flight, I wondered how I'd gotten on the plane in Sweden, after Indu had held me hostage. How had I gotten through? Who had taken me to the airport and bought the ticket?

Indu had to know his way around, with all his traveling between human cities. Isarna on the island in the Swedish

Bay of Bothnia, Doldastam in the Canadian subarctic, and Fulaträsk in the southern swamps of the United States. All of that was costly, and it required an understanding of human customs and laws across *multiple* countries.

That was the kind of thing that a tracker like Bryn would know. They had to be well versed in all parts of the human world to go among them and gather up the changelings—and their trust funds. Most changelings were left with families in relative proximity to their kingdom, but we couldn't exactly stop the hosts from moving whenever they wanted. Bryn had gone to Chicago, Seattle, Montreal, Atlanta, and she knew of others that went to London, Tokyo, and Dubai.

But that kind of travel, with the right documents, and the appropriate training for a sheltered teenage troll to blend into the cosmopolitan human world, was costly and time-consuming. The kingdoms sent young trolls to school to learn human etiquette, defense, and persuasion techniques.

How could an isolated tribe like the Älvolk have the money and know-how to do that, when they had no changelings or trackers?

It was late when we finally landed in Oregon. Bryn had to rent a car so we could drive to where Merellä is hidden along the coast. I could not wait to get there and take something for my throbbing headache, since I didn't know how human medications would work on a troll.

At some point, when we'd been in the air, the song had come back again. The baritone a capella singing of *enn morgana fjeurn on ennsommora orn*—the morning flower and the summer bird.

It began quietly, barely loud enough to be heard over the passenger snoring beside me. But as we traveled, it had gotten louder and louder. Even in the car, when Bryn had the radio on, it was still there, looping through my head.

grotta insa ihkku / anda cieri insa saddjavvi

she wept all through the night / until her tears became a lake

I closed my eyes and tried to sleep, resting my head against the window, but it was like a thunderous drum echoing through my brain.

lindanna fjeura blommid anyo / enndast efdar deen orn varrid torrid

linden flowers bloomed anew / only after the bird bled dry

Then finally, mercifully, the music started to subside, and I opened my eyes.

We drove along the coast, the moon illuminating the ocean crashing against the cliffs to our right, and a dense forest to our left. In front of us was nothing but a long, empty stretch of road. But then the air shimmered, and the mirage shifted into the night until the silhouette of the citadel slowly took shape.

The Mimirin was in the center of town, and even from this far away, it towered over everything. It looked like something from a gothic fairy tale, especially as we drew closer.

Bryn drove along the wall until we got to the large gate of wood and iron. Guard towers were on either side, and a guard came to meet us before opening the gates. Bryn flashed her credentials—her real ones, since a King's personal guard garnered immediate respect, even one from another tribe.

He waved us in, and we made our way down the dirt roads. The song fell silent in my head as small houses closed in around us. The Mimirin institution loomed over the city, and I leaned forward, looking up at the thirteen atriums that lined the top of the building.

The full moon shined brightly through them, making the Ögonen's semi-transparent ochre skin glow in the darkness. They were much too far away to see their eyes from here, but I had no doubt that they saw us, that they were watching us with their trollian eyes.

I told Bryn where to go, and the carriage house finally came into view. The apartment I shared with Dagny was on the second floor. Bryn parked in the narrow gravel spot underneath the stairs, and we grabbed our bags and went up the steps to our rustic little place. I'd called ahead to make sure it was okay with Dagny that we stayed here.

"It's still your place," she'd said simply. "I'll see you when you get here."

Since it was so late, I used my key instead of knocking, but Dagny was waiting up for us. Or at least she'd tried to. She was sitting on the couch, her head sagging to the side, a dog-eared copy of *Recovering Memories in the Troll Brain* on her lap.

Her long black hair was pulled back in a braid, and when she looked up at us, blinking groggily, I noticed the eyebrow above her left eye—one half was burned off, leaving a jagged ruddy pink mark in its stead.

"You're back with another houseguest," she said with a yawn.

I dropped my bag on the floor and stopped short. "When we talked on the phone, I told you about Bryn."

"I know, Ulla." She smiled as she stood up. "I'm only joshing you."

I hugged her. "It's good to see you, Dag."

18

lyrical

"Are you ready to face the pain this time?" Elof Dómari asked with a wink. The last time he drew my blood I had nearly fainted, but that had been a long time ago.

I smiled down at him. "Yeah. I made sure to eat before we came here."

"I made them both eat a big breakfast," Dagny said over her shoulder as she walked across the troglecology lab to get the equipment for the blood draw.

The lab was Elof's domain, as the esteemed docent from the Vittra kingdom. His main interest was blood—finding out as much as it could tell him about ourselves, our abilities, our ancestry. Trolls have always known that we had supernatural powers that humans could only dream of, but it was only recently that we started looking into *why*.

Some trolls were afraid of the science behind it, since humans were the ones that mastered it first. Others feared what they might find, or that it was going against "troll ways." Fortunately, trolls like Elof relentlessly pursued the truth, and they convinced the Vittra-controlled Merellä to join the human world in the twenty-first century.

That made Elof's sleek lab on the third floor of the Mimirin the best place within the troll kingdoms for Bryn and me to go to check our blood. The labs were a strange juxtaposition of original architecture, including stained-glass windows and barrel-vaulted ceilings, with slick lab equipment and modern islands.

Dagny had arranged for us to meet with Elof, which wasn't that hard because he hadn't resumed teaching his classes since he'd gotten back. Elof had been with Dagny, Pan, and me when Indu and the Älvolk held us for a month. While we'd been gone, his courses had been on hold, and when the planned trip of a few days stretched on for uncertain weeks, the Information Styrelse had suspended the summer semester.

Over breakfast, Dagny had told me all about it, but she thought it was for the best. It gave her and Elof plenty of time to work on recovering their memories.

"Did you remember anything when the Ögonen tried the aural healing on you?" I had asked her, as I sipped lemon tea.

She shook her head. "Just flashes of the cell they held us in. Nothing more."

"And you haven't heard anything from Eliana?" I asked.

She arched her eyebrow—the one still healing—and winced slightly. "Have you?"

"No. I was just hoping."

"I'm worried about her too," Dagny said finally. "But she's resilient."

Dagny was Elof's lab assistant, and they had gone back to working on the genealogical testing of the Inhemsk Project. While they had been gone, another docent and a Mästare had taken over testing the blood and comparing DNA.

"Are you ready for this?" Dagny asked as she laid her blood-drawing kit out on the counter beside me.

"Yeah, yeah." I was sitting on the stool, trying to pretend that I wasn't scared by the sight of the monstrous needle. Honestly, I would've classified it as a small metal tube. Needles were thin, petite, less aggressive.

Bryn was watching me with an amused gaze. When Dagny put on her gloves, snapping the latex against her wrist, I flinched, and Bryn laughed.

"I didn't know you were afraid of needles," she said.

I bristled. "I'm not *afraid* of them. I just don't like them."

Dagny continued the process—tying a tourniquet around my arm, and then probing with her fingers, looking for a good vein. Her brow furrowed as she searched, touching all down my inner arm.

"Is something wrong?" I asked.

"Not exactly." She frowned. "Your skin feels . . . thicker. I think you have some type of scar tissue building up. They must've taken a lot of blood from you."

"Is it safe to take more?" I asked.

"Oh, yeah. You'll be fine." Dagny must've found a vein she liked, because she wiped down my skin with a cold alcohol swab. "Just look at Bryn, and if you faint, she'll catch you."

I took a deep breath and looked over at Bryn. She stood with her arms folded across her chest, and gave me a thin, encouraging smile.

"If you need a distraction, you should try singing that song that you've been going on about," Bryn suggested.

"It's finally out of my head, and now you wanna bring it back?" I cringed.

She shrugged. "It distracts you."

"What song are you talking about?" Elof perked up. He sat across the island from me, resting his arms on the dark marble.

"She's had this song in another language stuck in her head for a few days, but it stops when she's in troll cities, so we think the cloaking magic interferes with it," Bryn answered for me.

"For a few days?" Elof tilted his head. "Did anything precede the earworm's implantation?"

"It started in a lysa," I said.

He looked to Dagny and asked her, "Is that the one you helped Pan with?"

"Yes, and I already went over it with Ulla, and I didn't notice anything strange with the lysa," Dagny said, and picked up the needle. "You're going to feel a pinch."

I quickly looked at Bryn, locking onto her blue eyes, and I recited the translation that had been stuck in my head.

the linden flower watched the sun
the bird of gold soared over the meadow
and in the summer morning light
the two fell in love
the flower stretched toward the sky
and the birds sang her songs all day
but they never last
for even the greenest summer
withers in the longest night
when the sky turned dark
the bird had gone and the flower saw
she wept all through the night
until her tears became a lake
and the flower drowned awaiting the bird's return
too late the bird came back
he plucked the feathers from his breast
until he bled on the meadows
linden flowers bloomed anew

only after the bird bled dry
over their bodies are the flowers and birds
singing his mourning song
the bird and the flower may fall in love
but they will never share a nest
the morning flower and the summer bird

Halfway through my recitation, I felt the needle pierce my skin, and the extra pressure of the effort Dagny had to use to get it through my thicker tissue. But I just inhaled sharply and kept on talking.

"That's not particularly catchy," Elof commented when I'd finished.

"It sounds better in the original language," I said.

"All done," Dagny announced, and I made the mistake of looking just as she was pulling the needle out.

I swayed to the side. "Oh, *jakla.*"

Bryn immediately grabbed my shoulder to steady me. "Easy."

"I'm okay." I blinked a few times and took another deep breath. "I'm okay," I repeated once Dagny had wrapped gauze around my arm, and I slowly got to my feet.

Elof brought me a glass of water, and Dagny finished labeling my samples—vials of my currant-red blood. He noticed me looking, so he put his hand on my arm, steering me away so I wouldn't make myself sick.

"What is the original language?" Elof asked.

"What?" I asked, then shook my head. "Oh, the song. I'm not sure. It *sounds* like something Old Germanic, like a rough Scandinavian dialect, but more guttural. And it has the harder consonants that remind me of Inuit or Sami."

"Interesting." He leaned back against the short island,

resting his elbows on the counter. "Could you sing me a bit? In the original language?"

"I can try, but I won't be able to match the pronunciations." I cleared my throat and concentrated, then gave it my best shot. "*Ennlindanna fjeur seern densolla / den orn av gullat svoavva ennung.*"

Elof's eyebrows shot up. "That sounds very familiar."

"Yeah." Dagny had stopped what she was doing to look up at me. "We've heard that before, haven't we?"

19

earworm

I walked down the hallways of the Mimirin, mostly empty because it was Saturday, and the stones felt cold and smooth under my bare feet. Bryn was still back with Dagny, getting her blood drawn while Elof questioned her about her biology. Though my light-headedness had passed, I'd left under the guise of needing fresh air.

But the truth was that while I had been sipping on my water, listening to Dagny and Elof discuss the strange familiarity of the song—though neither of them could quite place it—Dag had let slip that Pan was down working at the Inhemsk Project, making up for missed time.

I hadn't had a chance to see him yet, and I'd been hoping to do that this afternoon. But now, knowing he was a couple floors down, it was too close, too tempting to wait any longer. Since we'd already been playing phone tag, I hadn't told him that I'd be coming back, hoping I could surprise him.

The door of the Inhemsk Project had frosted stained glass in it, and instead of the name it was marked with a yellow flower dipped in blood. I opened it without knocking, and the large office space appeared deserted. There were half a dozen desks, partitioned off by bookshelves and file cabinets overflowing with papers, files, and binders—one of the side effects of trolls' distaste for technology. There were old, clunky laptops on most of the desks, but Pan said they mostly used them for typing reports and playing solitaire.

It was dark in the office, except for the light from a solitary desk lamp. Pan was hunched over his papers, his hand buried in his thick, wavy hair. He was so focused on his work, he didn't hear me until I was nearly at his desk.

He looked up, his dark eyes widening. "Ulla?" He blinked at me. "Is this a lysa?"

I laughed. "No, I'm really here. I got in at around two this morning."

"You're here?" He smiled as he got up and came around the desk. "I can't believe you're here."

Pan pulled me into a hug, wrapping his arms around me. And that's all it was for a minute, neither of us saying anything, just content to hold one another. I couldn't remember a single time in my life that someone had just held me like this, not pulling away or asking for anything more.

"I missed you," I said quietly.

"I missed you too." He kissed my forehead and finally we separated. "Not that I'm complaining, but why are you here?"

I filled him in on my brief visit to Doldastam and how Bryn wanted to confirm the truth through our blood. Then I finished it up by telling him about the song that had been stuck in my head since the lysa.

"'*Ennlindanna fjeur seern densolla / den orn av gullat svoavva ennung,*'" Pan said, doing a poor imitation of the extreme vocalization style of the song.

"Wait. You've been hearing it too?" I asked. "Like now? In Merellä?"

"Yeah. I mean, not *right* now. Only in my dreams," he clarified, and stepped back toward his desk. "As soon as I woke this morning, I wrote it down." He grabbed a wrinkled notebook page and handed it to me. "And when I came in this morning, I started looking up anything I could, and I actually found something."

Pan's sloppy handwriting was a little hard to read, but it looked like the same lyrics I'd had running through my head.

"I thought I'd have to wait until Monday, when Calder's working, because the archives are locked up over the weekend," Pan explained. "But the office is full of books from all over—even some snuck up from the archives, don't tell Calder. And then, as I'm coming in, walking in past a desk, my hip bumps this book hanging over and lo and behold—"

He picked up the book, mindful to keep his finger between the pages to hold his place, and he flipped over the cover so I could read it. *Folktales of the Arctic Peoples* by Belle Davies.

"Is this a human book?" I asked.

"Yeah, it is," he said. "Published in 1911 in London. It didn't have anything in the original language, but they have an abridged English version." He opened it to the right page, then handed it to me. "That's it, right?"

A flower of green and a bird of gold
fell in love under the summer sun.
Together they sang a song of old,
Until, in the meadow, they would be one.
Then the long night came and the flower did cry.
She shriveled and ne'r again did rise.
Without her, the bird knew he'd surely die.
He wept until blood sprung from his eyes.
The summer bird and morning flower did fall in love
and they both drowned in sorrow.

With one in the meadow and the other above
where they went, no one could follow.

"So, after each of the folk songs, the author explains what they think the folk song is about," Pan said when I finished reading it. "This one is about the long, dark winters and short, bright summers. Which sure, obvious take.

"But then the author goes on, saying that this particular song was found with artifacts relating to a skirmish between a Sami tribe and a Viking clan," he continued. "They fought over a patch of land where a flower grew. Both groups believed the yellow snowball flower *varrarassi* had medicinal properties. The Sami won the first battle, but the brutal Viking clan attacked them during the night. Almost all the Sami were killed, and those that were left were chased off the land. The author doesn't know what became of the Viking clan or the flower."

"Wait," I said. "You're thinking the *varrarassi* is the *sorgblomma* that the Vittra gave the Älvolk in exchange for us? The morning flower is the *mourning flower*."

He nodded. "That's *exactly* what I'm thinking, yeah."

"But how did the flower end up in the hands of the Vittra?" I asked. "And what are the 'medicinal' uses?"

"I don't know the answer to either of those questions," he admitted glumly.

"The book doesn't say anything about what the flower can supposedly do?" I asked. I flipped to the next page, which showed a big green dragon under the title "The Dragon Who Ate the Sun."

A watercolor painting of a long, serpentine dragon—a wyrm, I knew from Liam's book *Dragons of Every Size*— weaved between the lines of the short poem. Twenty stanzas told the short tale of a wyrm that ate fire, believing it was the sun, after the giants used a flaming elk heart as bait. Then the wyrm fell ill and died.

"No, the next one is just some weird retelling of the old Norse myths about Jörmungandr," Pan said with a disappointed sigh. "I've been reading through the rest of the book, but only these two were found with the artifacts from the *varrarassi* flower skirmish, and I haven't found any that mention a flower in a meaningful way, or hint at what the *sorgblomma* might be used for besides the vague term 'medicinal purposes.'"

"So . . ." I set the book back down on his desk and ran my hand through my hair. "We have a song stuck in our heads, in a language neither of us really knows, about a bird and a magic medical morning flower that may or may not have something to do with our missing month."

He smirked. "Aside from all the alliteration, I'd say you summarized the situation well."

"But why?" I asked. "Where did it come from?"

Pan looked at me intently, his eyes narrowed slightly. "The daughters of the Älvolk sang it to us when we were with them. It's one of the only things I remember from our time there."

And then I was suddenly there again—a memory of a large underground room, dimly lit by candles, as a choir sang on in their haunting way. Pan's warm, dark eyes cut through that, and it was only me and him in a dark corridor, but we were separated by iron bars. The singing stopped abruptly, and Pan's eyes went wide with panic. He screamed my name and reached through the bars for me, but something was pulling me, dragging me away.

"Stop all that squawking," Noomi growled as she hauled me off, her voice low in my ear.

"Ulla?" Pan was saying in the here and now, and his hand

was warm on my shoulder. I blinked, and then I saw him, worried, right in front of me. "Are you okay?"

I nodded. "Yeah. Sorry."

"Where'd you go?" He put his hand on my face, his thumb on my cheek.

"I've been getting these flashes of the last month. None of them make a lot of sense." I chewed my bottom lip. "You were there and ..." I trailed off. "I'm glad you're here now, and you're okay."

A soft smile played on his lips as he murmured, "Me too." He leaned in toward me and—

—and the overhead lights flicked on, flooding the room with bright light, and I stepped back from him.

"Oh, good," Sylvi Hagen said as she stepped into the office with her usual expression of aloof condescension, and her copper thermos in her hand. "I came down here in hopes that Panuk knew where to find you, but you're already here, Ulla, so that saves me the trouble."

"What do you need me for?" I asked, squinting nervously at her. "Am I not allowed to be here?"

"On the contrary." Sylvi strode languidly over to us and eyed me from under hooded lashes. "The Korva heard that you were here, and he wants an audience with you. As soon as I find you, I'm to send you up to Ragnall Jerrick's office."

20

korva

The Korva was the head of the Mimirin, and as such, had the nicest office in the institution. It was on the fourth floor, in the far southwest corner, with big grand windows overlooking the cliffside and the ocean crashing into it. The room was a long rectangle and sparsely furnished, giving it the same ominous feel as an empty swimming pool.

A large desk—a thick slab of obsidian with raw edges on an ebony hardwood base—sat at the far end of the room, with slipper chairs covered in soft Tralla leather on either side.

Sylvi had brought me up and left me with the guard at the Korva's door. He wore a crimson uniform and put a finger to his temple as he eyed me before letting me into the office.

When I went in, my bare feet padding quietly across the cold marble floor, Ragnall Jerrick was sitting at the desk. A leather-bound planner lay open in front of him, the pages blank, and a copper quill pen perched in an inkwell. His hand rested on his chin, and his dark eyes gazed out the grand windows.

With his glossy good looks—his head shaved smooth, his tailored mulberry silk suit, the rubies in the rings on his fingers—he looked posed for a magazine feature on successful businessmen. And my steps faltered because it hit me—this all felt very staged. Everything was posed so deliberately, so clearly aimed to impress, intimidate, brag. It was swagger as a design aesthetic.

He finally looked up at me and smiled wide—all toothy and shiny. "Miss Tulin! I'm so pleased to see you looking so well." He rose to greet me, then motioned for me to sit.

"Thank you," I said. "And thank you for doing all you did to get me back home."

"No need to thank me." He waved me off with exaggerated modesty. "It was a joint effort among the kingdoms, and we were only doing what is right by our citizens."

"I appreciate it anyway," I said, and then I cleared my throat. "What was it that you wanted to see me about?"

"You've gone through such an ordeal, and I wanted to check in with you," Ragnall said.

I thought he would say more, but he just smiled at me, and when the silence became awkward, I said uncertainly, "That's . . . kind of you."

He tilted his head, and his mouth turned to a bemused frown. "Why the hesitation? Is something troubling you?"

Plenty of things were bothering me, but I wasn't about to tell him that, so I said, "What happened . . . what I went through was an ordeal. But I know I'm not the only one in the citadel that went through something stressful recently. I can't imagine you're calling them all in to see how they're coping."

He laughed and leaned back in the chair. "No. I don't suppose I would have time for that. But you did experience something a bit more extraordinary."

"So you've met with the others then?" I pressed gently, since neither Pan nor Dagny had mentioned seeing him.

"I met with Dómari," he replied coolly. "Mästare Amalie talked to Kasten and Soriano. She apprised me of their conversation." He leaned forward and rested his arms on the desk. "You weren't here then, but you are now. I thought it'd be prudent to meet with you while you were around."

"Of course," I said. "I'm doing well now. I'm happy to be back with my friends in Merellä."

"If I understand correctly, you are here for more than a social visit," Ragnall said. "You were in the troglecology department, working in the lab."

"Yes, I—I came back to continue getting help in searching for my birth parents." I shifted in my seat, barely suppressing my urge to squirm away from his unblinking gaze. "That's what I came here for initially. To work with the Inhemsk Project."

"You met your father, didn't you?" he asked. "When you were in Sverige?"

"Uh, yeah," I stammered, thrown by his use of the Swedish name for Sweden.

It was common to hear it called Sverige in Scandinavia, like in the troll island city of Isarna, but here in North America, we kept to our neighbors' tongue. For most kingdoms that meant English and Spanish in the States, or English with some French and Inuit in Canada.

"You know who your father is, then?" he asked.

I nodded hesitantly. "I believe so, yes."

"Did he tell you about your mother?"

"Some. We didn't . . . I don't remember talking with him much."

"Because the memory was erased," Ragnall supplied.

"Yes."

"It's good you still retained the memory of meeting him," he said, smiling too brightly for the conversation. "You've finally gotten the answer to your question. You found your birth parents."

"I know their names, but I wouldn't say that I know *them*," I argued carefully. "That's why I came back to work with the Inhemsk Project. I want to know the whole truth about my family."

A bird flew by the window—a large condor, soaring precariously close to the glass. The wingspan left a long shadow splashing across the office. Ragnall watched it, staring pensively at the ocean and the circling bird.

"The pursuit of the truth is a noble thing, albeit an endless one," he said. "You never truly know when you've discovered it all or only parts of it."

"I think I'll know when I've found enough," I said.

"Getting your memory back would be a top priority for you, I would assume," he said, and looked back at me. "On your quest for the truth."

"I have been trying," I admitted.

"Any luck?"

I met his gaze evenly and shook my head. "None yet."

"Did you find Eliana?" he asked, startling me.

An image suddenly flashed in my mind—an angry girl with Eliana's face standing by a waterfall—but it was gone as soon as it was there.

"No, I never saw her," I said, and I wasn't sure if it was a lie or not.

And then, like a worm boring its way back into my brain, the song returned. It buzzed in the back of my skull.

"You don't remember anything from your time with the Älvolk?" Ragnall asked.

—Noomi dragging me down the hall, the tube in my arm draining my blood, the choir singing, a room full of vials and old books, a crumbling city built into the mountainside, Indu's

face as he crouched before me, saying, "You're making this so much harder than it needs to be," as crippling pain cut me down—

"Nope," I said firmly.

Ragnall narrowed his eyes, and I fought to keep my expression even. "Hmm." Abruptly, his megawatt smile returned. "You'll be sure to let me or Amalie know if you remember anything. We're very interested in finding out all that we can about the First City and the Älvolk."

"Of course," I lied. "I know that the Mimirin is a bastion for knowledge."

"Precisely," he said. "I'm glad we could have this chat."

"Me too," I said, and then I got out of there as quickly as possible.

I didn't know what was going on, but the whole interaction had left me unnerved. Everything Ragnall said *sounded* right, but somehow it all felt wrong.

21

eclipsed

"So . . . you think Ragnall can read minds?" I asked, and my stomach dropped even further.

"No, that's not what I said," Dagny corrected me with an irritated sigh. "He has psychokinetic abilities, but plenty of trolls do and almost none of them can read minds."

The four of us—Dagny, Bryn, Pan, and myself—were in the apartment. After my sudden meeting with the Korva, I'd gone down to the troglecology lab, and Pan was there, waiting with the others. By then, it was well after lunchtime, and Dagny's stomach was growling, so we decided to get something to eat, while Elof decided to stay behind and continue working in the lab.

We grabbed flatbread sandwiches on the walk back to my and Dagny's apartment, and I filled them in on how my conversation with Ragnall had gone. Bryn and Pan were sitting at the bistro table, while Dagny sat on the lumpy couch with her plate of food balancing on the arm of the couch and the Mimirin directory open on her lap, reading the brief biography of Ragnall at the back.

"Well, let's assume the worst," Bryn said between bites of

her sandwich. "The head guy *can* read your mind. Would it be so bad if he did?"

"I mean, I lied to him," I said.

Bryn swallowed her mouthful. "Why?"

"I don't know," I admitted. "Because I really don't remember much, and what I do remember is jumbled and confusing. And . . ." I took a deep breath, trying to define exactly why I'd held back from the Korva. "I don't mind talking to you guys about it, but I don't want to share a bunch of scattered, intense memories with strangers, especially before I get it all sorted out."

"You did the right thing," Pan said quietly, his dark eyes resting thoughtfully on me. "Not telling him. I never trusted Ragnall farther than I could throw him."

"Why would you throw him?" Dagny asked from the couch.

"No, I wouldn't. It's a figure of speech." Pan glanced between us and Bryn shrugged. "Do trolls really not know that expression?"

"No, it's nonsensical." Dagny snorted. "Ulla could throw Ragnall very far."

"Popular slang in the kingdoms takes hold in the strangest ways," Bryn said. "King Linus made a joke about something being 'on fleek' a few months back at a banquet, because Linus hasn't had any real contact with humans in five years, and now everyone is saying 'on fleek.'"

Pan smirked. "I think that was the last time that saying was cool. For a week in 2014."

"This doesn't say much about what Ragnall can do," Dagny said, and flipped the book shut in irritation. "They made sure to include plenty of effusive praise about his high intellect and visionary leadership without mentioning any actual specifics about his skills or qualifications."

"Even if Ragnall can read minds, that doesn't mean there was anything for him to read in your mind," Bryn said.

Dagny let out a loud "Ha!"

"No, I didn't mean it like that." Bryn rolled her eyes. "The Älvolk either erased your memory—so there's nothing there because it's gone—or they walled off your memory—so it's still there but with a barrier around it powerful enough that you can't see through it. That would be very hard for a mind reader to get through."

"Well, the directory did really run through the thesaurus section on the word 'powerful,'" Dagny muttered.

"And the memories are still there," I said. "They must be if some of them are coming back."

"Why do you think Ragnall might be reading your thoughts?" Pan asked. "He asked a lot of questions, but half the Information Styrelse interrogated me and Dagny."

"Yeah, you did actually get off easy," Dagny agreed. "I don't know how much Ragnall is even interested in Áibmoráigi. When I was looking for him in the directory, I glanced at Amalie's bio, and hers mentioned that she has championed multiple expeditions to find the First City. It's clearly something she's been pursuing for decades, but Ragnall's bio only talks of vague aspirations like 'helping the Mimirin Talo achieve even greater excellence.'"

"He didn't ask me anything about Áibmoráigi specifically, or how to find it," I said. "Actually, he didn't really ask me much at all. He only seemed focused on making sure I was okay and if I remember anything."

Bryn narrowed her eyes. "He was making sure you don't remember anything?"

"No, not like that." I shook my head slowly. "I told him that I didn't remember anything, and he didn't believe me.

And then . . . I felt the buzzing—" I moved my hand around the back of my head. "—and the song came back."

"The bird and the flower one?" Dagny asked.

"Yeah, it only lasted a few minutes, and it sounded dull and far away," I elaborated. "But yeah, it was definitely while I was in the Korva's office."

"Starting to feel left out because I'm the only one without this jaunty tune in my head," Bryn said dryly.

Dagny snorted. "It's definitely not jaunty."

"You're okay now, right?" Pan asked, and his eyes were solemn even though his voice was light.

I nodded and smiled to ease his worry. "Yeah, yeah, I'm fine. He didn't hurt me or anything. I was just a little weirded out after."

"Good," he said with a thin smile.

"On the good-news front, Elof said he thinks he'll have the results of the familial blood testing for you guys tomorrow," Dagny said.

"Good," Bryn said. "It'll be great to start getting some concrete answers."

We all talked a bit more, with the conversation turning to lighter subjects like Pan's reunion with his dog, Brueger, and then he got up and stretched.

"Speaking of Brueger, I should get home and let him out," Pan said. "He's been cooped up in the apartment since eight this morning."

"Do you mind if I go with you?" I asked, getting to my feet. "I could use the fresh air."

"Sure." He grinned and headed toward the door.

I turned to Bryn and said, "I won't be gone too long."

"I think Bryn and I will manage without you," Dagny said.

It was afternoon, and the sky was sunny and pleasant. Pan

and I went down the steps from the apartment and along the soft gravel alleyway.

"How has everything been going for you here?" I asked as we walked through the bustling avenues. Barrels of potted linnea and lavender aster lined the already narrow roads, and when we had to go single file to slide between the plants and a woman walking a pair of very pregnant angora goats, Pan put his hand on my back.

"Fine, honestly," he said, speaking loudly to be heard over the neighborhood sounds—talking, competing music, goats braying, babies crying, and children laughing. "Just trying to get back into the swing of things and make sense of everything."

There was enough room that we could fall in step beside each other. I knew we were getting closer to Pan's place because I could smell it. He lived in a studio apartment above a salmon tannery and only a street away from the giant woolly elk stables. The good news was that it wasn't quite as busy around here.

"How about you?" he asked, his voice lower now that it could be.

"Same." I sighed. "I just hate the feeling that something bad happened to both of us—*all* of us—and I don't know what it was."

The sun had been shining brightly, warming my skin, but clouds must've rolled in, casting shadows over us and cooling the air.

"The important thing is that we made it out, and we're okay," Pan said. "That's what I keep reminding myself until we can remember what happened."

"I think I remembered something new today," I told him quietly.

He stopped short. "What?"

"It's not much." I turned back to face him. "Probably not anything important."

"What was it?" he pressed.

"I was in a room I hadn't seen before, full of vials and old books and plants." I closed my eyes, concentrating on the snippet I'd seen in Ragnall's office.

—a dark room with high walls that stretched up and up, and the ceiling was a stained-glass skylight. In each of the corners was an ouroboros in dark green, and that's what I stared up at, what I always stared up at when they brought me there.

(How many times had I been there? How many times had they strapped me down to that bed?)

The whole room smelled sickly sweet, of lilies and potent copper. Restraints held me in place. I could feel them chafing my wrists and ankles and stomach, and no matter how much I strained at them, they didn't give. Panic surged through me—there had been so few times in my life that I wasn't strong enough to break free. With my strength, I could overpower most snares, but not this.

I craned my neck toward the voices, catching glimpses of the vials of currant-red liquid and Indu arguing with Lemak, the häxdoktor.

"This is taking too long," Indu was saying. "We're bleeding her dry as it is."

"It takes time for a correct ratio," Lemak protested. "But we've never been this close before."

"Close?" Indu sneered at the häxdoktor. "Almost? Nearly?"

I could see them with my head tilted back all the way, so they were upside down. From this angle, Indu's nose looked big, too large for his slender face, and his skin was noticeably weathered, with burst capillaries under his cheeks making him look like he was blushing.

The häxdoktor, *Lemak, was thin and tall, a sliver of a man really, with long slender fingers.*

(I had felt them on my skin many times before, probing my arms, his rough fingertips thirsty and demanding as they searched for viable veins.)

But now he shrank back from Indu, even though he towered over him, and Lemak held his arms up, as if shielding himself from expected blows.

"If a man dies but is nearly *saved, is he alive?" Indu asked him. "If you enter* almost *all the numbers into a codex lock, does it open?"*

"No, sir, but—" Lemak began to plead.

"Nej-li, it does not," Indu interrupted.

"I can help you," I said, even though I wasn't sure that I could. "Please let me go. I will help you."

Indu looked over at me, as if he'd forgotten I was there, and he gave me a wispy, sour smile. "Oh, my child, you are already doing all you can." His smile fell away the instant he turned back to the häxdoktor. *"You need to finish this. It's time to open the lock."*

"I can help you in other ways," I said, my voice trembling as I begged. "I have other skills. I'm strong, and I can read six languages."

"Ulla?" Pan was saying, and a cold wind rushed over me as I opened my eyes.

His hands were on my shoulders, and his thick brows were pinched together with worry. Everything seemed so dark, and I blinked to clear it, but it never changed. It wasn't a lingering haze from the memory—the sky was darkening.

"What's going on?" I asked.

"I don't know." He looked up at the cloudless sky and the shadow crossing over the sun. "Maybe an eclipse."

"I didn't know there was supposed to be one today," I said.

The streetlamps in the city were all kerosene, hand-lit before dusk, but with the unexpected night falling as the sun was blotted out, Merellä was soon going to be submerged in total darkness. Nearby, I heard confused shouts and uneasy rumblings as everyone reacted to the sudden changes in the afternoon sky.

The giant woolly elk bellowed in the stables, and we were close enough that we could hear them kicking and ramming at the doors, the wood and hinges rattling as their hooves stomped the ground.

"Shit, the woollies are freaking out," Pan said. "I should calm them down before they hurt themselves."

I took his hand, so he wouldn't run off and leave me alone in the dark. He squeezed it once, then we jogged through shadows and made it inside the stables just as the total darkness fell.

"I can't see anything," I said.

"Stay here." Pan pushed me gently, so my back was against the wall. The raw wood left a few slivers poking me, but I didn't complain. "I'll try to find a light."

Then he walked away, his stumbling footsteps receding, and he murmured words of comfort to the elk, though it didn't seem to be helping much. They brayed and kicked loudly. My eyes slowly adjusted in the dark—the outlines of the stacks of hay and stalls taking shape.

In the center aisles, outside of the stall and only a few meters away from me—closer than Pan, who I couldn't even see at all—stood an albino woolly elk. It was a massive beast, towering above me with wide, broad antlers, like a prehistoric moose. The antlers and thick fur were pure white, and the eyes of red seemed to glow in the darkness.

The animal started walking toward me, deliberate strides on long giraffian legs, and as it passed by the stalls on its way to me, the other woollies fell silent. The albino elk had nearly reached me when it stopped and leaned forward, chuffing as it sniffed my hair, and I reached out to pet its nose—

—and the lights suddenly came on. Pan had flicked them on, and I closed my eyes against the blinding brightness. When I finally opened them again, the albino elk was gone.

22

results

"There are no albino elk here," Pan told me with confused dismay, but I honestly wasn't that surprised. "Maybe it was your eyes playing tricks in the dark."

It was a reasonable suggestion, but I didn't believe it. I had seen an albino woolly elk once before. I had a hazy memory of following one through the ruins of a city as it led me . . . somewhere I couldn't quite remember.

Most of the woollies went out to one of the fields during the day, heading out at dawn and returning late in the evening. The ones that stayed behind were ill, old, pregnant, mothering a new calf, or the occasionally lazy elk that chose to stay in for the day.

I was comforting one of the calves, giving it a supplemental bottle of enriched formula to help fatten up the little runt, and through the windows, I saw the sun shining again.

Later, after I'd helped Pan with the rest of the woollies and gone back to my apartment, leaving Pan to take care of Brueger, Bryn told me that she'd timed it, and the eclipse had lasted just under seven minutes. Right after it ended, Dagny had run down to the Mimirin to find out what was going on, because of course she did.

Unfortunately, when she came back over three hours later, Dagny didn't have any real answers. They had even checked in with the human news and information from NASA, and while humans had seen it too, their experts were surprisingly mum. The "eclipse" covered an area of nine thousand square miles, and the best guess was that a large meteor had passed by at just the right time at just the right angle.

Already conspiracy theories were going around. The humans suspected an enemy nation, an alien ship, or a publicity stunt by a big tech company or the new superhero movie opening in a couple weeks. Trolls suspected the humans, other tribes, or maybe a small group of very powerful trolls.

"What do you think it was?" I asked Dagny. We were sitting on the couch, with a bowl of cloudberries and a cup of sweet honeyed cream between us, and we munched on the berries dipped in cream.

Bryn had put Halsey on Dagny's laptop, and she'd moved the bistro table and coffee table to the side of the room so she could use the space to shadowbox. She liked to work out when she was stressed or bored or anxious.

"Maybe a meteor," Dagny said, but she sounded unconvinced.

"But you don't think so?" I pressed.

"Honestly?" She glanced over at Bryn, bouncing around and punching the air. "I don't know if I should say."

"You can trust Bryn," I said defensively.

Bryn lowered her fists but seemed mostly unfazed. "I can keep my mouth shut. But I can also go out for a run if you'd like more privacy."

"No, no, I don't mean *you*." Dag shook her head. "I

mean . . ." She sighed and lowered her voice to a whisper. "The Ögonen. I don't know how much they can hear or see."

The Ögonen were the trollian beings that served as the guardians of Merellä. They were tall and sinewy with strange semi-opaque skins. The most alarming thing was that they had no mouths, but they had powerful psychokinetic powers that they used to cloak the citadel and hide it from the humans.

"Why don't you want them to hear?" I asked quietly.

"Because I think they're the ones that did it," she said. "Look, I'm not saying they did anything *wrong* per se. But I don't know *why* they did it, so I'd rather them not know that I suspect them until I figure out why."

"Why do you think it's them?" I asked. Bryn had gone back to fighting the air, and when she kicked quickly not too far from my head, I flinched.

"I don't know," Dagny admitted. "It's a feeling I had. There's something strange going on with them." She popped a handful of berries in her mouth and stared off as she thought, absently touching her half-burnt eyebrow.

"What do you mean by strange?" I asked.

"I've lived in Merellä for a long time, minus the Lost Month, and I hardly ever saw them around," she explained. "If they were outside their roof atriums, they'd be in groups, maybe five or six of them, and they'd be walking from the Mimirin to the edge of town where they live. They never socialized or tried to communicate, and I always thought that was because that's how they liked it, since it's difficult to communicate. They don't have mouths, and they eat sunlight.

"Elof and the troglecology department aren't really allowed to study them, but Elof suspected they might be something like a sentient plant," Dagny said, then quickly added, "a sentient *psychokinetic* plant."

"It sounds like they were strange to begin with," Bryn muttered between punches.

"Right, but their behavior is different. They've changed," Dagny persisted. "Now I'm seeing them all the time, wandering around town on their own. Hardly ever in groups. And when I pass by, they stare at me. They'll turn so their eyes follow me. And it's not just the one I met, the one that tried to recover my memories. That was Mu, and they're on the short side for their kind."

"They probably have a hive mind," Bryn said. "No mouths; they're telepathic. Some aspens have thousands of trees in a single organism. It'd make sense that if one of the sentient plants knew something, they could all know it."

Dagny frowned. "That's kind of disturbing."

"All of that does sound odd and maybe unsettling, but I don't see why you think they're connected to the eclipse," I said.

"On the map of the area that had total darkness during the event, Merellä was dead in the center," Dagny said. "Like the eye of the storm." She whispered again when she said, "The Ögonen are the most powerful beings in the citadel. If they worked together, they could easily pull off something like this. Maybe the eclipse was a side effect of something, or maybe they did it as a distraction, or maybe they wanted the cover of darkness."

She exhaled. "Or maybe they just wanted to blot out the sun."

"But if the Ögonen are as all-knowing and all-seeing as you think they are, how did Eliana sneak in?" I asked. "How could there be such a breach in the security?"

"Maybe she was powerful enough or small enough to slide by?" Dagny shrugged.

"Or maybe they let her in," Bryn suggested.

After that, Dagny changed the subject, saying she'd already talked about them too much, and we finished off the bowl of berries while talking about the woollies. Both Bryn and Dagny were surprisingly interested in hearing all about the baby elk I'd nursed after the eclipse.

We were all exhausted—especially me and Bryn—so we tucked in early, and I slept for fourteen hours straight.

Dagny woke me up the next day and told me that Elof had gotten the results from my and Bryn's familial blood test. I got up, got ready, and the three of us headed down to the Mimirin.

When we got to the lab, Elof took Bryn back to his office. It was a small room attached to the back of the lab. I sat on a stool at one of the islands, and Dagny grabbed a stack of papers and started reading through them, highlighting numbers and dates for Elof's research.

"Why did he take her back alone?" I asked her after Elof had closed the office door. "Does that mean it's bad news?"

"He likes to give everyone their results in private," she explained. "It can be very emotional for some, whether they get the confirmation they wanted or not."

"I guess he did tell me my original blood test results alone," I remembered.

"You are something," he'd told me then, when I'd asked what I was. *"You had significant markers for Omte, meaning that one of your parents was almost certainly from the Omte tribe."*

"What about my other parent?" I had asked.

"They're not a troll," he'd said.

"Okay, can you spit it out and tell me what it is that I actually am?" I'd asked in exasperation.

"That's the thing," Elof had told me finally. *"We don't know."*

Bryn was in the office with Elof for nearly a half hour, and by then I had moved to pacing around the lab, to Dagny's chagrin. When Bryn finally came out, her expression was unreadable—the stoic blank mask she wore when she was working as a guard—and her eyes downcast.

I started to the office, but Elof followed her out and held up his hand to stop me.

"Aren't we going to talk?" I asked.

"Yes, we are," Elof said with a smile. "But I thought it'd be better if we walked and talked." He headed toward the lab door and motioned for me to follow him. "Come."

23

olfactory

The bench seat in the back of the rickshaw did little to absorb the bumps and dips of the dirt roads, but I didn't have much room to complain since a driver was literally pulling the small, hooded cart across town. He looked Omte, based on his hulking frame and the ease with which he jogged while hauling me and Elof away from the Mimirin.

We were heading to the farming borough on the outskirts of Merellä, and while it was still within the sprawling city walls, it was an awfully long way to walk, especially for someone like Elof. Like many of the Vittra who had short stature, he sometimes needed accommodations.

Elof had once explained it to me this way: two types of dwarfism were found in the Vittra—hobgoblins, who had a series of comorbid conditions such as slimy skin, a benign but unpleasant form of acne, and exaggerated features, and little trolls, similar to Vittra trolls in almost all ways except for their height. Both conditions were often accompanied by assets—like superior strength for some—and negatives—like chronic hip pain.

Elof stood thirty-six inches tall, and by the time he turned thirty, he'd started using a cane when he walked long distances. Rickshaws were usually parked around the Mimirin, available for anyone to ride for a nominal fee, and they made the whole city much more accessible for hobgoblins and little trolls.

"Why are we going all the way out here to talk?" I asked Elof as we rolled past the woolly elk meadows, the big beasts grazing on the grassy fields. We were far enough away from downtown that we could speak without being overwhelmed by noise.

"I wanted to show you something, and we needed to talk, so I thought we'd hit two animals with one stone," Elof reasoned.

"Can you tell me now what the results are, or do we need to wait until we get to our mystery destination?" I asked.

Elof had told the driver where to go when he paid him, but I hadn't been close enough to overhear. I'd asked on the way down from the lab where we were going, but Elof had vaguely answered with "outside."

"I suppose I can tell you now if you'd like." He sat back in the seat and folded his hands on his lap as he looked over at me. "Bryn has no Omte blood."

"So . . . she's not my sister?" I asked, and it wasn't until then that I realized how much I was hoping that she was my sister, that I had a real connection to somebody I cared about.

That I had a connection.

"No, she is not," Elof said sadly.

My heart sank, and I swallowed back tears. "That's good for her. I mean, she really loves her dad."

"She has no Kanin blood either," he said, and I looked sharply at him.

"What?" I shook my head. "Iver Aven was born a Kanin

Markis. Bryn told me how her father came from a high-ranking Kanin family."

"Iver may very well have, but I didn't have a sample from him available," Elof said. "What I did have is a sample from Bryn that predominantly has markers for Skojare and some for the Trylle. And I have a sample from you that is half-Omte and half-unidentified."

"Indu said my mother is *álfar*, and that would be the unidentified half, so Indu is mostly Omte then," I said, my words rapid and uncertain. "He identifies as Älvolk, but that's—that's a cult, not a tribe, not a race, so he's Omte." My mind raced with the implications of Elof's words. "So Bryn's mom must've had an affair with another man."

He waited a beat, the wheels crunching loudly on the gravel, and the air sweetening as we passed the Sommar plum orchard, and then he carefully replied, "That is one possibility."

"What's the other?"

"Indu and the Älvolk live in Áibmoráigi, in northern Sweden," he said. "It's within a day's journey of Isarna, and although the memory of the exact location of Áibmoráigi is blocked from my mind, it's safe to assume that Isarna is the closest troll community to the Älvolk.

"As you know, Isarna is an unusual place," he continued. "A single island city belonging to two kingdoms—the Trylle and the Skojare. Given the proximity, I imagine that there are many Älvolk who had children with the Isarnans."

"You think Indu *is* Bryn's father," I realized.

"I would say it's likely that Indu is Trylle and Skojare, as opposed to being fully Omte, which is what he'd need to be in order for you to be half-Omte, half-*álfar*," Elof said. "I did only see him briefly in Sweden—that I can recall, at least—and I did not see much of a resemblance to you, or the Omte either."

"He's not my father," I said breathlessly, and as a wave of relief washed over me, I couldn't help but smile. "Noomi's not my sister. I'm not an Indudottir." I laughed to myself.

"I'm happy to see you're taking it so well," he said.

"Yeah, I really am." I laughed again. "I know that in a way, I'm worse off. I went from thinking I know who my dad is to having no clue once again. But all that I feel is a weight lifted off my shoulders, knowing that the kidnapping baby-crazy jerk isn't my father." I breathed in deeply.

And then I looked over at him. "So is Senka my mother?"

"I think that one *álfar* parent would explain the unusual nature of your blood, but I can't say for certain if it's your mother or father, let alone someone I've only heard about from you."

"Why did Indu claim he was my father?" I asked.

"Maybe he was mistaken, or perhaps he was lying. Or perhaps he was lied to himself," Elof said.

As we grew closer to the city wall, the scenery began to change. The elk meadow had given way to orchards and fields of sugar beets, but they appeared to be coming to an end a short distance in front of us. The lush gardens were replaced by squat dirt mounds, staggered around in circular patterns.

I sat up straighter, trying to get a better look, and I realized there were doors in the mound, slender and curved. And then I saw them—the tall and sinewy Ögonen, with their semi-transparent ochre skin leaving all their organs visible; they were trollian and otherworldly all at once. There were half a dozen of them, their heads just visible over the top of the dirt.

"Is this where the Ögonen live?" I asked Elof quietly. "Is this where we're going?"

"It is, and it is," he answered.

I looked over at him. "Is it safe?"

His brow furrowed. "Why wouldn't it be?"

"I don't know," I said quickly, remembering Dagny's fears that the Ögonen could read her mind. "I only meant, are we allowed there?"

"Of course. I'd never take you somewhere you weren't wanted," he said. "At least not without warning you first."

The rickshaw stopped in front of the Ögonen neighborhood, and Elof asked the driver to wait and assured him that we wouldn't be too long. He got out of the cart first, and I took a moment to steel myself before following him.

The last time I'd interacted with them hadn't exactly been pleasant. When I'd snuck down into the Catacombs of Fables, one of the Ögonen guarding it had given me a horrific vision of being chased by giant spiders. Admittedly, I'd been going somewhere I wasn't allowed to go, but their guarding technique of invading my mind and implanting realistic, terrifying visions had been very unnerving.

I had no idea if they could read minds, but it seemed plausible enough, and I wasn't exactly comfortable with them reading mine.

I didn't know if I could do anything to shield my thoughts, but I had to try something. In my head, I started spelling everything, hoping a cloud of benign thoughts would mask anything.

The paths between the mound houses were exceptionally narrow, maybe two feet wide, and I had to walk behind Elof. Nearby, seven Ögonen—

O-G-O-N-E-N-

—walking single file. They kept walking straight ahead but their trollian eyes followed us, unblinking, unwavering—

U-N-S-E-T-T-L-I-N-G

"Why are we here?" I asked Elof again.

"They have a special garden. The Ögonen believe it to be

sacred land, but they've allowed us to come and have a look if we promise not to touch."

"Are we looking at anything in particular?" I asked.

"Indeed."

I was about to ask for info, but we'd rounded another home, and a small, circular patch of overgrown plants sat at the center of the Ögonen neighborhood. It looked like nothing but wild, untended weeds, with the sickly-sweet smell of lilies and potent—

C-O-P-P-E-R

—and I was back in the häxdoktor's *office, my arms held with straps. The air was thick and my father—*

No, not my father. My kidnapper. Indu.

Indu argued with Lemak, "Nej-li, *it does not."*

"I can help you," I said, even though I wasn't sure that I could. "Please let me go. I will help you."

Indu looked over at me, as if he'd forgotten I was there, and he gave me a wispy, sour smile. "Oh, my child, you are already doing all you can." His smile fell away the instant he turned back to the häxdoktor. *"You need to finish this. It's time to open the lock."*

"I can help you in other ways." My voice trembled as I pleaded with him, talking fast, hoping anything would stick. "I have other skills. I can read six languages: Swedish, Inuit, French, Norse, Tryllic, and English. I can lift five times my body weight. I can—"

Indu looked sharply at me, his eyes narrowed and his nostrils flared. Suddenly animated with a fresh intensity, he rushed to my bedside and I flinched, pulling as far away from him as I could. Behind, over his shoulder, a wilting sorg-blomma *sat in a beaker, its golden yellow petals turning brown and shriveling.*

"*You can read Tryllic?*" *Indu asked, close enough that I could smell the death on his breath.*

"Ulla?" Elof asked, sounding concerned, and he put his hand on my arm to get my attention.

I blinked, the bright, lush plant coming back into focus in front of me. "The Älvolk already had the *sorgblomma*. When we were there."

"I thought they might," Elof said. "That's why I brought you here."

I looked over at him in confusion. "Why?"

"The sense of smell is closely linked with memory, and the *sorgblomma* has a very unique scent," he explained.

"Yeah, it definitely does," I said under my breath. "So you want me to . . . just try to remember?"

He nodded. "Go ahead."

I closed my eyes, inhaling deeply through my nose—

—*the* häxdoktor's *room again, but this time the straps were off. Indu wasn't there, it was only me and Lemak, with a row of wilting* sorgblomma *in the glass beakers, more of them now, their dead petals littering the apothecary table.*

"*These are what he wants you to work on today,*" *Lemak said, handing me a narrow tube of paper.*

Slowly, I unrolled the scroll, and I saw the jagged letters—

—a screaming shot of pain exploded in my skull and down my spine. I clamped my hands to my ears as tightly as I could.

24

walls

Once the pain passed and I had caught my breath, I tried again. I breathed in the scent of the flowers, the memory resurfaced—Lemak handed me the scrolls but when I tried to remember it, the pain came back again, only worse this time.

My brain felt like it was going to explode, and I pressed my hands to my head, as if I could hold it in. I collapsed to my knees and painfully began to retch. Once I stopped, I wiped my mouth with the back of my arm, and sat back on my heels, gasping for breath.

Elof's hand was on my shoulder and his voice low in my ear. "Ulla, are you all right?"

"Yeah," I said through gritted teeth. "I just . . . I can't remember. There's a wall of pain I can't get through surrounding the memory."

"Perhaps this isn't the best place to work through it," Elof said, and I finally looked up to see the Ögonen were standing all around us, watching us with their big brown eyes.

Elof offered me his hand, and helped steady me as I got to my feet. He stayed at my side, his arm around me, and my steps were still unsteady as we hurried through the narrow roads.

"Take us back downtown, please," Elof told the driver as I climbed up into the rickshaw. "And if it wouldn't be too much trouble, go as quickly as you safely can."

I was grateful that we didn't have to make the long walk on foot. The driver jogged onward, and a breeze cooled my face. Tangles of hair stuck to the sweat on my skin, so I slid the scrunchie off my wrist and pulled my hair up into a top-knot. The pain in my head had lessened to a dull throbbing, but my body felt weak and tired.

"I apologize for bringing you there," Elof said quietly. "I thought you would have a reaction to the flower, but I never suspected that it would be something like that."

"How'd you know I'd have a reaction?" I asked him.

"Because I had one," he replied. "When we returned, I went to get a sample of the *sorgblomma* to discern why the Älvolk had wanted it so badly. As soon as I smelled it, I remembered the dungeons we'd been held in, only for a moment. I was in a dark cell with Pan, and you were returning—Noomi and Tuva had you by each arm, and you were only semiconscious, your feet dragging along the ground. And the scent of the *sorgblomma* was coming from *you*."

"But you didn't have any pain with the memory?" I asked.

He shook his head. "None. But the memory didn't last very long." He leaned in, lowering his voice a little. "It seems that the Älvolk put special protections around your particular memory. I think you may have found what they wanted to hide the most."

"Great." I sighed. "Do you have any ideas on how I can get through the wall of excruciating pain that surrounds it?"

"Not at the moment, no," he said sadly. "But I've been

looking into different forms of memory recovery. I'm hopeful that I'll have an answer for you soon."

Elof had the rickshaw drop me at my apartment. Even though I was feeling well enough by then that I probably could've made the walk from the Mimirin, Elof preferred to err on the side of caution. I gave him money for the rickshaw, and Elof initially declined until I told him to add it to the driver's tip.

As I was walking up the steps to my apartment, I heard Bryn's voice, and I looked up to see her on the roof. The signal-amplifying dish was pointed to the sky, and her cell phone was pressed to her ear. She was speaking in a low voice, so I couldn't make out many words—just a terse "Ridley, I know what I'm doing."

I didn't want to eavesdrop, so I ducked into the apartment. Dagny was in the kitchen, warming up leftover sweet tomato soup and making fig jam and goat cheese sandwiches on the griddle.

"I wasn't sure when you'd be back, but I made extra just in case," Dagny said, and then she looked back at me. "You look all sweaty and pale. What happened?"

I sat down at the table and, while she cooked, told her about my experiences with Elof in the Ögonen garden. My stomach started rumbling by the time I finished, and she set a gooey, melted sandwich and a cup of soup in front of me.

"Thank you, this smells delicious," I said.

"Is Bryn still up on the roof?" She glanced toward the ceiling. "Should I yell up at her and let her know the food's done?"

I shrugged. "She's talking to her boyfriend and it sounded tense."

"He probably doesn't want her to go," Dagny said. "I thought it was a little abrupt when she brought it up, but she is a woman on a mission."

"Go where?" I asked. "What are you talking about?"

"To Fulaträsk," she replied. "Bryn says she knows a baby there, and she wants to find out who her dad is."

"What? That doesn't make any sense."

Footsteps rumbled across the roof, followed by a *bang* on the landing outside the front door as Bryn jumped down onto it. A moment later, she came in, her expression unreadable, and she set the amplifier on the shelf by the door.

"So." Bryn sat down in front of the plate Dagny had left for her at the table. "You found out we're not sisters."

"Yeah, Elof told me," I said.

"My dad's probably not Iver, but it might not be Indu either." Bryn took a bite out of her sandwich. She chewed and swallowed before saying, "And you're probably not Indu's daughter, but you might be. To know for sure, we need Indu's blood."

"And we're fresh out at the moment," I said. "Indu and his daughters are hiding out in the wilds of Sweden, and they've gone to great lengths to make sure that we don't remember how to find them."

"Not all his daughters," Bryn corrected me.

"That's the baby you know in Fulaträsk," I realized. "You're talking about Bekk Vallin. But she's still pregnant."

"Humans do in utero blood tests all the time," Bryn said with a shrug. "I looked it up online. Dagny thinks Elof can handle it."

"I said 'probably,' but you need to talk to him," Dagny said as she dipped her sandwich in the soup.

"At any rate, I'm going to Fulaträsk to get to the bottom of this," Bryn announced, and rested her blue eyes on me. "I want you to go with me."

"Wh-When?" I was caught off guard by her invitation.

"It depends on if Elof needs to come with to get the

samples, and what his availability is," Bryn said. "But the sooner the better, if I have a say."

"I understand," I said, and she was looking at me expectantly, waiting for my answer. "Um, yeah, sure. I mean, of course. I want to know what the deal is with Indu, and I want to help you."

"Good." She smiled and relaxed some. "Ridley didn't want me going alone."

"Why not?" Dagny wrinkled her nose. "You can take care of yourself."

"Yes, I can," Bryn agreed readily. "And Ridley agrees with that in most situations, but I have some history with Fulaträsk and the Omte Queen." She took another bite and talked around it. "She held me and . . . a friend captive for days. But that was five years ago, before the war. And during the Invasion of Doldastam, Ridley killed her advisor, Helge Otäck, and that's where she got most of her terrible advice."

"I've seen her since then without problems," Bryn finished nonchalantly. "But Ridley says that's different because it's always been at kingdom events and never on her own home ground in Fulaträsk."

"I . . . I will go with you, Bryn," I said carefully. "But I don't know how much help I can be if the Omte Queen wants to lock you up."

Bryn seemed to consider this as she chewed. "It would probably be better if Elof does come with us. He's already proven himself very capable at getting captives released."

25

strategies

Bryn worked with quick determination, and by noon the next day, she had everything in place. Elof was happy to come with, mostly because it would give him a chance to find out more about Indu and the Älvolk, and he even managed to convince the Mimirin it would be beneficial so he got to fly on their dime.

Unfortunately, since neither Bryn nor I were affiliated with the Mimirin, we'd have to pay our own way. Or rather, Bryn would be paying our way. I again tried to decline, telling her I had no idea when I'd be able to pay her back because I didn't have a job right now, but Bryn just shrugged it off and insisted that this was what she wanted to do.

"I worked hard for that money," she said. "I don't need much, so I've saved a lot. I did that so I'd have it if I needed it, and I need it now."

So I stopped arguing with her and just hugged and thanked her, and I let her buy us tickets.

Dagny was staying behind to hold down the lab while Elof was gone, so she went to work in the morning, like normal.

I stayed at the apartment, packing and watching Bryn make arrangements and work out.

Around lunchtime, a knock at the door interrupted our planning and packing. I answered it to find Pan standing on my doorstep. He ran a hand through his disheveled curls and gave me an anxious smile.

"Is everything okay?" I asked.

"Yeah, yeah." He nodded, but his gaze went past me, watching as Bryn moved around the apartment. "Can we talk for a minute?"

There wasn't anywhere private inside the apartment—only the bathroom and Dagny's room—and I wasn't comfortable hanging out with Pan in either one. So I ushered him out onto the landing and closed the door behind us.

"What's going on?" I asked.

"I saw Dagny at the Mimirin." His expression faltered. "She told me you're going to Fulaträsk."

"Yeah, it was Bryn's idea. Last night," I said. "But we just got everything finalized. I was going to tell you today when you were done with work."

"No, you don't have to rush and tell me the second you make plans. I wouldn't want that or expect that of you," he said, but he sounded sullen.

"You seem upset," I said carefully.

"I'm not upset. Exactly." He frowned at his own words and rubbed the back of his neck. "It's hard to explain."

I leaned against the railing beside him. "About me going to Fulaträsk?"

"Yes and no." His eyes were downcast, and he exhaled. "I think you know that I care about you."

"Yeah, I guessed that when we made out in Isarna." I laughed, hoping it would hide how nervous I felt.

He smiled crookedly at me. "I guess it was pretty obvious."

"Not *too* obvious," I allowed, and my stomach was twisting up.

Was he breaking up with me? How was that even possible when we weren't really dating? Were we? I hadn't even really had a chance to talk to him about us or what our romance really was. Every time we were together, we just *were*. And for me now—

—*my mind suddenly flashed back to the Älvolk dungeon, the dark stone, Pan's arm stretching through the iron bars, straining for me, and our fingers barely touching before Noomi and Tuva yanked me backward—*

—being with him was enough, and I hoped he felt the same way.

"But now . . . ." He looked away again. "I feel like I'm in such a weird place. That *we're* in such a weird place." There was a heavy pause before he quietly said, "We'd only just kissed and then—" He snapped his fingers, the sound startling me in contrast with his quiet voice. "—I'm back here and a month has passed.

"At least, in my mind that's how it plays out," he went on. "But there's this feeling that I have that . . . I *know* you." His eyebrows pinched as he tried to find the right words. "We went through something intense and strange and traumatic, and even though I don't remember, I still have these feelings, like faint emotional memories. . . ."

"I think I understand," I said.

He looked at me hopefully. "You do?"

"Yeah." I nodded. "I have all these lingering feelings that I can't always explain."

"And when I think about you, I feel so worried and helpless."

"Thanks?" I said uncertainly.

"No, that came out wrong." He grimaced and shook his head. "I only meant that I cared about you, and our time together deepened that. When we were with the Älvolk, I know they were hurting you, I know I couldn't do anything to stop it, and I know I don't want you to go through that again."

"Neither do I," I agreed.

"When Dagny mentioned that Bryn wanted you to join her in Fulaträsk because the Queen held her hostage once before . . . I kinda panicked," he admitted.

"I wasn't happy when she told me either," I said. "But she doesn't sound worried, and you and I didn't have any trouble when we went to Fulaträsk earlier this summer."

"We didn't go with Bryn," he reminded me quietly. "Who apparently has an antagonistic relationship with the Queen. And you're still recovering from your last hostage situation."

"I'm going to a major troll city with Bryn and Elof to visit a friend," I reasoned. "I think we'll be safe, and I also think it's the best place to find the truth about who my father is. Elof still says I'm half-Omte, and if it's not Indu, the Omte kingdom is the best place to find answers."

His jaw set as he thought, his eyes staring off into the distance. The Mimirin was just visible above the rooftops. From my front door, we could see the thirteen atriums on the roof of the institution, all of them housing an Ögonen that watched over the citadel.

"Let me come with you," he said finally.

"What?"

He looked over at me. "I want to go with you to Fulaträsk."

"What?" I repeated. "What about work?"

"I can help you," he persisted. "I've got some connections from working the Inhemsk. Sylvi told me I could take off more time if I needed it, and I think I actually do need it. And yeah, the plane tickets aren't going to leave me with much in my savings, but I can always save more, right?"

"Maybe," I said hesitantly.

"I can help you, and I want to make sure you're safe, and . . . I want to be with you." He licked his lips. "I really like you, Ulla, and I feel like I almost lost you in Áibmoráigi. I don't want to do that again."

"I really like you too," I said with my heart hammering in my chest. "I'm not asking you to do this, and I think I'll be safe, with or without you. But I won't lie; I'd be happy if you came with."

He leaned back on the railing, his hand beside him on the wood, and I tentatively put my hand over his.

"So I'm saying, it's up to you what you want to do from here," I said finally.

He smiled then, subtle but knowing, and it matched the dark heat in his eyes. "That's good, because I know of something I really want to do right now."

My stomach fluttered, and he leaned in toward me. He hesitated a moment—his eyes searching mine, almost as if looking for something, and I wondered if he remembered kissing me during the Lost Month.

But before his lips touched mine, Bryn opened the front door behind us, and it hit me painfully in the back. I tried to step out of the way, but the landing wasn't very large, and Pan put an arm around me, letting my body press against him.

"Sorry." Bryn stepped back and closed the door partway, giving us more room, and now only her head was poking out. "I was checking to see if your friend is staying for lunch."

"Um, thanks, but I should probably get back to the office and start getting things arranged for the trip." Pan moved away from me, toward the steps. "I'll call you when I get down to my desk and get details."

"Okay," I said, trying not to sound disappointed that he was slipping away without a kiss.

"I'll talk to you soon," he said, then looked to Bryn and gave her a small wave. "Nice to see you again, Bryn." Then he went down the stairs and down the path toward the Mimirin.

"Is he coming with us?" she asked me, and opened the door wider so I could go into the apartment.

"Yeah, he is. I mean, if that's okay," I said. "He's paying his own way, but it'll be easier if we travel together."

"Is he your boyfriend?"

"He's my . . . something." I tried to seem nonchalant even though my cheeks had felt warm since she'd caught me outside with him, near-kiss. "And he knows a lot about Fulaträsk. He can help us."

"Whatever works for you guys works for me," she said, and she went back to folding her freshly laundered clothes. "I went to Fulaträsk with a guy once. He said it was just to help."

"What happened?" I asked.

She paused and her face darkened. Then she shook her head. "Just be careful."

26

sutherlands

In the wee hours of the morning, when the sun was still dark and most of Merellä was sleeping, Bryn drove the four of us—herself, Elof, Pan, and me—to the airport in Eugene. It felt strange going without Dagny, but she wanted to stay behind and keep looking at what was happening with the weather and the eclipse incident a few days ago.

Despite the early hour, Dagny had gotten up to see us off and to take in Brueger, since she was dog-sitting for Pan again. When she hugged me goodbye, she told me to be safe, and I noticed the worry in her eyes—something I wasn't used to seeing her with.

I hadn't realized until then how much all of this had affected her. She always seemed so impervious and impassive. But it wasn't just concern, it was fear—not for me but of her own experiences. There hadn't been much time for any of us to process what we'd gone through.

It was nearly a three-hour drive to the airport, and I sat in the back with Pan, dozing on and off. As Bryn parked, I woke up with my head on his shoulder, and I immediately mumbled a preemptive apology about snoring and discomfort.

"Don't worry. I slept most of the time too," he assured me, and he kissed the top of my head while I was still leaning on him. Then he opened the car door and got out.

The flights were *long*—we had two stops before finally landing in Lafayette, Louisiana—and I sat by strangers each time. At least I was definitely getting a better hand on flying and making small talk with humans. They weren't all that different than trolls, really, except that they wore too much perfume and played on their electronics far more often.

After we landed in Louisiana, Bryn rented another car, and we drove until the paved roads gave way to a bumpy dirt road, so overgrown and wild it was almost taken back by nature. Bryn drove slowly as towering cypress trees surrounded us, blocking out the late-afternoon sun.

I had been to Fulaträsk before, with Pan, but we'd gone directly to his friend Rikky's house on the outskirts of the city. This time we were going right to the heart, for lodging at the Yggammi Tree Inn, an Omte hotel.

The road ended at the edge of a marsh, where the tall grass and reeds became a swamp. On the left side of the road was a dock, made with sun-bleached mossy boards. On the other side was a parking lot of sorts, with two dozen or so cars parked on the field. The ones closest to the road were newer and cleaner, but the ones in the far corner were rusted and overgrown; a couple were half sunk in the ground.

Bryn parked near the edge, and as we got out, I heard the familiar sound of the airboat's loud fan motor as it pulled up to the dock. On the side, *Yggammi Tree Inn* was painted, and the driver was a tall man with thick arms barely hidden under a dull orange work shirt. The logo for the hotel was just above where the name *Knut* was embroidered.

"Last time I came here, I didn't arrange a ride first,"

Bryn explained as we got our bags out of the car. "We had to wade through the swamp, and I definitely saw an alligator." She smirked. "I figured you guys wouldn't want to deal with that."

"You thought correctly," I said, and slung my bag over my shoulder.

"The last time I was here, I hadn't known to arrange transport either," Elof said. "Fortunately, an ogre was passing by, and he literally carried me into town. It was quite the journey."

"I didn't know you had been here before," I commented as we walked down the long dock.

"Ah, yes, I was in my early twenties," he explained. "It was after my second year at Stanford, and I was growing annoyed living among the humans. I thought there was no place better to get in touch with my trollian roots than a secluded Omte city."

"You didn't like your time here?" Pan asked.

"I wouldn't say that," Elof said with a weary sigh. "I was young, restless, and maybe a little cocky. The summer was long, but I learned a lot. Like to never sneak up on a gator."

"Did something happen with you and an alligator?" I asked in surprise.

"No, it's just good advice. The ogre told me that when I got here."

Elof sat at the back of the airboat, near Knut, and he chatted with him amiably about the city. Bryn stood, one hand on the back of the bench seat to steady herself. There was room to sit beside me and Pan, but she preferred standing, staring straight ahead.

It was hot, well into the nineties, and the air felt thick on my skin, so I was happy for the breeze as the boat weaved through the bald cypress trees. Fulaträsk was an oddly beautiful city—or at least the parts that I could see were. Most of the homes were built high in trees, embellished with scrap metal and found objects, and camouflaged with moss, vines, and tree branches. I couldn't even really see them until we were right under them, and I saw the ladders or occasional spiral staircases wrapping around massive tree trunks.

Wooden bridges connected some of the tree houses, creating a neighborhood in the sky. The Omte didn't have the kind of cloaking abilities the other tribes did, so they relied more on traditional means of hiding from the humans. Their city was in the middle of a swamp, with no roads. A few homes were on marshy islands or stilts, like Pan's friend Rikky's place.

As the name implied, the Yggammi Tree Inn was a tree house atop a trio of thick Southern live oaks that had grown close together, their branches spreading out and intertwining with each other like tentacles. Atop the multitude of hefty branches was the large octagonal building made of sun-faded wood. A staircase wound around the narrowest trunk, meeting with the dock at the base, where another airboat and two canoes were tied up.

After Knut parked the boat, he offered to carry our bags, but only Elof took him up on it, since Bryn and Pan had packed so lightly. Knut lunged up ahead, and we followed him more slowly, pacing ourselves as we climbed the dozens of stairs.

The hotel was rather nice, nicer than the human motels I'd stayed in before, and closer to the luxury tree house I'd seen on a glitzy TV show, but in a rustic, understated Omte sort of way. Polished wood floors, distressed wood on the walls. The check in counter was a solid chunk of raw-edged wood, and the wall behind it was a big mirror with gilded edges. An alligator head was mounted on another wall, wearing a pair of bronze sunglasses, but the centerpiece of the room was a vintage chandelier made with brass and mirror crystals.

Pan let out a low whistle as he admired the space—the leather bench, the vulture statue made from upcycled metal, a potted avocado plant growing in the corner. "This place seems pretty *hip*."

"The only places I could find for rent were this place and the palace," Bryn said. "And not only do I have bad memories of staying at the palace, but it was outlandishly pricy."

"There is actually one other place," the clerk behind the desk chirped. She was cute and chubby, closer to Elof's height than mine, and behind her horn-rimmed glasses, her green eyes were noticeably different sizes. Her dark curls were pulled back into short pigtails, and the name on her cheery yellow polo read *Margarit*. "But I wouldn't really recommend it."

"Why not?" Elof asked.

"I shouldn't talk ill of competitors," Margarit said, so she leaned forward and lowered her voice. "It's just two water-damaged trailer homes at the edge of the swamp, converted to have six rooms stacked with bunk beds, hostel style."

"I think we'll stay here," Bryn said.

"You definitely made the right choice," Margarit said with a smile. "All right, I've got you set with two rooms, each with two single beds, and you're planning to stay three nights." She grabbed two keys from under the desk, each one attached to a room-number keychain. "Who gets the keys?"

Bryn took one right away, and Pan shared a look with me—brief, uncertain, a little hopeful—but Elof spoke up before either of us could say anything.

"Pan and I made fine roommates before," Elof said as he reached for the key. "I suppose we can manage here."

Margarit told us where the rooms were, but the hotel wasn't big enough to get lost. We went to the hall to the left of the small lobby, and through the open breezeway that connected the three trees together. And there were our rooms—201 across from 202.

Bryn unlocked the door, and I gave Pan one last look over my shoulder before going into the room after her. It was small, styled nearly identical to the lobby, and it was clean. The three-piece washroom was about the size of ones I'd seen in motorhomes, and we had a teeny balcony through sliding glass doors that overlooked the swamp.

I grimaced at the beds. Not because they were narrow and hard—although they were. It was the duvet made of velvet the color of burnt sugar. For the life of me, I can't figure out why the Omte insist on combining their moist climate with tons of plush velvet.

"What's the plan from here?" I asked, lying back on the bed. It was really more of a cot than a true mattress, but it felt good to stretch out after a long day of traveling.

"Well, I need to contact Bekk." Brynn was taking her clothes out of her bag and hanging them up in the mirrored wardrobe, and she glanced at the flip clock on the nightstand. "Oh, shit. It's after six. I told her I'd call her by now."

"After you call her, then what?"

"Well, it depends—" she began, but her phone started ringing, and she pulled it out of her pocket. "It's Bekk." She answered and talked for a few minutes, but most of the conversation on her end was monosyllabic until just before she hung up and said the name of the hotel.

"So?" I asked when she hung up.

"Bekk will be here in about twenty minutes," Bryn said. "And we'll talk then."

27

ROOTS

"Are you sure it's safe for the baby?" Bekk asked again.

We were in the waiting room of the Omte clinic. It was a surprisingly modern little building sitting on top of a hill. The exterior walls were beige and overgrown with flowering vines. Inside, it was bright, clean, and almost cozy, reminding me of a country vet clinic I had been to once.

After Bekk called, she'd shown up exactly eighteen minutes later, and everyone had piled into our room to have a cramped conversation. Bekk was due in a matter of weeks, and with her belly, she sat awkwardly on my bed. I'd stepped out on the balcony, preferring the muggy fresh air to the claustrophobia of the five of us crammed in one small room (six if counting the baby).

Bryn and Elof explained the whole situation to Bekk, and he assured her that it was a safe, simple blood draw that he could use to confirm that her baby and Bryn were siblings. Bekk was hesitant at first, but Elof eventually persuaded her by telling her it could also be used to learn things about the baby, including possible genetic issues.

Since we'd flown, Elof had decided to leave the more

nefarious-looking parts of his equipment—namely syringes—at home, for fear of issues with humans' security. He had brought along his machine—a hefty cylinder that reminded me of a clunky food dehydrator. But for the actual procedure and analyzation, he needed better facilities.

That's where Pan came in. He'd called Rikky, who worked as a nursing assistant. She put Elof in contact with her supervisor, and he used his charm and credentials to secure the access and equipment he needed at the clinic and arranged for us to meet there at eight A.M.

So the next morning, after a complimentary breakfast of avocado toast and tea, we all ended up in the clinic waiting room. Elof was taking blood from Bryn, Bekk, and myself to compare them, and Pan had come along as a sort of emissary with Rikky.

"It's all perfectly safe," Elof reassured Bekk again. He sat across from us on a vinyl sofa, the analyzer machine resting beside him in a duffel bag. "I'll draw some blood and the baby won't feel a thing."

Bekk nodded, her eyes looking down at her belly stretching her T-shirt taut. Her dark hair was pulled back into a ponytail braid. Her face was puffier than when I'd seen her last, and the circles under her eyes darkened her olive skin.

She hadn't said much, mostly just nodding along and listening with a bit of a blank expression, not unlike a deer caught in headlights. When I told her that I'd gone to see Indu, she hadn't even reacted or asked about him.

"Hey, guys!" Rikky said cheerily as she strode through the swinging double doors at the far side of the waiting room. She looked lovely, even in her peach-colored scrubs. Her dark auburn hair was over her shoulder in a fishtail braid.

Pan had been sitting beside me, but he jumped to his feet to greet her. She threw her arms around him, hugging him tightly to her as if she hadn't seen him in years, instead of the reality that we'd visited her at the beginning of the summer.

She was also his *ex*-girlfriend, but that wasn't quite as defined as I'd liked, since she had kissed him the last night we stayed with her. And he'd kissed her back. For a second. He'd told me he only thought of her as a friend, but she made it fairly obvious she still had feelings for him.

"Thanks for helping us, Rikky," Pan said when she released him.

"No problem," she said with her easy smile, and she finally looked over at me. "Nice to see you, Ulla."

"Yeah, you too," I said.

Pan did brief introductions, since she hadn't met Elof or Bryn before. Then she offered to take Elof back to set up his makeshift lab, and Pan went with him, carrying the heavy analyzer and lending a hand where Elof needed it.

Rikky led the guys back through the swinging doors, while Bryn, Bekk, and I continued to wait in the stiff vinyl chairs. A nurse sat at the front desk to check patients in, but right now we were the only ones there. In the corner, a fish tank bubbled, and the air conditioner keeping the clinic pleasantly cool hummed loudly.

"I only did this because I wanted a baby," Bekk said softly, and the way she was looking down at her belly, I thought she was talking to the baby at first.

"You mean you were only with Indu because you wanted a baby?" I asked.

"I'd tried with other men, ones I actually cared about. I tried with Omte men, and when I lived in Doldastam for a summer years ago, I tried with Kanin men. But I couldn't get pregnant." She shook her head. "Indu fathered other babies. I knew one had died, but I didn't realize how many. Not until later. After I was already pregnant.

"I'd never do anything to hurt her," Bekk said emphatically. "Her name is Juno Bera. I named her months ago, when I found out I was having a girl. Indu told me he knew she'd be a girl, that he only has daughters, because he took *alvaroot* every time before he tried conceiving."

"*Alvaroot*?" I whispered, but neither Bekk nor Bryn seemed to notice.

"And then I found out the other babies died. I asked my midwife if it . . ." She went on, but I barely even heard her.

My mind was back on something I had read a while back when I was working in the archives of the Mimirin for Calder. I had put away a book called *Country Food Recipes of the Kanin,* but before I had, I'd skimmed through it for anything useful.

One of the recipes was titled "Tea Cakes with *Alvaroot*," and the introduction explained that *alvaroot* mixes with our blood in powerful ways, helping to manifest the wishes of whoever ate it. The Kanin had once called it the "luck root."

But a handwritten message scrawled in the margin had said: *WARNING! Do not ingest* alvaroot! *It is a potent root with attraction properties, but it causes severe birth defects in the offspring of both men and women who have ingested it. A small defect to the heart that grows worse over time and usually causes death in infants within the first two years of life.*

My stomach turned. Indu's hubris—his unwavering belief that he could control everything around him, that he could breed an army to ensure that everyone followed his will—was what had damned so many of his children to a young death.

I don't know if he knew about the risks of the *alvaroot* or not, since Bekk didn't seem to be aware of them, but I wouldn't be surprised either way. Indu had already proved that he put the needs of his daughters behind his own wants.

Bekk took a deep breath. "But I'm going to try anyway."

Bryn reached over and put her hand over Bekk's. "This is a step in the right direction. Elof is checking for abnormalities, and the sooner you know what's going on, the more prepared you can be."

"I hope so," Bekk said, and then she turned to me. "Did Indu hurt you?"

I'd been deliberately vague about my time with Indu and the Älvolk, mostly glossing over it all except the part where he said Bryn and Juno were sisters. Last night, when we'd been explaining it all to her, I hadn't been entirely sure where her loyalties lay. After all, she was carrying his child, and she had let him know that we were looking for him when we went to Isarna.

But with her looking at me now, worried for herself and her child, I thought she deserved the truth.

"He did, yes," I said.

She blinked and looked away from me again. "I'm sorry. He's a worse man than I thought."

"I'm sorry too," I said.

"But he has other daughters," Bekk said, sounding hopeful. "Grown healthy daughters."

"He claimed Noomi and Bryn, and they both seem okay," I said.

"Thanks," Bryn said dryly.

"Indu told you he took the *alvaroot*?" I asked Bekk carefully, but the doors swung open and cut me off.

Pan came out through the wooden doors and hooked his thumb back the way he'd come. "Elof's ready for you if you wanna go on back."

28

Daughters

The blood draw went smoothly, and although I got light-headed, I didn't faint. Once we were done, Elof didn't really need us all to wait around while he did his lab work, and Rikky offered to lend him a hand since she knew her way around the clinic.

Bryn, Pan, and I went back to the hotel. Pan said he hadn't slept well the night before—which made sense since the beds were horrible—and he went to his room to take a nap. Waiting made Bryn restless, and the room had little space to work out. She pushed her bed up against mine, and then she used the emptied space to do push-ups, crunches, and various other stationary exercises to burn off her anxious energy.

I stole the pillows from her bed and wadded them up to get halfway comfortable, and I settled in to read the Kendare Blake book I'd bought at the airport yesterday. Bryn's panting and banging around were rather distracting, and we would've been in serious trouble if we had downstairs neighbors. I didn't complain, because it seemed to be a healthy way to deal with the stress and confusion I knew she had to be feeling.

So if it took me ten minutes to read a page because I kept losing my place, well, so be it.

A strange ringing sound came from my bag, which I'd slid under the bed to save floor space. It was unzipped to allow for my laptop cord to wind out and into the outlet behind my nightstand. Last night, I'd plugged it in so Bryn and I could watch cartoons about "trolls" on Netflix to unwind and laugh at all the things they got wrong and marvel at the occasional thing they got right.

"I *wish* I could get my hair that pink or blue," I'd said, pining over the neon shades of the cartoon character's hair.

"Tell me about it!" Bryn chimed in, happy to complain about our difficult troll hair. "My hair is so light blond, if I were human, I'd be able to dye it any color of the rainbow. But I've dyed it black before, and it's literally dark for a matter of hours before fading to gray within a week. Our hair actively rejects dye."

After I'd finally been tired enough to sleep on the cot-bed with velvet covers, I had shoved my laptop under my bed and promptly forgotten about it.

Until it started ringing—an odd *da-da-da* sound—and Bryn popped from where she was planking on the floor. "What was that?"

"I think I have a call," I said uncertainly, and I pulled the laptop out and sat on my bed. I flipped it open to see a green phone icon flashing on the screen, and when I clicked on it, a video chat opened so my whole screen became Hanna's face.

"You answered!" She was all smiles and freckles, framed by her dark curls.

Behind her, I saw Mia holding one of the twins—I couldn't tell which from the angle—and she waved at me and said, "Hello, Ulla."

"Ulla!" Liam suddenly appeared in the frame, practically pushing his older sister out of the way to shove his face as close to the camera as he could get. He pointed to the fresh gap in his wide smile. "I lost a tooth yesterday!"

"That's awesome," I said as Hanna pushed him away.

"Mom, Liam's butting into my chat!" Hanna yelled, and somewhere in the background, I heard a baby crying—Lissa, it sounded like to me.

At the sound of the kids arguing and babies crying, Bryn stood up and excused herself to go shower.

"You don't own Ulla!" Liam pouted. "I can talk to her too!"

"I have something important to talk to her about!" Hanna argued, then she looked back over her shoulder. "Mom! I need privacy!"

"Liam, kids, come on," Mia said. There was some whining, but she herded the kids out quickly, and the sound of Lissa crying faded until I couldn't hear it at all.

Hanna let out a dramatic sigh. "Finally I get to talk to you. You're usually so hard to reach when you're gone."

"The Omte kingdom has great reception actually," I said. "The hotel even has Wi-Fi."

"Nice," she said, and looked impressed.

"How are you doing?" I asked. "How is everything at home?"

"We're all fine." She waved it off. "That's not why I called."

I heard someone mumble my name, and two chubby tan hands reached up for Hanna. She kept looking at me—well, the camera—but she reached down and pulled Niko onto her lap. He was nearly four years old, but he was small for his age, making his big brown eyes appear even larger under his mop of dark curls.

"Ulla!" he said, more clearly this time, and waved at me.

I waved back. "Hey, buddy."

"I have to talk to Ulla, so if you want to stay, you can't interrupt," Hanna warned him, and he nodded dutifully before making faces and watching himself in the corner of the screen.

"So what's up?" I asked.

"We're gonna do a three-way call with my grandparents." She wasn't looking at me then; instead her eyes searched the screen as her hands went to her mouse and keyboard.

"What?" I asked, feeling self-conscious. I ran my fingers through my tangles of hair and hoped that my eyeliner hadn't smudged too much since I put it on that morning.

Hanna was already calling—I heard the *da-da-da* of the ringing—and I glanced back at the blankets and pillows I'd mashed up behind me. I wondered if there was time to straighten up, but then there they were.

The video changed, becoming a split screen with Hanna and little Niko on the right side, and her bewildered but smiling grandparents on the left. The box where I could see myself got slightly smaller, tucked away in the corner.

Johan looked older than his wife; his thick hair and beard were only slightly blacker than they were silver. Sarina had long, fine hair in a rich maple color, and she was slender with intense dark eyes, giving her a brittle edge. Her smile was so tentative and fragile, like a bubble about to pop. The low resolution and Johan's beard made his smattering of freckles on his tawny skin hard to make out, but they were there, the one noticeable feature he shared with both his late son Nikolas and Hanna.

"Oh, there you are!" Sarina sounded delighted as her smile deepened.

"I told you it wasn't that hard," Hanna teased.

"We managed it," Johan said with a low rumble of laughter.

"Who is that little guy?" Sarina asked, and she wagged her fingers at Niko after he waved. "Liam?"

"Niko," Hanna said.

Sarina's smile went tight when she said, "They grow so fast."

"I talked to Grandma after we talked before." Johan put his hand on his wife's arm and gave her an encouraging smile. "She remembered more than I did."

"Johan's always struggled with recollections of his youth," she clarified sadly. "He doesn't have any memories of the time before Nikolas was born."

"That sounds rough," I said.

"It's all I've known," he said, giving his wife a loving look. "And Rina helps me remember."

"Johan told me everything that you talked about, but I didn't really understand what your intent is," Sarina went on cagily. "What are you trying to find?"

"Her parents and our friend Eliana," Hanna answered before I could.

"And how does that connect to a children's story that your grandfather wrote decades ago?" Sarina asked.

"Johan wrote about Jem-Kruk and Senka," I told her. "I met someone called Jem-Kruk who knows our friend Eliana and her twin sister, Illaria. I went to Sweden to meet with Indu Mattison—"

Sarina's eyelids fluttered; the corner of her mouth twitched ever so slightly at the mention of Indu's name.

"—and he told me that Eliana, Illaria, and I all share the same mother," I explained. "Someone called Senka."

Sarina pursed her lips but didn't say anything.

"Indu held me captive for a month," I said, choosing my words very carefully because I was acutely aware of Hanna and Niko listening. "I can't remember what happened, and I can't find Eliana. I want to know what's going on, and I think that you and Johan know something that might help me."

Sarina lowered her eyes then and put her hand on Johan's. He watched her with a look of sympathy and absolute adoration.

"I know when you left, we promised to never speak of it again," he told her softly. "But that was a long, long time ago."

Her jaw tensed. "It's about keeping everyone safe."

"My love," he said gently. "Ulla wasn't safe. We can help her, and we might be able to help her sisters."

She closed her eyes and took a deep breath. "I knew Indu and I knew Senka. In another life." When she opened her eyes again, she couldn't mask the pain, and she gripped tightly onto her husband's hand. "Before I left with Johan, I lived in Áibmoráigi. I was a thrimavolk, one of the daughters of the Älvolk."

29

parable

"The name given to me by my father was Rinatte Freya Som-dottir," Sarina said with a strange resignation on her face, like she always knew one day she'd have to say her given name again but it still left a bitter taste in her mouth.

I didn't like that it pained her to tell me, but I had to know the truth. Especially since others might still be in trouble, like Eliana and Bekk and her daughter, Juno.

"I never knew my mother, but she was from Isarna and I suspected she was Trylle," Sarina went on. "My father was Som Kerrson, an Älvolk like his father and his father before him, and he was one of the young men that had been ener-gized by the new leadership that focused on the teachings of Frey.

"As a mere thrimavolk, I wasn't privy to all of the mach-inations of the Älvolk," she said with a sneer. "But I knew enough. Throughout their history, the Älvolk were mostly peaceful, preferring to keep to themselves and protect their secrets and treasures.

"Áibmoráigi and the Bridge of Dimma are sacred to them, even in their ruination, and they want to protect what they have left," Sarina said. "That was all they truly cared about, until the young men embraced the wicked tenets of the Freyarian leaders, partaking in *blodseider magick* and *helifiske*. The latter was how the thrimavolk numbers quadrupled in a single generation."

"What are thrimavolk?" Hanna asked.

Niko had apparently grown bored and fallen asleep, his head lolling against the crook of her arm.

"The thrimavolk are the daughters of the Älvolk," Sarina answered. "They are warriors, the guardians of Áibmoráigi and the Älvolk. Our fathers are the protectors of the history and creators of order, and the daughters enforce their rule."

"So . . . they're the brain, and you're the brawn?" Hanna asked skeptically, but that was reasonable given Sarina's rather frail appearance.

"Something like that. But not all thrimavolk turned out the way the Älvolk intended." Sarina smiled briefly, but it quickly fell away. "Indu and I were born a year apart, the first children of the Freyarian Älvolk. My father, Som, and Indu's father, Mattis, were both devout followers and eventually chieftains among the Älvolk.

"Mattis died when Indu and I were still children," Sarina continued. "Indu couldn't have been more than eight or nine, and they tapped him for an important leadership role. I didn't see much of him after that, not until I was much older."

She stared off for a moment, thinking. "The life of a thrimavolk is order, discipline, sacrifice. My time was filled with ritualistic training and intensive chores. Exercise and combat in the mornings, cleaning and sewing in the afternoons, choir and quiet contemplation in the evenings.

"But I didn't know any better," she said. "When I was a teenager, I was allowed to venture outside Áibmoráigi for the first time, to forage and hunt in the mountains. If it went well, I might have eventually earned the privilege to trade with the humans and go to their villages. But it did not go well."

"She met me," Johan said with a squeeze of her hand, and she returned his adoring smile.

"That I did," she said wistfully. "I met Senka first, and we became friends, and she told me of a life that didn't involve complete servitude. And then I met Johan and we fell in love, and I knew I had to get out of Áibmoráigi."

"Where did Senka and Johan come from?" I asked. "Isarna? A human town?"

She took a deep breath. "They came across the Bridge of Dimma, from the hidden kingdom of Alfheim and the city of Adlrivellir."

My stomach dropped, and I felt dizzy. "They . . . Where is Alfheim?"

"I don't know." She shook her head once. "The bridge runs across a vast ravine. The south side is in Áibmoráigi, the north side is at the base of the waterfall. We guard the south side, but we can never, ever cross.

"Alfheim is on the other side of the bridge, and that's where Senka and Johan came from," she said.

"And you don't remember, Johan?" I asked.

"I recall hardly anything before 1989, I'm afraid," he said.

"I've always worried that it was something the Älvolk did." Sarina frowned as she looked at her husband and tenderly touched his hand. "Som learned of Johan before I left, and I tried to sneak out carefully so they couldn't use their *inovotto muitit* on me the way they had on the others that tried to escape from Áibmoráigi. But I fear they got to him somehow."

"It's all right, love," Johan assured her. "I remember you, and I remember Nikolas. That's more than enough."

"That's enough of this," she said quietly, and when she looked back at us, she blinked her moist eyes. "You didn't call to hear the story of my life. You want to know about Senka."

I cleared my throat. "Um, yeah. I mean . . . I would be happy to hear anything you might be able to tell me. At all."

"I didn't know her well," Sarina admitted. "The Älvolk usually prefer to keep outsiders away, but Senka was an exception, primarily because she was an ideal candidate to be a mother of the thrimavolk—young, *álfar,* and fertile."

Hanna's nose crinkled in disgust. *"Fertile?"*

"She had two daughters, twins, I think," Sarina said. "She brought them to the city once while I was still there, but I never met them."

"Wait. When did you leave Áibmoráigi?" I asked.

"In 1988."

"And how old were the twins then?" I asked, but as I did the quick math in my head, it didn't make sense.

I didn't know how old Eliana and Illaria were. When she'd been with us a couple months ago, Eliana had seemed like a naïve teenager, but Illaria seemed older, more like an adult in her mid-twenties. But it was 2019—for Eliana and Illaria to have been born before Sarina left, they'd have to be in their thirties now.

But I had spent a couple weeks living with both Eliana and Hanna, and there was no way that Eliana was over twice Hanna's age. In fact, if that math was correct, Eliana would be older than Hanna's parents.

"I'm really not sure," Sarina said. "I only saw them from a distance. Toddlers, maybe?"

"So how old would that make Eliana?" Hanna asked, and by her confused face, I guessed she was just getting to the same conclusion I had.

"I really couldn't say," Sarina said. "She was very protective of her daughters, and in turn, the Älvolk were protective of Senka, particularly the young men. Indu, Som, Lemak. She never seemed all that interested in them, not romantically, but that didn't stop Indu from following her like a hungry calf trailing its mother.

"I thought he was what drove her off, actually," she said, almost offhandedly.

"Indu drove Senka off?" I asked.

"Well, not entirely, I suppose," Sarina corrected herself. "At first Senka came around fairly often, with Johan. But soon, it was only Johan, and I'd always assumed she'd stopped visiting after we ran off together. I must have been mistaken, if you're her daughter."

She considered something for a moment. "Maybe she didn't feel safe going alone. Senka would mention wyrms, and Johan was a strong young man then. Perhaps she enlisted someone else later on."

"Do you know why Senka visited?" I asked. "If it was dangerous and she didn't like Indu?"

"Food, mostly," Sarina answered. "I don't know if it was scarce where she came from, but she referred to *älgost*—the cheese we made from elk milk—as an utter delicacy. She also seemed to enjoy us as a curiosity, like a tourist visiting a favorite destination.

"Not that I understood the appeal," she said, not hiding her distaste. "I know that the young men treated her like a goddess, but Áibmoráigi is an underground prison. Plenty of other thrimavolk and a few Älvolk tried to escape. Those that failed were met with the *inovotto muitit* or worse.

"But Sumi made a successful break two months before I did, and I—"

"Wait, Sumi?" Hanna interrupted Sarina. "Dark coils of

hair? A tattoo on her neck? Kind of intimidating even though she has a nice smile?"

"You know Sumi?" Sarina asked, sounding equally surprised.

"We've met briefly," I said. "She's friends with Eliana and Jem-Kruk."

"Are you saying that Sumi was a thrimavolk?" Hanna pressed.

"No," Sarina replied carefully. "Sumi had been an Älvolk. She was called Sumin Axelson at birth, and she was primed to be a chieftain, like Indu. Until she said she felt like she was truly a thrimavolk and asked to be called Sumi. Then things got very bad for her."

Her face darkened, then she forced a thin smile. "But Sumi got away, and I studied what she'd done, and that's how I was able to make a new life with Johan."

All of us fell silent, trying to process all that she'd told us. Johan moved to put his arm around her, and Sarina managed another brittle smile. Behind them were shelves of the hundreds of books that filled Johan's study. I remembered that when I had been there, it smelled exactly as it looked— earthy sandalwood and old paper.

"What was the point of all of it?" I asked.

Sarina lifted her head, her eyes wide like I'd startled her. "Pardon?"

"The Älvolk went to a lot of trouble and they're growing their numbers," I said. "To what end? What are they hoping to achieve?"

"Indu and his ilk were obsessed with a prophecy," Sarina said with disdain. "It was a ridiculous poem, really."

"*Enn morgana fjeurn on ennsommora orn?*" I asked.

Sarina gaped at me, then narrowed her eyes. "How did you know?"

"It's kinda been stuck in my head on and off since I left Áibmoráigi," I explained. "Do you know why they were so obsessed with it? What is it supposed to foretell?"

"The song is just nonsense," she said dismissively. "Just a parable about the seasons. As to why, they believed that the song would somehow lead them to finding a way to cross the bridge.

"The *álfar* can cross the bridge as they please, or so it always seemed to me," Sarina went on. "But we could only guard it. For centuries, the Älvolk had protected a place that they've never been. Alfheim became a treasure to them, something they had spent so long coveting that they felt entitled to it."

"The song is believed to be a prophecy that will enable the Älvolk to get their version of heaven?" I asked. "But how is it supposed to work? It's just a silly love story."

"I don't know how it would work," Sarina said with a bitter smile. "They never told me the details. All I know is that they were practicing *blodseider magick*, and they were trying to amass an army of thrimavolk."

30

The Bridge

My mind was racing, and I paced the room from door to door. Pan sat on the bed, one leg folded under him, and he'd been wearing the same thoughtful expression the entire time. I'd explained the conversation with Hanna and her grandparents, even the bit about how the connection had gotten sketchy at the end and we'd had to say goodbye abruptly.

"So my probably-father is a dangerous fanatic," Bryn said flatly. She was standing off to the side of the room, leaning back against the wall. "Unfortunately, that's not exactly shocking anymore."

"But if we figure out what that weird song is about, we can figure out what they're up to, and what they did to us," I said. "And maybe we can find Eliana and stop Bekk's baby from getting hurt like the others."

As soon as I had the chance, I would tell Elof about the *alvaroot*. Knowing the cause of the deaths would greatly increase any effort to keep Bekk's baby healthy, and if anyone could figure out an antidote to an old root, I had to hope it was Elof.

"That all sounds really good," Pan agreed tentatively. "But

it's basically a nursery rhyme. It doesn't mention a bridge or Alfheim or anything relevant. Other than that sad flower."

"What flower?" Bryn asked.

"The one the Vittra gave the Älvolk in exchange for us." Pan looked back over his shoulder at her. "The *sorgblomma*. It's a rare globeflower that bleeds aloe and smells like death, so they call it a 'mourning flower.'"

"They're doing something with blood," I said. "They took mine, they got a bunch of bleeding flowers. I don't know what exactly they're doing, but they obviously believe it will help them cross the bridge and get into Alfheim."

"But why can't they just go to Alfheim now?" Pan asked. "What's preventing them from crossing?"

"Some kind of magic?" I shrugged. "Maybe something like the Ögonen but much more powerful. I mean, trolls keep the humans out of our cities, and the Älvolk keep most of us out of Áibmoráigi. It's reasonable that the *álfar* figured out how to keep us all out of Alfheim."

Bryn rubbed her temple. "Can we do anything about this right now?"

"Um . . ." I looked to Pan. "At this very moment? I don't know."

"Good." She stepped away from the wall and nodded. "The last several days have been a major mindfuck for me, and I'm hungry and stressed and this room is making me claustrophobic."

"I think we could all use a break," I admitted.

"Margarit, the front desk clerk, told me that there's a bar and grill close by," Bryn said.

Pan snapped his fingers. "Oh yeah. The Ugly Vulture is connected to this place by a tree bridge, and I think there might be some other shops connected that way too." He looked up at me with slightly arched eyebrows. "What do you say, Ulla? Wanna give the Ugly Vulture another go?"

"Sure," I said, even though I honestly would've been happy to stay in the room, pacing and overanalyzing everything I'd learned this summer.

But Bryn was right—we could all really use a break. Plus, I figured that if I cleared my head for a while, I might be able to come back at the situation with fresh eyes.

The Ugly Vulture was kind of a roughneck place, but it was early afternoon so I figured it wouldn't be too busy. Pan and I hadn't had any trouble when we went there before, and I thought it sounded like a good way to unwind.

Bryn was freshly showered but Pan and I needed a little bit of time. I tried to be fast—I did a quick smoky eye with a suede lipstick, and I put on my black baby-doll minidress covered in big yellow and orange flowers.

But I took long enough for Elof to return from the clinic and for Pan to fill him in. The blood-analyzing process apparently took fourteen hours inside of the machine, so he had nothing to really do now except wait, and he decided to join us on our outing.

"When we get back to Merellä, I'll talk to Calder and have him pull the books on the *blodseider magick*," Elof said as we walked. He hadn't changed much to go out—he'd been wearing a vest and tie, and he'd ditched the tie, unbuttoned his top shirt snaps, and left his vest open.

We walked to the bar by way of the rope bridge that connected to the lobby. It was a little wider than a sidewalk, made with wooden planks, and it was suspended from the treetops with an intricate netting made with rope and vines, presumably for safety and camouflage.

The dark water of the swamp was fifty feet below, and I

watched it through the gaps between the boards and tried not to think about how it was only rope and branches preventing me from plummeting down into the alligator-infested waters below. Sun filtered through the canopy of leaves close above us, and the warm air was filled with sounds of birds and music from the bar.

"That probably is the best bet," Pan said as we walked. "Doing more research when we get home."

"Let's make a deal," Bryn said, just as we approached the entrance to the Vulture. Two driftwood vulture sculptures flanked the doors. "No talk about blood or family or conspiracies or work. For two hours."

"That doesn't leave us much to talk about," Pan joked.

She stopped short, her expression as no-nonsense as her outfit—tank top with jeans—her hair left hanging wild and curly. "I just want nothing stressful for a couple hours."

Elof smiled up at her. "It's a deal."

Inside the Vulture was an interesting mash-up of country and jungle safari. The ceilings were ten feet above us, supported by thick branches, and the floor was covered in sawdust, but that was only the entrance.

In reality, it was a sprawling bar with different-themed segments, with names like the Mudhole and the Dungeon. Last time I'd been here with Pan and Rikky, we'd gone to the Red Room, but this time Bryn bypassed it, and we settled on the Bridge. Its name was a real misnomer, since it was on the roof. But it was above the pathway that connected two trees, and it was outdoors, with only a vine trellis as a covering.

Bryn ordered us a round of shots. No sooner had she downed hers when she spotted the *økkspill* boards across the bar, mounted on the wall in the center of the roof patio.

She asked how to play it, and after a cursory lesson, she was off to try her hand at it for herself.

Elof switched to drinking water and chatting with the bartender, but I decided to be more adventurous and followed Pan's lead and ordered myself an Omte sangria. The shot of *eldvatten* had already made my stomach hot and bubbly, but the sangria left me pleasantly warm and relaxed.

The rooftop speakers played Dolly Parton's "Jolene," and I felt the tension I'd been carrying in my shoulders the last weeks finally began to uncoil.

"Bryn definitely had the right idea about this," I said as I rolled my neck.

"Yeah, she has some good ideas," Pan agreed. He looked back over his shoulder, watching her play *økkspill*. "You know she came up with another really great idea."

"And what's that?" I asked.

He looked back at me with a crooked smile. "That I should ask you to dance."

Confused, I glanced over at Bryn, then back at him. "When did she say that?"

"When she was ordering the shots. You were talking to Elof."

I laughed. "She really said that?"

"She did. But I would've asked you to dance anyway."

"Then why haven't you?" I asked.

"Dance with me."

I slid off the bar stool and took his hand, leading him out to the small dance floor. The song changed to Emmylou Harris, and Pan slid his arm around my waist.

As we swayed slowly together, Pan laughed to himself.

"What's so funny?" I asked.

"I was just thinking how nice it is that no matter what

happens, we always find time to dance together." He smiled down at me, his smoldering dark eyes holding mine.

With my arms around his neck, I leaned up and kissed him softly on the mouth. His full lips pressed against mine, and an excited heat grew inside me. This was the first time we'd kissed—*really* kissed—since our Lost Month, and I felt the sudden, dizzying sensation of a hundred other kisses I couldn't quite remember rushing over me. Stolen between iron bars, snuck around our captors—even in the darkest of places, we always found our way into each other's arms.

We'd given up any pretense of dancing, and we were just standing in the middle of the floor. We stopped kissing, his hands in my hair, and his eyes on mine.

"I'm so glad I found you again," he said, his voice low and husky.

"Me too," I whispered.

Behind me, there was a clatter of chairs, and Pan looked over my shoulder. His eyes widened in horror, and I turned around to see Rikky, standing beside an overturned chair and shooting daggers at us with her eyes.

"You dirty liar!" Rikky snarled.

"Rikky, listen." Pan immediately moved, stepping closer to her and putting himself between me and his livid ex-girlfriend.

"You didn't have to lie!" Tears stood in her eyes, and there was a slight slur to her words. I wondered how long she'd been at the bar before she discovered us on the rooftop Bridge. "I would've helped you anyway. Is that how little you think of me, Pan?"

"I didn't lie," Pan said, speaking calmly with his hands held palms-out toward her.

She shook her head furiously, her dark auburn curls

shaking. "I thought that you knew me better." Then, as if she was yelling at herself, exclaimed, "I've been so foolish! What was I thinking?" She cringed. "I kissed you! You let me kiss you!"

"I put a stop to it right away," Pan said quickly.

"But I wouldn't have done that if you'd been honest that she was your girlfriend!" Rikky shot back.

"You asked if she was my girlfriend, and I said no because we haven't . . ." He shifted his weight between his feet and glanced back over his shoulder at me. ". . . discussed labels."

Rikky glowered at him. "She's not your girlfriend but she's definitely your *something.*"

"Yeah, she is," he said.

"So you *lied,*" she countered, nearly growling out the last word.

Pan rubbed the back of his neck. "It's more complicated than that."

She rolled her eyes. "Oh, I don't doubt that." Rikky stepped closer to him, her hands balled up at her sides, but Pan didn't move. "You lied when you could've just told the truth. But you didn't. Because you don't know me at all, and you're a selfish coward."

"I'm sorry I wasn't more honest with you," he told her quietly. "I wasn't trying to keep anything from you or do anything to hurt you. But I was still figuring things out myself. I still am, honestly."

"Whatever you say." She looked around as if just realizing her loud confrontation had drawn the attention of other patrons.

Bryn had stopped playing *økkspill,* but she still held the kasteren axes and stood beside me, in case things got out of hand. I was a few feet behind Pan, standing awkwardly and unsure what to do.

Rikky cleared her throat and straightened up. "When your friends come for the results, it would be better if you stayed away." And then she turned and left the bar.

31

summoned

After the commotion, everyone went back to their own business. Pan righted the chairs that Rikky had knocked over, and then he slumped into one of them. I sat down next to him and put a hand gently on his arm.

"Sorry about all that," he said, frowning.

"It wasn't your fault."

"I never meant to lead her on or anything." He ran a hand through his dark curls and stared off at the sun slowly dipping below the treetops. "I was trying to let her down gently, and I didn't want to use you as an excuse not to be with her. Because even if I never met you, I don't want to be with Rikky anymore. But I guess I should've been more blunt about it with her."

Just then, a waitress came over and set a mug of ale in front of Pan. "This is from the little guy at the bar."

I looked over to see Elof, raising his own mug to Pan. Pan smiled and took a long drink. We sat at the table a while longer, him sipping his ale. I don't know that we ever completely shook the tension from Rikky's angry outburst, but by the time we decided to head back to our rooms, Pan was smiling and I felt a lot more relaxed. Bryn and Elof seemed in good spirits.

When we got to our rooms, we parted ways to freshen up before we figured out what to do next. Bryn went into our room first, but Pan took my hand and pulled me back toward him.

"I forgot to tell you before. You look really beautiful in that dress."

"That's funny because you did already tell me that," I said with a smile. "Twice."

He kissed me, gentle and sweet. "Maybe I can talk to Elof and see if he wants to hang out with Bryn for a little while, so we could have the room to ourselves." Then, quickly, he added, "Just so we can watch a movie on the laptop or something. I'm not suggesting Netflix and chill. Just the Netflix part."

"What are you talking about?"

"That was just a convoluted way of asking if you wanna hang out later?" he asked.

I nodded. "Yeah. Just come knock on my door when you're ready."

I finally went into the hotel room, and Bryn was lying on her bed, texting someone on her phone.

"You want me to clear out of here so you can have some time alone," she said as I sat on the bed and she never looked up from her phone.

"Uh, no, I would never ask you that," I stammered.

"So you guys weren't just making out in the hall?" she asked.

My cheeks reddened. "That was hardly making out."

She finally looked over at me. "I could just as easily go text Ridley from the lobby. They have a bench there that's slightly softer than this bed. It's no big deal."

"I don't know. I guess, maybe, if it's no big deal," I said

sheepishly. It felt rude kicking her out of our room, but she'd offered, and honestly, I would love to spend some alone time with Pan. We'd had hardly any since the Lost Month.

A knock at the door came before she could respond, and I hurried to answer, assuming it was Pan. But when I opened the door, it was Margarit, the bespectacled front desk clerk.

"Sorry to disturb you, but um . . ." She adjusted her glasses. "The palace called, and the Queen Regent has requested your presence, along with that of Mr. Dómari."

"Just the two of us?" I asked.

"Yes, they requested *only* Ms. Tulin and Mr. Dómari," she said.

"When do they want to see us?"

"Now, miss," Margarit said. "I went ahead and told Knut, and he has the airboat all ready to go."

"Okay," I said, because I didn't know what else to say about the Omte Queen summoning me for no apparent reason.

"If you need a moment, I still need to tell Mr. Dómari," she said.

"Yeah, thank you." I closed the door, and the sangria that had so nicely warmed my belly a couple hours ago now left it a burning sour pit.

Bryn was standing when I turned back around. I hadn't heard her get up, but she moved like a silent ninja when she wanted to. "Do you want me to go with you?"

"I mean, I don't think you should. Since the Queen didn't request you, and it sounds like she doesn't really like you."

"Do you know what she wants?" Bryn asked.

I shook my head. "No idea."

"I should go with." She moved toward her luggage, where she stored a dagger and calfskin sheath.

"No, no, no." I held up my hands. "I don't think that's

necessary. Elof and I have faced worse than Queen Bodil. We can handle this."

"Fine." Bryn straightened up. "But if I don't hear from you in an hour, I'm storming the palace."

With that settled, I went into the hall and met Elof. As we rode the airboat through Fulaträsk, we speculated about why the Queen was calling us down to meet her. Elof guessed it had something to do with Rikky, either our visit to the clinic or the incident at the Ugly Vulture.

"I don't know. It sounds like there's incidents there a lot," I said. "The King died there."

"I've heard that before," Elof said.

"He was a good King," Knut said, apparently overhearing our conversation. "A strong, just man who died among his citizens. It's a good death, because he died the way he lived, and our memory honors him."

The Omte palace finally came into view, but it was a squat building, nearly flush with the swamp around it, and moss covered the walls, so it wasn't that conspicuous, compared to all the other palaces I'd seen. The only real ostentatious features were the Gothic vulture statues on the eaves.

Knut waited in the airboat, and a palace guard led me and Elof inside. If he felt the same dismay I did when I first saw the musty interior of the palace, with its spiderwebs and snails on the walls, he didn't show it. Elof wore his usual expression of polite curiosity.

The Queen was waiting for us in the same parlor where she'd received me before. The large stained-glass window—depicting a black vulture stained with crimson blood—gave the room an eerie glow. The knickknacks on the shelves that lined the walls still managed to catch the dim light, glinting on the jewel-encrusted statues made of dark wolfram—the dragons encircling orbs and ravens on topaz trees.

Across from the window was a large painting of King Thor, his grinning face taking up nearly all of the wall.

Bodil stood in front of the stained glass, her back to us with her long black hair plaited down her back. The long black dressing robe she wore was sheer, revealing the silhouette of a black floor-length nightgown that showed off muscular arms.

She looked over at us. Her face was unusually devoid of makeup, making her look more tired than when I had seen her last. Her protruding eyes seemed a bit smaller, her lips even thinner, but she was still rather lovely, in her own way.

"Thank you for seeing me at such a late hour," she said.

"It's not that late," Elof assured her, and he wasn't even lying to be polite. The sky was still light.

We stood in front of the velvet love seat, but neither of us sat until Bodil took her seat across from us.

"Why did you want to see us now?" I asked.

"Because I only just learned that you were here," she explained. "My security told me that you were involved in an incident at the Ugly Vulture. They asked around and heard that you were here with a Mimirin official, doing blood tests at the clinic. I thought it would be best if I found out what kind of experimentation is going on in my kingdom."

"What I am doing is not experimenting, but simple, proven science," Elof assured her. "I'd be happy to explain the whole process I use for the comparative blood analysis I do."

She held up her hand, her long, pointed fingernails painted a metallic bronze. "That won't be necessary."

"All right," Elof said, but he sounded uncertain. "But I will tell you it's completely safe."

"Good." She pursed her lips and looked to me. "How are you involved with all this? Still stumbling through your pursuit for your parents?"

"That wouldn't be how I'd phrase it, but basically, yeah," I said.

"Did you find Orra, then?" Bodil asked with feigned indifference.

Orra Fågel—the woman who abandoned me as a baby—was Bodil's cousin. Indu had told me that Orra kidnapped me as a newborn, but he'd also told me that he was my father, and he'd either lied about that or been mistaken.

Indu had confessed that he'd tracked Orra down and killed her. But that I believed, since she hadn't been seen or heard from in nineteen years. And from what I remembered of Indu torturing me, I wouldn't put it past him to murder the woman who crossed him.

But I had no idea how much—if any—of that I should tell Bodil, especially considering how angry and eccentric she seemed.

"After much searching, I have come to agree with your assessment that Orra is dead," I answered carefully.

"It's as I said, then," she said, but surprisingly, she didn't appear happy to be proven right, nor saddened about the death of her cousin. "Perhaps you'll learn to trust the wisdom of a queen."

"I'm sorry, I didn't mean to doubt you," I said. I hated how slavish I sounded, but Bodil wasn't someone I wanted to upset.

"Is it true that you're traveling with Bryn Aven?" she asked.

I held my head up slightly. "I am."

"Hmmm," she mused. "One should always be prudent in the company they keep."

Before I could respond, the door to the parlor burst open and a gangly young boy rushed in, whining, "Mamma!"

"Furston, we have guests," she lightly rebuked him, but he appeared nonplussed.

Furston looked about eight or nine years old, with an unwieldy head of dark curls nearly covering his eyes. His height was hard to gauge, since he walked slightly hunched, and he wore a sleep tunic that barely covered his torso, leaving all of his wiry limbs exposed.

"It's past story time," he lamented with a passing glance in my direction.

Bodil's harsh expression softened, and she gave her son a smile of genuine apology. He stood a foot away from her, so she leaned forward and took his hand. "I'll be a little while longer, my love."

He scowled down at her hand, and for a moment, I thought he'd snatch his away, but he didn't. "But Mamma, I'm tired now."

"Go lie down, and I'll be up shortly."

"Why not now?" He glared back over his shoulder at me. "Why are they here so late? This isn't the proper time for the palace to have visitors."

"You're right, it is late." The Queen's smile was pained, and she looked to me and Elof. "I've kept you long enough, and I have the Crown Prince to attend to."

She stood up, so Elof immediately got to his feet, and I scrambled to do the same.

"I trust you can find your way out yourself," she said, still holding Furston's hand.

"Of course, Your Majesty." Elof bowed, and as Bodil and her son walked by, he reached out and boldly put his hand on Furston's shoulder. "It was truly an honor meeting you, Young Sire."

"Don't touch me," was all the prince said, and his mother led him out of the parlor.

32

confirmations

"I couldn't tell you what the Queen called us down for, but I can tell you that it was the most peculiar meeting I've ever had," Elof said when we were debriefing Pan and Bryn.

After we got back to the hotel, we went to his room, where Bryn was waiting with Pan. Pan hugged me as soon as he saw me, like he had been afraid that I wouldn't come back. Elof went across the room and shrugged off his vest before carefully folding it and putting it atop his luggage.

"So they go to bed at six o'clock?" Pan asked when Elof had finished.

I shrugged. "It sure seemed that way."

"When I stayed at the palace, we had dinner way later than that," Bryn said incredulously.

"Bizarre though their bedtime rituals may be, the most concerning thing was Bodil's fixation on Ulla," Elof said, turning his gaze to me. "You certainly touched a nerve with her."

"I haven't done anything really. She must not like anyone asking about her dead relatives," I said.

"Or maybe she just doesn't like anyone," Bryn muttered.

"That is a plausible theory," Elof said, ending his statement with a loud yawn. "You must excuse me. I hate to kick everyone out, but I really wouldn't mind getting to bed early tonight."

I didn't feel much like hanging out myself. My stomach was still turning, and I went to my room with Bryn. I read some more of the Kendare Blake novel and tried not to catastrophize all the reasons the Omte Queen might not like me. Eventually, I gave up and tried to sleep, hoping that the morning would bring along clarity with it.

But when I woke up, I felt the same as I had the night before, only now with a backache from the crummy hotel mattress. I had a quiet breakfast in the lobby and then Elof announced it was time to head down to the clinic to get the results. Bryn called Bekk to have her meet us there, and Pan stayed behind, the way Rikky had told him to.

I wasn't really looking forward to seeing her either, but she'd always been nice to me. Still, I felt better knowing that Bryn and Elof would be there too. We took the hotel airboat to the clinic, and a nurse in tangerine scrubs took us back to a patient room that had been set aside for us. Bekk arrived a few minutes after we did. Her olive skin was slightly ashen, and her expression was blank.

Rikky came in after that, but she never even looked at me. She kept her eyes fixed on Elof when she said, "I can take you back to the lab now."

Elof went with her to process the results and get the equipment he'd brought with him. That left the three of us—Bryn, Bekk, and myself—in the small patient room, waiting. Bryn paced, walking between the cream-colored walls with increasing urgency.

After what felt like an eternity, Elof returned with Rikky. She set his heavy machine on the floor. Before she left, I thanked her for all her help, since I didn't know if I'd see her again, and she mumbled "you're welcome" before departing.

Elof hopped up onto the wheeled doctor's chair and rolled closer to where Bekk and I sat. Bryn finally stopped pacing and stood beside Bekk with her arms folded over her chest.

"Usually, I give results individually," Elof said. "But given the unconventional nature of the situation, if it's all right with you all, I'll explain it all at once."

"Just tell me who my father is," Bryn blurted out, then added, "please."

"Given that Bekk's baby shares half of her DNA with you, I would say that Indu Mattison is your father," he said, and she cursed under her breath.

"Which means he's not mine," I said.

Even though it was as I suspected, the confirmation was less comforting than I thought it would be. Ruling out possible fathers—even psycho ones—wasn't nearly as satisfying as finding out who my father really was.

There was obvious relief in finding out a lunatic like Indu wasn't my father, but seeing the look of horrified resignation on Bryn's face dampened the mood.

Bekk looked up at her with a strained, bittersweet smile. "You have sisters now." She rubbed her belly, but Bryn only nodded once.

"Are you all right?" Elof asked her gently.

"Yeah, yeah." She looked up and blinked, like she'd just woken from a bad dream. "We should probably get out of here. Now that we got our answers. Real patients need the room."

"They could spare a few more minutes, if you need it," Elof said sympathetically.

She moved toward the door. "Nah, I'm good."

There wasn't much point in sticking around, not with Bryn bolting toward the door. So we all got up to go. I grabbed Elof's blood machine, since it was so heavy, and we headed out. Elof made sure to thank the front desk nurses for all their help.

It wasn't until we got to the airboats tied at the dock that Bryn asked, "Would anybody mind if I went with Bekk to her house? There are some things I'd like to talk about with her."

"By all means," Elof told her.

Bryn went in Bekk's boat, and Elof and I got in the hotel's, and we parted ways. It hurt a little that Bryn hadn't felt comfortable talking in front of me. But maybe she didn't want to deal with another set of emotions, when she was so clearly rocked to the core.

And she probably wanted a quiet conversation with someone who knew her father. Her whole life had been turned upside down. I understood the feeling, and if she needed space from me, I'd be happy to give it to her.

At the hotel, I went to my room, and Pan showed up at my door a few minutes later. His dark eyes were uncertain, and his hands were in the back pockets of his jeans.

"Elof told me what happened," he said. "How are you doing?"

I held the door wider to let him in. "I'm fine."

"Yeah?" He sat down on my bed, rumpled with a T-shirt on it, while Bryn's bed was made with military precision.

"I mean, essentially." I stood beside him and sighed. "I've gotten another question answered." Then I glanced around the room. "So that means we're done in Fulaträsk."

"That's a good thing, given that the Queen has been watching you," he said.

I frowned. "You make it sound so creepy."

"It is a little creepy," he reasoned, and he took my hand, gently caressing the back of it with his thumb. "All I really meant is that it will be nice to get back home."

"I don't know if Merellä is my home."

"You have an apartment and friends there . . . and me there," he said softly. "That's home enough for now, isn't it?"

"It's more than enough." I stepped closer to him, until I was standing between his legs, and I leaned down and kissed him.

He wrapped an arm around my waist, pulling me closer to him, and the awkward angle caused me to lose my balance, and we both fell onto the bed.

"Sorry." I laughed and lay on my side. "I thought that would be romantic."

Pan propped himself up on an elbow, and he laughed as he brushed a lock of hair out of my face. "Are you kidding me? Falling into bed with you is always romantic."

"What are we doing?" I asked as I looked up into his smoldering dark eyes.

"You mean right now or in a big-picture kinda way?"

"Both."

He took a deep breath and put his hand on my side. My shirt had ridden up slightly, so his fingers rested on the exposed skin of my hip, and my flesh shivered involuntarily, and a heat fluttered deep in my belly.

"Right now we're lying in bed together," he said. "And I was just thinking about kissing you."

"Just thinking about it?" I asked coyly.

His smile deepened, and he squeezed my side before pulling me close to him. Then his mouth found mine, and he kissed me more fiercely than he usually did (and that thought sent a delicious thrill through me, because there was a way that Pan *usually* kissed me). It was playful but urgent, the way his hand moved to my lower back, his fingers pressing into my skin.

Pan pulled away from me, a half smile playing on his lips.

"What?" I asked.

"I was just thinking about how much I missed this," he said, sounding almost wistful. "But then I realized we haven't actually done much of *this* at all. I think I missed you before I met you."

"Or maybe you just remember all the times we've kissed," I said, and his smile fell away.

"What do you mean?"

"I can't remember much, and the details are very hazy. But when I kissed you yesterday, I knew I'd kissed you a dozen times during the Lost Month. I don't know how, but we found ways to be together, even in the dungeon."

"That doesn't really surprise me," he said. "I'm very ingenious and persistent when I'm properly motivated. And I really enjoy kissing you."

I kissed him again then, wrapping my arms around him and holding him close to me. We made out like that for a while, mostly kissing but a bit of talking, though we both steered clear of anything heavy. Really, we were just relishing the time we had together.

He was lying on his back, telling me about an awkward high school dance, and I had my head on his chest, with his arm around me. Fortunately, we weren't in a compromising position when Bryn came back.

"Oh, good, you're all here," she said when she saw us. "Mostly."

"What's up?" I asked and sat up, pulling away from Pan. "How'd it go with Bekk?"

"Good, good." She brushed her hair back and exhaled deeply. "We're going to find my other sister."

"What other sister?" Pan asked.

"The one that's still alive," Bryn said. "Minoux Moen. She's nine years old, and she lives in a Skojare village. Bekk and I want to find her and talk to her mom, so we can figure out why she lived, and the others didn't. Bekk wants to prevent anything bad from happening to her baby, and I want to know what the hell Indu passed on to me."

"Okay," I said. "So what happens from here?"

"Bekk and I are going on to the Skojare village," Bryn said. "And you guys go back to Merellä to finish your search there. I'll be in contact with you, and I'll let you know what I find out. But I don't think I need to keep you from home any longer."

33

ARROW

It was at the airport, when my head was pounding, that the song came back in full swing. For the past couple days it had been pleasantly absent, but now the song of the morning flower and the summer bird was on a constant refrain. And it didn't really help that being around so many humans could make me jumpy.

It had only been seven hours earlier that Bryn gathered us all together, and we arranged our travel plans out of the Omte kingdom. We'd all gone to the Lafayette airport together, but Bryn and Bekk parted ways from us to head northeast. Everything happened so fast, there was no point in wasting money on a hotel room if we didn't need to be in Fulaträsk.

It was me, Pan, and Elof on a layover in Houston. Elof usually tried to make friends with anyone around, but he sprawled out on an airport bench, his carry-on luggage propped under his head like a pillow.

Pan, meanwhile, had left to find something to eat; his stomach seemed to fare much better with rich human food than mine did, if the way he'd slammed an energy drink earlier was any indication.

I was exhausted, my head was throbbing, and the song was on a never-ending loop. The human sitting beside me kept bumping me with their elbow, and I was sick of traveling.

Suddenly, I wanted to cry because I just wanted to go *home*, even though I didn't even know where that was. But when I closed my eyes and thought of home, the first thing that came to my mind was the loft bed in my apartment with Dagny. The sunlight through the windows and the open airy loft, with Dag, Pan, and Brueger hanging out on the lumpy couch.

I thought of my soft old bed and downy comforter, and I wondered if there would be enough room for Pan in the bed with me—

—but Noomi's voice cut through my daydream, practically growling as she said, "You're never going home, Violetta." She used the name my mother had chosen for me, spitting it out as if it were a slur. "You don't belong here. You don't belong anywhere. And once Father's used you up, I will throw you back in the hole you crawled out from."

"I got you an apple and a bottle of water," Pan was saying, pulling me from my thoughts, and when I opened my eyes, I was surprised to feel tears spilling down my cheeks. "Oh, jeez, Ulla, I can go find you something else?"

"No, no." I hastily wiped at my eyes. "That's fine. I'm just tired and . . . just really tired."

Pan sat down beside me and put his arm around me. "It's okay. I understand." I leaned into him then, and the song in my head finally quieted a little. "We'll be home soon."

"Soon" was definitely a subjective thing. It was another nine hours, making it nearly four in the morning when I finally crossed the threshold into my apartment. Dagny was snoring on the couch, and she didn't wake up to my unlocking the front door a few feet away from her, so I decided to let her sleep. I quietly crept up to my loft, and after changing into my comfiest pajamas, I crawled into bed and fell straight asleep.

The scent of burning rye toast woke me a couple hours later, and Dagny apologized profusely as she waved the toast in front of the open window.

"Sorry," she said as I slowly climbed down the ladder of my loft. "I wanted to have some toast quick and then run off to the archery range before work. I was trying to be quiet. I didn't want to wake you."

"No, it's fine." I poured myself a glass of lemon tea from the pitcher Dagny kept in the fridge. "I slept on the plane last night."

"You want a piece of burnt toast slathered in plum preserves?" Dagny asked as she spread purple jam all over the bread.

"Sure." I took what she offered and greedily chewed it down, since I hadn't eaten much yesterday.

"Since you're up, you could come with me to the archery range if you want," Dagny suggested. Her long black hair hung in a braid over her shoulder, and she pushed the sleeves up on her heather-gray sweatshirt. "You could fill me in about your Fulaträsk trip, and I could teach you to properly shoot an arrow. I have to leave for work in an hour, so you could come back after that and nap or whatever."

"Yeah, it sounds fun." I shrugged. "But I'm not getting ready. I'll brush my teeth and put on a bra, but that's it." My hair was in a messy bun and my face was puffy, but I didn't have the energy to stress about it.

Ten minutes later, I was walking out the door with Dagny and telling her all about Bryn, Rikky's fight with Pan, and my weird meeting with Queen Bodil. I even told her about making out with Pan, but I kept the details sparse.

"So," Dagny said as we walked into the archery range. "Where do we go from here?"

"Honestly, I was hoping you'd know, because I've got no clue," I said glumly.

"Remember, I'm not the only one who offers good advice," Dagny said. "I'm certain that Elof has something up his sleeve."

34

❧

morning flower

I dozed off on the couch while rereading *Jem-Kruk and the Adlrivellir.* I'd already read through it three times on the long flights, but I wanted to read it again. Any hint or mention of Jem-Kruk's friend Senka held such heavy significance now that I knew that Johan might've been making real references about my mother. I scoured the book, reading between the lines for any insights.

But I had been more tired than I thought after my archery lesson from Dagny. I barely made it two pages and I was out. I woke up a few hours later with a crick in my neck, and ringing in my head was the last phrase I'd read in the book— *the suns will set in the green sky when the good morning becomes the violent night.*

The nice thing about Merellä was that the magic seemed to block out that infernal ballad of the flowers and birds. While it was a nice reprieve, it was also rather disconcerting. The cloaking enchantments didn't keep out the average old earworm, like Taylor Swift's latest song, but they did this.

Which meant the song was in my head because of more

psychokinetic reasons. Was it a side effect of one of the spells the Älvolk had done? Or had someone cursed me with it on purpose? But why would anyone want me to hear that damned song all the time?

It had an obvious parallel to the *sorgblomma*—the mourning flower the Älvolk had gotten. But the lyrics didn't really tell me anything about what to do with the flower or what it was capable of.

A bird and a flower fall in love, but the bird flies away for the winter. The flower cries so much, the meadow becomes a lake. Which could maybe be a reference to Lake Sodalen that was near Áibmoráigi, according to the note I'd left myself during the Lost Month.

After all that crying, the flower dies, and the bird comes back. When he sees the flower dead, he freaks out and plucks all his feathers out, so he bleeds to death on the meadow. Then other flowers bloom in the field.

And that's it. A song about a tragic romance between a weeping flower and a bleeding bird.

Those were more apt names, anyway, than summer bird and—

"—*morning flower*," I heard Indu's voice saying, and I shivered.

Suddenly, I remembered something from the Lost Month. The first night we were there, we'd been invited guests of Indu, before he had snapped and locked us all up. But earlier that night, the Älvolk had held a dinner for us in a dark medieval dining hall lit by a hundred candles.

Before the meal was served, Indu stood and everyone fell silent. "Tonight we all have much to celebrate. It's not often that we have guests, but it is a fitting way to rejoice at the return of my daughter, my morning flower." He raised his glass and smiled down at me. "*Join in my welcoming them into our home!* Skol!"

And then, right after that, a choir of thrimavolk came in to sing the haunting song stuck in my head.

Indu had called *me* the morning flower.

And then he had stolen my blood.

The landline rang, a loud, clattering sound that jolted me out of my thoughts. I set aside my book and hurried to grab it, since it was probably Pan. I hadn't spoken to him since we'd gotten back to Merellä, which hadn't been that long, but I missed him already anyway.

I was smiling by the time I answered, "Hello?"

"Hi, Ulla, are you busy?" Dagny asked. Her voice sounded unusually pinched and anxious, but maybe I had just been expecting Pan's deeper voice.

"Uh, no, I don't think so," I stammered, since she caught me off guard.

"Good. Because you should come down here," Dagny said, and I decided that she *definitely* sounded anxious.

"Why? What's wrong?" I asked.

"Elof has something he wants to talk to you about. When can you get here? Twenty minutes?"

"Yeah, sure. I can do that."

"Great. See you then." She hung up before I could ask anything more.

I got ready lightning fast and jogged down to the Mimirin. I was out of breath by the time I made it up to the third floor, but I got to Elof's lab in just over twenty minutes.

"Dagny, what on earth did you tell Ulla?" Elof asked her as he appraised me, all sweaty and out of breath. Then, as he pushed out a stool toward me, he asked me, "Did she threaten you with bodily harm?"

"No, no." I waved him off and collapsed back on the stool. "She just said you had something to tell me."

"Take a moment to collect yourself and we'll get to it," he said, and again looked to Dagny. "Can you get her water?"

She sighed but did as he asked. Since she was working, she had on her luxe lab coat. It was a kaftan-style coat made of white linen embroidered with a pale gold quatrefoil pattern. A moment later, she returned with a paper cup of ice-cold water from the sink, and when she handed it to me, she said, "Why didn't you take the elevator?"

I shrugged and gulped the water down. I'd felt weird taking it without Elof, like I was breaking a rule or something.

"So," I said when I'd finally caught my breath. "What do you have to tell me?"

"I had a few suspicions I wanted to check out before I talked to you about them." Elof sat next to me at the island, his arms folded on the cold marble. "I don't want to get your hopes up, so I looked into a few things behind your back."

"Behind my back?" I asked nervously.

"Yes, but it's not as illicit as it sounds," he said quickly.

"Just spit it out, Elof," Dagny groaned in frustration. "This is torture."

My heart pounded so hard, they could probably hear it. "What is going on?"

"Elof knows who your father is," Dagny blurted out.

35

revelations

Elof glared at her from across the island, his nostrils flaring slightly. "That isn't exactly true."

"What is true then?" I asked.

He took a deep breath and looked at me with soft dark eyes. "When we were summoned to the Omte palace, I took the opportunity to procure a few hairs from Crown Prince Furston Elak."

"Why would you do that?" I asked.

"For comparison familial testing, the way I did with Bekk's baby and Bryn," Elof elaborated. "Against the sample I had just taken from you." He paused. "Ulla, Furston is your half-brother."

"What?" I shook my head. "Bodil is my mother?"

"We considered that possibility," he replied carefully. "But your sample did have markers that led me to believe one of your parents is *álfar*. I cannot say for certain that an *álfar* man did not impregnate Bodil in secret. Her fiancé was gone much of the year before your birth, so she had the opportunity, I presume.

"But then, that holds even more true for her husband-to-be," he went on. "Thor went on a mission that brought him to the First City, where the *álfar* Senka visited Sarina and other Älvolk. And then, Orra Fågel, who had been sent to Áibmoráigi to help Thor, is last seen in Iskyla, leaving behind a newborn baby.

"Thor was betrothed to Bodil in a marriage arranged by his father," he explained. "Indu was in a relationship with Senka when she fell pregnant, which is why he believed himself to be your father."

Elof paused, giving me a minute to absorb everything he was telling me. "Senka's relationship involved a controlling zealot, Thor's marriage was a political alliance, and they're both in the same obscure location at the same time leading up to your birth."

"They had the means and motive to hide their love child," Dagny said.

"And with good reason, since Indu killed Orra for taking you," Elof said.

"The Omte King is my father?" I asked, my voice hardly even a whisper.

Dagny nodded. "We think so, yes."

"Okay," I said, and then I ran and threw up in the sink.

This wasn't the reaction I expected I'd have when I found out who my father was. But then again, when I'd imagined finding out who my birth parents were, I'd always pictured them telling me themselves. Sometimes I feared the worst, that they gave me up because they hated me. Other times, they'd embrace me with open arms and apologize for all the years we'd lost.

But to do either of those things, they had to be here, and they had to be alive. Thor had died eight years ago in a stupid bar fight, and according to Indu and Illaria, Senka had died some time ago.

So my parents weren't here, and they never would be. They could never tell me why they abandoned me, or if they ever even loved me.

Had Thor known that I was his daughter, or did he think that I was Indu's? Did he know that I had been left in Iskyla?

Was it his idea to abandon me or was it my mother's? Did he want to see me?

Had he told Bodil about me?

Did she know about me?

"Ulla, are you all right?" Dagny asked, and put her hand on my back. I leaned over the sink, with cold water running from the tap, and I splashed it on my face.

"Yeah, I'm okay," I said, even though I wasn't sure if it was true, and I turned off the faucet.

"This is why I prefer to do things more slowly," Elof said, his tone meant to chastise Dagny as she walked with me back to the island. "It gives everyone more time to process info."

I sat on the stool and leaned heavily on the island. "I don't know why I reacted like that." I exhaled shakily and felt a painful lump growing in my throat. "I'm okay now."

But the truth was that I had no idea how I felt. I was strangely separate from my body, like I was hovering above myself, watching all of this happen to someone else. Another girl with blond hair sat across from Elof, listening patiently and nodding along as he explained how to process shocking information.

Was this shocking, though?

When I was younger, I used to tell everyone my parents were royalty and star-crossed lovers. As I got older, I made my peace with my adolescent fantasies as just that.

Except now it turned out it was sort of true.

I thought back to the huge portrait I'd seen back in the Omte palace. Thor had presumably sat for it, wearing a crooked bronze crown and a warm smile nearly hidden in his bushy beard. In the painting, he'd been larger than life. But he had to have been a big guy in reality, with a thick neck, barrel chest, and broad shoulders.

I must've gotten my super strength from him, I realized. How had the powerful king died in a bar fight?

The bottle had been on display at the Ugly Vulture. It was oversized, made of thick semi-opaque jade glass. The jagged points of broken glass had glistened in the light. That was what had killed Thor, the broken bottle gashing open his throat.

That was how my father died.

My stomach rolled at the memory of me staring at the weapon of my father's murder with only mild curiosity.

"Dagny, perhaps it's best if you went home early," Elof suggested. "Ulla could use some rest, and you could both use some relaxation."

"Sure," Dagny said, and I didn't bother protesting. I didn't really want to be alone.

Once we got back to the apartment, I took a long shower, and I helped Dagny make some quick grilled cheese sandwiches. After we ate, I finally started feeling better, and I was happy to spend the evening sacked out on the couch with Dagny, watching movies on the laptop.

I thought about calling Pan. I wanted to talk to him, to invite him over and cuddle with him on the couch. I could sink into his arms and pretend that everything was okay.

But then I'd have to tell him about my father, which meant I'd have to talk about it, and I didn't want to do that just then. Dagny understood, and she hung out with me all night without saying much.

I went to bed early, pulling the covers tight around me.

Sometime later, I woke up to a strange rumble. My phone was dead, so I couldn't see the time, but it was dark in the apartment without the waning moon filtering through the curtains. I sat up, blinking in the darkness, and I wondered if I'd only dreamt the rumble when it happened again.

Buh-bum. Loud enough to make the roof shake. A thunderous beat, like a booming, throbbing heart.

"Dagny?" I called out, but she didn't answer. "Dagny?"

I slowly climbed down the ladder, clinging to the rungs when the *buh-bum* shook the carriage house again. I still hadn't heard a sound from Dagny's room, and I worried something was wrong, because nobody could sleep through this.

I started toward her bedroom door, but then the room began to darken. The moonlight on the floor changed from white to red, and I pulled back the semi-sheer curtain and saw blood streaming down over the window, like a waterfall.

I screamed and jumped back from it. I shouted Dagny's name and ran for the front door. The sight of all that blood made me want to throw up or pass out, and I couldn't do that, so I needed to breathe.

And to breathe, I needed to be outside.

I rushed out the front door and leaned forward over the balcony, and I saw my breath fogging up the air. It wasn't night at all, despite the moonlight I thought I'd seen a few moments before, but rather early dawn, when the sun hadn't yet begun to rise but the sky was light and pink to the east.

I straightened up and felt the icy chill biting through the thin shirt and shorts I'd been sleeping in. It was mid-August in Oregon, yet it had to be near freezing out. My breath came out in plumes and my teeth chattered.

"What the hell is going on?" I whispered into the frosty air.

A loud bleating came from the bottom of the stairs, and I nearly jumped out of my skin. I looked down to see the albino giant woolly elk standing before me. The massive white antlers stretched out over three meters, and the large cinnamon-red eyes held my gaze.

"Am I dreaming?" I asked, but I didn't expect an answer.

The albino elk chuffed and then slowly turned and walked away. Still shivering, I wrapped my arms around myself as I descended the steps and went after the animal.

An eerie fog hung over the citadel, but the sky seemed to lighten quickly as I followed the elk through the empty streets. It was completely silent, except for our footsteps crunching on the soft gravel.

The elk traveled on Wapiti Way until it came to the Forsa River, then followed it out to the arched hole in the wall that allowed the river to meet the ocean. Once the massive beast had gone through the river and ducked low to clear the wall, it was out onto the beach.

That's where Hanna and I had found Eliana after she ran away. She'd gotten freaked out during a blood draw, and Sumi had pointed us in her direction.

As I followed the elk toward the ocean, I was thinking of Eliana and how we'd found her that day, sitting in the sand with her knees hugged to her chest . . . and then there she was.

Eliana turned to look at me, her hair a shimmering aquamarine color, blowing in the wind. When she saw me, her eyes lit up, and she smiled.

"Ulla, you're finally here!" she shouted, getting to her feet. Then she yelled back over her shoulder, "Ulla's here!"

I looked past her, and I saw Jem-Kruk standing with Sumi at the edge of the ocean.

36

enchanted

Eliana ran at me and threw her arms around me, hugging me tightly. "It's so good to see you." She squeezed so hard it hurt, and she smelled overly sweet, like cotton candy.

"This is a really vivid dream," I mumbled into her hair, and my arms hung limp at my sides.

"This isn't a dream." She finally released me, and she looked up at me fully with her big eyes. "I'm really here."

"No, I'm dreaming. I saw the albino elk and—" I glanced around, but the white beast was nowhere to be seen.

Jem-Kruk and Sumi came over to us. Jem, tall and lean, his black hair loose and lush, with an easy smile on his handsome face; Sumi, her dark coiled curls braided tight to her scalp on one side only, her expression more baffled than happy. Her hand hovered near the PSG holstered on her hip.

"How did you know we were here?" Sumi asked, her eyes narrowing.

"I—I didn't," I stuttered. "I don't. I'm still sleeping." I gestured to my pajamas.

Jem tilted his head, his smile turning quizzical. "But you are awake."

The air didn't feel quite so cold anymore, I realized, although there was still a chill to the ocean breeze. I folded my arms across my chest, acutely aware that I wasn't wearing a bra.

"What's going on?" I asked. "What are you doing here?"

"It's a long story, but we rescued Eliana and came here to hide from the Älvolk," Jem said.

Eliana dashed off, running at a seagull and twirling about. She sang a children's song I had heard before.

Sing, sing the heroes
The worm is full of flowers
Hush, hush the morning light
Down falls the darkest night
And now the end is ours.

"What's going on with her?" I asked. "And why do you need to hide from the Älvolk?"

"She hasn't been well enough for the journey home, and I've begun to fear that she won't ever be if we don't get outside help," Jem said. "And since we don't trust the Älvolk—"

"I told you that we shouldn't," Sumi interrupted.

Jem scowled and pushed up the sleeves of his cranberry-colored button-up shirt. A vest hung loose on his wiry frame and beaded leather bracelets adorned his wrists.

"Does it really matter, Sumi?" he asked wearily. "We're here now."

"Yes, we are, and Eliana's singing to the damn birds like she's bappers," Sumi retorted indignantly.

"We both made the same promise to Senka that we'd watch over Eliana," Jem said, growing frustrated. His hands were on his hips as he stared her down. "We're both doing what we think is best. This isn't a competition."

"Okay, you are here," I said uncertainly, since I still wasn't sure if I was awake or not. "And you need help, and I need help. So why don't we all go into Merellä and figure it out together?"

"We can't just *walk* in," Sumi said. "The cloaking spell won't let us pass through without permission."

"Okay, then ask the Mimirin for permission. They let you in before," I said.

"Sumi thinks it would be better if we moved under the radar," Jem explained.

She gave him a harsh look. "Something strange is afoot, and you know that, Jem. The Älvolk have been plotting for decades, but it never felt like this before. They've moved way beyond rhetoric and talk."

"So what are you doing here then? If you can't get in and have nowhere to stay?" I asked.

"I was preparing our own cloaking spell so we could sneak in," Sumi said. "I think that's how Eliana was able to get in here on her own before, but I can't say for sure because she doesn't remember."

"Do you know why she came here at the beginning of the summer?" I asked.

Sumi shook her head. "We have no idea how or why she ended up here."

"But she fondly remembers the time she spent staying with you," Jem said. "Which is why we'd been hoping that we could stay with you again."

"Yeah, of course," I said, because what else could I say. "Dagny won't mind. That much. Probably."

Thinking of cool, logical Dagny eased the nausea in my stomach. She'd make sense of this and know what to do. And she'd know for sure if I was still dreaming or not.

"We should go to my apartment, then," I said.

"I need to finish my cloaking enchantment," Sumi said. "It only takes a few more moments."

She went over to a small firepit that I hadn't noticed before, made of stones just beyond the edge of the water. She crouched beside it and pulled a fire-starter out from a small satchel she wore on a belt around her waist. Within seconds, an ivory flame bloomed in the pit.

From her satchel, she procured a few leaves—small and dark, like dried bay leaves—and a few fuzzy sticks—like tiny cattails. She mumbled an incantation, then crumbled up the leaves and sticks before sprinkling them into the fire.

The flame instantly became a luminescent bright silver and grew robust before quickly going out.

Sumi straightened up and nudged the rocks to the side with her foot, so the lapping waves would soon take away the ash. "We should go now. The cloak won't last long."

"Ellie!" Jem called out, and waved for Eliana to join us.

She was standing out in the ocean, the cool water splashing up to her knees. She wore a long, slightly oversized maxi dress made of white cotton with pastel flowers, and the long hem was mostly bundled up in her arms in a vain attempt to keep it dry.

When Jem summoned her, she seemingly forgot that attempt and immediately dropped her dress, soaking the length of it as she sprinted up to the shore.

"Will Hanna be there?" Eliana asked breathlessly when she reached us.

"No, she's not, but there're ways you can talk to her," I promised her.

We went into the citadel the same way I'd followed the albino elk out. We passed through the wall alongside the Forsa River, and Jem, Sumi, and Eliana had no problem with it. Eliana said she felt some tingles, but they didn't faze her.

It was very early in the morning, but the vendors were starting to set up the stalls on the main roads, so we took the back roads and alleys to my apartment. I wasn't sure if I needed to keep Eliana out of sight, but I figured it would be better if we did. Plus, I felt self-conscious walking through Merellä in my pajamas.

As soon as we got to my place, I woke Dagny up, and she answered her bedroom door looking irritated and tired, but that changed the moment Eliana threw herself at Dagny.

"I'm back and I missed you," Eliana squealed.

Dagny hugged her tentatively and looked over at me. "Ulla, what's going on here?"

37

fanatical

Dagny, Jem, Sumi, and I sat around the bistro table, sipping lemon tea. Eliana had gotten bored during the conversation, and she'd gone to take a bubble bath and wash off the sea-water.

Dagny listened intently and asked a lot of questions, as I'd known she would. The whole situation had left me rather dazed, and my brain felt sluggish and slow.

Jem had just finished explaining how he was a member of the Alfheim royal family, but eleventh in line for the throne, so he didn't have the pressures of his title but had the freedoms to travel and do as he wished for the most part. Sumi was his vizier, which was something like an advisor and a bodyguard, but she described it more as being a professional best friend.

"And we're both old family friends of Eliana," Sumi said.

"What exactly is wrong with Eliana?" Dagny asked.

"We don't know," Sumi admitted. "She's been erratic and depressed since her mother passed, but ever since she went across the bridge, her memory has been jumbled and inconsistent. She couldn't even remember any of us, which is why we had to take her against her will."

"You shot us with a psionic stun gun and kidnapped her," Dagny said dryly. PSGs were entirely nonlethal weapons, but could completely incapacitate, and they hurt like hell. "I remember that well. Where did you go after that?"

"To Áibmoráigi with Illaria, but we didn't stay long," Jem-Kruk said.

Sumi pressed her lips together grimly. "I haven't been welcome in Áibmoráigi since I left the Älvolk."

"Illaria convinced me that she was going to help Ellie, and I trusted her because they're sisters. I've known them both since they were born." Jem-Kruk stared down at the table, his dark lashes resting on his sharp cheekbones. "When they finally let us in to see her—"

"They *didn't* let us in," Sumi corrected him bitterly. "We had to fight our way in, and you had to threaten all kinds of violence."

"They think I'm more powerful than I truly am," Jem-Kruk confided sheepishly.

"Only because the Älvolk have fetishized every aspect of our world." Sumi rolled her eyes. "That's what all of this is about. I don't know what they were doing to Eliana, but I'm certain that whatever it was, they did it because they thought it would get them into Alfheim."

"When we finally got to see Eliana, the Älvolk were holding her in a dungeon." Jem grimaced. "Illaria claimed it was for her own safety, but Ellie was sickly and pale and hardly remembered anything."

"Her memory has been coming back over the past month," Sumi elaborated. "She still doesn't remember much from before she got sick in the first place, so she's foggy on us and her mother. But she has been able to remember the in-between, like Hanna and you."

"Which is why we're here," Jem said. "She's not getting better, and we don't know what to do for her."

"You said that the Älvolk fetishize your home. What did you mean by that?" Dagny asked Sumi.

"Growing up around them, they constantly spoke of the other kingdom, just across the bridge, and how it was our birthright that the *álfar* kept us from," Sumi said derisively.

"A long, long time ago, a powerful enchantment was put on the bridge between the kingdoms," Jem explained. "Only those with *álfar* blood can cross it."

"My mother was *álfar*," Sumi said, sounding proud for a moment. "The Älvolk men are trained in the art of *helifiske*. Meaning they're taught to charm and woo women into becoming carriers of their daughters. My father knew enough to lure my mother until she was trapped with him, much like Indu did with Senka."

My stomach rolled at the sound of her name. *Senka*. My mother. I wanted to tell them that she was my mother. But Sumi was talking, and it wasn't the time, so I sipped my tea to keep anything from spilling out.

"—rulers don't have any *álfar* blood themselves," Sumi was saying. "Perhaps they once did, but they need much more than a drop. So they were looking for other ways to break the enchantment. Thus far, they have not been successful."

"How do you know?" Dagny asked. "They could be crossing it as we speak."

Jem-Kruk smiled, crooked and uneasy. "If the bridge was open, what is on Alfheim would be here, and everyone would know."

"The Älvolk think that across the bridge will be their

rightful Valhalla." Sumi shook her head. "I followed Senka across, and what lies there is far more hell than heaven."

Jem bristled. "It has its own beauty to it."

"And its own monsters," she said, meeting his gaze evenly.

"Should we be worried?" Dagny asked.

"If the Älvolk ever break the enchantment, then yes," Sumi said. "But it's held for nearly a thousand years. Even with their fanaticism, I don't see why they could do it now."

"What can we do to prevent them from undoing the enchantment?" Dag asked.

"We don't even know what is required to break it, so it's difficult to say what one shouldn't do," Jem said with a dismal shrug.

"They're collecting blood," I said. Everyone looked at me with a start because it had been so long since I'd spoken. "They took so much of my blood, and they've got all these flowers that bleed."

"I bet they took Eliana's blood," Dagny said. "That's probably why she freaked out so much when Elof tried to draw her blood back in June. If they held her and drained her the way they did Ulla."

"And I could probably handle it better, because I'm Omte," I realized.

In the bathroom, Eliana was loudly singing the song of heroes and worms of flowers.

Dagny looked at the door with pity in her eyes. "They stole her blood."

"And they still can't get across the bridge," Sumi said with a heavy sigh.

"So where do we go from here?" Dagny asked.

And then they launched into the logistics of it all. Where they could stay—to keep it under the radar, they'd have to make do with extra blankets and pillows in the living room;

what they would do about Eliana—Dagny would arrange to sneak her in to see Elof tomorrow; what everyone else would be up to while Dagny and Sumi would be helping Elof and Eliana—Dagny assigned me and Jem to go to the archives to convince Calder to help us find anything we could about the Lost Bridge of Dimma and how to cross it.

After Eliana came out of the bathroom, she complained of being hungry, and Sumi admitted they'd had trouble finding food on the road, which was a problem I understood all too well.

Dagny and Sumi headed down to the market to get more food, since we didn't have nearly enough for five mouths, while I stayed back to help Eliana and Jem settle in.

I felt strangely on edge with just the two of them, an electric current of anxiety threaded through me, so I couldn't sit still. I set up the laptop so Eliana could watch her shows while curled up on the couch, but I moved around, mindlessly dusting things that didn't really need dusting.

Before she'd gone, I'd pulled Dagny aside and in a hushed voice, made her reassure me that this wasn't still a dream.

But this still felt so unreal and bizarre. Eliana was back, and Jem-Kruk was in my apartment, watching me with a bemused expression as I paced the room. My stomach flipped the same way it had every other time I had seen him—a mixture of butterflies and a hint of trepidation. But I had never felt both quite so intensely before.

It had been weeks since I saw him last, with the Lost Month in the middle, and now he was here, in *my* home, telling me that a cult had stolen my blood to open a bridge to a dangerous, mysterious kingdom.

38

BAHSUTT

I'd climbed up to my bedroom loft to gather up all the blankets and pillows I could spare, and I didn't realize that Jem had followed me until I heard his voice behind me.

"It's cozy up here," he mused, and I looked back to see him perched at the top of the ladder at the edge of my loft.

I knelt on my bed, my heart racing in my chest, and I realized this was the first boy I'd had in this bedroom. Although the term "room" was being generous. It was an open loft above the bathroom.

Wood railings surrounded it to keep me from falling eight feet in the middle of the night, and the slant of the roof meant that I didn't have a ton of headroom. The floor space wasn't that much bigger than the mattress, with a nightstand and outlet squeezed in by the head of the bed, and I had some storage in the shortest part of the room, past the foot of the bed.

To brighten the small space up, I'd strung fairy lights around the loft, and I'd tacked up pictures of my friends and the kids in Förening on the wall by my nightstand. It *was* cozy, actually.

And there was Jem, his dark eyes taking it all in. The warm

glow of the fairy lights played wonderfully on his tawny skin, highlighting his sharp cheekbones and the playful smattering of freckles across his face. His black waves of hair hung mostly free, except where a few small, well-placed braids kept the rest of his hair out of his face.

He was so handsome, he seemed unreal, and his smile cut through me like a knife through melted butter.

"Is it okay that I'm up here?" Jem asked. He must've noticed something off in my expression.

"Yeah, yeah." I nodded weakly. I had just thought that Pan would be the first guy I had in my bedroom, but I didn't say that.

Jem-Kruk came farther up, and he slid back on my bed so he was sitting beside me.

"I know I don't know you that well, Ulla," he began cautiously. "But you seem especially shaken up since we arrived. Is there anything I can do to put you at ease?"

"No, I . . ." I trailed off. I looked over the railing to make sure that Eliana was fully engrossed in her shows, but I still lowered my voice when I said, "I think Senka was my mother."

His eyes widened, and in an awed whisper, he said, "You're the dead baby."

"Wh-Wh-What?" I gasped. "What are you talking about?"

"Senka fell in love and left our kingdom," he explained. "I visited her once, and she was pregnant. Sometime later, when she came back, she said the baby had died. She never talked much of her time in Áibmoráigi, only saying that it was too painful."

"She thought I was dead?" I asked around the lump in my throat.

"That is the only way she would've left you behind," Jem said. "She was a devoted mother, and she was never quite the same after she lost the baby. Lost *you*." He gave me a sad smile.

"She sounded daring and bold in the book," I remembered.

"She could be quite daring and bold, but what book are you talking about?" he asked with a puzzled expression.

I took the *Jem-Kruk and the Adlrivellir* book from off my night table and handed it to him. "This book is about you and Senka and Jo-Huk."

He stared down at it in confusion and ran his fingers over the cover, tracing the triskelion triangle with its swirling vines on the inside—the Älvolk symbol. "What does it say about us?"

"It just talks about the adventures you had when you were younger," I said as he flipped through the pages. "The man who wrote it, his wife was friends with Senka."

"Senka must've told her all our stories." He blinked back tears as he looked down at the book wistfully. "I hope she portrayed me in a favorable light."

"You came off looking good," I said with a smile. "What was she like?"

"Senka was . . ." He exhaled and stared off. "Brave and bossy, but only because she cared so much. She would be as fierce as a *kuguar*, but she was warm and funny. We have a word where I come from, *bahsutt*. It means to be aggressive without anger. She was kind and generous, but never angry, and always bold and motivated.

"Illaria was more like her than Ellie, but Senka never had the bitter streak that Illaria does," he said.

"What happened with Illaria?" I asked.

"I don't truly know. The time she spent with the Älvolk when she was young shaped her heart and mind more than I had ever imagined. Indu and his rhetoric burrowed deep inside her and slowly ate away her brain." He scowled. "That's the only way I can explain how she could betray her sister—and her mother's memory—the way she has."

"How did Senka die?" I asked.

"She was bitten by an *etanadrak* in the spring. The venom didn't kill her but she never fully recovered. When she later fell ill with a bloody cough, it was too much for her."

Another weight around my heart tightened, like a noose squeezing so tightly that every heartbeat ached. I had known she was dead, but hearing Jem say it—right after finding out my father was also dead—it was hard for me not to cry.

"Hey, hey, are you okay?" Jem sounded alarmed as tears spilled over my cheeks.

"Yeah." I wiped at my face and sighed. "Life has just been . . . *a lot* lately."

Jem moved closer to me and put his arm around me, loose but comforting. "I know precisely what you mean."

I shook my head. "I feel so silly. All this time, I thought I would feel better just knowing the truth about my parents. And now I found out the truth, and I'm blubbering."

"You haven't exactly been getting good news," Jem said reasonably.

"That is very true," I agreed with a weary laugh. "But I'm glad that Eliana is safe here, and I'm safe." I looked over at Jem, so close to me, with his dark eyes on me. "And you."

"And Sumi," he added because I didn't.

Heat flushed my cheeks and I looked away from him. "Right, yes." I swallowed hard. "I am grateful everyone is safe and sound."

"I know," he said with a playful squeeze of my shoulder, and my stomach flipped.

"I have . . ." I trailed off because I didn't know how to finish it. Or if I needed to say anything at all, or if I would just make myself seem even more ridiculous than I already had.

I wanted to tell Jem about Pan. That we were . . . something.

And maybe I was misreading the situation. Jem was trying to make me feel better, and my tears had stopped. But I still felt like crying, and I did also kind of want to kiss Jem, even though I mostly just wished that Pan were here instead, and I wanted to throw up.

I was all over the place, and I swear at that moment, I felt every single thing all at once.

"You have what?" Jem asked, because I'd never finished my sentence.

"I have no idea what I'm doing anymore or how to feel about anything," I said finally.

Jem moved, taking his arm from my shoulder, so he could face me more fully. His knee pressed against mine, and he took my hands in his. "You're going through something, and no doubt the journey is treacherous at times. But you must remember that you are not alone, and you still get to decide where this journey ends."

"But what if I don't know where I want it to end?" I asked.

He smiled. "You'll find the way as you go."

A knock at the front door interrupted the moment, and Eliana bounced up from the couch and announced, "I'll get it!"

I let go of Jem's hand and moved toward the railing. "Eliana, I don't know if that's a good idea."

"But maybe it's Elof or Hanna," Eliana argued cheerily, and she never slowed as she threw open the front door.

"Holy shit, you're back," Pan said. I couldn't see him yet, but he sounded shocked.

Eliana made a delighted noise before grabbing him and pulling him into a hug. As she embraced him, he looked over her shoulder, and when he spied me, sitting up in my bedroom with Jem, his expression faltered.

"What's going on, Ulla?" he asked.

39

*

risks

Pan leaned back against the counter, his hands beside him, his palms resting on the butcher-block with his fingers drumming along the edge. All the while that I'd been telling him about how Jem, Sumi, and Eliana came to be here—with Jem expounding occasionally and Eliana interjecting whenever she felt like it—Pan's expression had only contracted: his eyebrows pinching and his full lips pressing into an anxious frown.

He'd come over to check on me and invite me to brunch, since we hadn't seen each other since we'd gotten back to Merellä. Instead he was getting everything dumped on him, so I understood his growing unease.

Jem and I stood across from him in the small kitchen. Eliana was in the living room, practicing an exercise dance that Sumi had taught her.

"Sumi is an Älvolk, right?" Pan asked when we'd gotten to the end, and he looked to Jem for confirmation, who nodded. "Does she know why they stole so much of Ulla's blood?"

"We don't know exactly what they're doing with it, but

we think that her unique parentage makes her tolerate it well, so they took as much as they could," Jem said.

"Unique parentage?" Pan echoed, and looked at me in surprise. "You *know* who your parents are?"

"Yeah, it all just came together," I said sheepishly. "Thor Elak and Senka."

"*Thor?*" His eyes widened. "The Omte King?"

I nodded. "Elof did a familial match with Furston."

"Wait," Eliana said, and stopped her dance exercise. "Did you say Senka is your mother? But isn't she my mother?"

I took a deep breath and faced her. This wasn't how I wanted to tell her, but I guessed this was how it was happening. "I think we're half-sisters."

She put her hands to her face and let out an earsplitting scream. Her skin started changing—her usual deep tan became a rapidly shifting kaleidoscope of colors, and her long hair rippled bright green.

"This is the best news!" She ran over to me and literally leapt so I had to catch her. When I put her back down, her skin and hair returned to normal, and she smiled up at me with tears in her eyes. "I was looking for you, wasn't I?"

"I don't know," I admitted.

"You must've been why I came here," Eliana insisted definitively. "I had to find my sister."

"Maybe, Ellie," Jem allowed. "But we don't know anything for certain."

"No, I know it in my heart of hearts," she persisted. And then she twirled around and went back to doing her dancercise.

"I don't mean to change the subject, but I find it hard to believe that Sumi grew up with the Älvolk, yet she has no idea what they did to Ulla or Eliana," Pan said, a harsh skepticism hardening his words.

"Sumi hasn't lived with them in quite some time, and their motivations never made sense to either of us," Jem said.

"She thinks they're trying to open the bridge to Alfheim," I said.

"And that's a bad idea because Alfheim is dangerous?" Pan asked, still sounding dubious.

"Forgive me. I overstated myself," Jem replied with a sharp smile. "I can only truly say that nothing I have seen in your kingdoms would withstand a single attack from a wyrm."

Pan looked away then, chewing the inside of his cheek as he stared down at the floor. "The Älvolk stole Ulla's blood to let monsters from your land into ours, and we don't know how to stop it."

"We would know a lot more about what's going on if I could just remember the Lost Month," I said.

"Yeah, it'd be nice if any of us could remember," Pan muttered.

"But maybe I can," I said.

Pan narrowed his eyes. "What do you mean?"

"Elof tried something with the Ögonen and Dagny," I said.

"The thing where Dagny nearly died?" Pan asked incredulously. "No way. That's way too dangerous."

"She didn't *nearly* die," I argued—though, truthfully, he probably knew better how it had gone, since he was there and I wasn't.

But the way Dagny had explained it to me, it didn't sound *that* bad. Elof had brought an Ögonen into his lab, and they did something like what Sunniva and Tove had done with me back in Förening. Dagny lay down, the Ögonen put their hands on her head, and in their attempt to restore her memories, she'd overheated—dramatically enough that she had singed off her eyebrow and required healing for internal injuries.

"You don't know that," Pan replied.

"I know that she's fine now," I persisted. "And I'm stronger than her."

His jaw set, and he inhaled deeply through his nose. Then, almost quietly, he said, "I don't want you getting hurt."

"Neither do I." I gave him a weak smile, but that did nothing to assuage the worry darkening his eyes. "I survived the Lost Month. I think I can survive remembering it."

"The Älvolk magic is very old and very powerful. It's not something to combat lightly," Jem advised.

"I won't," I assured him before Pan could latch on to his comment. "And Elof would not let me do anything like that."

"So that's what you're doing today?" Pan asked. "Contacting Elof?"

"Yes," I said, as if that had been my plan all along and not something that had just occurred to me when Pan suggested it. "That, and helping everyone get settled." I motioned around.

Jem took that as a cue and went into the living area to join Eliana in her dance.

"So brunch is off the table," Pan said.

I walked over and leaned back against the counter beside him. "Dagny and Sumi went to get food and supplies. I'm sure there'll be enough for one more."

"Thanks." He hesitated, holding my gaze heavily, and I once again marveled at the beauty in the depth of his warm, dark eyes. "But I think you've already got your hands full here."

I tentatively put my hand on his. "There's always room for you."

"Ulla, can I talk to Hanna again?" Eliana asked loudly.

They'd already chatted for an hour that morning, and so

I wasn't depriving her when I told her, "Not right now. Can we talk about it in a little bit?"

"Fine," she said, but her expression turned poutier than normal. She always looked kinda pouty because her bottom lip was slightly larger than the top, but now she was especially sour.

"Actually, I should head out, so you can talk about it now," Pan said, and stepped away from the counter.

"Pan, you don't have to go," I said.

"I know," he assured me. "I thought I'd hit up Calder and see if I can find any books that might help us figure out what the Älvolk are up to." He looked back at me. "You can see me out, though, if you want."

Once we were out on the landing and the front door was closed behind us, I asked, "Is everything okay?"

He nodded. "Yeah, yeah. I think I'm still in shock seeing Eliana and everything." Then his expression shifted. "And you! You found out who your parents are. How are you really doing with all of that?"

"Truthfully, I don't know." I shook my head. "That's why I didn't tell you about Thor being my . . . my dad. I just didn't want to talk about it with anybody."

"Hey, no, you don't owe me an explanation," he said. "You don't have to tell me anything until you're ready."

I squeezed his hand. "Thanks for understanding."

"And . . ." He paused and glanced back toward the door. ". . . and I don't need to worry about you and Jem, do I?"

"No," I said emphatically, hoping the shameful heat in my cheeks didn't show. "It's not like that at all."

"I'm sorry, I shouldn't have asked." He shook his head. "I'm feeling a little insecure, and that's not your problem. Especially not right now. Sorry."

"It's fine."

"I don't know if it is, but anyway." He forced a smile at me. "I should get going. But I'll talk to you later, all right?"

"Yeah. Of course."

He leaned over and kissed my forehead, and then he jogged down the stairs.

40

Ögonen

The next day, I headed down to Elof's lab. It was the soonest he could see me, since he was busy trying to figure out something to help Eliana. Pan came with me, albeit grudgingly, because he still wasn't convinced this was safe for me to do.

I was tired and walked slowly, so I didn't mind his pace anyway. Yesterday had been a long, exhausting day, and I hadn't gotten much sleep. Eliana had bunked up in my bed with me, where there was hardly enough room for us both. Not to mention she was a tiny furnace, and when I finally did fall asleep, I woke up drenched in sweat.

Plus, she'd wanted to stay up all night, bonding over sisterly things. The hardest part about that was that she couldn't tell me much about herself, so she was mostly asking me questions.

And I just . . . didn't feel like bonding.

It was bizarre, because I'd spent so much of my life *longing* for family, and now I'd discovered some of my only living family members, and that I was related to someone that I already knew and cared about . . . and I felt stunningly blank about it.

Maybe because I'd already gone through the roller coaster of thinking that I had many sisters—including my good friend Bryn and my nemesis Noomi—to finding out that I didn't.

Then I found that my real siblings were the amnesiac Eliana, her evil twin Illaria, and the unusual, wild Prince Furston.

And I was still digesting my parentage confirmation.

Something about all that left me feeling sorta numb and disconnected from Eliana. But I hoped once I had absorbed this all and gotten all the Älvolk/Lost Month mess behind me, I'd be able to really embrace Eliana as my sister.

That's why it was so important that I remembered what happened during the Lost Month. So I could deal with it and move on with my life. Until I understood fully what Indu had used me for, it would all feel like unfinished business to me.

Well, that and Jem and Sumi seemed to think it would be mighty bad for everyone if the Älvolk got the bridge open.

The Mimirin was quiet because it was Sunday, and Elof was alone in the lab when we got there. He'd forgone his usual kaftan-style lab coat, and he just wore a burgundy dress shirt with the sleeves rolled up and the top buttons of his collar undone.

"Are you ready for all this, Ulla?" he asked, and his tight smile did little to ease the anxiety bubbling in my stomach.

"Yeah, of course!" I forced myself to sound confident and upbeat because Pan was looking at me, and he already had serious safety concerns about this. I knew his fears weren't exactly unwarranted, but I thought (hoped) I was strong enough to handle them.

"Wait, what is that?" Pan asked. We'd been walking toward where Elof sat at the island, but Pan stopped short.

He pointed to a big metal tub sitting nearby, filled with slowly melting ice cubes.

I winced because I distinctly remembered Tove Kroner dumping me in a cold shower in the Trylle palace bathroom. His sister had been helping to recover memories when I over-heated.

"It's only a precaution," Elof said. "Because of how things went with Dagny."

"Are you sure this is safe?" Pan asked.

"No," he admitted with a rough exhale. "But I've made it as safe as I can." He'd been holding on to a small jar of sky-blue liquid, and he slid it across the island toward me. "This is an elixir to help prevent inflammation and keep your body temperature down. You should drink it before the Ögonen arrives, so it has time to take effect."

"Inflammation?" Pan sounded alarmed, and I grabbed the jar and gulped down the bitter, milky liquid before he could talk me out of it.

"Dagny had some mild brain swelling, and I hope to avoid that this time around," Elof said, keeping his tone as matter-of-fact as possible.

Pan opened his mouth like he was about to protest, but the door at the back of the lab opened, and a slender Ögonen ducked as they came in. I'd seen them plenty of times by now, but I never got used to their appearance.

They were trollian but only in a vague, androgynous way. They were totally nude always, but they were hairless and without any obvious outward genitalia or sex characteristics. Their skin was the color of burnt ochre, but it was thin enough to let some light pass through, highlighting their veins and organs. Though I could see it wasn't true, they moved like they were made of jelly, oddly graceful and fluid.

I hadn't been this close to an Ögonen since I had the run-in with the guardian of the catacombs back at the beginning of summer, and that had been a rather traumatic experience. I gulped down my fear and smiled up at the mouthless face towering above me.

Creepy, creepy mouthless face with troll eyes, I thought, before remembering that the Ögonen can read minds. Or something like that. I tried to think of nothing, but my mind immediately went back to the brief and unfairly chaste make-out session I'd had with Pan the previous night on the landing outside my apartment.

He'd come back over for supper, after an unsuccessful trip with Calder down in the archives. It had been a fun, chaotic dinner, and the only moment alone we could get was at the end before he'd left.

I thought we'd only do a quick goodbye, but he pulled me into his arms and kissed me passionately. I wrapped my arms around his neck, and he pushed me backward, until my back was against the wall. Then I buried my fingers in his dark curls, and—

"This is Ur." Elof interrupted my thoughts, and my cheeks flushed with embarrassed heat as he motioned to the Ögonen, who merely blinked down at me.

"Hello," I said uncertainly, but I didn't notice a reply from Ur the Ögonen.

"Ur doesn't communicate much," Elof said, somewhat apologetically. "Earlier, I arranged this all with Amalie and Ur, so they know what to do."

With their long slender finger, they pointed to the island beside us.

"I think they want us to get on with it then," Elof said. "So I'll have you lie back on the island."

"You want me to just climb up and lie down on the counter-top?" I asked.

"It'll be a bit cold, but I think that will work to your benefit," he said.

I hopped up onto the island. Pan took my hand to steady me, even though I didn't need it, but it made me feel better anyway. I scooted back on the counter and lay back.

Ur walked around until they stood right behind my head, and then they knelt on the floor. They brought their hands up to either side of my face, and I felt their fingertips—like ten cold pools of water pressing against my skin. The thumbs on my temples, the rest staggered down my cheeks.

"Ur needs you to try to remember something from—" Elof was saying.

But I was already there. And it wasn't like I was remembering. I was there. Back in the Lost Month.

41

Ablaze

I was cold and wet, my hair dripping in my face. A thick, stiff robe of elk fur was wrapped around me, but aside from that I was naked. I was in an octagon made of stone, with wooden benches around the edge. In the center, a bin of burning coals slowly warmed the room.

I was alone, but I could hear water running nearby. Somehow, I knew this was our weekly bath, when Noomi and our captors let us use the bathtubs and the sauna, assuming we behaved in the days between.

And I'd behaved, but I was here alone.

Until the door opened, and Pan came in. His dark curls were wet, and his robe was snug across his broad shoulders.

"Ulla," he gasped when he saw me, and he rushed over. When he held me and we kissed, I knew from the way my skin trembled that it had been so long since we last touched.

"How are you here?" I whispered, and I held his face in my hands.

"I don't know. They left me alone to bathe, and when I finished, I came in here," he said breathily. "Maybe they

forgot about me." He put his hands over mine, but his thumbs brushed the raw skin of my wrists, and I winced.

"Sorry," I said as I pulled my hands away. "The cuffs they use burn my skin."

"My god, Ulla." He sounded horrified as he gingerly took my hand to get a look at the red, swollen skin. "What are they doing to you?"

"I've been translating old documents from ancient Tryllic, but it doesn't make any sense. It's like a recipe for blood pudding but written in the style of a limerick. I've been stuck on several words that I can only translate into literal gibberish, but they've been bringing me these documents in Old Norse and Irytakki for reference."

"They're torturing you just to get you to work in the archives again?" Pan asked.

"Yeah, it seems that way," I said with a thin smile.

His eyes were pained and his voice was husky. "I'm sorry." He put his hand on my face, caressing my cheek gently with his thumb. "I wish I knew how to save you."

"I wish I knew how to save us all," I replied softly.

He bent down and kissed me, gently at first. His lips were soft, pressing against mine, until I pushed on my tiptoes, leaned deeper into his kiss. His arms went around my waist, holding me tightly against him. I buried my fingers in his thick curls, letting them wind around my fingers.

Heat rolled over me, and it wasn't from the steam coming from the heater bumping up against me. And then I slid my hands down and under the robe. It wasn't so much a sexual thing—and I didn't want to have sex with Pan in the sauna of the dungeon we were held captive in—but I suddenly needed skin-to-skin contact. It had gone far beyond craving, and it was an impatient need to feel his flesh warm against mine. To feel something soft and safe and warm in a place so cold and unforgiving.

"What are you doing?" he asked thickly.

"I just need to feel you, nothing more." I paused—his robe half open with my hands on his chest. "Please."

In response, he kissed me again, and his hand moved down, untying my robe so it fell open. His hand found my hips, pulling me toward him, and then there was this wonderful relief of warmth enveloping me.

We were kissing again, hungrily, greedily. Then Pan's mouth trailed along my jawbone, down to my neck, and in a low voice, he murmured, "I love you, Ulla."

"I love you too, Pan," I said without hesitation, because I knew it was true, the same way I knew my heart was pounding in my chest.

He kissed me again, on the top of my head, and hugged me to him. I looked over his shoulder, and on the wall behind me, I spotted a big spider crawling along it.

"Pan."

"I know, but . . ." Pan said, his voice nearly lost in my hair as he held me. "I've wanted to say it for so long. I'm so glad I finally did."

"No, Pan, I'm saying there's a huge spider." I detangled myself from him enough that I could point at the fat black spider with a jagged green stripe, but he didn't turn back to look.

"I know," he said gravely. "Me and Elof have been doing everything we can."

"Wait. What?" I stepped back from him and refastened my robe tightly. "You know about the spiders?"

And by now it was spiders. I spotted another even larger one creeping along the ceiling, and a few smaller ones crept out from under the benches.

"Well, what does Indu want?" Pan asked.

I looked sharply at him. "What? Are you saying Indu wants the spiders?"

There was hardly any steam in the room anymore, but the heat kept rising. I could already feel the beads of sweat forming on my back.

"What have you translated so far?" Pan asked.

"Nothing about infestations, so I don't think it really matters right now." I was nearly shouting by now, because I could see more spiders sliding through the cracks between the bricks in the wall. I grabbed Pan's hand. "We have to go!"

He frowned. "Blood pudding? Is that what they're using your blood for?"

"Pan, I don't know what's going on with you, but we've got to—"

"Yeah, I'd say that is cannibalism," he interrupted me.

He was looking straight at me, but it was like he couldn't see me. I let go of his hand and waved in front of his face, but he only stared blankly forward.

"Pan?" I said plaintively as the room rapidly became a furnace. The once-cold stone floor tiles scorched the bottoms of my feet.

"An elk heart?" Pan asked, and he was backing up, toward the bench overflowing with arachnids.

"Pan!" I shrieked, but he just sat back on the bench. His expression never changed, not even as dozens of spiders crawled over him.

"Sorry, a white elk heart," he said, as a spider languidly crawled across his eyeball. "Is the heart white or is it the heart of a white elk?"

It was so hot, the spiders started to burst into flames. The tinier arthropods on the floor were popping like popcorn all around me, and all I could do was scream.

42

manipulations

I was screaming into the ice water, then I surfaced, gasping for air, and Pan was kneeling beside the metal tub.

"Are you okay?" he asked.

"Let her breathe, Pan," Elof said, and I saw him standing just behind Pan.

"Did I get too hot?" I asked.

Pan nodded. "Heat was radiating off your body, and then you started to scream, so I dumped you in the ice bath."

"Do you remember anything?" Elof asked me.

"I think. Sorta." I looked over to the Ögonen, staring placidly at me. "They implanted something."

"What do you mean?" Pan asked.

"Spiders. They filled a room in the dungeon with spiders and then the spiders burst into flames." My teeth started to chatter, so Pan took my hand and helped me out of the tub.

"How do you know that didn't really happen?" Elof asked. "That it wasn't some kind of bizarre torture by the Älvolk?"

Pan handed me a towel and I wrapped it around my shoulders.

I shook my head adamantly. "No. The Ögonen used

spiders to scare me before." I glanced over at Pan, thinking of the moment he'd confessed he loved me—a moment he no longer remembered. "And Pan was there, and he started acting strange when the spiders showed up."

I dried my face with the towel, and I looked up to Ur the Ögonen. "Why did you do that? Why did you infiltrate my memories?"

Ur blinked at me, then looked to Elof.

"What are they saying?" I asked Elof.

"Nothing to me." Elof shook his head. "Ur, we thank you for your help, but if you wish not to converse with us in whatever way you can, perhaps it's best if you go."

Ur blinked and then walked out of the lab. Though they were gone, that didn't mean they couldn't still read my thoughts from far away. I shivered again, thinking of the spiders covering Pan's face.

"What did you remember?" Pan asked.

"We were left alone, by accident, I think," I said, and I'd already decided that I was going to skip over all the kissing bits—at least until Elof wasn't around. "Just me and Pan. And you asked me what Indu was doing with me, and I told you about the documents I translated for him. Some kind of gross blood pudding recipe with an elk heart as an ingredient. You called the Älvolk cannibals."

"Shit," Pan said. "Do you remember anything else?"

"That's when it was overrun with spiders and fire." I chewed my lip. "I have to remember what I translated for Indu."

"You can't do that again with the Ögonen," Pan said. "You weren't under that long before you got way too hot. It's not safe."

"I'll never do that with an Ögonen again," I said definitively. "I can't trust what they show me."

"Maybe you can't completely trust anything you see when someone else is digging around in your head," Pan said. He leaned against the island; his button-up was wet on the rolled-up sleeves and chest, so the fabric stuck to his muscles.

"I can trust Sunniva Kroner," I said.

"That's the younger woman who does the aural healing back in Förening?" Elof asked.

I nodded. "She's been working on her healing since I've been gone. I'm sure she's made progress by now."

"That's a bit of a leap, don't you think?" Pan asked, not unkindly.

"Fine. I'll call Finn before I go back and get the scoop."

"Whoa, what?" He straightened up. "You say that like going back to Förening is a sure thing."

"I have to get these memories back," I insisted. "There's something in those translations, and I have no clue what it is. But since they let us go, I must've figured it out, which means that the Älvolk know what it is. They stole blood from me and my sister for it. We need to know the truth."

"I'm not arguing with that," Pan said. "I just don't think it's worth you dying to find out. Are you sure that you can trust Sunniva Kroner? Not to muck around in your brain *and* not to go further than your body can handle?"

"Her brother is one of Finn's oldest and most trusted friends, and Finn is the most honorable man I know," I said. "Tove is doing this with Sunniva."

He was silent, considering it. "They wouldn't let you do it if it wasn't safe?"

"No, Finn definitely would not," I said, and he let out a relieved sigh, his fears temporarily placated.

"When did the spiders appear in your memory?" Elof asked.

He pulled up a stool and had a seat. I was still standing, alternating between my feet, because I didn't want to sit. I felt too antsy, and my skin had a sunburnt feel to it, so any touch burned a little.

"It was right before Pan started asking me about the translations," I said.

"What had you been doing before he asked you about that?" Elof pressed.

My cheeks burned, and I mumbled, "Like . . . kissing."

"Ah, understood," Elof said.

Pan cleared his throat. "What did the spiders do?"

"Crawled around." I shrugged. "They swarmed the room."

"Maybe they were meant to highlight something?" Elof asked.

"But . . . they ruined the memory." I frowned. "I was panicked and I didn't understand at all what memory-Pan was saying, because I couldn't recall what my half of the conversation had been." I shook my head. "I need to get to Sunniva and get the rest of my memory back."

"Well, before you head out, let me do a quick checkup to make sure that there wasn't any serious damage done," Elof said.

He checked a few things—my heart rate, blood pressure, pupils, reflexes—and then he cleared me to go. Pan walked me home, and he stayed long enough to be interrogated by Dagny while I had my phone call with Finn.

The verdict from Finn was that Tove and Sunniva had made significant progress, and he thought it might be time for me to come back to Förening.

"So it's settled then, isn't it?" Pan asked, once I finished summarizing the phone call. "You're going to Minnesota."

I nodded. "It's where I need to be."

"It's where I need to be too!" Eliana piped up, and she threw one arm around my shoulders. "With Hanna and my sister."

43

❧

worldly

Pan slid open the barn-style door on his friend Hugo Rohm's garage. Hugo worked with him as a peurojen, and he fixed cars on the side. Over the summer, he'd been very slowly working on the Jeep that Finn had lent me to drive to Merellä from Förening. It was from the Trylle kingdom's fleet, and Eliana had crashed through the fabric top when I first arrived at the citadel.

Hugo had stopped working on it while we'd been busy, because he wasn't sure what to do with it, and that had slowed his progress. But he'd gotten it all fixed up in time for me to drive back to Förening.

The bright mojito green Jeep Wrangler was dusty, but otherwise it looked good as new. The canvas canopy was shiny and intact, and the scratches in the paint were gone.

"This looks really great," I said as Pan and I inspected the Jeep. "Thanks again. How much do I owe you?"

"Two hundred and fifty dollars." Hugo stood beside us, half leaning on the vehicle. Grease stained his white shirt, his dark brown hair tangled curls that landed just above his jaw.

I hid my wince as I pulled the cash out of my bag. It really wasn't a bad price, but that was 250 fewer dollars that I had to fund my two-day road trip to Minnesota. I wasn't flat broke yet, but my savings were very, very scant.

That was another reason I had to get back to Förening. I wanted to ask Finn and Mia for a small loan. Just something until I could get a paying job again. When I'd lived with the Tulins, I'd worked at the inn, and when I lived with Finn and Mia, I helped watch the kids (and cook and clean) for ten-plus hours a day.

So I was used to working, and I hadn't been sitting idly. Dealing with the fallout of being captive in another kingdom took time, and it felt like I was so close to understanding and remembering what had happened to me.

I might have to spend every penny I had, but it would be worth it to know the truth and to stop something terrible from happening. And then I could move on. Decide where to live and find a job. And spend quality time with Pan.

After I paid Hugo, he gave me the keys to the Jeep, and Pan and I got in and began the short drive back to the apartment.

"I wish I was going with you," Pan said quietly.

Yesterday, when I'd been making the plans, we'd decided it was best if he stayed back. Eliana insisted on going, and we all thought that Jem and Sumi shouldn't be separated from her. With the four of us, that was basically a carload. Plus, Pan had been missing a lot of work, and he was needed here.

Dagny and Elof were continuing their research into what was wrong with Eliana, what the Älvolk were up to, and how to recover our memories safely, and Pan could help them with that. It all made sense, and he understood and agreed with all of it.

But that didn't really do anything about this trepidation. I knew that Pan was nervous that something bad might happen with Sunniva and the memory recovery, and he didn't completely trust Jem-Kruk and Sumi.

Those are the things he'd told me, when he voiced his concerns the previous day. But I also suspected there was another silent fear lurking under everything: the fear that I wouldn't come back. That I would go to Förening and stay, the way Rikky had done before.

That was the only way I could explain the way Pan kissed me after we said our goodbyes. Jem and Sumi had put the last of their things—they only had a few bags between the three of them—in the back of the Jeep while Eliana hugged Dagny.

"I'll call you when I get there," I told him as we stood by the driver's side door in the warm morning sun.

And then suddenly, he grabbed me, pulling me to him, and he kissed me fiercely, deeply. It stole my breath away and made my knees weak. Fortunately, his arm around me stopped me from going full swoon.

When we stopped kissing, he rested his forehead against mine and breathed in deeply. "Come back to me, Ulla, safe and sound."

"I'll always come back to you," I promised him.

I hadn't told him what I'd seen in the memory—the two of us saying "I love you" to each other—or that I knew I loved him still. Just before I left didn't seem like the right time, especially when we hardly had a moment alone.

So with that goodbye, I got in the Jeep and got on the road. Things took a bumpy turn right at the start, with Eliana and Sumi getting into a heated debate about what music to listen to, but they finally shut up when I put on Queen.

The drive was supposed to be split between two days, with us ending up in Bozeman, Montana, very late the first night, if we stayed on track, but Eliana was dead set against keeping to our schedule. She was an exuberant tourist. Everything that even remotely counted as sightseeing—including a very, very large tree and a woman giving away puppies at a gas station—she wanted to stop for.

When we were through a long, open stretch of road, she yelped in the back seat and slapped the window with the palm of her hand. "Look at them!"

I slammed on the brakes, only to see the danger Eliana was alerting me to was half a mile away. A pack of six silvery gray wolves raced through a grassy field that ran alongside a twisting shallow river.

Since the vehicle had stopped moving, Eliana opened the door and dove out.

"Eliana!" I shouted, and I turned the Jeep off, since there wasn't another car around for miles.

"Ellie, don't go near them!" Jem warned as he slid out of the back seat after her. "They look dangerous!"

"I won't!" she yelled, but she jogged a few more feet before stopping.

Some of the wolves stopped, apprehensively looking our way, but the rest kept on running.

"Stay back!" I told Jem and Sumi, since I was probably the strongest one, and I didn't want the wolves getting spooked. They were close enough and big enough that they could do real damage if they decided to attack.

Eliana stayed still, her hair shimmering golden brown in the evening sun, and a cool breeze blew through the nearby evergreens and over the river, ruffling the wolves' fur. One giant canine looked like it was holding Eliana's gaze with his golden amber eyes.

I walked slowly behind her and grabbed her arm. "Eliana, come on."

"They won't hurt me," she said, and didn't budge.

"You don't know that."

"I do," she insisted, then looked up at me. "Be still, Ulla. Enjoy the moment."

I sighed and didn't let go of her arm, but I also didn't throw her over my shoulder and carry her back to the Jeep. Compromise.

The wolf kept looking at her, until another wolf howled somewhere in the distance. Then he cocked his ear and took off with the rest of his pack.

"Thank you," Eliana said quietly as she watched the retreating canines. "I know we're in a hurry, so thank you for letting me have this moment. They were stunning creatures, and I want to see as much of this world as possible while I can."

"Well, I'm glad you got to enjoy this," I said, softening. Another five minutes wouldn't destroy our timetable. "But you can't scream and jump out of a vehicle. You have to ask and wait for me to pull over."

"I understand," she said with a wistful smile. "I knew this would be special, though." Suddenly, she whirled around and hugged me. "I'm so happy that you're here. I always wanted a sister."

"You have a twin sister," I reminded her.

"That doesn't count. She's not like you." She released me and frowned. "She can't love."

"What do you mean?" I asked.

She shrugged. "She didn't love me."

"Has the danger passed?" Sumi asked as she walked up behind us.

I nodded and glanced back at her, her lovely long coils of hair hanging past her shoulders. Her loose tank top and tight leather pants made her look like a boho rock star, like an olive-skinned Janis Joplin.

"The wolves are gone." I pointed to the trees they'd disappeared in, about a hundred meters away.

"They didn't seem so dangerous," Jem said as he joined us. "Our *kuguars* are twice that big back home."

"Were you hoping to end the day with a mauling?" Sumi asked him wryly.

He laughed. "I suppose not." He breathed in deeply. "It is lovely here. The sunsets remind me of home."

"Maybe that's why I like them so much," Eliana said as she stared at the pink sunset.

"The good news is that we can enjoy them from the car," I said, and started back that way.

44

whimsical

After the second grueling day of fifteen-plus hours on the road, we finally arrived in Förening at nearly midnight.

Following the winding roads on the top of the bluff along the Mississippi River, we passed through a metal gate after a guard waved us through. Förening was a lush green town, with many cottages both quaint and chic hidden deep among the trees. Over five thousand trolls lived here, but the streets were quiet, with only hints of life visible through the branches—a swing set, smoke from a chimney, a bleating goat.

The place where we were staying was an inn on the north side of town called the Wisteria & Whimsy Bed & Breakfast. It was the smaller of the two hotels in town, but the other was more expensive and extravagant, catering to visiting dignitaries, traveling Markis and Marksinna, and friends of the royal family.

Wisteria & Whimsy Bed & Breakfast had gone with a more fairy-tale, cutesy approach. From the outside it was positively charming, with a curved roof and lavender flowers hanging from the thick vines covering the stone walls. The flower gardens in the yard were practically overgrown, with cheery little gnome statues hidden around. It was dark out, but little lights scattered through the front gardens made it rather bright.

Inside was more of the same whimsical décor. Pastel walls and a curved front desk greeted us. The woman working the desk was someone I knew from around town, Birdie Vinstock. She was plump and lovely, with an energetic smile, even when the ornate grandfather clock behind her was ticking even closer to midnight.

She gave us our keys—big brass keys with butterfly room numbers on the key rings—and directed us to our rooms on the third floor. As we checked in, she told us about the communal washrooms and complimentary breakfast of appleberry scones and green tea.

Each room had two narrow beds, and Eliana called dibs on bunking with me. That was probably my preferred sleeping arrangement anyway. Our room was small and lavender, with elaborate paintings of fairies on the walls and an overabundance of pillows on the small beds.

I was exhausted and just wanted to sleep, but Eliana once again had other plans.

"I can't sleep," she announced after we'd been in bed for all of five minutes.

"You haven't even tried," I said, and snuggled deeper into the pillows.

"I just can't believe I'll see Hanna in the morning," she said, barely containing her excitement.

Finn and Mia already had a houseful, and I didn't really think they could squeeze the four of us in. I'd considered staying with them, but I knew that both Eliana and Hanna would be hurt if I stayed and Eliana couldn't. So it was better this way.

"Do you think she'll remember me?" Eliana asked softly.

"Yeah, of course. You weren't apart *that* long. And you've talked to her on the phone."

"Well, both you and I forgot a lot of things, and it happened all at once. One day we knew things, the next we didn't."

"That's different. Hanna didn't have the Älvolk playing with her memories." I'd been lying on my side with my back to her, but I rolled onto my back and stared up at the ceiling.

The curtains were lacy and let in more of the glowing yard lights than I would've liked. The branches of the large weeping willow made dancing shadows across the room that looked like arms reaching out for us.

Eliana had finally fallen silent, and the *enn morgana fjeurn on ennsommora orn* playing in my head reached a fever pitch. Since we'd left Merellä, the song had been on its usual loop, dully playing in the back of my skull no matter what else I heard or did. And now that I was finally trying to sleep, it grew louder and the baritone went screechy. It was like an audible headache.

So now I was the one that wanted to talk. Not just to drown out the song, although that was a key motivation, but there were a few things—a lot of things, actually—that I wanted to talk to Eliana about, but it hadn't felt like the right time. It wasn't the right time now, probably, but neither of us could sleep, so why not now?

"Do you remember our mom at all?" I asked.

"No. When I think of the *mumuh,* I feel warm and safe," she answered carefully. "But I have no memory of *her.* I tried to talk to Illaria about her, but she refused to tell me anything. She liked that it hurt me, not knowing."

"I'm sorry she's so awful."

"It's okay. She's your sister too," Eliana reminded me.

I grimaced. I'd been so relieved that Noomi wasn't my sister that I hadn't really thought about how I'd traded one evil half-sister for another. At least with Illaria I understood she hated me because she hated literally everyone.

"We should go to sleep," I said finally. "It'll make time go faster."

"I'll do my best," she said wearily.

It felt like I'd only just closed my eyes when Eliana bounced on my bed, waking me up, but the sunlight streaming through the curtains let me know that she had at least let me sleep through the night.

Eliana could barely contain herself while I got ready, and she wouldn't even eat Birdie's complimentary scones and tea. I drove the four of us across town to the Holmes's house, and I swear that Eliana could sense when we were getting close. She leaned forward in her seat, practically pressing her face to the window.

As soon as I pulled into the driveway in front of the large peridot cottage, Hanna burst out the front door and ran toward us. Eliana leapt out of the Jeep before I put it in park, despite the fact I'd just explicitly told her not to do that, and they ran to each other and hugged. They both made excited squeals that sounded like a cross between laughing and crying.

Finn and Mia came outside with their gaggle of children, and that began the twenty minutes of introductions between everyone. Once that was over, Mia invited us all in, but Hanna had already taken Eliana's hand and started giving her a tour.

"I talked to Tove last night and set everything up for tomorrow," Finn said as we made our way into the house.

"Excellent," I said with a nervous smile. It was what I wanted, but I was still scared of the pain and what I might find out.

Mia led us into the living room, where we all sat around and made stilted, polite conversation. Or at least we attempted to, but it was hard with all the kids. Lissa climbed onto Sumi and kept playing with her hair, Emma kept interrupting to ask questions, Niko sat on my lap babbling, and Luna started crying.

"How are you liking Förening so far?" Mia tried to ask over all the chaos.

"We haven't seen much," Jem admitted with an uneasy smile.

"Is that a real knife?" Liam pointed to the one sheathed on Sumi's waist.

"All right, that's enough." Finn stood and picked Lissa up, carefully untangling her chubby fingers from Sumi's curls. "Liam, Emma, go up to your room and play." He scooped up Luna with his other arm. "I'll take the twins upstairs for my mother to watch."

Niko fell silent and sank deeper into my arms as he played with the polar bear necklace I always wore.

"Sorry about all that," Mia said once Finn had herded Liam and Emma up the stairs.

"It's no problem," Jem said with a smile, and Sumi looked relieved now that it was quieter.

Hanna suddenly bolted down the stairs, her laptop under her arm, and Eliana followed just behind her.

"We just had the most wonderful idea," Hanna announced. She set her laptop down on the coffee table and knelt in front of it. "We're going to video chat with Grandpa Johan and Grandma Sarina while Jem and everyone are here."

"Your grandparents might be busy," Mia warned as the laptop made its *da-da-da* ringing sound.

But then the ringing stopped, and a moment later, I heard

the familiar voice of Johan saying, "What a pleasant surprise, Hanna!"

The way Hanna was situated, with Eliana sitting beside her, the laptop was facing the couch, where Jem and Sumi sat. I was on the chair off to the side of the room, and I couldn't see anything from that angle, so I stood up, carrying Niko with me.

There was Johan, readjusting his oval spectacles and grinning into the camera through his bushy beard.

"I wanted to introduce you to some of my friends." Hanna leaned back, so he'd more easily be able to see Jem and Sumi.

Jem glanced back at me, a bemused expression on his face, and to encourage him to interact with Johan, I said, "He's the one that wrote the book about Jem-Kruk and his adventures."

"Oh." He uncrossed his long legs and leaned forward, closer to the laptop. "Good morning, sir."

"And good morning to you," Johan said with a laugh.

Slowly, Jem's expression changed. His brow furrowed, his eyes narrowed, and his jaw dropped. He leaned in closer to the screen, and in an awed voice, he said, "*Oleva,* Jo-Huk? Is that you?"

45

time

It took quite a bit of back and forth, especially with everyone talking over each other. Finn came back just when it was reaching a fever pitch, and he held up his hands. In his most commanding voice he said, "Everyone, quiet! One at a time, please!"

Johan went first—maybe the threat of Finn's angry-dad voice didn't translate fully through the laptop speakers. He sat back in the chair of his study, a befuddled expression on his face, and cleared his throat.

"As I was saying, I don't . . ." He trailed off and squinted at the screen, at Jem-Kruk smiling uncertainly back at him. "I *have* a brother." He put a hand to his mouth, and his eyes welled with tears.

Hanna looked between the handsome, much younger Jem and her elderly grandfather. "You guys can't be brothers. The age difference is . . . *a lot*."

Eliana leaned over the coffee table, her chin propped up on her hand. Her eyes watched Hanna intensely, and her heart-shaped face was sweet and youthful.

"How old is Eliana?" I asked.

"Ellie's . . . well, she's—" Jem said, then looked to Sumi, who just sighed.

"It's a harder answer," Sumi said. "Eliana was born in Alfheim around four years ago, but in that time, thirty-two years have passed in your kingdom. Time moves differently in our lands, and she's spent time in both places, so it's very hard to say precisely how long she's been alive. I would put her age at about seventeen."

"Illaria's older because she spent much more time here with the Älvolk," Jem added.

"She's closer to twenty-five," Sumi clarified. "Jo's been here for much longer than Jem, obviously." She smiled at Johan. "I remember when Rinatte met you. She fell head over heels for you."

Johan chuckled softly. "I remember you now, Sumi. You've aged well."

"I've cheated," she said with a rueful smile. "I spent time in Alfheim."

"Okay, I don't mean to interrupt," Finn said. "But what do you mean by time moves differently in our lands?"

"One year on Alfheim is about eight years here," Sumi answered.

"After Eliana and Illaria's father was killed by a *kuguar*, Senka took them across the bridge," Jem elaborated. "She used to travel with Jo-Huk, then she had the babies, and he fell in love with Sarina and ran away with her."

"I'm sorry, Jem," Johan said, his voice thick. "Sarina wasn't safe with the Älvolk, and I loved her. But I never thought I'd forget you. I never wanted that."

"I'm sure the two of you have a lot to talk about, and you definitely should, but I'm having a hard time with the whole time thing, so can we go back to that for a moment?" I asked.

I moved Niko, holding him more on my hip so I could

sway and bounce him more easily. Not that he was fussing. I just needed to do something.

"When Senka left, the twins were just babies, crawling around," Jem said. "For me, in Alfheim, that was only three and a half years ago. When I visited her once, she was trapped in an unhappy relationship with Indu and very pregnant with you."

"That's when I met Jem," Sumi explained. "I'd been living on my own, moving around the various villages and the wilds of the arctic lands around Áibmoráigi. I never ventured too far into the human world, and I did odds-and-ends jobs for trolls. I was recruited by the Omte King to help find the Lost Bridge, and I became friends with Senka through the whole ordeal."

"You knew my parents?" I asked, feeling dazed. "When they knew each other?"

She nodded. "I knew Senka and Thor, but I didn't know they were involved or had a child together. And I didn't spend much time with the two of them together. When Jem visited Senka, I followed him back to Alfheim. And that's where I stayed until Eliana went missing."

Finn sat down on the arm of the chair beside his wife. "But *how* does time move differently?"

"The Älvolk always thought time moved more slowly because Alfheim is home to the gods," Sumi said with a derisive snort. "After I was excommunicated, I did my own research, even using human resources. And that answer seems to be more scientific than mystical. The farther someone is from a gravitating mass, the faster time passes. Alfheim is just much closer to a much larger gravitational field than you are."

"Is the bridge to Alfheim incredibly long?" I asked, thinking of something I'd heard before: that the bridge took ages to cross.

"Not that long, but the bridge isn't how you actually get to Alfheim anyway," Sumi explained. "It's merely a gate, a lock to keep out those that don't belong in Alfheim. On the other side of the bridge, there is a waterfall, and that's the entrance. You pass through, and you're in Alfheim."

"Then how does it have different gravity?" Finn asked.

"Alfheim is much farther away than the journey implies," Jem said simply.

"So wait, are you my uncle?" Hanna interjected.

"Great-uncle. I think," Sumi said.

Hanna stared at Jem a moment longer, then looked back at the computer screen. "How come you didn't remember him anymore?"

"I—" Johan shook his head, at a loss for words, and he was visibly choking back tears. "I have no idea how I could ever forget my brother. My family."

"A few things could be at play." Sumi offered up an explanation. "The Älvolk are fond of playing with memories. They even know how to do something called *fúinn muitit* that causes memory to decay over time.

"Then there's the fact that going through the entrance to Alfheim is exhausting," she went on.

"I thought you said it was fast," I said.

"It is," Jem assured me. "But it leaves you bone-tired and discombobulated. Usually, it passes within a few days, but if you're not well when you go through, it can be much, much worse."

"That's why we haven't brought Eliana home yet," Sumi elaborated. "But that puts us in a difficult position. I've begun to suspect that staying here long term is deleterious to pure-blood *álfar.*"

She held up her hand and ticked off her fingers as she spoke. "Senka came back ill and died shortly after spending over a decade with the Älvolk, Illaria's spent even more time here and she's very unstable, and Eliana and Johan have serious memory issues, to say the least."

"Wait, wait," I said. "The *fúinn muitit*. How do you know if that's been done to you? How long will it take your memory to decay?"

Sumi gave me a grim smile. "You don't know. It can take years before you notice, and even then, there's not much you can do about it. It's one of the most powerful incantations known to the Älvolk."

46

veloma

Hanna begged her parents for a sleepover, so Eliana stayed behind, but that worked because I had the hotel room to myself. All of us had spent the day talking about the Jem-Kruk/Alfheim situation. Niko even stayed for all of it, although he fell asleep halfway through.

Once I got back to my hotel room, I flopped back on the bed. I didn't know what to think about everything. The Älvolk had already messed with my mind so much, and now it turned out they might take even more? Sumi had spent a long time explaining the time differences, but I still wasn't sure that I fully understood it.

Not that it really mattered. My hope was that I'd stop the bridge from opening—not cross it myself. I didn't want to go somewhere I could lose entire days for an overnight trip.

And Sumi knew my parents. When they were together. I wanted to know everything she had seen. Were they in love? How did they meet? What did they think of me? *Did* they think of me?

But Sumi said she wanted a nap. And I doubted she

knew the answers anyway. I imagined that Senka and Thor's relationship—as much or as little as it may have been—was presumably clandestine.

Or maybe Sumi had known, but she'd forgotten it. The way Johan had.

Throughout the conversation, both he and Jem had intermittently cried. They truly seemed to love each other, and Johan had once remembered his childhood well enough to write a book about it. But all of that had been stripped from his mind.

It was a cold, horrifying thought that I could lose everything I cared about, everything I'd ever done. It could all be gone. The Älvolk could make me forget everything.

A knock at the hotel door stopped my rumination, and when I answered it, I found Jem on my doorstep.

"Sumi's sleeping, but I'm not tired. I was hoping you might want some company," he said with his razor-sharp smile.

"Yeah, sure." I stepped back and let him into my room.

"How are you handling everything?"

"I don't know," I admitted wearily. "How about you?"

"Well, for me, I reunited with my long-lost brother, so it's been a happy day," he reminded me.

"Of course. Yeah. I'm so happy for you both."

Jem sat on Eliana's bed, leaning back with his arms behind him, and he looked up at me with his dark eyes. He'd left his hair loose, and when he shook his head to get a curl out of his face, there was something oddly sexy about the gesture. My belly warmed, and once again I wanted to blurt out that I was seeing Pan.

Instead, I played it cool and averted my gaze as I walked over to sit on my own bed. "Yeah, I'm just trying to keep moving forward," I said, like I knew what that meant.

"That's the best way to live, I think," Jem said.

"If I ask you something, will you give me an honest answer?" I asked, giving him a sidelong glance.

He was slightly taken aback. "I always try to be honest."

"You really didn't know who I was?" I asked. "When you met me in Merellä. You didn't know I was Senka's daughter or Eliana's sister?"

"No, I had no idea. I was looking for Ellie, and then I met you." He raised a shoulder in a nonchalant shrug. "Maybe subconsciously I saw a bit of Senka in you. You don't look much like her. She looked a lot like Ellie, only taller. But there's something in you that reminds me of her, an open kindness. There's a warmth about you that she had."

I smiled. "So Senka had a kind face?"

"The kindest." He nodded. "Big, wide, dark brown eyes, and she had a contagious laugh. It was impossible not to feel happy around her. And she was an amazing fighter. She was so fast and light on her feet, and she'd always stop to help anyone that needed it."

I suddenly remembered a passage from *Jem-Kruk and the Adlrivellir.*

After they had gathered all the fruit they could carry, they lounged in the meadow. Jem-Kruk smiled at Senka, and it was the smile of a boy who has never been happier and who had never seen a girl prettier.

"She sounds amazing," I said.

"She really was," he agreed with a wistful smile.

My phone vibrated in my pocket, and I pulled it out to see a text from Pan asking how things were going. I hadn't talked to him yet that day, so he was probably getting a little worried.

"Is everything okay?" Jem asked.

"Yeah. Pan's just checking in with me."

"Is he your boyfriend?" he asked, surprising me.

"Yeah. Sorta. I think."

"Like *veloma*?" Jem asked, using the *álfar* word that meant "the one you choose to be with."

"Yeah." I smiled. "Pan is my *veloma*."

"Good," he said with an unreadable smile of his own. "I'm glad you have someone who cares for you so much." And then he gestured broadly around. "You have so many that care about you. Senka would be so happy. All she ever would've wanted for you is a life full of love."

I swallowed hard, barely holding back the tears, and I managed to eke out, "Thank you. I needed to hear that."

"It's good that I stopped by then."

I wiped my eyes hurriedly and looked over at him. "I'm sorry. I've just been talking. You found out your brother is alive!"

He laughed. "I last saw him four years ago, and now he's an old man. I'd always hoped he was alive and well, that he had love and a family. It's good to hear that that's mostly been true."

"I'm sure he and you have a lot to talk about," I said.

"We do," he agreed. "I'm looking forward to talking with him more tomorrow."

Hanna was going to help Jem and Johan do a video chat tomorrow while I did the aural healing with Tove and Sunniva. Johan was going to make sure his wife was home, so Jem could finally meet her.

Jem and I hung out in the room for a bit longer, talking about the strange twists our lives had taken, and then we went down to grab something to eat at a café around the corner. After that, we parted ways. I checked in with both Dagny and Pan, and everything sounded like it was fine back in Merellä.

That left me free to spend the evening fretting and pacing. When I finally felt tired enough for bed, I ended up tossing and turning for a long time, but finally I fell asleep.

And the next time I opened my eyes, I was in the dungeon again.

Not the prison cell, but the corridor outside it. Narrow and dark, although the stones seemed more rust colored than I remembered. Or maybe it was because all the lamps were lit.

The hallway ended in an almost blindingly bright light, and as I walked into the atrium, lifting my arms to shield my eyes, I realized something.

"I've been here before," I said softly, and lowered my arms. I squinted up the tall silo of a room. A staircase wound around the walls, and the roof was all glass, letting in so much sunlight. "I've done *this* before."

"All of this has happened before, and all of it will happen again, *binrassi*," a woman said in a sultry baritone, and I looked over to see her standing on the steps.

Her wide eyes were dark, like her long hair floating ethereally around her. She wore a gossamer gown, adorned with goldenrod and poppy red flowers, and a shawl of soft bird feathers. She was lovely and luminous, but her expression was grim.

"But this time, you're the one that must stop it," she said in her deep, seductive voice. "You must hurry." She raced up the stairs, her long train billowing out behind her.

"Wait!" I shouted after her, but she never slowed. "Where are you going?"

She was nearly at the top of the stairs, so I ran as fast as I could. When I got to the landing at the top, the only way out was a set of large doors, and I hurried through, but there was no sign of her.

Outside, the air felt warm and crisp, and the beautiful mountainside city around me was eerily silent. Carts were left unattended in the dirt roads, and front doors left open on empty houses.

The air turned cold and dark clouds rolled in, and I knew that a dense fog would follow behind it.

"What am I to do?" I shouted into the still air. "You told me to stop it, but how do I do it? What am I even stopping?"

"You're stopping the end of everything you know," she said, and I whirled around to see her standing there as the fog thickened around her.

"How do I stop it?" I asked, and as the harsh air burned my throat, I realized it was smoke, not fog.

She came closer to me, and sadly she said, "You will give your heart and your blood. That is the only way you will kill the wyrm."

"What?" I asked incredulously, and the ground shook beneath my bare feet. "How could I possibly do all that?"

"When the time comes, follow the lone white elk." She was nearly shouting to be heard over the rumbling. Stone buildings crumbled all around us, but she didn't move, so neither did I.

"What are you talking about?"

"When the time comes, follow the lone white elk. If you don't, the whole world will burn," she warned me, and suddenly, everything erupted in screams.

The city that had a moment ago been devoid of life was abruptly filled with running, terrified men, women, and children. Some were bloodied, some singed, all of them screaming and shouting in a language I couldn't understand.

My lungs and throat burned and flashes of green lit up the smoke. The woman in her gossamer gown was gone, and I was dodging strangers and collapsing buildings. I ran around a burning barn, narrowly avoiding a panicked crowd rushing toward me.

I heard a guttural growl, and the last thing I saw was a burst of green before an inferno engulfed me.

47

A journey back

Tove and his husband, Bain, lived in a surprisingly luxe townhouse at the peak of the bluffs. It was the end unit in a row of six, and they had panoramic views of the vibrant green forest and deep blue Mississippi River cutting sharply through the land.

Honestly, their house looked like something out of one of those home-decorating shows I sometimes watched with Hanna, Mia, and Finn. Soft gray walls like downy clouds, white marble tiles around the fireplace, wood floors so dark they were nearly black, and elegant crystal light fixtures. There were also a few chic rustic pieces, like a silver moose head made of mercury glass mounted on the wall and a chunky knit mohair blanket on the back of the sofa.

When I got there, Bain answered the door and showed me to the sitting room, where Sunniva was already waiting. A cup of tea—mint flavored based on the scent—was in her hands, both carefully cupping the mug so her rings clinked against the ceramic.

"Tove, your guest is here!" Bain shouted up the stairs. He smiled nervously at me. "He'll be down in a minute."

Though he'd been the Chancellor for years, Bain lacked a politician's knack for hiding his true feelings. Part of that was his boyish face and his wide blue eyes. His features were otherwise very Trylle, but his light eye color meant he had Skojare in him too.

Tove jogged down the stairs a moment later, his hair still damp from the shower. "Sorry to keep you waiting. I finished filling the bath in the guest room with cold water." He glanced at me, his mossy green eyes landing on me for a split second. "Just in case."

"That really doesn't sound safe," Bain said, his voice tight with worry.

"We've got this," Sunniva told him, and set her cup on the mirrored coffee table. "I've been training." Long, thick lashes framed her earnest brown eyes, and her dark hair hung in a thick Dutch braid.

"Didn't you have a book club you wanted to get to today, hon?" Tove asked Bain.

"I did." Bain took a deep breath. "Be safe." He looked to me. "All of you." He kissed Tove, then gave me and Sunniva a polite goodbye before departing out the front door.

After he'd gone, I told Sunniva and Tove about the hyperrealistic dream that ended in me burning in green flames.

"Why are you telling me this?" Sunniva asked flatly, while Tove went into the kitchen to get a wet washrag and an ice pack.

"I'm not normally the type to tell everyone about my dreams," I said. "But this seemed *so* real. Like it was really happening. Or the memory of something that did really happen." I shuddered involuntarily at the thought of the way my flesh burned and smoke filled my lungs. The scent of ashes and smoke still clung to the inside of my nostrils.

Sunniva shrugged. "Maybe it did happen, but it didn't happen to you. You didn't die in a fire."

"Not yet," I muttered.

"I'll be keeping tabs on your body temp," Tove said as he returned. "I won't let things get out of control."

"Let's do this," Sunniva said, and pointed to the furniture. "Move this out of the way."

I stepped toward the couch, preparing to lift it, but with a wave of Tove's hand, the couch slid back to the stairs, the coffee table toward the fireplace, and the chairs went back toward the dining room. He tossed a throw pillow down in the middle of the wool floor rug, and I lay down on my back.

As he positioned the ice pack under the back of my neck and laid the washcloth across my forehead, I looked past him and asked Sunniva, "If it was a memory, can you recover it?"

"I can recover the memory of a dream." She got a stepladder from the closet under the stairs and set it up at my feet. "But you already seem to remember it pretty well, so it doesn't seem like the best use of our limited time. Your body can't handle doing this for too long."

"You're right." I sighed. "Could it have been a lysa?"

"I have no idea. Lysas have nothing to do with aural healing." She was on the top step of the stepladder and she pushed up the sleeves of her green blouse. "Now, are you ready?"

"Yeah, of course." I closed my eyes and lay still.

"I need you to try to remember what you want me to recover," she commanded.

Since she'd asked me this last time, I had come prepared and already decided on the moment I most wanted to remember. The memory that surfaced when Elof took me to the Ögonen neighborhood to see their secret *sorgblomma* garden, but pain stopped me from being able to see it all the way through.

I squeezed my eyes shut and lay perfectly still—

—and I was back in Lemak the häxdoktor's *office. The bed with restraints was behind me, and I sat shackle-free at an old wooden desk. My wrists still bore the red, blistered reminders that my freedom was only temporary.*

It was only me and Lemak. And all of his dying flowers. Glass beakers lined the apothecary table with wilting yellow sorgblomma *littering dry petals everywhere.*

"These are what he wants you to work on today," Lemak said, handing me a narrow tube of paper.

Slowly I unrolled it, and I saw the jagged Tryllic lettering.

РЕЦЕПТ ДЛЯ ОБРАТНОГО ПУТИ

Tryllic was a runic bastardization of Russian Cyrillic with a Finnish influence. The Trylle had invented it centuries ago, after the Vittra intercepted royal correspondence and laid siege on the kingdom. Because of that, the Trylle wanted to create a language that the other tribes wouldn't be able to decipher, and so they kept the Rosetta stone secret for many, many years.

Now it's a nearly forgotten language, with hardly any Trylle even bothering to learn it. Finn knew it, and he wanted me to study it because he thought it was important to remember our heritage and that it might be useful, the same reasons he had me learn Norse and Swedish. I had hated learning it at the time, but now it was literally saving my life.

I still wasn't fluent in it, not by a long shot, and I hadn't read any Tryllic in quite a while. Lemak and Indu had gathered me various old documents to do comparisons and help decipher it.

The main scroll that I had spent the most time on—days? Weeks? How long had we been there? I could feel memories overlaying it, a dozen different days at that desk, my wrists healing only to be bloodied and raw again, the flowers crumbling in their beakers replaced by fresh ones that wilted again—was called "A Recipe for the Journey Back."

In my attempts to finish the recipe, I made a few "unrelated" translations, or at least, that's what Lemak would say each day I didn't solve the puzzle they'd been working on for years. Lemak would lean over me, his long bony fingers on my shoulder, his breath reeking of fermented elk meat with his words in my ear: "You're wasting time, and we're losing patience. You need to stick to what truly matters."

I had futilely tried to explain to him that I didn't know if a passage or word was relevant until I translated it, and the archaic wording made it very hard to decipher without some time and effort. But he wouldn't listen, so I merely said, "I'm doing my best."

Then I'd uncovered the passage that made Lemak lose it—he struck me across the face, twice, and when I crouched down on the floor, trying to hide from more blows, he began hitting me over the head repeatedly with an old book. Dazed and in pain, I tried to fight back, but he hit me with a PSG before I had the chance.

That had been my punishment for translating about the formation of Áibmoráigi:

"Frey took the kingdom and was called the King by the Swedes, and they paid taxes to him. He built a great temple in Áibmoráigi. Then began the Älvolk domains, which have been ever since."

Another passage that earned me a beating on a different day: "The sky last will turn green on the most violent night, but good morning brings light to us all."

The room was heating up, and I felt like I was slowly roast-ing in an oven, but I kept my head down and did my best work. I didn't know what Lemak would do to me—or Pan, Dagny, and Elof—if I didn't. So even when the flowers began to crumble right before my eyes, and the sweat dripping off my brow smeared the scrolls, I kept working without com-plaint.

Until finally—as the days rushed together, all the hours mashed into a matter of moments—I had completed the rec-ipe for a disturbing blood pudding:

- 1 drinking horn of *álfar* blood
- 1 mug of spring lamb stock
- 3 whole goose eggs
- corn cockle seed flour
- lard of *hvalnum* melted over an open fire
- mashed cloudberries
- *sorgblomma*, stem and liquid, mashed into a paste
- dried mugwort, powdered in a mortar
- Induian pear, minced
- albino elk heart, minced

Stir it all together, cook in a full-sized cauldron until firm.

"Why is the recipe so special?" I asked as Lemak read it over.

"It's not what the recipe is," he said. "It's about what can be done once it's consumed."

He was so delighted, his thin lips pulled back to reveal his yellowed teeth in a sickly smile, and when I asked if I could translate the bit that was scribbled at the bottom, he grunted, "You can waste your time if that's what you choose," without backhanding me.

Still, I wasn't sure how long his mood would last, since some of those ingredients sounded hard to come by. The hval-num may even be an extinct water mammal, though it sounded like it could be a harbor porpoise. They'd been taking my blood, but I wasn't álfar. At least not completely. At the thought of someone cooking my blood and eating it, my stomach rolled, and I coughed to suppress my urge to vomit.

As I hurried to translate the scribblings, the heat in the room continued to rise. Over the course of a few days, actually. Lemak ordered me to continue translating it now, after Indu demanded more information about the ingredients. But it had been several days, and they had never been patient.

The stone walls were sweating, and the paper kept rolling and warping from the rising temperature.

"Can you turn down the heat?" I asked, nearly gasping from the suffocating warmth.

"It's fine down here," Lemak snapped, and then he was reading over my shoulder. "Finish your work."

But the truth was that I thought I already had. The words at the bottom simply said, "Frey's father has closed the bridge for the *ekkálfar,* and to cross it is to undo his words, and his word is bond."

The water in the beakers began to boil, and the stone tiles scorched the bottom of my feet. I lifted them up, resting my heels on the edge of the chair to keep the skin from melting off.

"I can't stay here anymore," I said, practically shouting.

Lemak looked at me, and from his mouth, I heard Tove's voice: "We're getting you out of there now."

Wind rushed through the room and the walls began to shake. The papers on the desk burst into flames, and I screamed.

"Ulla, I need you to open your eyes," Sunniva said, and her voice shook the entire room.

48

annul

My hair was still wet from the ice bath, but I changed out of my clothes as soon as I got back to the hotel. Jem and Sumi were already there, him sitting in the rocking chair in the corner, Sumi pacing in front of the lacy curtains, but we were waiting for Finn. I wanted to talk this all over with him almost more than anybody.

He'd know what to do.

At least, that's what I kept telling myself.

He arrived a moment later, pounding on the hotel room door, and when Sumi answered it, he rushed in and over to me.

"Are you all right? You sounded so panicked on the phone." Finn sat down on the bed beside me, and his dark eyes were frantic with worry.

"Yeah, I'm fine." Then I shook my head and corrected myself. "Mostly fine. Pretty much."

"You sure?" He put the back of his hand against my forehead, checking my temperature, and he frowned. "You're still very warm."

I leaned away from him and his overbearing parental

mode. "It takes time to cool down completely, but I'm getting there."

He let his hand fall. "What did you remember?"

"I know what the Älvolk are doing and what they want," I said. "They're making some kind of mystical blood pudding with rare, disturbing ingredients."

I'd written them down in a notebook, and I held it out to him, but Sumi snatched it before anybody else had a chance to, and she quickly read through it.

"They think if they consume it, they'll be able to cross the bridge and enter Alfheim," I explained.

"Why'd you write this on here?" Sumi tapped the bottom of the page where I'd jotted down *Frey's father has closed the bridge for the* ekkálfar, *and to cross it is to undo his words, and his word is bond.*

"That was the last thing I remember translating," I said.

"Oh, sweet sister *Hel,*" she said under her breath. "They mean to cross the bridge and enter Alfheim. They want to undo the word of Frey's father, annulling the enchantment that kept the entrance to Alfheim closed. But if they do what Frey said was impossible by crossing it, then the bridge would be open to everyone." She looked to Jem with wide eyes. "On both sides."

Jem cursed and rubbed his chin. "They're not prepared here. They'll be slaughtered."

"I had a dream. Or maybe a lysa. Or a vision," I said. "I don't know. But I think it was about the fall of Áibmoráigi. There was a woman, and she told me that I needed to prevent it again."

"How?" Sumi asked.

"When the time is right, I need to follow the lone white elk," I said uncertainly.

Finn scoffed. "That sounds like a stress dream."

"No, Finn, it wasn't," I insisted. "I've been seeing an albino elk, and now I'm told I've got to stop something terrible from happening. So what do I do?"

Nobody said anything, and the sick feeling I had in my stomach only intensified.

"Okay, then." I sighed. "What about the ingredients? Can we stop them from getting them?"

"The mugwort, cloudberries, corn cockle, and goose eggs are all fairly common in Áibmoráigi," Sumi said. "It's not an everyday thing, but they often have *hvalnum* lard and spring lamb stock in their pantry. And Jem just traded them a bushel of Induian pears in exchange for 'helping' Eliana."

"That was before we realized they were abusing and exploiting Ellie," Jem muttered.

"And they got all the *sorgblomma* from the Vittra," Finn said dully.

"The only thing they need is the albino woolly elk heart," Sumi surmised.

"How common are those?" I asked.

She shrugged. "I've never seen one."

"You said you had, though," Finn said, looking to me.

"Only in my dreams. Or visions or whatever they are." Then I corrected myself. "At least I think they're dreams or something."

"Doesn't your friend Pan work with the woolly elk? Maybe he would know more," Finn suggested.

"I should talk to him." I wished he were here, discussing this all with me. He always made me feel better, even when everything seemed impossible.

"We mustn't let them finish the recipe," Jem said. His fingers were tented together and his eyes were downcast. "My grandfather told stories of the last time the bridge was open, when the wyrm got through. So many lives were lost. Cities fell and the world burned."

"We'll do all we can to stop this, but what does that entail?" Finn asked carefully. "What can we do? I don't even know how we can prevent them from obtaining the elk heart, other than not giving them one ourselves."

A moment passed before Sumi said, almost reluctantly, "The only way we can be sure that the Älvolk won't follow through on the crusade they're on is if we make them submit to our will. They only respond to force." She exhaled roughly. "We must attack them."

"They trained Sumi to be a warrior," Jem said, looking up at her. "She knows how they fight, and how they think."

"If you have any military, I'd be happy to tell them what I know," Sumi said to Finn.

"Thank you," he replied. "I will probably take you up on that."

"I have to go back to Merellä," I realized.

"But you just got here," Finn said.

"And I'm needed here," Sumi said.

"You should stay," I told her. "Maybe Sunniva and Tove can help Eliana with her memory, and she can spend more time with Hanna, while you two help Finn decide how best to handle the Älvolk.

"But I need to go back to the Mimirin and get to the bottom of the vision I had," I said. "I need to learn as much as I can about the albino elk, and I can help Elof and Dagny figure out a way to stop the Älvolk from crossing the bridge."

49

✢

Humanity

I drove by myself for nearly two days, minus pit stops and the seven hours I slept in the Jeep at a rest stop in Montana. It was a long, boring trip, but I did notice that I'd gotten better around humans. It used to be that I tensed up every time I pulled into a gas station. But now it didn't bother me. They were all so busy worrying about their own stuff, most of the time they never even noticed me, and if they did, they were mostly polite.

Still, I was happy to be back in Merellä and relieved that the guard let me pass with my old acceptance letter. It was late on Saturday, and Pan should've just finished up his night shift as a peurojen. As tired as I was, seeing Pan sounded better than sprawling out in my bed.

His apartment was on Market Street, and all the shops on the row were closed, so I parked right out front. The entrance was around back, and I rang the doorbell and waited in the dimly lit alley.

I heard footsteps pounding on the steps, and then he opened the door wearing an Ottawa Senators hockey T-shirt.

His hair was disheveled, like he'd been sleeping, but his eyes were bright and his breathless smile seemed genuine.

"I hope you don't mind that I just stopped by."

"Are you kidding me?" His crooked smile deepened, and he stepped closer to me. He cradled my face in his hands, then he leaned in and kissed me.

"I missed you too."

"I *did* miss you," he said, then stepped back so I could enter his apartment. "Come on in. I know you had a long trip."

I'd walked Pan to his door before, but I had never actually been inside.

There was a small entryway right inside the door, and then a set of stairs leading to his second-story flat. Outside, it smelled strongly of smoked salmon, which attracted more than a few stray cats, but inside, Pan had strategically placed infusers around so it smelled nicely of a rainy meadow.

His place was smaller than mine and Dagny's. It was all one room, other than the tiny bathroom in the corner. He had a queen-sized bed, a desk, and a small kitchenette with a hot plate and small fridge. The roof was pitched, so he didn't even have full head space at the edge of the apartment on the north and south walls, and he used that space for storage—an oversized dresser, a squat bookcase, and a crate of records and battered paperbacks.

His style seemed more functional than intentional, with most of the furniture pieces looking like well-maintained thrift store finds. The bed was made with a slate gray blanket, and there were framed pictures on his dresser—him as a scrawny tween and a beautiful older woman hugging him, presumably his mother. The only art on the walls were band posters.

"Do you want anything to eat or drink?" He moved toward the kitchenette portion of the room and motioned for me to sit down on the short futon near the end of his bed. Brueger, the dog, was sprawled out on the rug, gnawing on a thick bone.

My stomach growled. Eating on the road was always challenging. "I would, actually, if it isn't too much trouble."

"I never keep my place super stocked, but I do have some plumberry wine and honey butter that's great on wheat bread," Pan said, and he was already pulling the wine out of the fridge.

I settled back into the futon and exhaled deeply. Two days ago, Sunniva's aural healing had taken a lot out of me, and the next morning I hit the road. I was exhausted through and through, and this was the first time I'd truly been able to relax in days.

"That sounds amazing, thank you," I said gratefully.

Brueger finally set aside his bone and came over to greet me, his tail wagging happily. He was a big, beautiful puppy—a dog really. A sturdy Belgian Malinois with a coat of dark fawn and black, and his left ear drooping instead of pointing straight up like a triangle the way the other one did.

I scratched him between the ears and asked Pan, "How have things been here?"

"Fine." He leaned back against the counter, waiting for the bread to toast. "Nothing's really changed since I talked to you this afternoon."

I'd called him from the road, and told him all about Jem and Johan and time dilation, and about my seemingly prophetic dream, and everything I remembered, and the conclusions I had come to with Finn, Jem, and Sumi.

He, in turn, told me about the goings-on here in Merellä. Dagny and Elof had been incredibly busy, and they'd been taking hours of meetings with Mästare Amalie and sometimes the Korva, Ragnall. Pan didn't really know what for, but between his two jobs and Dagny's long hours, they hadn't had a chance to talk much. I had only briefly talked to her on Thursday to let her know I'd be home, and I'd just barely caught her between meetings.

"I still have to interrogate Dagny when I get home," I said.

"I am interested in finding out what's going on with her and Elof," he agreed, and his eyes rested warmly on me. "How are you doing?"

"Right now I'm really tired and really glad to be here."

The toast popped up, and he slathered it with honey butter. He brought it over to me, along with two coffee mugs filled with plumberry wine. He handed me the mug with the color-changing light sabers, and for himself, he kept the one with the peurojen symbol—a heart with antlers.

"Thank you." I gulped down the wine greedily. "This is very tasty wine. The mug is nice too."

"Are you a big *Star Wars* fan?" he asked with a smirk.

I nodded. "Not like a fanatic, but I like the movies. At least the ones I've seen."

"It's so weird to me that you know what *Star Wars* is when you're so sheltered."

"I have to agree," I admitted between bites of toast. "But I know some things, especially those that are too ubiquitous to hide from."

"What else do you know that would surprise me?"

I laughed. "I don't know? You tell me."

"Well, what about Bastille?" Pan motioned to the band poster on the wall.

I shook my head. "Nope."

"Oh, they're the best. You'll love 'em." He got up and rummaged around his records before putting one on, and a mellow song with beautiful vocals began. "I saw them years ago back in Canada." He came back and sat down beside me. "It was so great. Have you ever been to a concert?"

"I mean, I've seen bands and orchestras, but all of them were made entirely of trolls in troll kingdoms, so I don't know if that counts."

"I've seen troll orchestras, and no, they do not count," he said, and I laughed again.

"Oh, come on, we've got some really talented musicians."

"We do," he agreed readily. "But the whole experience is different at a rock show. You'll see when I take you."

With my toast finished, I took another long drink of my wine, enjoying the warmth it left in my belly. Then I leaned back on the couch and moved my legs up, lying them across his lap. He smiled at me, and cautiously, he rested his hand on my thigh, barely below my shorts.

"What other things have I been missing out on?" I asked. "From the human world. Rock shows? What else?"

"Oh, that's a good question." He thought for a second. "Food, for sure. I know most trolls have tough stomachs, but there're foods that are allergen friendly and very tasty cuisine. There's this amazing vegan place in Portland that a lot of the Mimirin students check out on breaks, and they love it."

"Try more food? All right, I'm up for that."

"Oh, and beaches. Like, warm sunny beaches with crystal-clear water," he said. "All sorts of animals, like elephants and pandas."

"I see nature documentaries," I reminded him.

"I guess I don't know then." He ran a hand through his messy curls. "The truth is that I haven't seen that much of the world either. But I know there are plenty of amazing places to explore."

"I used to be so anxious being out in the human world, but they're not that different than anyone else. Plus, I've seen some really beautiful things." I thought of the wolf pack I saw with Eliana, and a beautiful veil waterfall. "I'd love to see more of it."

He grinned crookedly. "We'll start with a vegan place and a rock show."

"It's a date then," I said. "When stuff is straightened out, and we have time." I yawned. "Sorry. I should be getting home."

"Or . . ." Pan paused. "You could spend the night here." Then quickly, "We don't have to do anything. I can even sleep on the futon."

I leaned over and kissed him. "We've spent enough time apart lately."

50

slumber

He lent me a shirt—an oversized Guns N' Roses tee—and I went into the washroom to change. When I came out, nervously pulling the hem of the shirt farther down my thighs, Pan had turned off the overhead lights, so the apartment was dimly lit by a bedside lamp. He was on the other side, shirtless, bent over and petting his dog.

"I was just letting Brueger know that he has to sleep on the floor tonight," he said.

"I didn't mean to kick him out of bed. Now I feel bad."

"Nah, don't worry about him. He doesn't mind." He straightened up and smiled over at me. "That shirt suits you."

"Thanks." I blushed and climbed into his bed so I could hide under the covers.

Pan got into the bed and clicked off the light. He slid over to me, but not quite close enough to touch. "Do you need me to set an alarm or anything?"

"Wait, what day is tomorrow? Thursday?"

He laughed, enough of a rumble that it shook the bed. "Sunday."

"Ugh." I groaned. "I think I got jet-lagged from all the driving I've done this week. Is that a thing that can happen?"

Pan laughed again. "I honestly have no idea."

"Do you have to get up by a certain time tomorrow?" I asked.

"At four-thirty A.M.," he said, and I gasped.

"That's so early! And I've been keeping you up so late!"

"I'm used to it."

My eyes had adjusted to the dark, and I could see his profile as he stared up at the pitched ceiling. I was lying on my side, studying his handsome features. His strong jaw and full lips. His long eyelashes lay on his cheeks, and one of his hands rested on his stomach.

"What?" He looked over, apparently aware that I was watching him.

"I was just thinking about how far away you are."

He moved one arm up to the pillow and tilted toward me, opening his arms, and I slid across the bed and into them. I pressed my body against him, and as his strong arms enveloped me, I kissed him.

A heat in my belly simmered, the way it did every time we touched, but an oppressive weariness was barreling down on me. Pan noticed right away and he stopped kissing me.

"Is something wrong?" he asked as he brushed a lock of hair out of my face.

"I'm just really tired," I said with a yawn.

"Let's just get some sleep then."

He settled back into the bed, one arm still around me, and I rested my head on his chest. The rhythmic thump of his heart slowly lulled me to sleep.

With his arm around me like that, firm, warm, safe, enveloping, I wondered, is this what it feels like to be loved, really and truly, all the way through? Because that's how I felt in his arms.

I woke up to the bed moving, with the sunlight lighting up an unfamiliar space. I sat up with a start, and Pan was standing beside the bed, clad only in a pair of jeans.

"What time is it?" I asked.

"Seven."

"You overslept!"

He laughed. "No, I made it to work on time, and I just got back from my shift. I thought I'd crawl back in bed, and I was hoping not to wake you."

"That sounds wonderful," I said. "But I should probably get up and go to the apartment. Dagny will start to worry if I'm not back soon. And I need to get my next move sorted out."

Pan had been in the process of undoing his jeans, but he zipped them back up before sitting on the edge of the bed. "What exactly is your next move?"

"I was actually hoping you might be able to help me with that." I pulled my knees up to my chest and hugged them to me.

Brueger jumped up on the bed, lying between me and Pan, and Pan absently scratched him as he gave me a quizzical look. "What do you mean?"

"Remember, weeks ago, when you visited me in the lysa?" I asked.

He smiled in a sly way, his skin slightly darkening, and I knew he was thinking of the rather intense kiss we'd shared within the confines of the psychic dream. "Of course."

"How did you do it?" I asked.

"Why?"

"That dream I had before, with the city collapsing in green fire, I think that might have really been a lysa. It was so real, and I remember it the way I remember a lysa, not all hazy the way dreams usually are."

"But who would be doing the lysa? It takes two," he said.

"I don't know exactly." I licked my lips. "I think it's the woman in the dream. The one in the dress made of flowers and the shawl of feathers. She kept telling me that I had to do something, but I don't know what I need to do."

"So you wanna do a lysa with her so you can ask what's going on?" he surmised.

"Exactly."

"But you don't know who that woman is?" he asked.

"Unfortunately, no, I don't."

He exhaled and stared off, thinking. "I am no expert on lysas, and I don't know if what you're suggesting is possible. But if it is, Dagny would be the one to know how to do it."

Forty minutes later, when I was back in my apartment and had finished explaining everything to Dagny, she sat silently on the couch, taking it all in.

"Okay," she said finally. "I think I can do that with you."

"Really?" Pan asked in surprise. He'd come back with me to find out what she would say.

"Yeah." Dagny nodded. "But I'll need help from both of you."

51

⚜

lysa

Clouds covered the sky, and the wind coming off the ocean had a bite to it, especially up here on the widow's walk at the top of the Mimirin institution. The narrow pathway ran along the length of the highest point of the roof, and it was maybe five feet across, with wrought-iron railings running along either side before the roof sloped sharply downward. Up here, we had a stunning view of the city of Merellä to the east and the Pacific Ocean to the west.

Thirteen towers protruded around the edges of the building, and atop each one was a glass atrium containing a solitary Ögonen. They stood tall and motionless, staring emptily at the far-off horizons.

I warily eyed the Ögonen, and their semi-opaque skin looked murky in the gray light. Dagny knelt down, writing on the tiles with the ashy end of burnt sage, and Pan took out the things we'd gathered for the lysa, all brought in the large wicker purse Dagny had.

I suddenly remembered the time a few years ago when Finn and Mia had taken me and the kids on a picnic up high in the bluffs. It had been quite the hike, and the air was cold

and windy. Finn had started a fire and we'd roasted marsh-
mallows, all crowded around together. To entertain the kids,
I had read from Liam's favorite book, *Dragons of Every Size*.

With the seven of us crowded around the fire—Mia was
pregnant with the twins at the time—Finn, Mia, and I took
turns doing voices of different mythical reptiles. Finn did the
gruff dragon with two wings and four legs, Mia, the excit-
able wyvern with two wings and two legs, and I took on
the smarmy wyrm with no wings and no legs. All the kids
stared up at us, laughing, their eyes big and wide and glowing from the dancing flames.

Their eyes looked much like those of the Ögonen, and the
warm memory suddenly went cold.

"Do we really have to do it up here?" I asked. I didn't exactly feel safe around the Ögonen, not since they kept giving
me horrific visions of spiders. Just being up here, I felt like I
could feel bugs crawling on my skin.

"Yes," Dagny replied firmly. "Normally, their cloaking
would dampen our attempts, but if we get close enough, and
we tweak a few things, we can use them to amplify your lysa.
This is especially necessary because you don't know who exactly you're looking for."

"But we can do it?" I asked nervously, and as she sketched
a few runic symbols on the tiles, I began to wonder if this was
a mistake.

"Lie down," Dagny commanded. "I want the top of your
head to rest against my knees."

I did as she said, and the cold from the tiles quickly seeped
through my sweater, sending a chill down my spine. It reminded me of the times Sunniva and the Ögonen had tried to
do memory recovery, and the burning agony that followed it.

I shivered at the thought of it, and Pan noticed and draped
the fleece blanket over me.

Dagny held crystals against my temples—twin violet fluorspar crystals that I'd spent the morning tracking down in the market while Pan had gotten the sour withania root juice I drank before we climbed up here. Dagny said it would take time for me to soak it all up.

"So," she said, "I need you to close your eyes, like you're going to sleep, and start imagining the setting. Once you've got a clear image, let me know, and then you need to project who you want to invite into the lysa."

"I don't know how to do that," I said.

"Yes, you do. All trolls have at least a tiny bit of psychic power," she insisted. "We can do persuasion, so we can project. Lysa is the same basic principle as persuasion, except that persuasion is a command and a lysa is a conversation."

"Okay." I closed my eyes and tried to envision a setting.

I chose the meadows in Sweden. Verdant green fields of bright wildflowers rushing up to meet the snowcapped mountain. It all felt so vast and infinite, like staring up at the starry night sky far away from the cities.

Despite the size, and even though I'd only been there once before, it felt familiar and safe. A lot like coming home.

"Ready," I said finally.

"Now just project," Dagny said.

I thought of her, the ethereal woman with her long wavy hair, and I tried to will her into the meadow in my mind. Slowly, the meadow grew around me, feeling more solid, more real. The grass tickled my ankles, and the sun warmed my skin. I could even smell the linnea flowers.

But the woman remained a ghost, a mere memory of when I last saw her.

"You need to *project*," Dagny repeated emphatically.

"Push out your thoughts," Pan clarified. "Like you're shouting in your mind."

I took a deep breath and tried again, picturing her in my mind and shouting for her. As I did, the world shimmered and bowed, and the sun seemed to shine brighter, haloed by a bright sun dog. The ground trembled underneath my feet.

And suddenly, she was there, standing on the other side of the meadow.

I ran toward her, excitedly yelling, "You're here! You're actually here!"

"You summoned me?" The wind blew her silken hair and ruffled the feathers that dripped around her shoulders.

"We needed more time to talk."

She turned, walking toward the mountains on the far side of the meadow valley, and the long flowered train of her dress dragged along the grass. "You didn't find my message clear?"

"Not really, no," I admitted as I followed her. "You said I needed to stop something, but you didn't tell me how. Or who you are."

"Oh, *binrassi*, isn't it obvious?" she asked with a weary smile.

"I'm sorry, but it really isn't." I stopped and let out a frustrated sigh. "Are you here to help me or not?"

She turned around and smiled more broadly at me. "That might be the first sensible thing you've said."

"You didn't answer the question."

"Yes." She stepped toward me. "I'm here to help. Do you remember what I told you?"

"That the world will burn if I don't stop it," I said, but she only stared at me, so I added, "And to follow the lone white elk."

She cocked her head, listening to a far-off rumbling. "To stop the world from burning, you must do as I say."

"Okay," I replied uncertainly.

"Do you hear that?" Her wide, dark eyes set on the horizon, toward the increasingly thunderous sound.

Before I could answer, she took off running toward it, and I chased after her. Over the rolling hills, I saw the antlers, and then the herd crested the hill. Hundreds of giant woolly elk with their broad velvety antlers; their massive hooves shook the earth. They curved across the land, rounding their way down into the valley, loping toward us.

"We should get out of the way," I said nervously.

"No." She smiled serenely. "We called for them."

"Why?"

"It's the only way." She stayed perfectly still, and the elk parted around us. The giant beasts trampled the earth as they flowed past us.

And then, walking slowly and towering over the rest, was the albino woolly elk. The cinnamon-red eyes were on me as he broke away from the others, taking cautious strides toward us.

I stepped closer, and when he lowered his head, I reached out, gently petting the coarse fur of his snout.

"What are you doing here?" I asked softly.

Pale, long lashes fluttered as the beast blinked at me, and then suddenly, he threw his head back and let out an ear-shattering bleat. He stumbled backward, and the rest of the herd scattered.

The white elk fell to the ground with a final, laborious breath, and that's when I saw the blood pouring from the underside of the animal, spilling into the ground.

The woman started laughing, cackling really. Both of her arms were soaked with blood. In one hand she held a massive dagger, and in the other she held the giant, still-beating heart of the elk.

"What did you do?" I screamed.

"I got what I needed." Her appearance shifted—her lips puffier, her eyes slightly smaller, and the hook-shaped scar appeared on her cheek.

The woman in the gown of flowers was Illaria, Eliana's twin sister.

"You were the only one the albino elk would come to, so I disguised myself as Senka and invaded your mind. You fell for it much faster than I thought you would."

"What have you done?" I felt dazed and sick, and the sky was crumbling around us. Clouds fell like meteors and crashed into the dirt.

Illaria just threw back her head as she laughed, and before my eyes, she disappeared into the air, letting hostile winds carry her away.

I collapsed to my knees, next to the body of the beautiful albino elk. Tears spilled down my cheeks as I petted his snout one last time. "I'm sorry." And then the lysa collapsed around me.

52

authority

"Calm down, Ulla," Dagny repeated. "You're not making any sense."

"Illaria was there, and she stole the heart." I pushed myself to my feet, and as I stared out from dizzying heights, all I could think of was the fear in the elk's eyes as it bled out. "They have everything they need. They're going to cross the bridge and open the entrance to Alfheim."

"How?" Dagny asked.

Pan stood beside me, and he put his hand on my arm. "What happened?"

"Illaria was there, but she was disguised as my mother," I said breathlessly. "I didn't know it was her."

"You know what your mother looks like?" Dagny asked.

"I don't." Tears were streaming down my cheeks—they had been since before I opened my eyes—and I wiped at them with trembling hands. "Illaria chose her image to mess with me. And then she ripped the beating heart from the elk, and when she vanished, she took the heart with her."

"How is that possible?" Dagny asked, more in awe than incredulous. "Are things in the astral plane able to transport in a tangible way to our world?" Her brow scrunched. "If the elk only existed there, the lysa could work as a conduit between the ethereal and the tangible. But that would require amplified power, more than . . ." She trailed off and looked to the Ögonen.

"She used the Ögonen to manifest the astral essence into a physical body," she finished, sounding slightly dazed. "They're powerful enough, or at least Illaria is powerful enough with them that she was able to literally pull what she wanted *out of thin air*."

"We have to warn someone," I said.

"Warn them of what?" Pan asked.

"The Älvolk have everything they need," I said. "They're going to cross the bridge and unleash something dark and terrible."

"Illaria knows that's what will happen?" Dagny asked.

"She *showed* me what will happen." I swallowed hard, trying to calm myself. "She wants the world to burn, and she enjoys torturing her sisters."

Pan studied me a moment, squinting into the wind, and he nodded. "I still don't fully understand what's happening here, but I agree with you that we need to talk to somebody about all of this."

Dagny had been kneeling the whole time, but she stood up now. "I'll call Elof."

"I was actually thinking we should take this up with someone with more military contacts," Pan told her. "I mean, tell Elof too. But this sounds like something that needs more . . . national defense." Something must've occurred to him because his expression changed abruptly. "Should I alert the human governments?"

"Not yet," Dagny said quickly. "It'd be a waste of time trying to convince them of something they might never believe, and if they do, there is the unfortunate likelihood that they would overreact and bomb all the kingdoms."

Pan sighed. "I want to argue with you but I can't."

"Then we should make some calls so we can see Amalie and Ragnall," Dagny said.

"We should get off the roof, and then figure it out." I hugged my arms around me, but it wasn't the cold that drove me off the Mimirin. As I turned and walked toward the spiral staircases, I could still feel the eyes of the Ögonen on me.

Pan used his key to let us into the Inhemsk Project offices downstairs, and we used the landlines to make calls. It took nearly an hour of scrambling and calling around, but Dagny finally managed to get Ragnall's assistant on the phone.

"Thank you," she kept repeating as Pan and I expectantly watched her finish up her call. "The good news is that Ragnall's agreed to a meeting in—" She paused to check her watch. "—in exactly thirty-nine minutes."

"What's the bad news?" I asked.

"He's willing to meet with only Ulla," she said.

I leaned back. "What? Why?"

"That seems strange, doesn't it?" Pan stood beside me, his hands on his hips.

"His assistant said he doesn't want to deal with a whole gaggle of us on a Sunday morning, and that he'd previously met with Ulla." She shrugged. "Make of it what you will."

"The important thing is he's meeting with one of us soon, and I need to make it count," I said. "What can I do to convince him to take this seriously?"

We spent the next half hour discussing different ways to approach the topic, things to highlight, phrasing to avoid to keep me from sounding like a maniac. All the prep work we did helped little in actually helping me feel prepared, though.

I went to the bathroom to freshen up. My makeup had

smudged from all the crying, and when I reapplied my eye-liner, my hands were still shaking. I felt sick to my stomach, and I wasn't sure I was up for any of this.

But time was running out, and someone had to do *something*. If that someone had to be me, then so be it. I would get it done.

I went up to Ragnall's office alone, with Dagny and Pan waiting in the Inhemsk office until I came back down.

He worked all the way up on the fourth floor, in the far southwest corner, and he always had a guard in a crimson satin uniform. While I waited for the guard to finish his security scan, I faintly heard voices from the Korva's office. A man and a woman talking indistinctly. Dagny didn't say anyone else would be here. Maybe Amalie or his assistant had decided to sit in.

The guard stepped to the side. "Go on in, Ms. Tulin."

I mumbled thanks and opened the door. It was a long rectangle of a room, with the entrance at one end and Ragnall's obsidian desk at the other. Windows gave a view of the ocean crashing at the cliff far below, and my footsteps echoed softly as I walked in.

Ragnall sat in the chair at his desk, while a young woman sat on the desk itself, facing him with her back to me. Her long dark hair was woven together in multiple braids, and she wore a cloak of cobalt blue. In her hand she held a vicious-looking weapon. It was a bardiche—similar to a spear with a wooden pole, but instead of the spearhead it had a long, curved battle-axe.

"Ah, our guests have arrived!" Ragnall said with his razor-sharp grin.

As I walked toward the desk, the young woman looked back at me, and I froze. She only appeared a few times in my recovered memories, but I recognized her instantly.

It was Tuva, the head of the thrimavolk, who had held me prisoner along with the sadistic Noomi. They were the exact ones I had been trying to prevent from being able to cross the bridge.

And she was with the man I had gone to for help in stopping her.

Ragnall rose to his feet, rebuttoning his suit jacket. "I see you still remember my daughter, Tuva Ragnasdottir."

"D-daughter?" I stammered.

"Her memory is resilient, but she's not great with words," another voice said with a short cackle of a laugh.

I'd been so stunned to see Tuva I hadn't noticed Illaria standing by the window.

53

BENEVOLENT

"What are you doing here?" I asked. I'd meant it to come out angrier, but the shock left my voice breathless and weak.

Illaria had been leaning against the glass, and her hair nearly matched the overcast sky—a steely gray. She smiled at me, and it had the disarming effect of making her look like an evil doll. Her bottom lip was fuller than the top, giving her wicked smile a pouty twist, and her big eyes were framed by long lashes.

When she stepped away from the window, coming toward me, her hair changed color to match the interior of Ragnall's office—first shifting to the rich brown of the Tralla leather chairs before landing on inky black to match the obsidian slab of Ragnall's massive desk.

"I already got what I wanted, or did you already forget that?" she asked coyly.

My mind flashed back to her arms covered in blood, and the pain in the big red eyes as the albino elk died before me.

"Fuck you," I growled, for real now, because my rage brought my strength back with it.

I lunged at Illaria, but she jumped out of the way like a damn grasshopper, and I slammed into the desk. It was hard enough that it went flying backward, and Ragnall dove out of the way in time to avoid being pinned against the wall.

Tuva wasn't quite as quick and agile as Illaria, but she still jumped up and landed on the desk with ease, riding it like a surfboard until it crashed into the wall.

I wheeled around and ran at Illaria, but Tuva jumped off the desk and landed on my back. In an instant, she had the stick end of the bardiche against my throat, pressed so hard I could barely breathe.

"Ulla, there's no need for this." Ragnall rounded us so he stood in front of me, and he was smoothing out his suit. "I meant for this to be a pleasant conversation."

"What the hell is going on?" I croaked out around Tuva's weapon.

I tried to push the stick back, and it started to give—I had to be stronger than her—but then she kneed me in the back, so hard I felt a white-hot pain shoot from my back and through my entire abdomen. I fell forward on my hands and knees, gasping for breath.

"We haven't even been properly introduced yet," he said.

I took a deep breath and fought back the angry tears stinging my eyes. I lifted my head slowly, and when Tuva didn't strike me with the stick, I sat back on my heels so I could look up at Ragnall.

"You know me as the Korva of the Mimirin Talo," he said with his dreadful smile. "But for a very long time, I have been the chieftain of the Älvolk. I am your father's boss and mentor."

Apparently, they really did believe that Indu Mattison was my father. Since I suspected that was something that might help keep me alive, I decided that now wouldn't be the best time to correct them.

"That makes you sort of like my uncle then?" I asked.

Tuva struck me in the side of the head with her stick, so fast and so hard I barely had time to register what happened. Everything flashed white, and I was dimly aware of Ragnall laughing, a bombastic sound that echoed off the stone walls. I blinked and looked up at him, and when I put my hand to my head, my fingers came back wet with blood.

"You're funny. You didn't get that from your father." Ragnall wagged his finger at me. "Indu's loyal, ambitious, and impressively devout, but he's never had much of a sense of humor."

"Did you invite me here to reminisce about my dear ol' dad?" I asked him.

His smile instantly fell, and he gazed down at me beneath his harsh black eyebrows. "No, I did not invite you here. You *begged* for an audience through your lackeys, and I allowed you to come up. You wanted this, but you are only here because of my benevolence. I want you to remember that."

My hair had fallen across my face and I brushed it back. "Why are you being so *benevolent*?"

Illaria snorted. "That is a good question."

"First, as a favor to your father, and then because you were useful," Ragnall answered. "But your usefulness has run out, and I consider any favors to your father repaid." He unbuttoned his suit jacket and crouched down to my eye level.

"I let you up here so I could tell you that it's over," he said, his voice firm, cold, emotionless. "I have been looking for a way to cross the bridge and return home for a very, very long time. You had an important role to play, which is why you're still alive. But your part is done."

"You can't cross the bridge," I warned him. Tuva hit me in the back of my head with the pole, but I had already gritted my teeth, preparing for it. I winced but I didn't fall forward this time. "There are dragons on the other side, and if you cross the bridge, you'll unleash them on this world. They will burn it down to the ground."

He laughed again, but it was completely devoid of any happiness or joy, and it stopped abruptly. As he looked down at me, scratching his eyebrow, he said, "I'm honestly disappointed that you fell for their lies. Until now I thought you were smarter than that."

I looked over at Illaria. "You know the truth. That the earth can't withstand the life in your world. That's what the Grændöden was. Áibmoráigi fell in a matter of minutes. The whole city and all the life within it."

"I don't care about this place at all," Illaria said. "Our mother's fondness for this stupid blue world was always her greatest downfall." She walked closer, so she stood just to the side of Ragnall, and sneered down at me. "I've been on the other side. I know the Älvolk will be revered like the gods they are when they return to claim what is rightfully theirs."

"Jem-Kruk and Sumi—" I began, but that's all that made it out before Tuva hit me in the head again. This time, gritting my teeth wasn't enough, and I blacked out for a second.

"—not say the name of the heretic and traitors," Tuva was saying as I blinked.

"It's dangerous," I said in a strained voice. "What you're doing. Lives will be lost."

"You don't know what you're talking about, Ulla," Illaria snapped. "You are just a stupid, spoiled girl."

"Our time for talking is done." Ragnall looked to Tuva, and she put the weapon to my throat again, pressing hard enough that I could hear it grinding against my trachea.

Ragnall straightened up, rebuttoning his jacket as he did. "It is over, Ulla. It's too late to stop any of this, and I have no reason to ever see you again." He looked down at me. "If I do, I will kill you. I have no more time or patience for these childish games."

54

EXILE

My head throbbed as I ran down the steps. Somewhere, I heard a door slam, and I glanced back over my shoulder. By the time I reached the Inhemsk Project main offices, I was out of breath, but I never slowed.

"Ulla!" Pan jumped up from his desk when I came in. "What happened?"

"Are you okay?" Dagny asked at the same time as Pan.

"Get your stuff." I leaned over, resting my hands on my thighs, and tried to catch my breath.

"You're bleeding!" Dagny gasped.

She stepped toward me, like she meant to inspect the wound on the back of my head, and I straightened up to deflect her concern.

"I'm fine, but we gotta go now," I said more authoritatively. "I'll explain later. But make sure you grab everything you want to see again. Shit. And Elof. He should come with us."

"Wait, are we being kicked out?" Dagny asked.

I shook my head and winced at the pain in my skull. "I don't know."

Pan, for his part, had been gathering up his stuff, and he came over to join me.

"Well, why else wouldn't we come back?" she asked.

"Because it's not safe!" I shouted, in fear and frustration. "Ragnall's the leader of the Älvolk, Tuva is his daughter, and they're working with Illaria to cross the bridge."

Dagny opened her mouth, then thought better of it and went over to shove her laptop in her bag. She got all of her things together in a hurry, and the three of us walked very quickly out of the Mimirin. I glanced back at the ancient building looming behind us, and I wondered if I'd ever see it again.

Pan took my hand, holding it as we walked through the winding streets.

"What are we going to do?" Dagny asked.

"I don't know. Ragnall said he'd kill me if he saw me again, and he and Illaria are dead set on crossing that bridge," I said. "I have to get out of Merellä, and we have to warn somebody that has the power to stop this."

"Well, you've got friends in high places," Dagny said. "Isn't Hanna's dad close to the Trylle Queen? And Bryn is the Kanin King's guard, right?"

When we got to the apartment, the three of us scrambled. Pan took the Jeep back to his place to load up his stuff and find pet care for Brueger, and Dagny took the landline first to call Elof. While she did that, I raced up to my loft to grab all the stuff that mattered most to me.

As Dagny candidly told Elof about the situation, I worried that Ragnall might be listening. But then I remembered the Ögonen were probably reading our minds, so it didn't matter. I had to assume that everything we said and did inside the walls of the citadel, Ragnall and the Älvolk knew about.

I wondered if Mästare Amalie knew the truth. Or had

she been duped by Ragnall like the rest of us? It didn't really matter right now, I supposed. There were far worse things to worry about.

Pan returned about five minutes before Elof showed up. Elof had only brought along a laptop and a satchel bag with some clothes.

"Elof, we're not coming back," Dagny reminded him as she forced her steamer trunk suitcase closed. When she finished, she carefully set her bow and arrows, safely stored in a leather quiver, on top.

"I've got what I need," Elof assured her, and patted his satchel. "Everything else is replaceable."

"Did you know that Ragnall was the Älvolk chieftain?" Pan asked him.

Elof shook his head. "No. I never had any indication. But he didn't interact much with me either. He seemed to have disdain for troglecology in general."

I slung my duffel bag over my shoulder. "Is everybody ready then?"

Dagny took one last forlorn look around the apartment. "Yeah. I think so."

We loaded up the Jeep, and Pan drove us out of Merellä. I closed my eyes and rested my head back against the seat.

"Don't you wanna see the city one last time?" Pan asked softly. The vehicle slowed, and I knew the guard post at the gate out of Merellä had to be coming up soon.

"No," I said.

Nobody else said anything more until we were beyond the walls, and the air felt easier to breathe.

The song had come back, a dull buzz gnawing through my killer headache. It wasn't at full volume yet, but it was enough that I knew it was the *enn morgana fjeurn on enn-sommora orn* playing on an infinite loop inside my skull.

"Now, why is it that we can never go back?" Elof asked, speaking deliberately. "I don't think I got the full breadth of the situation."

"The leader of the group that held us hostage and tortured us for a month is the leader of the Mimirin institution and basically the entire city of Merellä," Dagny said, her tone exaggeratedly flat and monotone. "He attacked Ulla and threatened to kill her, and he plans to open the bridge to hell."

"It's not hell," I corrected her, and I opened my eyes finally to see the thick forest of towering firs and hemlock trees surrounding us. "It's just somewhere different, a world we're not acclimated to."

I remembered reading about the bottom of the ocean in Mr. Tulin's nature magazines. The pictures made it look like a desolate hellscape with alien monsters. Like the angler fish with its horrific mouth of spiky teeth. I was terrified of the ocean after that, but Mr. Tulin told me that I needn't fear. Their world was a paradise for them and they were happy to be there.

"Just because their world isn't for us doesn't mean it's worth any less or any more than ours," Mr. Tulin said. "Life—all life—is worth something."

"We have half a tank of gas, and I'm heading east," Pan said. "Any ideas on where I should go?"

"My family's in Ningrava," Dagny said. "It's just a small Kanin village on Newfoundland island, but it's a fairly welcoming place. For a Kanin village."

"I have a home in Ondarike in Colorado. You're welcome to stay with me, if you'd like," Elof offered. "We can make a game plan from there."

"I'm going to Sweden," I said. "You all go wherever you like, but I need to go back to Áibmoráigi to stop the Älvolk."

"Ulla, you can't go up against them alone," Pan said incredulously. "We basically already tried that before, and it did not work out so well for us. We're not soldiers."

"I do *dödstämpel* and archery," Dagny interjected, referring to the intense form of martial arts she practiced for self-defense.

"That doesn't change the fact that the Älvolk held us in a cage for a month, and we couldn't get free," Pan said.

"I'm not planning to go alone." I looked down at my phone and the full service bars at the top. "I'm going to call Finn and then I'll call Bryn, and we'll get backup from the kingdoms. They need to stop this just as much as we do."

"I have contacts in the Vittra," Elof said. "They can lend a few troops, I'm sure."

Everyone was quiet for a minute. The way Pan's hand was twisting on the steering wheel, I knew he was especially anxious.

"Should I book flights to Sweden then?" Dagny asked.

I looked over at Pan. "You don't have to do this."

"You oughtta know better than that by now, Ulla," he said with a crooked smile. "We started this together, we finish this together."

I reached over and squeezed his hand.

"So four seats?" Dagny asked.

"Not exactly," I said. "Pan and I have to make a stop first."

55

Bolster

Even with the airboat speeding through the swamp, the wind wasn't enough to cut through the thick, hot air. It had been just over twenty-four hours since we left Merellä, and this morning, Pan and I split from Dagny and Elof at the airport. They went north to Sweden, and we went south to Louisiana.

"You still wanna go to the hotel and freshen up?" Pan asked, as Knut drove us on the Yggammi Tree Inn airboat.

"Yes, that's the first thing I have to do." My hair was up in a ratty bun, and the back of my neck was still slick with sweat. Not only did I feel super gross, but nobody at the palace would take me seriously if I came around demanding an audience looking like this.

"And then we're just gonna roll up to the castle and stroll on in and visit the Queen," Pan said, not hiding his unease. "That's the whole plan?"

"You're oversimplifying, but yes. The plan hasn't changed."

"And why are you certain this will work?" Pan asked.

"Because." I lowered my voice so Knut wouldn't be able to overhear. I didn't necessarily think that Knut was listening to us, but I was more paranoid since Ragnall's threats against my life.

Pan leaned in closer, his shoulder against mine, and quietly asked, "Because why?"

"I think she knows the truth." I looked over at him. "About who my father is. Or at least she suspects it."

His mouth opened as realization hit. "That's why she's keeping tabs on you."

"Yeah, that's what I think."

"But if she suspects . . ." He glanced back at Knut, and then he lowered his voice so much, I could hardly hear him over the fan engine, even with him nearly speaking in my ear. "You're a threat to her position and her son's. The Omte have absolute primogeniture succession. The firstborn child of the dynastic monarch inherits the throne, regardless of gender."

I shook my head. "My mother isn't Omte. I have no claim."

"Your mother wasn't," he agreed. "But Orra Fågel was. And you once thought she might be. It wouldn't be unreasonable to make the same connections you once did. But without the counterevidence that Indu and Elof gave you."

"*Alai*," I whispered. "You're right. She thinks I'm a claimant."

"You still think we should do this?" he asked.

I stared out at the swamp and the canopy of trees around us. My heart pounded hastily, as if trying to escape my chest, and my stomach convulsed.

"She hasn't threatened my life yet," I reasoned. "Unlike the man we're asking her to help us stop." I looked over at him. "We have to stop the Älvolk. This will help us do that."

At the hotel, we checked into our room. We just got one room this time, only partially to save money. My savings were gone, and Pan had just enough to get us to Sweden. After that,

I had no idea what we would do next, but I tried not to think about the fact that I was basically a homeless drifter now.

I didn't have time to worry though, at least not yet, and I hurried to shower and dress. Since my hair was still wet, I did a quick fishtail braid. For my eyes, I did bronze on the lids with a smoky liner, and I paired it with a maxi dress dyed like an ombré sunset.

Pan looked gorgeous in snug jeans and a burgundy dress shirt, but I hardly had time to notice it because we were out the door and on the way to the palace.

The guard at the door let us in, but he waited with us in the foyer while the butler went to see if the Queen Regent would see us or not. I had tried to plead my case, but he refused to listen to anything beyond my name.

We waited long enough that I had started counting the snails on the walls to keep myself from freaking out. Pan kept shifting from one foot to the other and sighing.

A door slammed somewhere deeper in the palace, followed by bare feet stomping loudly on the cold stone floors. Then she appeared at the top of the steps, already in her dressing gown, which I should've guessed, since it was after six P.M.

"Why do you keep coming back?" Bodil asked, sounding incredulous as she descended the stairs toward us. "Have I somehow mistakenly given you the impression that you have a standing invitation to my home? Because you do not."

"I need your help," I said.

She glared down at me, her arms firmly folded across her chest. "I am not a magic fairy here to grant you wishes. I am the ruler of an entire kingdom. Who in the hell do you think you are to ask anything of me?"

I glanced over to the guard, and then I looked back at

Bodil and tried to give her a knowing look. "Please. I promise this will be the last time I ask for your help."

Her nostrils flared as she glowered at us a moment longer. "I'll give you ten minutes, nothing more."

"Thank you," I said, but she didn't say anything more as she strode down the stairs in a huff, her long robe billowing out behind her.

When she reached the main floor, she turned and stalked down the hall, and Pan and I hurried after her. It was dark in her parlor, no lights at all, and the black-and-red stained-glass window let very little of the setting sun in.

I hesitated in the doorway until Bodil lit two kerosene lamps, bathing the room in dim, warm light. The painting of King Thor was so large, the top half of his head was still in the shadows. Bodil had gone to a drink cart at the back of the room, taking a lamp with her so it illuminated her shelves of bejeweled figurines and wolfram statues while she poured herself rose-colored liquor from a decanter.

While she did that, I stepped over to the painting to get a better look at Thor. At my father.

His hair was short, but it was the same color as mine. His eyes were different, but his smile—lopsided, like his full lips—was mine too. The picture was much larger than life, but he was obviously a huge guy, with burly shoulders and a thick neck.

There was something playful in his expression, and a knowing twinkle in his eye. He looked like the kind of man who loved life, and I wondered if, when he laughed, he threw his head back. I bet he had a loud belly laugh that could be heard all through the palace.

"Is *he* what you wanted to talk about?" the Queen asked. She stood just behind me now, and I looked over my shoulder to see her taking a long gulp from her glass.

I would've loved to ask her about Thor, to listen to everything she was willing to tell me about him. But the Queen had only given me ten minutes, and I couldn't squander it.

"No, I'm not here for that," I said.

She arched an eyebrow. "I suppose we should sit down then." As Pan and I went to the velvet love seat to sit, she said, "I'd offer you a drink, but I'm afraid you'd accept, and I don't want you staying long enough to finish it."

"Thank you for seeing us at such an inconvenient time like this," Pan said, attempting to defuse the tension. "We should never have asked this of—"

"Just get on with it," Bodil commanded.

"The Älvolk are doing something stupid and dangerous, and we need warriors to help us stop them," I said bluntly.

"Of course it's about the damned lost bridge," she muttered, and she took another long drink.

"They're going to cross it and enter Alfheim," I said.

"Let's make it short then: no." Her lips twisted into a bitter smile. "I won't help you."

"This isn't for us," Pan persisted, and he leaned forward, resting his arms on his knees. "This is for everyone and everything. The creatures that cross the bridge are not anything that this world can handle, and if they're allowed to roam free, thousands of lives will be lost."

"Thousands of lives are lost every single day." The Queen gave an empty shrug. "What do I care about anyone dying on the other side of the planet?"

"There's no reason to believe the death toll will stick to Scandinavia," Pan said. "An unstoppable monster would wreak havoc everywhere. Humanity's governments could turn to nuclear weapons, leaving devastating fallout."

"Sounds like humanity's got it covered then," she replied wryly.

I cleared my throat, and when she looked over at me, I said, "You should care about this because I care." She snorted at that. "You know who my father is."

She'd been about to take a drink, but she froze with the glass to her lips.

"We both know that I'll most likely never ascend the throne," I went on. "But I have enough evidence of a legitimate claim to make your life and Furston's very difficult."

Her eyes narrowed, and she slowly lowered her glass.

"Except, of course, I don't actually have the evidence on me," I said. "That would all be in the hands of Elof Dómari. You remember him, right? The Vittra Markis and the Mimirin docent? He plans to pursue a case with the Inhemsk Project, if I don't return from this trip. You know, in case you decided it's easier to kill your stepdaughter than parcel up your late husband's estate."

Suddenly, the glass shattered when Bodil clenched her fist too hard. Pan and I flinched away, but she was unfazed. She wiped the broken glass from her lap, and took a tea towel off her side table and wrapped it around her bloody hand.

"Ten of my soldiers," she said finally. "That is all I will spare." She looked at me, blinking slowly. "Now get the hell out of *my* palace."

56

Falling

When we got back to the hotel room, I went out onto the balcony, and watched as bearded vultures languidly soared above the treetops. Twanging rock wafted softly from the Ugly Vulture bar nearby, and the air buzzed with insects and wildlife. Even though it was late enough in the evening that the stars were coming out, it was still so hot, the air seemed to stick to my skin.

But I liked being outside anyway. Being able to see the amethyst sky, to hear the sounds of life, to feel the air around me. I leaned against the railing and pushed away thoughts of the Älvolk dungeon from my head.

The Omte palace reminded me a bit of that. The low ceilings, the darkness, everything smelling of must and decay.

Despite the heat, I shivered.

"Are you okay?" Pan joined me on the balcony.

His shirt was unbuttoned. He'd been undressing to change out of his nice dress shirt, but had stopped halfway through to check on me. My hands still trembled, and I let out a shaky breath.

"I'm okay," I told him with a weak smile. "I thought for

a minute that . . ." I swallowed back tears, and he slid his arm around my waist, hugging me to him. "I thought she was going to lock us up and throw us in the dungeon. I never would've forgiven myself if I got you pulled into that again."

"You took a risk to save the kingdoms," Pan said. "And we're not locked up. We're free, and we're okay.

"You did cash in the one and only favor you'll probably ever get from Bodil," he added after a long pause.

"I know, but it seemed like the only option," I said. "She wouldn't be swayed by anything other than self-preservation. And we need everyone we can get."

"Ten Omte soldiers are worth fifty from the other kingdoms," Pan said, repeating a common expression. But based on all the misinformation I'd learned about the Omte, I assumed that was a half-truth at best.

I leaned into Pan, resting my cheek against his bare chest, and I wrapped my arms around him. "I hope so."

"You are brave for going up to the Queen like that." He kissed the top of my head, and then, with his words nearly lost in my hair, he said, "I love you, Ulla."

Four simple words, and my whole body felt light and tingly. I had heard him say it before, in the memory, but that didn't lessen the way it felt hearing him say that.

I had never in my entire life heard anyone say that. At least, not anyone over the age of twelve.

Breathless and elated and warm and terrified and safe, but mostly I felt totally and completely in love with Pan. When I looked up into his eyes, so warm and dark like black tea on a winter morning, I knew that I loved him with every part of my being.

He put his hand on my face, his thumb caressing my cheek, and in a husky voice, I told him, "I love you."

He kissed me then, and I think he meant to be gentle, but

his fervor matched mine, and his hand pressed to the small of my back.

When we parted, I breathlessly confessed, "You told me that once before."

"Did I?" he asked in confusion.

"You did." I put my hand to his chest, suddenly worrying that I was doing the wrong thing by telling him. Or maybe I had done the wrong thing by not telling him sooner?

He tilted his head. "What do you mean?"

"When we were in the dungeon." I lowered my eyes, staring down at the exposed bronze skin of his chest, and I toyed with the collar of his shirt. "I remembered it when the Ögonen tried to recover memories. We kissed and . . . you told me you loved me. Before the spiders came."

He waited a beat before asking, "What did you say?"

"That I love you too."

"Why didn't you tell me about this sooner?" he asked in a quiet way where I couldn't tell if he was upset or not.

"I don't know. I felt like it wasn't my place . . ." I trailed off. "I mean, you didn't remember it, and maybe your feelings changed."

Pan laughed warmly, and then he put a finger under my chin, gently forcing me to look up at him. "Ulla, I was falling for you when we went to Sweden, and the only thing that's changed about my feelings is that I care about you more every day that I spend with you."

I kissed him then. My hand slid around the back of his neck, pulling him to me. His arms were around me, and I felt his hands through the thin fabric of my dress. We were moving but I hardly noticed until I backed into the window next to the balcony door. The glass was cool from the A/C in the room, and it sent a delicious shiver down my spine.

Pan was still kissing me, pinning me between his body and

the window, and I loved the way it felt—his body blocking out the rest of the world so it was only me and it was only him.

I knotted my fingers in his thick curls and arched my back to press myself against him as a heat intensified in my belly, and a small moan escaped my lips.

"Maybe we should go inside," Pan murmured.

"Let's go." I took his hand and led him into the room.

He ditched his shirt as soon as we were inside, and then we were kissing again. He fell back onto the bed, then propped himself on his elbows. I pulled my dress up over my head.

For a second, I stood in front of him, only in my bra and panties, so my pale, chubby body was completely on display. I fought the urge to hide all my exposed flesh with my arms, and when I saw Pan's eyes—dark and smoldering with lust and hunger—I stood taller. In that moment, I knew I looked as beautiful as I felt.

Pan reached forward, pulling me down onto the bed with him. His mouth was on mine, hungrily kissing me, as his fingers explored the tender parts of my body, and I moaned against him.

"I want you," I breathed.

In a flash, he'd slid off his pants and boxers, and I took off my bra. From the pocket of his pants, he pulled a condom out, and he hurriedly tore it open and slipped it on. He kissed me again, and his hand went down, looping his fingers through my panties to help me slide them down.

Finally, wonderfully, he eased himself inside me, and I moaned in relief. Quickly, he found a rhythm, and I dug my fingers into his back as he kissed my neck. We moved together until I felt the heat rising inside me. I bit my lip to keep quiet, and Pan moaned in my ear before covering me in kisses.

He collapsed on his back beside me and pulled me into his

arms, so I rested my head on his chest. He kissed the top of my head and rubbed my back.

"So," he said. "I know we talked about our relationship status before, but a lot of things have changed."

I laughed. "That's putting it mildly."

"And I know how you're feeling." He paused, taking a deep breath. "But I would like it if you were my girlfriend."

I looked up at him. "I think I would like that too."

He kissed me on the lips. Our hands were intertwined—my right and his left—and with my other hand, I absently ran my fingers through his hair.

"Jem-Kruk told me about this *álfar* word once," I said.

"What was it?"

"*Veloma* means the one you choose to be with," I said.

"*Veloma*," he repeated. "That has a nice ring to it."

"It does," I agreed. "But I'm very happy to be your girl-friend."

"And my *veloma*," he said, and then I pushed myself up so I could kiss him again.

57

The Ten

"Come on. The view up there is amazing." Pan smiled and extended his hand to me.

We'd been traveling from Louisiana for well over twenty-four hours, but even as exhausted as I was, I couldn't say no to the excited look on his face. I let him take my hand and lead me to the upper deck of the ferry.

When we'd been here before—one of the last things I remembered before the Lost Month—it had been misty and cold. Today it was sunny and fairly warm, although the upper fifties did feel rather chilly after the oppressive heat of Fulaträsk.

"You can see everything from up there!" Pan sounded exuberant as he led me up the stairs, and I had no idea where his energy came from.

But he wasn't wrong. From the top level of the ferry, we had stunning panoramic views of the dark waters of the Bay of Bothnia and the lush evergreen islands that populated it.

"*Alai*, it's breathtaking," I said in a hushed tone, and leaned against the metal railing that surrounded the boat.

"It really is," he agreed. Pan stood behind me, with an arm

on either side of me and his hands on the rail. "I knew you'd love it up here."

"Thank you for making me come up here to see this."

"I figured they could spare you for a few minutes," he said.

No sooner had he said that, than a loud commotion broke out on the lower level, and Pan groaned and dropped his head.

"The Ten," he grumbled.

The Omte Queen Regent had been kind enough to lend us ten "warriors," and the motley group had shown up at our hotel room on Tuesday night, and we'd been traveling with them ever since. It had not been easy or pleasant getting a sheltered, unruly bunch of trolls through three separate airport layovers, but we had somehow managed.

The Ten—as we had nicknamed the group—were Knut, the airboat bellboy with no military training; Benner, a sixteen-year-old guard in training; Jennet, a veterinarian and volunteer firefighter; Alfie, the middle-aged bouncer with anger issues; and several other equally qualified Omte citizens.

All of them could, at best, be described as having minimal training to fight a warrior cult and interdimensional monsters. But they were also better than nothing, so we'd have to make do with what we had.

"I should go down and make sure they don't break another chair," Pan muttered.

There had been an incident at the Newark airport, but fortunately, Jennet had powerful enough persuasion to convince the human security that there was nothing to see long enough for us to get out of there.

The ferry was the first time I'd been able to relax a little, since it was only trolls on board. The boat was open to humans, but September was off-season for tourism in northern Sweden, so most of the islands were closed up for the winter.

But even without human witnesses to worry about, I

didn't want them trashing the boat. Pan and I went back downstairs, where Knut was holding back Alfie, while Alfie pointed and swore at Jennet.

"You're losing it, Alfie!" Jennet yelled at him.

"You're a lousy *sliffa*!" Alfie shot back.

"Hey, *hey*!" Pan shouted, using the deep, authoritative voice he used as a peurojen to keep the giant woolly elk in line.

Everyone fell silent, and Alfie finally stopped struggling to get free from Knut's restraint.

"We are almost there," Pan said. "Can you keep it together for fifteen damn minutes?"

"What changes when we get to the island?" Alfie asked.

"What happens there is that I am no longer responsible for you all." Pan put his hands on his hips and surveyed the group of large Omte. None of them were ogres, but most of them were tall, muscular, and a tad overweight.

"Who is our commander?" Alfie asked, not for the first time.

"I still don't know yet," Pan said. "I'm going to hand you off to the Markis Ansvarig Patrik Boden. He's in charge of Isarna and their military, but I don't know if he's been appointed Överste or not."

In times of war, the Överste was the officer in charge of commanding the soldiers, although declarations of war and actual battle plans still needed to be decided by the King or Queen.

Pan and I had been in contact with Elof and Dagny as we traveled, so we had gotten some updates on how things were going, but they had also been very busy getting the army ready.

The trip across the bay had been clear and crisp, but as we approached Isarna, a heavy fog cloaked the island. The ferry went through the dense fog for a few minutes, and then it began to clear.

As the fog cleared, I saw forms taking shape. I recognized the big carriage and the two massive Tralla horses—a silver mare called Agda and her nephew, a dapple steed named Eldil. It wasn't until the ferry had almost docked that I noticed Dagny and Finn waiting for us.

Dagny waved and smiled on the dock, and Finn stood beside her, eying the Ten, who leaned over the railing and gawked at the island. I was so excited and surprised to see him that I shouted his name and ran straight off the boat down to him, and he hugged me tightly.

"What are you doing here?" I asked once he released me.

"After we talked on the phone a few days ago, I knew you needed all the help you could get," Finn explained. "Queen Wendy is getting the Trylle army ready, and they should be following soon. But I didn't want to leave you here alone for that long."

"I'm so glad you're here," I said, and then I turned to Dagny—who had been greeting Pan—and I pulled her into a hug. "Both of you."

"Jem-Kruk, Sumi, Eliana, and Sunniva came with Finn too," Dagny said. "But they're back up at the Öhaus with Elof and Patrik."

"Sunniva's here?" I asked in surprise.

"She thought you might need her help," Finn said.

"She's an intense chick," Dagny said, sounding impressed.

"We're taking any help we can get," Pan said.

"I'm sorry, I don't believe we've met," Finn said, turning to Pan.

"I'm Pan Soriano. I worked at the Inhemsk Project with Ulla."

"He's my boyfriend," I added, and slipped my hand into Pan's.

"*Finally,*" Dagny muttered under her breath.

Finn's eyebrows raised. "Oh." He was stunned for a moment, then smiled and shook Pan's hand. "I'm Finn Holmes, and Ulla has been like a daughter to me."

"She's told me all about you," Pan said, giving him a nervous smile.

"Are you the commander?" Alfie interrupted.

"I am the Överste," Finn said. "So yes, I suppose I am."

58

together

In the Öhaus in the center of Isarna, Finn and Patrik Boden were briefing everyone. The large main room was a museum of sorts, with display cases of artifacts and ancient tapestries on the walls. They had moved some of the displays to the side, and set up wooden folding chairs on the antique Swedish rugs, more than we needed for the group we had. Isarna had a small guard of less than thirty Trylle and Skojare, but Finn warned me that most of them weren't combat ready.

In addition to the Isarna guard, there were about a dozen volunteers, most of them far less equipped than the guard. Like an old Skojare fisherman, a couple Trylle farmers, and Minnie, the teenage girl that worked the Grand Bottenviken Hotel.

Plus the Ten we brought with us, and Pan, Dagny, Sumi, Eliana, Sunniva, Finn, Patrik, and me. About sixty of us altogether, and almost none of us prepared to take on a warrior cult.

I sat near the edge of the room, in between Pan and Dagny, and after a few minutes of Finn and Patrik talking,

I was slumped down, with my head on Pan's shoulder, falling asleep. I wanted to stay awake—what Finn was saying was important—but I hadn't really slept in the past day and a half, and my body basically passed out. Pan had managed to get a few winks on the flight, but I'd sat vigilant, in case the Ten acted up, though they'd ended up spending most of the flights snoring.

"Ulla," Pan said softly, rousing me from sleep.

"Ulla, get up," Dagny said, and her chair banged as she stood up, startling me awake.

"What happened?" I glanced around the emptying room and wiped my mouth in case I drooled.

"You slept through everything," she said, and held up a notebook covered in her delicate scrawling. "But I took notes, so I can go over it with you later."

"We thought you needed the rest more," Pan explained.

"Thanks, I think I did," I agreed sheepishly, and I stretched. "Where's everyone going now?"

"Everyone's free to do whatever they want until tomorrow morning," Pan said. "We're meeting here at five A.M. to suit up and make the long trek out to Áibmoráigi."

"So we're going right into it then?" I was wide awake now, and slightly terrified.

"Yeah," Dagny said. "Jem and Sumi remember how to get there, and we know that the Älvolk have everything they need to cross the bridge and enter Alfheim. It'll be easier if we can stop them before the murder monsters get through, and we really don't have much time."

"But it's just us going to fight the Älvolk?" I asked. "Nobody else is coming to help?"

"The Trylle and Skojare kingdoms are sending troops, but they take time to mobilize," Pan explained. "The other tribes haven't officially said one way or the other if they'll join."

"What about Bryn?" I asked. I had talked to her on the phone a few days ago, telling her all about the situation, and she said she'd get help, but I hadn't heard from her since.

Dagny shook her head. "I haven't talked to her."

"Ulla!" Eliana shouted as she burst in through the large front doors. She was grinning widely, and her shimmering blue hair hung down in a pair of braids, swinging past her shoulders. "There you are!"

I stood up as she ran over, preparing for her to hug me for the tenth time today. "I've just been here."

"Everyone's meeting at the bar at Grand Bottenviken Hotel," she said, and instead of going for a hug, she grabbed my hand. "Come on. You have to go too."

"Why? Is something wrong?" I asked.

"No, they're meeting for fun!" Eliana laughed. "Sumi called it the last drink before we die."

I frowned. "That doesn't sound fun." She laughed again, and I let her pull me away, with Pan and Dagny following more slowly behind us.

The last time I had been in Isarna, it was during the summer midnight sun. Now the sun set before eight P.M., and we walked to the hotel in the dim twilight with the roads lit by lampposts.

"I've felt a lot better since I've been here," she said as we walked. "Like I can breathe easier and think more clearly. My memories haven't been coming back at all, but I'm happier here, I think."

"Why do you think that is?" Dagny asked.

"Patrik said maybe because the air is cleaner," Eliana said.

"Hmm." Dagny didn't sound entirely convinced, and she looked around at the blue shops and fluffy pine trees that lined the road.

The Grand Bottenviken Hotel was up ahead. It was a

charming lodge that attempted to marry the Skojare and Trylle communities in its design, with cornflower blue ship-lap and flowering vines winding over it.

When we'd been here before, it hadn't exactly been de-serted, but business was slow. Now it was packed.

Off to the right of the nautically themed lobby, the hotel had a restaurant with a bar. It was a long rectangle of a room with green and gray *gädda* fish mounted behind the bar. One wall was a large picture window, framed with blue stained glass, that had a view of the dark bay. A bench ran all the way down the interior wall, allegedly made from the wood of an old Skojare Viking ship, with tables and chairs, and the rest of the room was all pub tables and bar stools.

I managed to find a spot on the bench with Eliana beside me, and Dagny sat down across from us while Pan went to get us some drinks at the bar. I knew most everyone in the bar, or at least recognized them from the Öhaus briefing. Patrik and Finn were noticeably absent, but I suspected Finn was video chatting with the kids before going to bed.

That was probably what I should be doing, and I would—soon. But with everything that was about to happen, I wanted to spend some time hanging out with my friends, because I didn't know if I'd be able to do it again.

Eliana linked her arm through mine and rested her head on my shoulder. "I'm so glad you're here. Jem and Sumi don't talk to me about everything."

"Are they here?" Dagny asked.

"Yep," Eliana said.

Across the room, I spotted Jem. He was laughing at some-thing Knut said, his dark eyes twinkling and his long dark waves flowing free. Sumi wasn't too far from him, sipping a drink and leaning against the window. She surveyed the crowd with a look that reminded me of an especially snobby lioness, and when she locked eyes with me, she stalked over to join us.

"Oh no, she's coming over," Eliana complained.

Sumi stopped at the table but she didn't sit down. "I thought you might sleep through this too."

"Hey, it's been a *long* . . . summer," I said, and the truth of the statement hit me all at once. "It seriously has been one long-ass summer."

"The good news is that it's going to end with a bang," she said with a wry smile.

"You strike me as the brutally honest type." Dagny looked up at Sumi, who just shrugged in response. "What do you think our chances of surviving tomorrow are?"

"Well, the Älvolk and the thrimavolk have been train-ing for this exact scenario for generations, and if a large enough *etanadrak* gets through, it could easily take out half our fighters." Sumi took another drink. "But this is the only chance we have to stop them so . . . we must fight tomorrow. Tonight we drink and pray that the gods fight with us."

Then she drained her glass. "I should get another."

"Ugh," Eliana groaned after Sumi left. "She's always like that."

"You say that like it's a bad thing," Dagny said, watching Sumi walk away. "Maybe I should get a drink."

She got up and went after Sumi, while Eliana remained glued to me. Pan joined us a moment later, taking Dagny's seat and setting cranberry juice in front of me.

"Did I miss anything?" he asked.

"Sumi told us we're all doomed," I said with a crooked smile, and he nearly choked on the drink he was taking.

"You," someone said, and I looked over to see Sunniva Kroner pointing at me. "You, I know." I hadn't talked to her since she recovered my memories in Förening.

"Hey," I said. "How are you?"

She shrugged and sat down in the chair next to Pan. "Fine except I don't know anybody here. It's weird having your last hurrah with strangers."

"You know Ulla, and you met me," Eliana said brightly. "And that's Pan. We're not strangers."

"Fair enough," Sunniva replied with a slight smile.

"I hope you don't take this the wrong way, but I'm surprised to see you here," I said.

She lowered her gaze, and her long, slender fingers absently toyed with a napkin on the table. "Aural healing isn't the only thing I can do. I also have something else known as auditory precognition."

"You can hear the future?" Pan asked uncertainly.

"Not all the time, but yes, sometimes I hear snippets of the future. I can't control what or when or anything about it," Sunniva explained. "What I've been hearing the last few days is fire and the earth rumbling." She licked her lips and then looked up at me. "And I hear you, shouting my name."

"I'm shouting for you?" I asked.

She nodded. "I don't know why, but I feel like I'm supposed to be here. That you need me here for something. So here I am."

"Thank you for being here," I said. "I don't know what I'll need you for yet, but we're happy for all the help we have."

Eliana changed the subject after that, suddenly quizzing Sunniva about the color of everyone's auras. Dagny had silvery white ("she's all honesty and hard work"), Eliana's was a vibrant lavender ("a confused hopeful daydreamer"), Pan's was cheery green ("except for when he's around Ulla, then it goes all pink"), and mine was still murky orange and bright yellow ("your optimism is trying to push through the damage that's been done").

Pan and I stayed down there a half hour longer, chatting with our friends old and new, and then we slid away up to our room.

We hadn't been up there long, maybe fifteen minutes. I had only just changed into my pajamas, and Pan was brushing his teeth in the bathroom, when someone knocked at the hotel room door.

"Hi, sorry for bothering you," Sunniva said. "But I was talking to Eliana and . . . Can I just come in? I think I need to do something for you."

59

summer bird

"You're sure this isn't dangerous?" Pan asked again. He stood to the side of the room, his arms folded, as he watched Sunniva and me with trepidation.

Sunniva knelt at the headboard of the bed, and I lay on my back with my head at her knees.

"I never said that," she reminded him. "I said that since the Älvolk aren't blocking this particular memory, it shouldn't be difficult or painful recovering it."

When Sunniva had gotten here, she'd told us about the conversation she'd had with Eliana. Eliana was telling Sunniva all about how we were sisters but neither of us could remember our parents.

"For different reasons, obviously," Eliana had elaborated. "Mine because the Älvolk messed with my mind so my memories are all bappers. But Ulla's is because she was only a baby when she was taken away."

As soon as Eliana said that, Sunniva explained, she'd had another of her auditory precognitions. The fire and rumbling and me shouting her name was only one of them.

"I think I'm supposed to help you remember your mom,"

Sunniva had finally told us. "I know you can't remember being a baby, but your brain was still there, recording everything. It's hidden away by natural barriers, your mind's own
processes, and that is much, much easier to circumvent than
the Älvolk's magick."

That's how I ended up on the bed with Sunniva, with Pan
pacing apprehensively. The process was different this time,
because Sunniva wasn't using her abilities to repair the damage the Älvolk had done, but rather to make a connection
between latent memories and my conscious mind.

She put her index fingers on my temples and stared down
at me. Her black hair was pulled into a thick braid, and her
dark eyes were framed by long lashes. Multiple pairs of spar-
kling earrings were in her ears, and I stared at them instead
of meeting her intense gaze.

"Stop that," Sunniva commanded.

"What?" I asked.

"Averting your gaze. I need to look into your eyes."

"Sorry," I mumbled, and looked up at her.

"Should I run a cold bath?" Pan asked.

"You can do whatever you want as long as you stay quiet,
okay, buddy?" Sunniva asked, not bothering to mask her an-
noyance at all.

"Sorry," he said sulkily, and I heard him sit back in the
chair, while I stared up at Sunniva the way she commanded.

Her eyes were nearly black, with inky lines spiraling
through her irises. And as she looked at me, I swear they
started to move. Pulsing subtly but hypnotically, and it was
like a black ocean rushing for me.

*Then I was gasping. My throat felt raw from crying. The
darkness around me finally broke with a painfully bright light,
but all the shapes were blurry. Then a blob of amber came toward me, breaking up the monotony of gray.*

"Shh," a woman's voice cooed, and instinctively, I knew it was her. My mother.

Her face came into view, and she was close enough I could see her more clearly, though she still had a warped quality to her, like I was looking through a foggy pool up at her.

She looked just as she had in my lysa, when Illaria had taken her form. Her hair was very long and wavy, and she wore it with a waterfall braid woven through it. Her dark eyes were large and bright, and they were almost hyper vivid.

"Hush, my binrassi," my mother said. Her voice was low but warm and sweet, like summer tea sweetened with honey and milk. But there was a nervous undercurrent to it, and I noticed the panic in her eyes.

A door cracked open, and she cast a fearful look back over her shoulder. Her breath caught in her throat, then she whispered, "My love. I didn't think you'd be able to get away."

"I had to make time." The man's voice was low; I felt it rumbling through me like bass. He sounded pained, but there was a softness underneath that felt familiar and safe. "I couldn't let my daughter leave without saying goodbye."

And then he was there, towering over us. My father, Thor Elak, seemed just as large as he had in his portrait hanging in the Omte palace. He was broad and burly and at least a foot taller than Senka. His eyes were wide and kind, and they were the same color as mine.

He reached down, gently stroking my cheek, and he smiled sadly as he said, "Goodbye, my Princess Violetta."

"What if Indu sees you here?" my mother asked, and put her hand on his thick biceps.

"He didn't. I made sure of it." He spoke to her, but his attention was focused on me. When I squeezed his finger, tears formed in his eyes.

"Are you sure this is the right thing?" Senka sounded desperate now.

Thor turned to her and put his meaty hands warmly on her shoulders. He bent down, so he was closer to her eye level. "Senka, we've gone over this. I love you, and I love the baby, but we can't be a family right now. It's not safe for her."

"If we wait longer, until she's old enough to make the trip back to Alfheim—" She was pleading with him but he cut her off.

"Indu will realize she's not his daughter," my father said calmly but firmly. "She has my eyes, Senka, and she's a strong Omte baby. He's going to know, and he's going to kill her."

"You're strong and you're King!" Senka argued. "You can stop him."

"I can stop him, but I can't stop all of them," he said. "And Helge won't approve sending any more troops. I need to go back to Fulaträsk and get my kingdom to loosen the purse strings. But you and the baby need to be safe first."

She looked up at him and put her hand to his face. "But is sending Violetta away safe?"

"Orra is my most trusted guard, and she's practically family," he said. "She'll take the baby far, far away, and she won't leave her until she knows she's safe. You'll stay here to placate Indu until I can return with the troops."

Her lips quivered. "What if he doesn't let the twins go? He has Illaria with him always."

"When I come back with the troops, I'll make sure we get the girls to safety," Thor promised her. "And once everyone is free and safe, I will be able to end my engagement with Bodil, and then we'll get the baby, and we'll be together as a real family—me, you, Illaria, Eliana, and Violetta."

They kissed then, even with Senka crying. "I am trusting you that this is true."

"I'll never stop trying to reunite with you," he said. "I love you more than I love myself, my kingdom, my world."

She smiled up at him. "I love you, my summer bird."

"And I you, my morning flower."

I started fussing, and they both looked at me. My mother picked me up, and she held me in her arms with tears streaming down her cheeks.

"Orra will be here soon to get the baby," my father said, putting an arm around her.

"I know." Senka sniffled. "This is probably the last time the three of us will be together."

"For a while," Thor agreed in his warm rumble. "But not forever. Not for long. I'll get the army we need to properly deal with the Älvolk. Then I will come for you, and we will get the girls and live freely, happily ever after."

As I looked up at my parents, embracing each other as they held me, a fat spider dropped down from the ceiling. It landed in Senka's hair, and I started crying; wailing actually.

"Shhh," my mother said, but the spider was still there, crawling in her hair.

"Hush, little one," my father said, and put his big hand on my head, trying to comfort me.

But still I cried, watching the spider climb from her hair and onto his shoulder.

"Maybe she knows." Senka's voice was soft and thick. "She knows we're sending her away." She looked at Thor, frantic. "I could take her to Alfheim. There's a way that you can cross the bridge. Indu is looking for an enchanted recipe. It will allow anyone who eats it to enter Alfheim. It may take some time, but you could find it, and you could eat it and join us."

"I would join you tomorrow if I could," Thor said. "But is the land where you've slain monsters with poisoned arrows, the place you already fled from with your young daughters after their father was killed, is that where you want to bring our infant?"

"She won't be a baby, not by the time it's safe for her to cross the bridge." Senka was crying again, and the fat spider crawled off my father's arm. I could see the fangs as it came toward me.

"We will find a way to be together," he promised her again. "But now Violetta must go into hiding. Orra is here."

And then, somehow oblivious to the spider biting into my cheek, my mother fiercely said, "My love, you must remember—only together can we slay the monsters that chase us."

The door opened, and Orra Fågel slipped into the room. She was nearly as tall as Thor, with ruddy cheeks and honest golden eyes.

"Are you ready, my lord?" she asked him.

"No, but there isn't more time, is there?" Senka asked through her tears.

"No, there isn't," Orra said, her voice firm but sympathetic.

"Here." Thor pulled a weapon from his waistband—a wolfram dagger with a bronze hilt and the Omte sigil of vultures. "This is the weapon of a warrior. Use it to protect my daughter and protect yourself."

"I will," she promised him. She sheathed the weapon, and then she took me from my mother and fled with me into the night.

60

EN MASSE

In the darkened room, Pan held me in his arms, even though I had stopped crying a while ago. After Sunniva had finished helping me with the memory, I was a blubbery mess.

For the first time in my life, I *saw* my parents, and I felt how much they loved me. How much hope they had for the future. They truly believed we'd all be together again.

But I knew how their story ended. Orra left with me, and they never saw me again. My father died twelve years later, and my mother returned to Alfheim, where she stayed until she died. I didn't know if they ever even saw each other again.

"How are you doing?" Pan asked, when I'd been silent for a while. He stroked my hair back from my face, and I rested my head on his chest.

"I don't think I'll know the answer to that question for another week at least." I sighed. "I don't know. But I just keep thinking of what my mother said."

"That only they can stop the monsters that chase them?"

I tilted my head to look up at him. "We have to be prepared

for that. We need to tell Finn to make sure that the arrows are tipped with *sorgblomma* poison."

"Sumi and Jem should know about that," Pan said. "We'll talk to them in the morning."

"Why do you think my parents didn't see the spider?" I asked.

He exhaled loudly. "I have no idea. I mean, I didn't see the memory."

"Yeah, I know, but . . ." I paused, thinking about why the spider had bothered me so much. "Spiders make me think of the Ögonen. They chased me out of the catacombs with spiders, and my memory filled with spiders when the Ögonen tried the aural healing."

"Are you saying that you think they implanted a spider in the memory Sunniva just showed you?" he asked—not so much dubious as confused. "Why would they do that? And *how* could they do that out here? We're so far from the Mimirin."

I sat up and looked down at him. "The Älvolk have Ögonen helping to mask their location. And someone told me that they have a hive mind."

"So wait." He scooted so he was sitting up with his back resting against the headboard. "Why are they putting spiders in your memories?"

"I don't know if they're trying to tell me something or scare me off." I shook my head. "Maybe it's a warning."

"You think they're warning you that a monster is coming?" he asked.

My breath came out short. "What if they are?"

Pan ran a hand through his hair. "Why? Why warn *you*?"

"Because I was nearby? Because I'm Omte so I can handle the aural healing better? Because I'm half-*álfar*?"

"Dammit." He glanced over at the alarm clock on the nightstand. "Elof's probably asleep now. We'll have to wait until the morning to talk about the Ögonen with him."

"And we should get some sleep." I sighed and lay back down, resting my head on his chest again. "Or try to, anyway."

He wrapped his arm around me, and I snuggled deeper against him. I tried not to think about the terrifying things crashing around us. And even as tumultuous and frightening as things were, being with Pan did make it easier. In his arms, I felt like his love could protect me from everything.

Deep in the logical part of my mind, I knew that wasn't true. Love hadn't been enough to protect my parents—or *me*—from harm, and it wouldn't protect us now.

But I managed to fall asleep quickly, and morning came too soon. It was still dark when we got dressed and headed down to the hotel restaurant to meet with everyone.

Over harsh nettle tea and stale pastries, I told Finn, Elof, Dagny, and Sumi about the memory of my parents. The most pertinent bit seemed to be the arrows, and Finn immediately set about getting the very limited *sorgblomma* supply to tip our weapons.

"Sumi and I were up late trying to figure out a way to do the *leat fámus* en masse," Elof explained with a suppressed yawn. "We think we got it now."

Áibmoráigi was protected by such a thick cloaking spell that even trolls couldn't see through it. The entrance to the city looked like it was blocked by a giant boulder, but the Älvolk and thrimavolk alike had a powerful and painful incantation that allowed us to see through the spell. It was called *leat fámus,* and Sumi was capable of performing it.

But there were nearly fifty of us going to Áibmoráigi, and it would take a very long time for her to do it to everyone.

Not to mention that doing the *leat fámus* fifty times in a row could be very draining and likely damaging to her.

"Have you tried it yet?" Pan asked. He sat beside me, his arm on the back of the bench behind me. Elof and Dagny sat across from us, with Sumi sitting at the corner with her feet propped up on Finn's now empty chair.

"On a small scale," Elof said tentatively.

"Two drunk townies and that fella named Knut," Sumi amended, and sipped her tea.

"But it's impossible to know if it works until we get to Áibmoráigi," Elof clarified.

"So how do you do it?" I asked.

"I channel Eliana," Sumi said.

I shook my head. "*What?*"

"*Álfar* blood has unique properties," Sumi said. "It has an amplifying effect on our supernatural abilities, but its potency fades with time. So Eliana is more effective than Jem."

"Wait, are you stealing her blood?" I asked in horror.

Sumi snorted. "No, of course not. I just hold her hands."

"And you think that will work?" Pan asked.

"We hope it does," Elof said.

61

summit

Patrik had arranged the transport, a series of Mercedes Sprinter fifteen-passenger vans. They were more luxe than we needed, but they held all of us in four vehicles, so it worked.

Pan, Jem, Sumi, Eliana, and I joined the Ten in their van, and Sumi drove because she knew the way best. It was a long drive across the Swedish landscape. Eliana sat in the back, chatting up the Ten, but eventually, even she ran out of things to talk about, and the van fell into silence.

At some point in the afternoon, when the road had been long but there was still a long way to go, and we were all getting restless, the Omte among us had to do something to pass the time.

Knut started first, low and slightly tremulous, then Jennet joined in, harmonizing with him, singing an old Omte folk song.

Sing, sing the heroes
The worm is full of flowers
Hush, hush the morning light

Down falls the darkest night
And now the end is ours.

They had stopped singing before we reached Lake So-dalen, which is when we left behind the vans and switched to traveling on foot, but the haunting melody lingered with me on the long trek across the valley and up the mountain-side. It was a hard journey for all of us, but Elof especially struggled, and I carried him most of the way up to Áib-moráigi.

As we rounded the summit of the snowcapped moun-tain, the path growing more narrow and treacherous, Eliana slipped once, and her heavy pack threw her off balance. Pan saw and grabbed her arm, just in time to catch her before she tumbled miles to her death on the rocks below.

"How much farther?" Pan asked.

"Just around the bend," Sumi said without slowing as she led the way.

The path widened a few yards before the giant boulder blocking the path, but it was still only wide enough for two or three of us to stand shoulder to shoulder. Sumi crouched down in front of the boulder, then summoned Eliana to help her with the *leat fámus*. Everyone else waited in a long line behind us.

"The boulder isn't really there, right?" Pan asked.

Sumi and Eliana crouched down facing each other, and Sumi didn't break eye contact with her, even when she an-swered Pan, "It's not and yet it is. It disappears like mist but you cannot pass through, even when you know the truth."

"How are you going to make it so we all can go through?" Dagny asked, hovering just behind Sumi.

"I will do it the way it is done." Sumi cast an irritated glare toward us, and then she looked back into Eliana's big doe eyes.

"Will it hurt?" I asked, remembering how my skull felt like it was going to explode when Indu did the incantation on me.

Sumi put her hands on Eliana's face, so her thumbs were over Eliana's eyes and her pointer fingers were on the temples. "Yes, it will." And then quietly, Sumi said, *"Leat fámus."*

It was like being cracked in the head—a quick but blinding pain. I heard others crying out, and I leaned back against the mountain face, steadying myself on the rocky wall.

When I opened my eyes, with the pain already just a dull ache, the boulder was gone. The grassy plateau was covered in the ruins of a civilization. Crumbling structures of stone and iron had mostly been taken back by nature, with weeds overgrowing and birds nesting in the remains of a tower.

I hadn't heard anything a few moments ago, but since the *leat fámus* had removed the boulder and cloaking, now sound could travel through. And now I heard it, the haunting choir singing the *enn morgana fjeurn on ennsommora orn.*

While the others gathered themselves as the pain subsided, I slid past Sumi and knelt with Eliana, her eyes tearing and her hair rippling through every vibrant hue of the rainbow.

"Is she all right?" Elof asked, sounding concerned, and I was dimly aware that I should be worried too. Eliana had collapsed, others were still groaning in pain, and I had no idea how the Ten had handled the *leat fámus.*

And deep down, the fear was there, the urge to stay and listen as Sumi explained that the incantation took a lot out of Ellie but she would recover soon. But the song was calling me, pulling me into Áibmoráigi.

As I walked through the ruins, winding between the tall grass and broken-down shells of homes, I heard someone shouting my name, but I didn't stop. Not until Pan grabbed my arm, and then I whirled around to face him.

"Where are you going?" he asked, and put a gentle hand

on my face. "Are you okay? You're walking like you're in a trance."

"Yeah . . ." My voice sounded far away and I shook my head. "I was following the song."

"You're best not going alone," Sumi said as she joined us. Dagny followed a few steps behind her, her bow and quiver of arrows strapped to her back.

Behind them, I saw Jem standing with Eliana, whose hair had finally settled into her natural chartreuse. Finn was near them, getting the troops into formation.

"Why are they singing?" Dagny asked.

"I don't know." Sumi scanned the ruins, her lips pursed and her hand hovering above the weapon sheathed on her hip. "They never sang up here when I lived here. The children are hardly even allowed on the surface."

"We shouldn't wait," I said with a certainty I couldn't explain. "It's happening now."

"What?" Dagny asked incredulously. "How do you know?"

I slipped out of Pan's grip. My Omte strength meant that I could easily overpower him, so instead of wasting time fighting, he fell in step beside me and let me lead him through the crumbling remains of Áibmoráigi's glory days.

As we walked, I remembered flashes of the lysa Illaria had shown me. *The walls falling, the smoke blotting out the light, the men, women, and children running as they screamed in terror. The air smelled of sulfur and blood.*

At first, I had thought the lysa was showing what I needed to prevent. But now I understood the truth was far darker. Illaria was taunting me, showing me the horror she was about to unleash on the earth, because she didn't think I could do anything to stop it.

The song echoed off the mountains, and I hurried toward

the stable. It was a large building, weathered and worn, but not overgrown or a pile of rubble like everything around here.

As we approached—Pan, Sumi, Dagny, and I—slinking along the walls, I noticed a strange buzzing. And then I saw the dark cloud of flies swarming around bleeding elk hides, still with clinging hunks of meat and fat and bits of bone. So much blood that the grass had become a sanguine swamp outside the main doors.

At the edge of the growing pool of blood, I paused to see the carnage inside the dimly lit stables. The corpses of the great giant animals were piled all down the corridor. Some of them still had the skins on, others' skins were partially removed. Broken antlers, shattered hooves, a long tongue in a puddle of fur in bile littered the floor.

They'd slaughtered their entire herd.

Pan had only peeked into the stable before dry-heaving, and Sumi was ashen and cursed under her breath after she saw it.

"She should move on," Dagny suggested as she swatted at flies.

Pan wiped his mouth with his shirt, and I took his hand. He walked more slowly, still in shock over seeing the majestic animals he'd cared for as a peurojen butchered in such a violent way.

"Are you sure we should find them? After what they did?" he asked in a low, thick voice.

"The suns will set in the green sky when the good morning becomes the violent night," I answered darkly.

Sumi looked sharply at me. "What did you say?"

"Hush," I said, because as we rounded the collapsing tower, I finally spied them.

The Älvolk and thrimavolk were surrounding an unusual turret-shaped gazebo. All of the walls were open, to the cauldron and large pit in the center. The roof was tall and shaped like a teardrop, with a point at the top and curved eaves at the bottom, and it was covered in scalloped crimson tiles.

62

temple

Beneath the temple, a cauldron boiled over an angry pit of fire. The bloodred flames licked at the iron cask, and above it, flat tins simmered on a grate, their maroon contents curdling over the sides.

The Älvolk and thrimavolk circled around the temple. The men and boys knelt in the closest circle, the choir of younger girls in the second, and the young women brandishing weapons in the outermost ring.

The Älvolk wore kaftans of red, and the choir wore kaftans of marigold. Their hair hung in twin braids, and they wore crowns of reeds and *sorgblomma* flowers. Behind them, the thrimavolk wore uniforms of cobalt that were more fitted, with breastplates made of elk hide and bones. Bold slashes of cobalt were swiped across their eyes.

Ragnall emerged from the crowd, and he grabbed the tins from the fire, unbothered by the hot metal searing his skin. In a booming voice, he shouted an incantation I couldn't understand and raised the blood pudding over his head.

"No!" I shouted, and Noomi snarled at me from across the circle.

Ragnall faltered, but only for a moment, then he plunged his bare hand—blistering skin and all—into the tin and brought a handful of the gelatinous muck to his mouth.

I ran toward him but Noomi rushed me, hitting me with a bardiche. The first time, the stick connected painfully with my shoulder, with the blade of the axe just nicking my skin, but the second time, I caught it before the blow hit. I yanked it from her and broke it over my thighs, but Noomi charged at me again.

I punched her—hard enough that my knuckles split—and she collapsed back on the ground. Sumi knocked Tuva back, and Dagny set her bow only to be thwarted by Indu.

Finn shouted behind me, and I looked back to see him arriving with the small army. The thrimavolk charged at them head on. The younger children screamed and scattered, as did some of the Älvolk, but the rest of them clamored toward the cauldron to get their hands on the boiling blood pudding.

I dodged another stick attack and lunged at the cauldron. The hot iron burnt my skin, but I easily tipped it over, covering the earth with boiling blood and spilling the tins of pudding.

The flames exploded in a black smoke, and I jumped back out of the way and fell in the dirt. I saw a man reach for a tin that fell in the fire, howling as the flames ate his flesh.

"I should've killed you when I had the chance," Indu growled, and I looked up at him just as he pressed the tip of his sword against my throat.

And then Pan was there. He grabbed Indu by the throat and threw him back against the temple wall. With his other hand, he took Indu's arm and bent it back until he dropped the sword.

"Don't ever touch her again," Pan spat at him.

Indu looked at me over Pan's shoulder. "I brought you into this world, and I will take you out."

I got up and sneered at him. "You're not my father, you worthless worm."

His eyes widened, and then Knut came crashing through the wall as he tackled a pair of thrimavolk warriors.

I grabbed Pan, pulling him out of the way so he wouldn't be buried under wood and fighting trolls, the way Indu was.

The ruins were in chaos. Sumi and Dagny were lost in the fray, and I had no idea where anybody else was. It was a blur of bodies running—the bright colors of the thrimavolk and Älvolk, the subdued greens, browns, and pale blues of the Trylle, Omte, and Skojare.

Pan and I leaned back on the exterior of the half-broken wall, and I tried to catch my breath. I was strong, but I had never been in a real fight before, let alone a battle. What little preparation I had gotten in beforehand had hardly been enough.

Then, through the crowd, I saw him running away. Ragnall Jerrick was taller than most—other than some of the Omte—and he had a bloody handprint splattered on the back of his shaved head. He was escaping from the mess he'd created here and going for the bridge.

I couldn't see the bridge from where I was—the plateau of Áibmoráigi curved slightly around the mountain, and that's where it connected with the bridge.

—as I had once before, when I followed the white elk through the ruins and Illaria found me at the waterfall—

I couldn't let Ragnall cross the bridge or enter Alfheim, so I raced after him. Someone dove at me, but I ducked out of the way, and I punched another Älvolk soldier and pushed him to the side.

I ran faster than I ever had before. My lungs burned, and

I pushed myself as fast as I could, and I was managing to close the gap.

The Lost Bridge of Dimma was just before him, a stone arch stretching over the canyon between the two mountains, and I shouted, "Ragnall! Wait!"

He paused long enough to look back at me, smirking over his shoulder, and then he charged across the bridge.

"You're going to kill us all!" I yelled after him.

He laughed loudly—the bombastic sound ricocheting off the mountains—and he ran so fast he was nearly across the bridge before I'd even reached it.

"Maybe," he called over his shoulder. "But I will live eternal."

I stopped at the bridge, hunched over with my hands on my thighs as I struggled to catch my breath.

Ragnall made it across the bridge. He laughed again, almost hysterical, and he ran his bloodied hands over his smooth scalp as he looked around in delighted amazement.

The air rippled, and I heard a strange sound. A crackling bleat strangled by a guttural growl. Behind Ragnall, water sprayed out from the ethereal waterfall. From the correct angle, the way the water fell, it looked like a woman in her bridal veils.

But now a beast was emerging from it.

It had a broad snout covered in iridescent evergreen scales and a mouth of jagged teeth. With emerald eyes and spiky protrusions all down its spine. It had no legs or wings, and yet it flew through the air, like a snake slithering through the clouds.

It was the dragon known as a wyrm.

Ragnall stared up as the beast circled over his head, casting a dark shadow over him. The wyrm was large enough that giant woolly elk would have only been a snack for it.

The wyrm let out another crackling howl, then dive-bombed down from the sky. Ragnall was too stunned to do anything, even when the dragon bit into him. As the wyrm flew higher, chomping down on Ragnall's body, blood dripped down, and his severed leg fell and landed on the bridge with a wet splat.

63

❧

crossing

"This isn't happening," I said in a voice that was barely more than a breath. "This *can't* be happening."

I blinked, but the wyrm still languidly hovered in the sky above me, gulping down what was left of Ragnall Jerrick.

And something else was crawling through the waterfall.

It had a long leathery neck protruding from a bony ginger-colored shell, and it had a mouth lined with razor-sharp teeth, like a gharial crocodile. The rest of the body was a primeval mash-up of a snail and a snapping turtle. It slithered along the ground at a horrifyingly fast pace, considering it was the size of a Tralla horse.

I had seen enough of what was coming from Alfheim, and I didn't want to be anywhere near the bridge when that thing decided to cross.

I ran back around the mountainside, where everyone was still fighting around the temple. Many of them were bloodied and ragged, and a few of them lay in the dirt, unmoving.

A group of Älvolk were still crouched behind the blazing red flames raging underneath the temple. They clawed through the dirt and ash, desperate to get any last drop of the blood pudding.

But none of them had tried to cross yet—no one except Ragnall—and everyone else was focused on staying alive. Dagny climbed halfway up the stone remnants of a once-great tower, giving her a good vantage for shooting her arrows. Sumi was facing off against three thrimavolk herself, Alfie had backed another into a corner, and Pan was in a fistfight with a teenage Älvolk.

They didn't know about the dragon.

"Run!" I shouted—screamed to be heard over the noise—as I ran toward the fighting. "You all need to run! There's a dragon!"

Most everyone kept fighting. Maybe they couldn't hear me, like they hadn't heard the monstrous roar. But Pan decked his opponent, knocking him out, and he looked at me in confusion.

"There's a bloody dragon!" I yelled as I reached him. "We have to run!"

"What?" he asked as I gasped for breath.

"The monsters are coming." I blinked back the tears in my eyes. "I don't know how we can stop them."

"We'll . . ." Pan swallowed. "We have to try."

I nodded. "I know."

The wyrm roared again—loud and close so everyone stopped and looked up as it rounded the peak. When it dove down toward us, everyone screamed and took off running, including Pan and me.

We ran past the temple, and the wyrm swooped down, exhaling a plume of green flames. Pan dodged to the right, while I went left, but I was close enough that I felt the intense electrical heat crackling near my skin.

I could see Pan getting swept away by the crowd in the

opposite direction of me, but I didn't want to push back against others running in panic, maybe pushing them into the mouth of the dragon. I ran toward the elk massacre in the stables, joining the others going for the entrance to the safety of the underground Älvolk city.

But the wyrm doubled back and swooped around us, cutting off the path. It landed on the ground and slithered quickly on its belly, going over to inspect the bloody animal corpses.

"Shit." I stopped short, and I spied Eliana, standing near the wyrm's long tail. She stood frozen, watching as it sniffed the corpses and burnt them with its breath.

I jogged over and grabbed Eliana. She let out a surprised mewling sound and I threw her over my shoulder.

"Over here!" Dagny shouted, and motioned for me to join her behind a tall stone wall.

It had once been a building of some kind, but three of the walls had collapsed into a pile, now long overgrown with grass and weeds. A lone wall remained, and we hid behind it with our backs pressed against the stone.

Along with Dagny, Elof and Jennet were crouched low. Dagny had a scrape across her arm and a bruise forming on her cheek, and all of them had wild-eyed shell shock, but they seemed otherwise okay.

"Ragnall crossed the bridge, and all the monsters are getting through," I said as I sat Eliana down. She slumped against the wall and sat down beside Elof.

"*Monsters?*" Dagny asked. "You mean there's more than a dragon?"

"Yeah." I leaned against the wall, and I flinched when the wyrm let out another crackling roar. "They're going to eat the world."

"We have to contain them," Elof said.

"I am happy to do that, but do you have any suggestions on how we go about it?" Dagny asked.

"The Älvolk are masters of the incantation," he said, speaking more quickly as he went on. "And they've already proven they're capable of channeling the Ögonen's magick to create the most intense cloaking in the troll kingdom." He looked around, his eyes resting grimly on the sheer mountainside across from us, his gaze traveling up toward the peak.

But I didn't follow his gaze. Instead, I peered around the wall, checking to make sure the wyrm was still occupied by the elk massacre. I couldn't see the whole beast—just its long tail twisting in mud made of ash and blood.

"I'm certain that, using the Älvolk's own methods and tools here, we should be able to come up with some kind of psychokinetic cage," Elof went on. "I don't know how long it would hold—maybe not that long at all—but it would give us more time than we have now."

"What do you mean?" Dagny asked. "Time for what?"

"Time to figure out how to get them back home, or kill them if we must," Elof said. "Time to stop them before they eat the world, as Ulla put it."

A sounding horn let out a loud, oddly triumphant sound that broke the yelling and screaming, the chuffing of the dragon and the crackling of the flames.

"Oh, *alai*," I said. "What fresh hell is this?"

This time Dagny poked her head around the corner, and she let out a gasp.

"What?" I rushed over to join her, and looked around the wall to see troops marching into Áibmoráigi. They were decked out in uniforms of sage green, sky blue, crisp ivory, crimson red, and golden amber. The five tribes had all sent soldiers—real soldiers—and leading them into battle was Wendy, Queen of the Trylle.

Only a few steps behind her was my friend Bryn Aven, but she'd forgone her usual crisp clean uniform signifying her elite rank in the Kanin guard. Instead she wore black slacks and a gray tank top, with arm and shin guards, but the scars down her arms were clearly visible.

The wyrm roared again before taking to the air. It cast a dark shadow as it circled over us, and Bryn drew her sword as she stared up at it.

64

calvary

BRYN

The days I had spent raising an army and traveling to the First City weren't nearly enough to prepare me for a dragon flying overhead and spewing green fire into the air. I heard Tove Kroner curse under his breath, and his hands hung limply at his sides as he stared up at it.

"I didn't really think there would be fucking dragons," he said.

Someone screamed, and I gripped my sword tighter and snapped my attention back to the battlefield. Áibmoráigi was larger than Doldastam, and the ruins and vast empty spaces between crumbled buildings and rotting barns gave it a more sprawling and spread-out feeling. Like Doldastam, the city was walled off—in this case by the sheer mountain to the south and the steep cliff to the north.

The ruins provided a fair amount of coverage, but most everyone appeared to be running around like chickens with their heads cut off. The sight of a fire-breathing monster had sent everyone to chaos.

A fire burned in green and yellow, but the largest blaze was set at the far northeastern end of Áibmoráigi, before the plateau ended. A tall gazebo with a teardrop-shaped roof of crimson-blue was engulfed in a red fire.

That's where everyone seemed to be coming from. A few of them seemed to be charging at us, ready to fight, but the rest were just running in terror.

I shifted my stance—rolling my shoulder and flipping my sword—and I stepped toward them. I had no idea how to kill a dragon, but I sure as hell knew how to handle a guy in a red cloak running at me with a spear in one hand and a kasteren axe in the other.

He grunted as he raised the stick, but I blocked it easily with my blade, and his spear snapped in two. He tried to come at me with the axe, and I ducked down, dodging out of the way. While crouched down, I grabbed the broken staff and used it to knock his legs out from under him.

He cried out—something in a language I didn't understand—as he fell back to the ground. I straightened up, and I saw the shadow darken his face—

"Bryn! Look out!" Ulla shrieked at me from the cover of a nearby wall.

I dove back out of the way in time to see the Älvolk I'd been fighting go up in a green burst of flames as the wyrm lit him up. I was still close enough that I could feel the heat singe the bottoms of my feet. The Älvolk's screams died almost as soon as they started, so at least the death was quick.

I scrambled back from the burning corpse as the wyrm flew on, lighting more of the city on fire. It was enough to darken the sky, the smoke creating a thick gray-green fog that settled over anything.

Coughing, I got to my feet and looked up, watching the wyrm. My eyes were drawn back to the cages on the mountain. I had noticed them when we were first marching up to the plateau. Cages of stone and iron had been carved into the mountain face, making it look as if bird cages had somehow grown into rocky formations.

Each one of them contained a sinewy Ögonen, standing with their long fingers wrapped around the bars, their eyes following the battle below.

Despite the wyrm's best efforts to burn the First City down to dust, the Älvolk and their warrior daughters kept coming back at us.

But they weren't the only ones. The smog was destroying the visibility, but I could see the odd, lumbering silhouettes of the other monsters that had followed the dragon here.

I didn't entirely understand what they were or where they came from. Ulla hadn't exactly sounded certain when she'd called to ask for my help three days ago. But I had spent my entire life protecting the troll kingdoms, and I wasn't about to stop now.

Especially since my biological father was one of the ones that had helped create this mess. Indu Mattison had to be here somewhere, and I wondered dimly if I would recognize him from the few grainy photos Bekk Vallin had shown me.

As I stalked across the battlefield—knocking out an over-zealous tween Älvolk with the hilt of my sword—I heard rocks falling behind me. I turned around to see a spider the size of a small Siberian husky climbing down a pile of stone, but its spindly legs kept knocking rocks loose.

Despite the unstable footing, it was horrifyingly fast, and I moved quickly to drive my sword through its thick abdomen. Viscous lime-colored blood oozed out onto the ground and the spider let out a high-pitched shriek as it died.

I pulled the sword out and looked back to see a tall blonde with a bloodied lip arguing with a shorter girl, who had black hair coiled on her head and blue makeup smeared across her eyes.

"Tuva, this is madness!" the blonde yelled at her.

"I am the chieftain!" Tuva shot back at her, and she held her bardiche like a staff as she glowered up at the blonde. "We fight until all our fathers cross. And only then do we follow."

A spider jumped at her from behind, and with a flick of her wrist, she spun her pole weapon like a pinwheel around her body. She slipped it behind her back, and in a matter of seconds, she'd sliced through the arachnid.

One of the Skojare guards that followed me here was nearby, fighting an Älvolk, and the blonde rushed over to assault him.

I went to Tuva, intercepting her before she could join her comrades in attacking my ally. She immediately swung her weapon at me, and I blocked it with my sword. But she used enough force to knock me back on the ground. Tuva shouted at me in another language, but it definitely sounded like an angry slur.

I kicked her hard in the abdomen, but my blade was wedged in her wooden pole, so it went with her. An abandoned kasteren axe was just to the left of me, and I rolled over to grab it.

The dragon cried in the sky, and I looked up, searching the green fog for a shadow. Instead I caught sight of another monstrosity slithering toward me. It was bigger than my horse, Bloom, with skin like leather, a thick shell, and a long mouth of angry teeth.

It was a murder snail, and it was coming right for me.

I got to my feet, and Tuva stood on her bardiche to pull my sword free. For a moment, she wielded both weapons, and I stood a few feet away with the murder snail barreling toward us.

She looked to it, then tossed me my sword. I chucked the axe at the monster, and it landed in the shell with a *thwack*.

Tuva swung her weapons until the blade caught in the skin did not give easily. The creature whipped its long neck around, and Tuva barely got in another blow—chipping off a chunk of shell—before it bit her.

She let out an agonized scream as the murder snail chomped into her arm. I could hear the teeth grinding against her bone.

I grabbed the kasteren axe still stuck in the shell, using the handle to pull myself up. I straddled the muscular neck of the snail, and it finally released Tuva. Before it could snap back at me, I drove my sword through the top of the head with a wet squelching sound, and it fell dead.

Tuva lay on the ground, convulsing, and her fresh bite wound dripped with red blood and frothy green venom.

65

❧

encamped

wendy

This was not going as I had planned.

Finn had come to me three days ago about the Älvolk threat, and I had prepared my army accordingly. I had hurried to get here, hoping if we arrived in Áibmoráigi soon enough, I could meet with the Älvolk leaders, and this could end in diplomacy instead of war.

I had dressed for that occasion—an emerald military-style jacket with brass and jeweled buttons paired with pleated culottes—but my hopes for mediation left me feeling foolish as I ran across the battlefield. Yet I didn't let that slow me down.

I gave out orders as I moved, directing my guards and aides to get the base camp set up. We had a main camp at the mountain summit, but that would be too far and too treacherous a journey for our wounded. With a dragon lighting the First City on fire, injuries were a certainty.

In my nine-year reign as Queen of the Trylle, I had unfortunately seen my kingdom through two wars. I had personally fought and killed in battle. But as I watched my friends and allies clash under the green fog of dragon breath, the ground already bloody and burning, I had never seen anything lay siege so quickly.

It would kill us all if we didn't find a way to stop it.

"Wendy!" Loki, my husband the King, called for me.

He was behind me, helping to hurriedly erect tents. The tarps were made of tanned Tralla hides, imbued with cloaking and protection, which the enchanters thought would help them withstand fire and minor assaults.

I turned back to see him discarding his jacket and taking up a sledgehammer, presumably to pound the tent stakes into the ground. His hair was damp with sweat despite the chill in the air, and his dark honey-colored eyes were wide with worry.

"If you must stay on this damned mountain, will you at least go inside the shelter?" He motioned to the tent. "You can't command if you're burnt to a crisp."

He had a point, so I told him to stay safe, and I went into the tent to see that the others were already getting a makeshift medical station set up. Patrik Boden—the Markis Ansvarig I had spoken with many times when the Älvolk had held Finn's foster daughter captive—seemed to be heading up the effort, along with a few Trylle healers.

But wounded were already coming. Someone pulled in a Skojare soldier, his body half burnt and bloodied, crying out in pain. One of the Omte that joined my volunteer army—a lovely young woman with dark auburn hair and peach-colored scrubs—dropped to her knees beside him and immediately went to work.

"What do you need?" I asked, since all the other available hands were busy constructing the medical tent and base camp.

"Gloves and gauze to start," she said. When she glanced up at me, her eyes widened in surprise. "You're the Queen."

"And you're the medical professional," I said. "Tell me what you need."

"Gauze, scissors, and disinfectant swabs," she said, and her focus immediately went back to the patient.

I ran over to the trunks of equipment—helpfully labeled and carried up the mountainside by Vittra hobgoblins—and quickly gathered what she needed. When I returned, she'd moved the patient onto a cot and was injecting him with a painkiller in his unburnt arm.

"Thank you, Your Majesty," she said as she pulled on the gloves I had brought her.

"Call me Wendy," I said, and I slid on my own pair of gloves so I could assist her.

"I'm Rikky," she replied with a quick smile. "Rikky Dysta."

"Nice to meet you," I said, and went to work helping her.

We got the soldier stabilized—as much as we could given the situation—and the sounds of the battle raged on outside. Swords clashing, fires crackling, monsters roaring, and trolls screaming . . . mostly screaming.

Two more injured were brought in, and Rikky enlisted a healer and Patrik to start doing triage.

Across the canvas covering the tent, a pattering sound trickled above us, and the sound reminded me of hail. The canvas rippled, and I heard a girl scream right outside the front flaps.

I ran out and saw that a pack of spiders the size of fat house cats were on the tent, descending on a teenager. Two of them launched themselves at her—one clung to her leg while she tried to pull another smaller one off her arm.

I focused my energy at them—when I was angry or frightened I had the ability to harness it and direct it at other living things. In other trolls, it caused a pain inside their head, short but intense, like they were being slapped.

In the spiders, apparently, it had a much more aggressive effect. Because all at once, the spiders exploded—their thick abdomens bursting with gooey innards. The girl lifted her arm over her face, but she couldn't hide from the gooey lemon-lime splatter. And then she just stood there, screaming.

"Hey." I took her shoulders, and she finally stopped. Soot and ash clung to her long brown hair, and blood—red and green—was smudged across her cheek, and I realized she was only a few years older than my son, Oliver. "What's your name?"

She stared blankly forward and blinked slowly. "M-Minnie."

"Minnie, you're okay." I wiped the blood off her face. "You're going to be okay."

Nearby, I heard my husband yelling. I couldn't see him—I thought he'd been out here, securing the tent, but his voice sounded like it was coming from around a crumbling tower nearby.

"Go inside," I told Minnie, and let go of her. "They'll make sure you'll be fine."

She nodded and started toward the tent, and I turned and took a step toward where I heard Loki shouting, "Fall back! Fall back before they eat you alive!"

And then he rounded the tower. Thrown over one shoulder, he carried a limp body in a Trylle uniform, and he had his other arm around a Kanin soldier with a bloody stump for a right leg. Thanks to Loki's preternatural Vittra strength, he carried them easily.

"Get back, Wendy!" he yelled as he hurried toward me. "There's a lot more coming."

66

underground

ulla

With the wyrm otherwise occupied circling above us, the entrance to the underground city of the Älvolk was open, relatively speaking. To get to the stairs, we had to pass through the stables, where the mutilated corpses of the giant woolly elk had been piled.

The air was thick with buzzing flies and the scent of sulfur and ash. I led the way, since I remembered our time here better than the others.

Eliana was at my heels, and I kept taking her hand because I didn't want to lose her. Elof and Dagny were a few steps behind, with Dagny using her bow and arrow to take out several giant spiders that rushed toward us.

At least we made it to the stables without crossing any thrimavolk or Älvolk, but I suspected that they had their hands full with the monsters they'd unwittingly released, the ones we were trying to contain.

"Why would they do this?" Eliana asked in quiet horror as she surveyed the carnage.

"I don't know," I admitted, and swallowed back my revulsion. "Stay with Elof. I'll clear the path."

She and Elof waited near the entrance while Dagny and I went over to get the heavy bodies out of the way. I took a fortifying breath, closed my eyes, and I moved the dead elk out of the way enough to clear a path.

"Ulla!" Sunniva yelled in surprise, and I looked over to see her standing in the doorway. "I've been looking for you!"

"Why? What's going on?" I asked, and wiped my hands on my jeans in a vain attempt to get the blood off.

"Other than the end of the world?" she asked as she stepped over a bloody elk antler. Her expression was grim as she reached me. "I just feel like I'm supposed to be with you."

"For what?" I asked.

She shook her head uncertainly. "For whatever comes next."

"We should get downstairs," Dagny said, wiping her forehead with the back of her arm.

"Where are you going?" Sunniva asked as Dagny helped Elof over the animal remains that still littered the stable floor.

"Down to the Älvolk living quarters," I explained. "We're trying to find a way to contain or stop anything that comes across the bridge."

"I'm in," Sunniva said, and she joined us as we made our way through the stable massacre and down the spiral staircase.

As we descended the stone stairs into the earth, it seemed darker than when I had been here last. There was the earthy mildew smell that I remembered all too well, but it was currently being overwhelmed by the strong scent of burnt sulfur and metallic heat.

I ran my fingertips along the wall, using it as a guide,

until my fingers grazed a bloody handprint smeared across the stone—still warm and sticky.

The stairwell ended in a large stone room with an archway that led to the two respective wings: the Älvolk under their triskelion sigil, and the thrimavolk under an ouroboros of a serpentine dragon biting its own tail.

"I know they had a lot of texts in the *häxdoktor*'s office in the *medica*," I said. I had a sharp memory of running down the hall from the thrimavolk dormitory, and then down a narrow stairwell. That's where the *medica* was located.

"Wait." Eliana grabbed my hand and peered into the darkness of the thrimavolk wing.

"Why?" Dagny asked.

"There's something . . ." Eliana trailed off and went toward the room, gently pulling me with her.

Then I heard it too. A whimpering sound and ragged breathing.

Elof pulled out a torch, flooding the thrimavolk living room with amber light. Huddled in a group behind the sofa were twenty or so children—boys and girls, none of them older than nine or ten.

They cried out when they saw the flame, and Eliana rushed over to comfort them.

"No, no, it's not the wyrm," she said, and crouched down in front of them so they could see she wasn't a fire-breathing monster. "I won't hurt you."

"Eliana, leave them," Dagny said. "We should go."

"They're terrified," Eliana protested.

"But they're safe," Dagny persisted. "As safe as they can be until we find a way to close the bridge."

"We can't just leave them alone like this!" Eliana argued.

"Why don't you stay with them?" Elof asked. He handed

her another torch and a dagger from his belt. "Keep them safe until we come back for you."

She took the blade tentatively, and her hair color rippled—it matched the flickering golden flame of the torch.

"You're strong and brave," I told her, remembering the impressive acrobatic stunts I'd seen her do in the past.

Eliana straightened up and gave me an uneasy smile. "I can do this. You go do what you need to."

I wanted to hug her, but Dagny told me we needed to hurry, and she wasn't wrong.

We were on the move again. Elof handed another torch to me, to light the way as we ventured deeper into the dark underground. Down another stairwell—much more narrow this time, but shorter—and the *medica* was right off the stairs.

When the air smelled of dry lilies and rotting fruit, I knew we were getting close. The scent of the *sorgblomma* permeated the *häxdoktor*'s office, and I saw dim light coming through the door left ajar.

Glass shattered inside the room, and I pushed open the door to see the man from my nightmares. Lemak, the *häxdoktor*, his long, slender frame cowering in the corner, behind the contraption that he used to steal my blood.

patriarch

вryn

Tuva convulsed on the ground beside the dead murder snail.

"What the hell's happening to her?" Pan asked. He stood a few feet away from me, and his arms were extended back behind him, holding a stretcher. It was empty, and he carried it alone, the rear handles dragging in the dirt.

One of Pan's sleeves was torn, there was a fresh gash across his runic clock tattoo, and mud and ashes were tangled in his curly hair. Around his waist, he wore a satchel marked with a green cross—the Trylle First Aid symbol.

"She's dying," I told him.

Her eyes began to bleed as she writhed and moaned, so I drove my sword through her throat, severing her brain stem with a slick crunch.

Pan winced and looked away.

"You couldn't have saved her," I said, and wiped my blade clean on her tunic. "Ending her pain was the only kind thing to do."

"I don't know that I can save anyone," he said quietly. His

face was pale, and his eyes were dark as he stared down. "I'm not a medic, but I'm not a fighter either. A nurse I know needed help, and I wanted to help . . ."

"You can't think too much out here," I said. "You gotta keep moving. You gotta help those you can help. You gotta keep yourself alive." I pointed to the dead shelled monster behind me. "And stay away from the murder snails if you don't want to end up like her."

"Thanks." He nodded grimly, then jogged off with the stretcher in the direction of someone crying out.

From a crumbling stone house half hidden in the fog, I heard swords clashing and men arguing. I went closer to it to get a better look, and I saw them walking backward up a mossy staircase.

Jem-Kruk was on the defensive, nimbly blocking the aggressive blows of a man in a cobalt kaftan.

"It never had to be this way," Jem was saying.

His Älvolk aggressor retorted through gritted teeth, "No, this was always how it ended. You dying by my hand."

"Your arrogance will be your downfall, Indu," Jem said, but he sounded weary, and he stumbled on the stairs.

"But I will be yours," Indu snarled.

I raced up the steps, running at Indu's back as fast as I could, but I wasn't fast enough. Indu stabbed Jem-Kruk through the chest, and then he tossed the body off the third-floor landing and it fell on a pile of rubble with a wet thud.

He finally turned around and looked down at me. And for the first time in my life, I was face-to-face with the man that impregnated my mother. I was a few steps below him, and he tilted his head, giving me a curious expression, like he recognized me from somewhere.

Indu looked more like Iver—my father, the man who raised me—than I had thought, and it was disorienting. I had expected a stranger's face, but the familiarity was unsettling.

Just before I had left Doldastam a few days ago, I had gone to see my parents. I forgave them for keeping this from me—I knew they had their own complicated reasons for it. Dad told me that he'd always love me, no matter how I felt about any of this, and I told him that he was my dad and always would be.

I cleared my throat and asked, "Indu Mattison?"

Realization flashed across his face, and he smiled. "You're Runa's daughter. *My* daughter."

"My father is in Doldastam," I corrected him, and tightened my grip on my sword. "As far as I can tell, you're nothing but a womanizing sycophantic murderer, and you just killed my friend."

His smile fell away and his eyes hardened. "Not to sound like an overprotective father, but Jem-Kruk is slime. You shouldn't be spending time with a worm like that. I did you a favor."

"I suppose I ought to return the favor," I said, and I charged up the stairs at him.

Indu didn't hesitate to swing at me, and I caught the blade with my arm guard. "We don't need to fight. You can join me."

"You opened a portal to hell, and you think you can tempt me with an invitation into the fire?" I sneered at him.

We crossed swords. He held his with both hands as I backed him up, but I wielded mine with only my right. My left hand twisted behind my back to lift the dagger from my belt. The ornate handle of ivory felt hot against the palm of my hand. They were beautiful daggers, but most importantly, they had long sharp blades of silver.

I blocked his strike, but he pushed hard, his blade hovering mere inches from my face. With my left hand, I swung wide and drove my dagger deep into the side of his neck.

His eyes widened in surprise, and he made a gurgling sound as blood filled his mouth. I pulled the knife from his neck, and he fell back onto the steps. His sword fell to the ground, and I used my foot to kick him, and he rolled off the stairs.

Indu tumbled to the ground two stories below, his body landing a few feet from Jem's.

68

venom

wendy

Rikky had taken charge of the triage, quickly giving out orders to any available hands, and that included me, but honestly, it was a relief. This wasn't my usual role when the Trylle went to war. Acts of diplomacy often kept me from the front lines.

But this was too important. All five kingdoms had united for this because the enemy was so fierce. They had followed me here, and I couldn't stand back and do nothing. My captains with their military expertise were leading the troops, but my talents lay elsewhere.

Right now, following Rikky's orders seemed like the best way to be useful. Minnie had overcome her initial shock, and she had snapped into action beside me. We applied a tourniquet on the calf of someone who'd had their foot ripped off by some kind of monstrous animal. Our main goal was to stop the bleeding until a healer or medic got to them.

But I had no idea when that would be. Rikky had her hands busy with a trio of violently convulsing patients infected with a powerful venom. The medical tent itself—despite its large size—was already filling up.

The injuries and casualties were far more than we were prepared for, but I couldn't let that knowledge overwhelm me. I kept my head down and moved quickly, doing as much as I could as fast as I could.

While Minnie cut away the fabric around a wound, I went to grab an elixir for the pain from a nearby cart, the way Rikky had shown me. By the time I made it back, Minnie had stopped her frantic work and just stared down at the wounded troll.

"Minnie, what are you doing?" I asked.

"He died." She nodded at the motionless body on the cot in front of her. "While I was trying to help him, he just died."

"You did what you were able," I said, but any more words of comfort I might've given were overridden by someone shouting from outside the tent.

"Can someone help me?" he shouted, and I ran out through the tent flaps and saw Rikky's friend Pan struggling to bring more wounded to the tent.

Rikky had sent him off with a stretcher and a medic kit, and he'd returned with two burnt soldiers in blue strapped to the stretcher, and a large Omte with an arrow in his back was leaning on him.

I rushed over and put my arm around the Omte and let him put his weight on me. He was a big guy with broad shoulders, and he somehow managed to be even heavier than he looked. I struggled to hold him up but I managed.

"Sorry," he said when he stumbled.

"It's okay. I've got you," I said, digging deep to hold him up. "What should I call you?"

"Knut," he said in a low grunt and tried to stand up straighter.

Try as we both did, we weren't moving fast at all. Even Pan, pulling two soldiers with only the petite Minnie helping him, was ahead of us.

As we walked, I could hear the wyrm roaring, and I looked up toward the sky. I couldn't see the creature through the haze, but the mountain wall was close enough that I could see the cages made of stone and iron, filled with bizarre beings with trollian eyes and extended hands.

"What in the world do they have caged to the mountain?" I asked.

Pan looked up, and his expression changed to confusion. "Those are Ögonen, but I don't know what they're doing up there like that."

I had heard of the Ögonen before, but I had never seen them. Merellä rarely extended invitations to the Kings and Queens, and I hadn't yet had the pleasure. The official briefings I'd had on the Ögonen described them as cousins of trolls, more in tune with nature and plants. They volunteered their powerful psychokinesis to help protect our kind and our way of life, which Merellä and the Mimirin institution professed to be their true purpose.

I don't know what the Älvolk were doing with the Ögonen, but they certainly didn't look like they were here of their own free will. They strained at the bars, and their large eyes stared down at us in desperation from their haunting, mouthless faces.

"We have to free them," I said.

Pan and Minnie were now too far away to hear me, but I was speaking more to myself, making a promise I hoped I would keep.

But now wasn't the time to worry about what came after. Now I had to focus on surviving and getting Knut to the tent as quickly as possible.

Beneath my bare feet, the ground began to shake, and a loud rumbling came from within the mountain. I picked up my pace, the adrenaline giving me the strength to start dragging Knut along.

"Run!" I shouted at Minnie and Pan.

69

Girjastu

ᴜʟʟᴀ

Lemak whimpered when he saw me. I grabbed him by the shoulders and tossed him roughly into the apothecary table.

The memories came rushing back all at once, as vivid and raw as if it was happening now. Dozens of times, Lemak restraining me with the wolfram metal cuffs.

All the times he'd watched as stronger trolls than him held me down so he could steal my blood. But now he was on his own, and the wolfram restraints were secured on the *medica* bed across the room.

Lemak fell to the ground, and beakers and instruments on top of the apothecary table rained down on him. As he lay simpering before me, his bony fingers skittered across the floor, reaching for a giant needle attached to the end of the rubbery tube.

But I stomped on his hand before he could grab it. His bones crunched and he yelped as he recoiled back against the wall.

"Not this time." I glared down at him. "Not ever again."

"Please," Lemak begged. "I was only doing as Indu ordered—as—as your father told me to do, so that we could claim the kingdom we were denied, with our treasures and land waiting for us on the other side of the bridge. We never wanted it to come to this! This is the only way we could get what we were owed!"

"Indu is *not* my father, and nobody ever owed you anything," I said. "How do we stop this?"

"You—You can't," Lemak stammered.

"How did you maintain the cloaking spell?" Elof asked. He stood at my side just behind Lemak.

"I didn't," Lemak answered. "My work was in *blodseider magick,* not in the incantations and reveries."

"Where would we find someone who could help us with incantations and reveries?" Elof asked.

Lemak's small, bloodshot eyes went up to the ceiling. "We were all at the ceremony. I alone left when I saw you return."

"Of course you did, you coward," I sneered at him.

"What about your books and scrolls?" Elof asked Lemak. "Where do you store your incantations and spell books?"

"The *girjastu* holds all the books," Lemak explained in his sniveling way. "It's on the east wing of this floor, past the armory."

Sunniva was waiting in the corridor with a torch, keeping a lookout of sorts, though it seemed deserted down here. We couldn't be too cautious with radical Älvolk and killer spiders lurking about.

Dagny went out to join her. "It's just straight down that way." She looked back at me. "It'll be easy enough to find. We don't need him."

"Nobody does." I turned and started toward the door.

With my back to the *häxdoktor,* I heard Elof grunt and a loud clatter. I whirled around to see Lemak gripping the needle in his non-broken hand, and Elof breaking a beaker over his head.

Lemak snarled and turned his rage toward Elof. I grabbed him to stop him, and he turned on me with the monster needle. I caught his arm, and without too much effort, I snapped his forearm with a loud crack.

He screamed in agony, and I kept bending his arm back until the needle tore into his throat. His eyes widened, and he fell silent—aside from a raspy breath—as the metal cut through his jugular and windpipe.

When I felt his blood hot and sticky on my hand, I released him. Lemak immediately fell to the floor, his blood pouring out from him as he stared vacantly at the ceiling. The blood pooled quickly and I jumped back to keep it from getting on my feet.

"Ulla." Dagny put her hand on my arm. "We need to go."

Elof nodded and pulled his gaze away from Lemak's death rattle to look up at me. "You did what you had to do. You saved our lives."

"I know," I said, but my voice sounded empty. I wiped my hands off on my jeans, and I followed Dagny and Sunniva as they walked down the long, narrow corridor.

I tried not to think about what I had done or what it meant. The belief that Lemak deserved it, that he had given me no choice, was a cold comfort, and we had to keep moving.

Dagny paused to look in the armory, long enough to let out an impressed whistle, but I stayed on task. We could check out the weapons once we had the monsters contained.

The *girjastu* was a long room with low ceilings and dusty shelves. We didn't have enough torches for everybody, so I stayed close to Sunniva, hurriedly pulling books off the shelf and flipping through them.

Suddenly, Sunniva froze and cocked her head. "What was that?"

"It's just Dagny and Elof a row over," I said.

"No, not that." She frowned. "This is something else. . . ."

She grabbed me and pushed me back against the wall, and then I heard it too. A loud rumbling, and the room started shaking. Books and shelves tumbled over, and I put my arms over my head to shield myself.

70

brimstone

bryn

I ran down the stairs of the ruins and nearly got hit with a giant cat. Tove Kroner stood only a meter away from me, his hands held palms out and his face twisted up in concentration. He had used his psychokinetic abilities to throw the monster cat into the mountain wall.

But the cat was on its feet almost instantly. It was a massive, stocky beast, built like a tiger mixed with a bulldog. The fur was mottled silver, with spots and rosettes of black splattered all over it. It had paws the size of baseball mitts, each lined with five hooked claws like a damn velociraptor's, and its two sharp incisors extended several inches below its powerful jaws, making it some kind of saber-toothed pit bull of a cat.

As soon as the cat was up, it started charging at Tove. He slammed it back against the wall, pinning it against the stone as its feet thrashed wildly in the air.

Sumi finished killing a supersized spider, and she went

over to the cat. While Tove held it in place, she stabbed it through the heart, killing it instantly.

"The *kuguars* won't stop coming once they have a taste for our blood," Sumi said as she came toward us. A small spider scurried at her, and she absently crushed it with her foot. "But I can handle them. It's the wyrm that's beyond my skill set."

She nodded up to the sky where the shadows circled through the smoke.

"You never faced one before?" I asked.

"We stay in the valley, and the wyrms live in the mountain and caves that surround the entrance to Áibmoráigi," Sumi explained. "We sneak by when we go through, but otherwise, we avoid each other, and on the rare occasion the wyrms hunt in the valley, we hide from them."

"So your tips for combating the wyrm are running and hiding?" Tove asked.

She shook her head, making her dark coils of hair sway. "I'm only saying that I've never seen anyone or anything take a wyrm down, so I can't speculate on how it's done."

"There's always a first time for everything," I muttered.

"I'll need to get closer." Tove squinted up at the sky. "It's been flying high."

"There's a crumbling tower back that way." I hooked my thumb over my shoulder.

"That might be—" Tove began, but he was interrupted by the screeching call of the wyrm.

It dipped low to the ground, its breath lighting up the smog. Trolls ran toward us, away from the wyrm flying at their heels, both allies and Älvolk alike.

When Finn darted past us, we ran after him, following him down the winding trails through the crumbling, burnt remains of ancient buildings.

Behind us, I heard screaming and smelled the burning air. It was brimstone and chlorine, smoky and chemical all at once. We stopped behind the stone-and-wood skeleton of a barn, hiding in the small area between the barn and the mountain wall, trying to catch our breath with air that burned our lungs.

Sumi and Finn leaned against the back wall of the barn, while I paced slowly in place, my hands on my hips. Tove stepped a few feet away from us, nearly bumping into the wall as he stared up at the sky.

Suddenly, the wyrm crashed into the barn—flying straight through the walls—making the crumbling structure explode in stone and rotten wood. I jumped out of the way and landed roughly in the dirt, and I held an arm over my head to protect myself from the shrapnel and splinters.

Tove stood against the mountain, his hands out, and his face contorting in pain. The wyrm was frozen in the air, its mouthful of jagged teeth only inches away from him.

The primal, emerald eyes of the beast narrowed—maybe in anger, maybe in confusion—and the veins on Tove's forehead looked like they were about to burst. I grabbed my sword and charged at the wyrm, and I swung as hard as I could against the monster's neck.

But the thick, iridescent scales held strong, and it was my sword that gave. It broke in half, and I was left stumbling back with only a hilt in my throbbing hand.

"I don't know how to stop it!" I yelled, and smoke fumed out through the wyrm's nostrils.

Tove grunted, and his face was beet red. He wouldn't be able to hold the wyrm for much longer, and I scanned around for anything that I could use as a weapon.

Before I could find anything, Tove let out an anguished cry, and he flung his arms upward. The wyrm's body followed the motion as Tove threw the hundred-pound reptile into the mountainside as hard as he could.

Tove collapsed to the ground, and I rushed over to him as pebbles rained down on us. As the rumbling began, I realized that he'd inadvertently triggered a rockslide.

71

***

quaking

wendy

Inside the tent, we tried to pretend like it didn't sound like the world was ending outside. I helped Knut sit on a cot and made him as comfortable as I could, as the earth shook and the Tralla leather walls quaked.

Throughout the loud shaking, a few trolls had been running in, dazed and battle-weary. I kept glancing back at the tent flaps that served as the door, hoping everyone I knew and loved was safe. I wanted everyone that had followed me here to be okay, but I hadn't been so naïve, and this tent was evidence of that.

But when my husband pushed his way in—dirty and dazed, his shirt torn, his chest scratched and bleeding—I let out a breath of relief. Knut was sitting up, and I asked Minnie to keep an eye on him before rushing over to Loki.

The rumbling and shaking had finally stopped, but I could still hear the wyrm raging.

Loki wrapped his arms around me and kissed the top of my head. "I'm so glad you're safe."

"Are you okay?" I put my hand on his chest and tried to get a better look at him. His hair lay wildly across his forehead, and a bruise was growing dark purple on his cheek.

"Yeah, it's only a scratch," he said with a smirk.

Loki had been in plenty of battles in the past. Before he knew me, when he lived in the Vittra kingdom, he had been touted as the Warrior Prince. His childhood had been especially rough, but his super strength, quick wit, and endless compassion had gotten him through it.

I knew he could handle himself, that he was one of the best soldiers we had, and that we needed him out there in combat if we were to have any chance of defeating these monsters.

But I wished that, just this once, he wasn't the King of the Common Troll. That he didn't believe that if a war was worth fighting, he should be in it. I wished that he could stay back and stay safe, but I loved him because he knew that "safe" wasn't where he needed to be.

Someone outside screamed, and Loki looked through the gap in the tent. He swallowed hard and said, "I've got to get back out there. The rockslide is over now, and there might be trolls trapped under the debris."

"That was a rockslide?" I asked.

He nodded, then looked back down at me and put a hand gently on my cheek. "You need to go, Wendy."

"What?"

"I don't know if we can win this battle," he said thickly, and his eyes were pained. "But if we have any chance of winning the war against an unstoppable enemy like a dragon, we need leaders who know what they're doing."

"Loki, no." I shook my head. "I am the Queen. I am of service here."

"Wendy." His voice was firm, but there was a slight tremor to it. "Our son needs a mother. Not all the choices we make can be for the kingdom. Sometimes we must choose our family."

"He needs you too," I argued.

"I know," he admitted quietly. "But I can save them. I have to go back out there."

I stood on my tiptoes and kissed him fiercely. I loved him with everything I had, even more than the day I married him, almost ten years before. And even though it killed me to, I let go of him.

He went out through the door, and I held the flaps open, watching as he jogged off into the smoke, toward the rockslide. A few larger boulders had piled up just beyond the tent, but the worst of it had sounded farther away, to the northeast.

Rather strangely, all the iron and stone cages on the mountainside had broken open, some of them crumbling down. The slender, jelly-like Ögonen were free, climbing down the sheer mountain face with surprising grace and dexterity.

But my attention was immediately on the animals crawling on top of the rock pile. A pair of spotted saber-toothed cats and a whole horde of spiders.

None of us were going to survive up here much longer.

"We need to evacuate!" I shouted, and I looked back to see Rikky and Patrik with panic in their eyes. "We have to get everyone down to the valley, and we have to do it *now*."

72

wolfram

ulla

Sunniva and I had stuck close to the wall, and we'd mostly been spared from the book avalanche. I don't know how long it lasted—it felt like forever—with the entire room shaking and the thunderous rumble booming.

By the time it ended, all the shelves had fallen over, some of them splintering and broken. A pair of wrought-iron sconces fell to the floor with a loud clatter, and I heard the creaking groan of a door opening at the end of the *girjastu*.

But I couldn't see because the only light came from Sunniva's torch. Elof's had gone out, and I could see neither him nor Dagny.

"Dagny?" I said once the quake had stopped. "Elof?"

I heard a mumble, so I climbed over a fallen shelf and started hurriedly tossing books aside. Then an arm popped up from a pile of books, and Dagny sat up. Beside her, the books moved, and I hurried to help Elof out.

"I'm okay," Dagny said, but Sunniva offered her a hand anyway, and Dagny let her help her up.

"I'm a little banged up, but I'll be all right," Elof assured me with a thin smile.

Dagny was on the move, already searching through the piles of books for the right incantation.

"Dag, are you sure you're okay?" I asked.

"Yeah, I just need more light." Her hair had come loose from her ponytail, and she brushed it back from her eyes. Then she gave Sunniva an irritated glance. "Can you bring the torch closer?"

I waded into the books, digging around where Elof had been, until I found the torch he'd dropped in the chaos.

I got it lit with the intention of helping them search. Elof used his good arm to sift through the books near him, and Sunniva stood between Dagny and Elof, so they could both use her light, and she picked through things with her free hand.

There was another loud *boom* above us, and more dust and pebbles trickled down from the ceiling. That's all there was this time, no prolonged quaking that followed, and I heard the high-pitched groan again, coming from the door swinging at the dark end of the *girjastu*.

I went down to get a better look, and I discovered a thick copper door, oxidized green around the edge, standing ajar. I ducked under a spiderweb and peered in the doorway. The dim torchlight instantly picked up on the shelves lined with treasures—glittering jewels, works of art, dusty artifacts, and ancient tools.

This must be an Älvolk vault, where they locked away their precious valuables. I stepped inside the crowded room, looking around at all the strange treasures. I was about to call for Dagny, thinking she'd like to see what was in here, but something caught my eye, and I froze.

The large amber stone glimmered in the bronze hilt, beneath a sigil of the Omte—a trio of vultures. It was a short dagger with a wide blade made of wolfram metal. Runic symbols were carved down the center, along the blood groove. Though the dagger was battered and scraped, with the ridges on the handle dull and worn down, the edges of the blade were exceedingly sharp.

It was the weapon of a warrior. The same one I remembered Thor giving to Orra Fågel, the one that Mr. Tulin had seen her carrying the night she left me at the inn in Iskyla.

And then, after she'd left me, Indu had tracked Orra down and killed her. She died protecting me from him and his oppressive cult, and he had stolen the dagger from her. He had stolen my father's blade.

The leather sheath lay underneath the dagger, on a pile of gold coins and loose gemstones in red and blue. The belt was long—Thor had been even wider than me—but there was a smaller handmade notch on it, one that fit almost perfectly. Orra must've been about my size.

I secured the belt around my waist and sheathed the dagger at my hip.

"Ulla! We found something!" Dagny shouted.

I jogged back over to them, where they were crowded around a large, dusty book. It was at least two feet tall and even wider than that, and Dagny turned the vellum pages carefully. They were covered in drawings, pressed flowers and herbs, and writings in a runic language.

In the margins, translations had been made in delicate calligraphy. Dagny read it aloud when I crouched down beside her to have a better look.

"'Take a flame to the blood of *álfar*; twice more than a drop will do,'" she read. "'Together you bow and pray upon the earth, repeating these words: *omorbba vid all sihkka-matön*.'"

"What does it do?" I asked.

Dagny tapped a paragraph near the top of the page, next to sketch of a twisting flame. "'If an enemy is too great, armor can be applied to the air. No arrows shall pass through, no warriors or beast. Time passes quickly under this protection, so prepare wisely for when it lifts.'"

It was called "An Impenetrable Sphere."

"Do you think my blood will work?" I asked. "Since I'm only half-*álfar*?"

"We'll try four drops instead of two," Dagny said, and looked up at me. "You can handle that, right?"

I nodded. "Let's do it." I unsheathed my dagger and answered Dagny's questions before she could ask: "It's my father's dagger, I found it in the vault. I'll explain more later. Let's get this over with."

Elof tore some pages out of a book for kindling. Sunniva used her torch to get it going, and I slid the blade against my finger, wincing at the pain.

I held my hand over the fire and squeezed four big drops of blood. The flames flared up, turning gold and violent, and Elof handed me a handkerchief to wrap around my small wound.

"Okay, now we all read the incantation together," Dagny said.

"We should hold hands?" Sunniva asked, and Dagny gave her a funny look. "It said to say it together."

"It's better safe than sorry," Elof agreed.

Dagny sighed and held her hands out. I took her hand, mindful of my cut, and with my other I took Sunniva's. Dagny held Elof's hand, and we circled the fire.

"*Omorbba vid all sihkkamatön.*"

73

unearth

bryn

My head and back throbbed. I had thrown myself over Tove when he collapsed, shielding him from the rockslide. Fortunately, he had enough strength to catch a large boulder with his abilities, because it certainly would've crushed us both if he hadn't.

The smaller rocks, some dirt, and debris still got through, leaving me bruised and sore when the rockslide ended. Tove tossed the boulder aside and immediately passed out. I pushed the rubble off me and Tove, and I pulled him up so he was sitting slumped against the wall, and his eyelids fluttered.

Above us, the wyrm cried out in anger, and I watched him spew fire and fly erratically until his smoke made the air too thick to see through.

With Tove safe—relatively speaking—I ran over to where Finn and Sumi had been standing. They were buried in debris from the barn—mostly stone, wood, and moldy hay—and rocks from the recent slide, which were heavy enough that I found them difficult to move.

My whole body ached, my head throbbed, and my vision blurred in my bad eye. I worked as hard and fast as I could to unearth Finn and Sumi, but I worried that I didn't have enough strength to move fast enough.

"Help!" I shouted as I dug through the rubble. "Somebody! Please *help*!"

Loki—the King of the Trylle—suddenly rounded the barn, running toward me.

"Hurry!" I shouted at him. "Finn and Sumi are trapped under the rocks!"

"Finn's there?" Loki blanched slightly, and he sped up. He lifted rocks I'd been unable to move like they were pillows.

"Help!" Sumi's voice barely carried through the rocks.

When her hand came through, I grabbed it and started pulling her up. Loki kept moving junk out of the way while I pulled her out. She coughed hard as soon as she was free. Wood chips, dirt, and hay were tangled with her hair, and some of it shook free as she doubled over.

"Are you okay?" I asked her, as Loki kept searching for Finn.

She nodded and struggled to catch her breath. "All the old crap from the barn softened the blow of the rocks. It would've been great if I hadn't breathed in so much dust and mold."

"Got him!" Loki announced, and I looked over to see him helping Finn out of the rock pile.

He coughed hard enough that he threw up, and he was bleeding from his temple. But he stood on his own, once Loki helped him off the rocks.

"What the hell happened?" Finn asked, looking around in dismay.

Loki put his hand on Finn's shoulder. "What's the last thing you remember?"

"The dragon chasing us," Finn said.

"We can't kill it." I clenched my jaw, holding back the frustrated tears that stung my eyes. "Tove used everything he had to hold it, and I broke my sword on its scales." I lowered my gaze. "That was probably the best chance we had, and I couldn't . . ." I grimaced. "I don't think we can hurt it at all. We just pissed it off."

Nobody said anything for a moment. Loki stared down at the ground, his arms folded over his chest, and Finn looked up at the dark sky. Sumi sat down next to Tove, catching her breath.

"I told Wendy to evacuate with everyone she could," Loki said, and he exchanged a look with Finn. "You should go too. They'll need you."

"You'll need me if you wanna stop this thing," Finn countered.

"She says we can't stop it." Loki motioned to me.

"I don't know *how* to stop it," I amended. "But there has to be a way. There has to be something we can do."

"Maybe the thing we can do is step aside and let the humans go after the dragons with their bombs," Loki said quietly.

Finn scoffed. "They would blow us all up along with the dragon!"

"Then we run and hide!" Loki yelled. "But we don't know how to stop the wyrm, and it's already taken out so many of us. We can't defeat it if we're dead!"

"Guys?" Sumi said. "Tove isn't doing so well."

He was awake—ish. His eyes were open, and he rubbed at them with the palm of his hand.

"Tove?" Finn asked.

"He's been mumbling nonsense," Sumi said, sounding concerned.

"No, it's just head dizzy," he said. "Once I get two feet, it's on the fine." He started pushing himself up, and Loki rushed over to catch him before he fell.

"It's okay, I got you, buddy," Loki said, and put his arm around Tove. Then he looked solemnly at the rest of us. "We need to get to the tent. We can decide whether to fight or evacuate from there."

Sumi got up and started back the way we'd come, around the barn and to the base camp at the southwestern side of Áibmoráigi. Finn followed a step behind her, and Loki half carried Tove to keep with Sumi's fast pace.

I went after them more slowly, staring into the dank smoke and listening to the animalistic groans and nearby screams. The ruins were crawling with monsters I couldn't see, and I had broken my sword.

A burnt Älvolk corpse lay across the path, his sword still gripped in his hand. I pried the hilt from his stiff fingers, snapping two of them off in the process.

A *kuguar* roared, sounding much too close, and I lost sight of Loki and the others in front of me. I held my sword out, and I wanted to charge on ahead, but the ground was littered with bodies. They were bloody and torn up, some completely eviscerated. They had been mauled to death.

As I stepped over a body, I heard whimpering. A girl lying facedown in front of me moved slightly, crawling away from the body of a child. Her dark hair shifted colorings, changing to a pale yellow-green.

"Do you need help?" I asked her softly, so none of the nearby predators could hear me, and I crouched beside her.

She finally looked up at me, and I recognized her as Ulla's *álfar* sibling, Eliana.

"Eliana, are you all right?" I asked, and she nodded meekly. "Come on. Let's get you to the base camp." I took her hand and hoped I was leading her toward somewhere safer.

74

✦

escape

wendy

Patrik Boden stood in front of the rows of injured and dying that already filled the tent. He was ashen and blood stained his shirt and arms. He was the Markis Ansvarig of Isarna, with thousands of trolls under his care, and he'd brought along so many to fight in this battle.

And I understood the look on his face completely. The horror and icy resignation that all of this was happening because of the decisions we made. That lives were lost today because we asked them to be here, fighting this impossible enemy.

Only time would tell if it had been worth it, if what we gained outweighed all that we lost, if we'd gained anything at all.

But now wasn't the time to wax philosophic, and I shouted at Patrik again, "We need to evacuate!"

"We can't!" He shook his head, and behind him, Rikky looked up at us while she wrapped a wound. "There's too many wounded, and some of them will die if we move them right now."

"We're all going to die if we don't get out of here," I said.

Outside of the tent, the saber-toothed cats let out guttural roars, and they were loud enough to be heard over the screams.

Patrik looked back over his shoulder at Rikky and said, "Start with the ones we can move the fastest."

Then, in a strong voice, Rikky barked out orders—directing the other medics and healers to start gathering patients and gear for the arduous journey down the narrow mountain trail.

I went over to Knut to help him to his feet, but he only shook his head.

"I'm too slow," he said. "Help others."

"I'll come back for you," I said, and went to aid Minnie with her work securing a wounded teenager to a stretcher.

We worked quickly, getting as many of the wounded ready as fast as we could, but it felt like a Sisyphean task. I ditched my jacket, using the ripped-off sleeves for a makeshift tourniquet, and now I ran around in a camisole with blood drying up, and my long curls pulled up and secured with a tassel from the jacket.

The flaps of the tent burst open, and Loki came in, helping a limping Tove along, and Finn followed a step behind. They'd helped Tove into a chair by the time I got to them.

"What happened?" I asked.

"Overexerted myself," Tove said wearily, and ran a hand through his tangles of hair. "Need a minute. But I'm okay."

"I thought you were supposed to be halfway down the mountain by now," Finn commented. He was banged up and dirty, but his expression was stoic as usual.

"We're trying to evacuate," I said. So far, only a half dozen of those that could move themselves had gone. Everyone was rushing around trying to get the immobile patients ready to go.

"Finn, you could help them down," I suggested before anyone could say anything more about me getting out of here. "You and Tove can lead them safely."

"Are you going down?" Rikky interjected, and wiped her forehead with the back of her arm. "I've got some kids ready to go." She motioned to three children under the age of seven with various limbs wrapped and splinted.

"Yeah, I got them," Finn said without hesitation, then looked back at Tove. "You can walk yourself down, right?"

Tove slowly got to his feet and nodded. "Yeah. Get the kids."

"What do you need me to do?" Loki asked Rikky.

"Are you staying or going?" she asked him.

Loki didn't look at me when he answered, "Staying."

"Great." Rikky sounded relieved. "You're strong, right? I've got a four-hundred-pound ogre I'm trying to splint. You think you can help with that?"

"Yeah, of course," he said as he followed her.

I helped Finn get the children situated on a stretcher, and Tove held the flaps open for them as he took the kids outside. I didn't watch them leave, because I didn't want to think about what they were walking into, and if they would make it out of the city.

Minnie started screaming at the other side of the tent, and I ran over to see smaller spiders—these were only the size of a small cat—crawling under the tarp.

Pan rushed over to help her, stomping on the arachnids, and Minnie swatted at them with a long pair of medical clamps. I used my psychic mind slap to pop a few of them, but they were coming so fast. My head throbbed in pain as I struggled to keep up with them.

They finally stopped coming in, but I could see the long legs poking into the tarp as they climbed over the tent. I slumped back against a cart, taking a moment to breathe and let my head rest.

Then I heard Finn yelling, the panic in his voice unmistakable. I ran out the front flaps, barely stopping a spider—squashing it with my foot this time—before it pounced on me.

"We're trapped!" Finn shouted when he saw me. He was running, pulling the stretcher of children behind him. He held it by the handles on one side and let the handles on the other drag on the ground behind him.

"What?" I asked, but my words were drowned out by the sound of the wyrm roaring.

I looked up, and through the haze, I saw the serpentine dragon thrashing at the sky. A burst of flame from its mouth bowed, as if stopped by an invisible curved wall.

"We can't get out!" Finn yelled.

As the wyrm raged against the sky, I finally understood. We were trapped under a dome with all the monsters, none of us able to escape.

world ender

ulla

"Did it work?" I asked.

After we said the incantation, we stood in silence, holding hands around the fire burning gold and violet. As far as I'd been able to tell, nothing had happened. No sounds, no shaking, no changes in the fire.

"Should we say it again?" Sunniva asked.

"It's not necessary," Elof said, and Dagny let go of our hands. "If it works, it worked. And if it didn't . . ."

"If it didn't, then what?" I asked, since he'd trailed off.

"Our time is better spent finding a way to kill the monsters or send them back where they came from." Dagny had already put her back to us and gone back to the books.

"What should we look for?" Sunniva asked.

"We don't know," Elof admitted. "I only found the incantation book because a spider fell on it, and the title sounded promising."

I stopped cold. "A spider?"

A loud banging in the hall interrupted us, and Dagny

grabbed her bow from where she'd left it by the entrance of the *girjastu*. Her quiver and arrows were secured on her back.

"Someone's in the armory," I whispered.

Dagny cursed and jogged down the hall, moving silently on the balls of her feet. I didn't keep up with her, so she was basically going in blind since I had the light.

There was another bang, then Dagny shouted, "Don't move!"

I arrived in time to see Dagny holding her bow and arrow on Noomi Indudottir. She was holding a spear with a forked head, but she slowly raised her hands above her head. Her makeup was smeared across her face, the skin on her right cheek was red and blistered from a fresh burn, and her blond hair was singed and jagged on that side.

Every time I had seen her before, she was so strong, angry, and sneering down at me. Now she was trembling, with tears in her eyes.

"You were right," Noomi said when she saw me, squinting in the torchlight. "About everything. I have been *jallaki*."

"So you're saying that we should put you out of your misery?" Dagny asked.

"No!" Noomi shouted. "Please! I have seen so many of the ones I care about slaughtered today. I only want to protect those I have left."

Reluctantly, Dagny lowered her bow. "Do you think you can kill the nightmare creatures running rampant on the surface?"

"I've already taken out a few. With proper weapons, I can take out more." She held her weapon up higher as an example.

"How do you kill the wyrm?" I asked.

Noomi laughed, a dark sound with a high-pitched lilt of

hysteria. "As far as I've seen, the flying serpent cannot be killed. It is Jörmungandr, the world ender."

"Everything ends, even wyrms," Dagny said.

"And what of me?" Noomi asked. Her hands had slowly fallen back to her side as we'd been speaking, and she stood taller, even when her chin quivered. "Are you ending me today or are you allowing me to fight alongside you?"

Dagny looked over at me, deferring to my judgment about the woman who had helped torture me during the Lost Month.

"I remember what you did," I said, and she visibly gulped. "Not all of it. But enough to know that you're a sadist, and you don't deserve forgiveness."

Noomi lowered her eyes and sniffled as a tear fell down her cheek.

"But life isn't about what you deserve," I said finally. "And we need anyone we can get to fight these fucking things."

"You can join us," Dagny agreed with a sigh. "But don't make me kill you."

76

Betrayals

BRYN

I only made it a few steps, leading Eliana by the hand, as we stepped over the bodies of Älvolk and allies alike. Some of them were even children, and I paused to make sure they were dead. I didn't want to leave them behind if there was still hope.

"We shouldn't stop," Eliana said, frantically looking around while I crouched over a toddler whose burnt body had already gone cold. "It's not safe."

"Talking too loud isn't safe," I told her with an icy glance back over my shoulder. "Checking for survivors is prudent."

Her jaw tensed and her mouth twisted into an irritable scowl.

"If we don't help those that need help, we're no better than the monsters," I said.

She looked like she wanted to argue, but then her eyes widened when she looked past me. As I turned back, I already heard the slurping wet sound of the thick mucus trail the murder snail left behind.

It stretched its long neck outward, snapping at me with a narrow mouth of crooked fangs, and I leaned backward, grabbing Eliana's arm as I did, pulling her down and out of the way, and I somersaulted back onto my feet.

Eliana ran away, leaving me to face the snail alone, but it was better that way. I remembered the way Tuva had screamed and writhed after the venom got her.

When the snail came at me again, I dodged to the side at the last second and swung my sword to quickly slice through the stalks that held up its big ginger-red eyes. Now blinded, its head moved erratically, and I had to move quickly to evade the gnashing teeth.

But it couldn't see to block me, and it only took two strong blows to get through the neck and decapitate the murder snail.

I took a deep breath and ran on, after Eliana and toward the tent.

I could hear yelling before I saw them through the smoke and haze. Sumi cursing, Finn yelling about no escape, someone else just screaming bloody murder. As the tent took shape through the smog, I saw the full horror of the situation.

Spiders were crawling all over it, while Sumi and a few others tried to fight them off. Finn and the Trylle Queen were arguing outside, but the spiders were coming faster so he dragged her inside.

I stayed outside, fighting alongside Sumi, taking out as many spiders as I could. Until I saw an arachnid the size of a hobgoblin tear a hole into the tarp, making a new entrance in the side.

I went after her—cutting through a pair of fat, angry spiders on the way—and made it inside the tent in time to see the spider wreaking havoc with the medical equipment. Standing in front of the rows of cots were Eliana, Minnie, and a few others creating a troll wall before the wounded.

At the far end of the tent, I spied Pan and Rikky fighting spiders that had broken through at their end. Finn and Wendy were having a heated discussion in the relative safety near the center of the room.

I took my battle stance, looking for the right moment to strike the massive spider. The arachnid had turned its attention toward the wall of Minnie and Eliana, and I charged at it.

And then, as I ran, the spider had its eyes fixed on Eliana. But then Eliana took Minnie by the shoulders, and she pushed her directly into the waiting fangs of the spider. I shouted *no* and Eliana screamed, but it was cut short by the sound of fangs tearing through bone and flesh.

I leapt onto the back of the spider, driving my sword through the jagged green line down the back. The gelatinous innards spilled over the ground, and Minnie's body was submerged beneath it.

When I stood up, I wiped the spider gunk off my hands and stepped toward Eliana. "What the hell is wrong with you, Eliana?"

"That's not Eliana," Sumi said from behind me. "That's Illaria."

The girl I'd thought was Eliana suddenly laughed, and Sumi frowned.

"I promised your mama that I would take care of you and your sister," Sumi said. "The problem is, Illaria, I don't think anyone can be safe with you around."

Sumi stalked past me, her chin down and her eyes on Illaria. She moved like a *kuguar*. I stepped to the side, leaving Sumi to deal with the evil twin, while I took care of the spiders that kept invading the tent.

After Illaria had murdered Minnie to save herself from a spider, everyone that could move scattered away. Illaria stood alone, spider corpses surrounding her feet, and her hair kept shifting through different shades of red.

"You and Mama cared for a world that tormented you, isolated you, rejected you both," Illaria said. "But it cannot reject me. It's cold and it is cruel. This world deserves to be destroyed."

As soon as she said that, Illaria snarled and lunged at Sumi. In an instant—a quick flick of her wrist—Sumi had drawn her blade. Illaria moved insanely fast, but Sumi seemed to anticipate all Illaria's strikes in advance.

And then Sumi's blade found Illaria's heart. Illaria gasped in surprise, and Sumi jammed the knife in deeper. Iridescent burgundy blood spilled from her mouth and she staggered back.

The wyrm roared, sounding just above us, and the scent of sulfur wafted in the tent.

Illaria collapsed back on the ground, and the tarp of the tent bowed in from the pressure of fire blowing at it. The Tralla leather was supposed to be flame retardant but the electric heat from the dragon breath was extreme, and it started to blacken and burn.

The only "safe" spot I knew of in Áibmoráigi was on fire and surrounded by the wyrm and giant spiders.

77

stable

wendy

Finn stood in front of me, his dark eyes full of fear in a way that I had never seen before.

We were in the tent, and even with all the chaos and spiders and screaming, time seemed to have slowed since he'd come running back to tell me we were trapped, like moths in a jar. He pulled me inside the tent, ostensibly to figure out what to do, but what could we do?

"We can't leave, we can't stay," I said. "So we fight."

"Wendy . . ." He shook his head helplessly. "I don't know how to fight this. I can't think of an option where we don't all end up dead."

My first thought was of my son, Oliver. He was back at the palace with my brother Matt, his wife, Willa, and their children. Safe, secure, loved. But if we didn't find a way to stop the wyrm from eating the world, how long could Oliver or anyone be safe? Even in Förening?

I closed my eyes, picturing Oliver—his hair sandy like Loki's, his eyes dark like mine, and a smile that lit up my world.

For him, I would do anything. Even the impossible.

"Underground." I opened my eyes and everything seemed to be moving hyper fast. Bryn was fighting spiders at the far end of the tent. But I focused on Finn.

"The Älvolk live underground," I said. "How do we get there?"

"Stables," Pan said.

He was leaning on a cot behind me, his breath ragged. His curls were damp with sweat and blood, but based on the lime green color of the blood, it wasn't his.

"What'd you say?" I leaned in closer to hear him better.

"The stables," he answered. "You go through the stables at the center of the city, and it'll take you underground." Then he pointed toward the screaming going on near Bryn, by the entrance. "Sumi knows where to go."

"Finn, go with Sumi," I commanded. "Take the children and anyone you can with you."

"What'll you do?" Finn asked.

"I'm going to get everyone else going," I said. "And you're going to make a path for us."

The wyrm roared again. Within minutes, the entire roof of the tent was on fire, but by then Finn was already gone, taking everyone he could with him. As ash rained down from above and the air clouded with smoke, I struggled to help Rikky, Patrik, and Pan get a large unconscious ogre onto a makeshift stretcher.

Pan and I got in front, carrying the cot backward, with Rikky and Patrik bringing up the rear. It was slow going with all the weight and stepping over the carnage. The heat from the flames was overwhelming and sweat dripped into my eyes.

Then, with a loud *whoosh,* the half-burnt tarp above us collapsed down on us. It was heavy and hot, like a smoldering weighted blanket. I tried to tear through the tarp, but it wouldn't give and the fire burned my fingers.

I coughed as smoke filled my lungs, and a blade tore through the leather and a hand reached in. It took mine, strong and rough, and Loki pulled me free. He scooped me up in his arms, and I wrapped mine around his neck, and he ran through the burning remnants of the tent.

"You saved my life," I said hoarsely.

"I figured it was time I returned the favor." He set me down once we were far enough away, and brushed the silver lock of hair from my eyes. "Are you all right?"

I nodded. "I'll live."

A grunting sound from the tent caused us both to look over to see Pan dragging Rikky out of the fire. Loki rushed away to help them, and I collapsed to the ground on my knees, coughing and trying to breathe.

Loki carried Rikky over—her left leg was bloody and burnt, and she seemed dazed. Pan staggered over and collapsed beside me, coughing hard.

"What about Patrik?" I asked. "And the ogre."

Pan shook his head. "They didn't make it."

Tears stung my burning eyes when I asked him, "Can you show us the way down?"

78

ouroboros

ulla

Dagny finally lowered her bow, but she didn't put it back in her quiver. We were about to leave the armory when I heard yelling and running on the stairs.

"Go as far down as you can!" a familiar voice commanded, and I ran out in the hall to see injured survivors coming down the steps.

"Where should they go?" I asked, looking to Noomi. "Where can they be safe from the wyrm?"

"Um . . ." She thought for a second. "The *girjastu* should be good."

Dagny stepped out and started directing the dazed survivors. "I'll take you down to the *girjastu*." Then she turned to Noomi. "Come with me and help me get them safe and comfortable."

Noomi knew her way around here, and Dagny wanted to keep an eye on her, I'm sure, so it made sense. Dagny didn't ask me to join her, but she probably knew I wanted to be here, watching and waiting.

Pan had gotten split up from us a while ago, but I hadn't let myself think about what he might be doing or if . . .

Finn I saw first, and he hugged me tightly—hard enough that it hurt. When he released me, I noticed his red-rimmed eyes under the amber torchlight.

The only time I had ever seen him look this shattered was after his sister died, but this time he was all bloody and banged up like he'd been in a car wreck.

"Go, rest while you can," I said.

He didn't say anything. He only nodded and then moved down the hall, shuffling like a weary zombie. As survivors continued down the stairs, most passed me by without saying anything—like Sumi with her head down and an injured Jennet. They just followed Dagny's voice, directing them to the *girjastu* with promises of water and blankets.

Tove went by very slowly, until he saw his sister, Sunniva. Then they both ran at each other and hugged. He had dried blood in his ears, and Sunniva cried when she got a good look at him.

I was waiting in the doorway to the armory, and Bryn paused as she reached me. Her arms were covered in both scars and fresh wounds, and sweat left trails through the blood and dirt staining her arms.

"Glad you're safe," she said, and that's when I went in for a hug. She let me hug her, but her arms hung limply until she finally squeezed me back.

"I knew you'd be okay," I said. "You always are."

She coughed and pulled away from me. "Right now, I need to get something to drink."

"Yeah, go," I said. "I'll see you in the *girjastu* soon."

At least that's what I hoped. The more time passed without seeing Pan, the more anxious I became. The survivors were trickling down slowly, but there really weren't that many.

The Trylle Queen and King descended the stairs, and right behind them, Pan was helping Rikky down the stairs. I ran over to them, and I wanted to embrace Pan and cover him in relieved kisses, but Rikky couldn't stand on her own, so I swooped in and put my arm around her.

"Thank you," she said quietly.

"What are you doing here?" I asked as we walked down the hall.

"The Trylle Queen sent messages to all the kingdoms asking for volunteers," Rikky explained. "It sounded too important to sit out just because I was mad at Pan."

"Well, it's very brave of you to be here," I said.

"I've always helped those who need it." Rikky put too much weight on her injured leg, and she winced.

"Lean on me," I told her. "I got you."

When we made it to the *girjastu*, Dagny and Sumi were organizing the space to be a makeshift camp. They had pushed the shelving toward the back to create private spaces for the more seriously injured to be treated, while the rest of the room had pillows and blankets for everyone to get comfortable and water buckets to start allowing them to drink and clean up.

Eliana had a spot right near the front door, where she had set up a cozy sitting area with blankets and hay for herself and two younger girls. As soon as she saw me, she invited us to join her, and Pan and I helped Rikky get settled in with her.

Once we'd finished, Pan and I offered to take water pails down to the well at the end of the hall. Everyone was coughing and dirty, not to mention many of them had serious wounds.

Someone had lit the torches that lined that hall, so Pan and I walked in the warm glow down the cool stone floor. We didn't say anything at first. The relative silence—the sounds of talking muffled and echoed from the *girjastu*—was comforting after all the noise and violence of the day.

We were almost to the well when Pan stopped. I paused, looking back at him. His biceps had been wrapped in gauze, taut around the muscle as he stood with his hands on his hips.

"Pan?" I asked.

He stared down at the floor and rubbed his chin. "I . . ."

I set the pails down and stepped closer to him. Then he looked up at me, his lips slightly parted and his eyes dark as night. Without saying anything, he moved in a flash. His mouth on mine, one hand on my face and the other on my waist. I wrapped my arms around him, and he pressed me back against the wall.

He kissed me fiercely, hungrily, in a way I felt all the way through me. The way his hands felt, gripping me like he was afraid to lose me.

He rested his forehead against mine, and he inhaled deeply.

"I love you so much, Ulla," he said, his voice husky. "I need you to know that. In case anything happens today."

"I do know," I said, and he looked me in the eye. "I love you so much. But nothing's going to happen. We're going to make it out of this, and we're going to make our own happily ever after."

He smiled wanly and kissed me again. "We should go. They need water."

On our way back from the well, we passed by a brightly lit underground greenhouse of sorts, filled with all kinds of lush plants and vegetables. I stopped to peek in the open door, and Finn was standing in a circle, talking with Bryn, Sumi, and the Trylle Queen and King.

I couldn't hear what they were saying, but Pan and I had our hands full with water, so I kept on moving.

After all the water had been dispensed, I went over to where Dagny and Elof had holed themselves up in a corner with a pile of books. I sat down on the floor beside them, taking a quick break.

"How are you doing?" Dagny asked me.

"Okay. I just need a minute." I looked over at her and Elof scouring dusty pages. "How are you guys doing?"

"If the situation wasn't so dire, I'd be happier than an elk in spring," Elof said dourly. "All these old books are a dream come true, but everything else is a nightmare."

"The biggest obstacle is that most of this is written in runic chicken scratch," Dagny said with a heavy sigh. "They're difficult to read at best and impossible at worst."

"I do have plenty of experience with that." I leaned over to read over her shoulder.

"I've been struggling with this passage." She held the book out to me. "I know it says something about Jörmungandr, the world ender, but the ink in the passage is smeared, so it's nearly illegible."

The page was written in an Old Norse derivative, and it had survived water damage at some point in its history. Beneath the smeared words was a relatively intact drawing of an *ouroboros*—a wyrm biting its own tail.

A few words stood out to me—*allhardr, morginn, groenn*—and I suddenly remembered, *"The suns set in the green sky when the good morning becomes the violent night."*

"What?" Dagny asked.

"I think I know what I need to do," I said.

79

resolve

BRYN

The room the Trylle Queen chose was an overwhelmingly green indoor garden. She had wanted to meet with advisors about what to do, away from the prying eyes and ears of everyone in the *girjastu*, and that meant she'd assembled her dream team of Finn, Loki, and a very dazed Tove.

Sumi and I exchanged a look, and then we both followed Wendy and company down the hallway. When she did notice us, she motioned for us to join them, but we would've come on in without an invitation. I had pushed my way into meetings with royals, and I wasn't about to let anybody hold me back now.

That was contrary to what I'd told my boyfriend, Ridley, last night. It had been late, and I had been traveling, and I called him from a rest-stop bathroom.

"Just be safe, Bryn," Ridley had said, his voice thick and far away.

"I will do my best," I'd promised him.

He sighed. "I should be there with you."

"No, you shouldn't," I said firmly. We'd already gone over this before I left. After the Kanin Civil War—and after Ridley had been tortured—he'd suffered very debilitating PTSD.

We all did, really—everyone in Doldastam—to varying degrees. But Ridley had been through things that left him unfit for combat. He panicked and froze if he heard certain things or when he smelled blood.

Coming here would have only made him a liability, plus I'd be way too busy worrying about him. So I asked him to stay in Doldastam to help coordinate and do what he could from there.

"I still hate that I'm not there with you," Ridley said finally.

"I know." Tears stung my eyes. "I love you, Ridley."

"I love you too," he said. "Come home safe."

Now, in the underground greenhouse of the lost city of Áibmoráigi, I wondered if I could keep my promise to him.

Wendy surveyed the small group of us standing in a semicircle around her, in a humid room that smelled like lilacs and dirt. Her expression was grim, her clothes bloody and torn, and I realized that I'd never seen a Queen look so worried and disheveled.

"Does anybody have ideas about what to do?" she asked, and the silence that followed was deafening.

"We have enough food to stay here awhile," Tove said, and absently played with a leafy vine from a plant hanging above.

"That's not a permanent solution," Wendy said.

"It might end up one," Sumi said, sounding resigned as she looked around the room.

"No, it won't," Finn said with strong conviction. "I will get back to my children, or I will die trying."

"I know," Sumi said. "I'm saying that you'll probably die."

Finn bowed his head slightly and pinched the bridge of his nose. "We have to come up with something more than just sitting here."

"Isn't that docent Elof looking into the old scrolls?" Wendy asked. Her hands were clasped in front of her, twisting together. "Looking for an incantation or some way to fight this?"

Loki scoffed. "That's how we got trapped in this snow globe from hell."

"They trapped us in this mess before the wyrm could do more damage," Sumi argued.

"That's all well and good, but we should've evacuated everyone first," Loki said, and cast a look over at his wife.

"Yeah, we should've done a lot of things differently, but here we are," Tove muttered.

They went round and round like that, sniping at each other out of frustration. I don't know how long they spent debating the merits of undoing the protection spell, but I had stopped contributing.

I sat on a garden stool, hunched over with my hands buried in my hair, listening to Wendy and Finn argue their opposing points again.

"We can't risk unleashing this horror upon the world," Wendy insisted.

"Then we will all die!" Finn shot back.

"Then that's how it must be!" Wendy yelled.

"I think I know what to do," Ulla said, her clear but soft voice cutting through the tension, and I looked back to see her standing in the greenhouse with her friend Dagny.

"What?" Finn asked her.

"I know what to do." Her expression was nervous, but she stood tall. "I have to kill the wyrm."

"Ulla, you're strong, but you're not trained," Finn said. "The wyrm laid waste to many, many Omte soldiers today."

"But I'm not just Omte," Ulla reminded him. "I'm also *álfar*. I am the morning flower and the summer bird, and I'm the good morning that ends the violent night."

"That's . . . very poetic," Loki replied carefully. "But that doesn't tell us how you are going to go about killing the unkillable."

"With her dagger and my arrows," Dagny interjected.

"What are you talking about, Ulla?" I asked, since none of what she was saying made any sense to me.

She took a deep breath and looked uncertainly over at Dagny, who nodded her head in encouragement.

"I don't know how to explain it exactly," Ulla began. "I was reading an old text, talking about this prophecy—*the suns will set in the green sky when the good morning becomes the violent night*. I just *knew* what I needed to do."

"I'm going to coat the tip of my dagger—" Ulla's hand went to the ornate Omte weapon sheathed on her hip.

"And my arrows," Dagny repeated.

"—with *sorgblomma* blood," Ulla continued. "We're going to kill the wyrm and the monsters, and when we're done, everyone can evacuate."

"Elof, Noomi, and Sunniva are currently looking for a way to close the portal again," Dagny said. "Elof can hide out, surviving with the remaining Älvolk and thrimavolk, and seal themselves in again until they find a way to close the portal."

"But what if another wyrm gets through?" Wendy asked. "Or something worse? If the portal is open, we're all still in danger."

"You can help Elof look through the books," Dagny suggested. "That's what I'll be doing as soon as the wyrm is taken care of."

"I don't know what it is that you think you know, Ulla," Finn said. "But if you go up against the dragon, you will die."

"I know it's not a perfect plan," Ulla said. "But it's the best one we've got."

I stood up and looked at Ulla. "What can I do to help?"

80

✣

abyss

ulla

Dagny, Sumi, Wendy, Bryn, and I stood around the map of Áibmoráigi that Sumi had sketched in the dirt. Finn had kept arguing against the idea—even after everyone agreed that it was the best course of action—so Tove and Loki took him back to *girjastu*.

Sumi's map helped us lay out possible vantage points and potential coverage. It was hard to know what exactly we'd be walking into or how many of the Alfheim monsters would be waiting for us, so Sumi and Bryn ran through multiple scenarios and how to deal with them.

"Whatever happens, you two need to get as high as you can as fast as you can," Bryn summarized. "The rest of us will run interference so you can take care of the wyrm."

"How much *sorgblomma* do you have?" Wendy asked.

Dagny slipped her bag off her back and pulled out a corked bottle. It was half full of red liquid, and she sloshed the bottle. "We took everything the *häxdoktor* had on his shelf."

"Are you sure that's enough?" Wendy asked.

"Well, it's all we have, so it has to be," Dagny replied, and Wendy frowned.

"Ulla?" Sunniva called for me from the hall.

"Yeah?" I said as I went back toward the door.

"There you are." She came into the room looking relieved, and Noomi was right behind her.

"Is something wrong?" I asked.

"Not anything you don't already know about," Sunniva said. "And my auditory precogs are getting louder."

"What do you mean?" I asked.

"Maybe nothing, maybe something," she replied vaguely.

"What are you doing here?" Dagny asked Noomi.

"I heard you were going to kill the wyrm," Noomi said. "I want to help."

"It would've been a lot more helpful if you hadn't let the damn thing in," Dagny countered icily.

Noomi's jaw tensed and she met Dagny's gaze defiantly. "I cannot go back in time. I can only fight forward."

"You can fight with me," Wendy said to Noomi. "We need all the help we can get."

Suddenly, there was a far-off boom, and dust rained down from the ceiling.

"You all heard that, right?" Sunniva asked uneasily.

"What was that?" Wendy asked.

Sumi looked up at the ceiling. "Another rockslide maybe?"

Sunniva was standing beside me, and she reached over and took my hand. Then she took a few steps backward, leading me more into the center of the room.

"What are you doing?" I asked.

"No matter what happens, we stay right here," Sunniva said firmly, and her dark eyes were locked anxiously on the door.

There was another boom, louder this time, and more dust and pebbles came down from the ceiling.

"Noomi!" someone yelled, and a young thrimavolk came running in. "Noomi, the wyrm burnt down the stables, and it's trying to get in through the front door!"

"Go back to the *girjastu* and take the youngens to the vault," Noomi commanded. "Tell everyone else to take what they need from the armory to fight the wyrm."

"Is there another way out of here?" Bryn asked once the girl ran off.

Noomi looked back at us. "Not a way that we could get everyone out. If the wyrm gets back down here, we're all cooked."

Another boom, but this one had a long rumbling aftershock, and the ground shook. With my free hand, I grabbed Dagny's arm and pulled her back beside me.

The floor kept shaking—the stones clattering together—and then warm, humid air suddenly rushed up as the floor gave out. We went into a free fall, plummeting into a dark pit below.

81

knightfall

bryn

I opened my eyes, staring up through the water at the white light above. I sat up and took a deep breath. I had no idea how long I'd been under, but my Skojare blood meant I was capable of being underwater for a very long time.

My eyes adjusted, and I saw everyone scattered throughout a cave with pools of hot water and several small steaming geysers. Wendy, Noomi, and Sumi sat nearby at the edge of the water, coughing and getting their bearings. Farther down, Ulla and Sunniva were sitting while Dagny paced through the shallow water.

"Where are we?" I asked as I stood up. The pool of water only came up to my knees.

"The hot springs are under the indoor gardens. The floor gave out"—Sumi motioned around to the chunks of floor and overturned plants littered around us—"and now we're trapped in a steamy cave while a dragon burns down the world around us."

"Doesn't this water feed into the well?" Ulla asked, and

she pointed to the darkest end of the cave. "Is the well down there?"

"The ladder!" Sumi and Noomi shouted in unison.

Dagny got the torch lit, and Sumi took it from her so she could lead the way. The springs ended in a small stream that passed through a narrow gap in the stone. We followed it through. The well was a stony tunnel up toward a green sky, and a mossy ladder ran up along the wall.

Sumi went up first, climbing up the slippery ladder without hesitation, and I went after her. It took about ten frightening minutes, moving upward with a small dot of light guiding us up.

Not that things were bright on the land. The air was all a green haze, and it smelled of ash and death, and it burned my nose and lungs.

From where we came up, I could see the serpentine dragon writhing around in the ashes of the stable and the bones of the elk that blocked the entrance. Only a portion of the tail was still out, as it used its head like a battering ram, taking down the winding staircase. The stairs were a narrower width than the massive room, so it had to tear down brick walls to get through.

"Ulla, how strong are you?" I asked as she climbed out of the well behind me.

"Pretty strong, why?" she asked uncertainly.

"Do you think you can pull that thing out?" I pointed to the wyrm tunneling its way underground. "Or at least pull on its tail enough to piss it off?"

She thought for a second, chewing her lip, then nodded. "Yeah. I can piss it off, at least."

"Great, because there's no way you're getting through those scales," I said. My hand was still bruised and throbbing from when I broke my sword over it. "You'll have to aim for the eyes, so we need to get its head out before you take your shot."

"You get the wyrm out," Sumi told Ulla. "As soon as you do, then you and Dagny need to get to higher ground. The tower ruins are the closest. Me and Bryn can go south to distract the wyrm while you two get in place."

"Wendy and I will lead the wyrm back so Ulla and Dagny can take their shot," Noomi said.

"Are you ready, Ulla?" I asked.

She took a fortifying breath and nodded. "We've got this."

Then she turned and ran over to the wyrm. She winced when she grabbed the tail, covered in spiky scales, and dug her heels in the ground.

As Sumi and I ran around to the south side of the stables, I looked back and saw Ulla straining. Her face was already red and sweaty as she pulled the wyrm with all of her considerable might.

Sumi and I took cover behind a burnt-out snail shell. She immediately took her sword and used it to break off a large section of the shell in the shape of a lopsided diamond and handed it to me.

"What's this for?" I asked.

She flipped it over, and on the underside she used her ankle dagger to quickly take out a small chunk. She picked it up, using the gouge as a hand grip, and held it in front of her. "*Etanadrak* shells are fireproof. They make a great shield."

Then she held it out to me. "Here. You take this one. I'll make another."

"Thanks," I said, and glanced around. A smoldering *kuguar* corpse lay a few feet away. The one good thing about the wyrm's rampage of killing every living thing was that that included the *kuguars* and the murder snails.

Ulla still pulled at the wyrm's tail. The ground rumbled

as the wyrm wriggled and fought. It whipped its tail, yanking her through the ash and dirt, despite her best efforts to keep her footing.

The wyrm was scooting backward out of the stairwell, and with more of its body out, it was whipping her around with more and more force. Until finally it threw her, and she landed in a pile of rubble.

"Ulla!" I shouted, and started toward her, but she sat up, coughing, and I stopped short. "Ulla! The wyrm's almost out! Go with Dagny and Sunniva to the tower! Sumi and I will take it from here!"

She nodded, then took off to where Dagny and Sunniva were waiting by the tower.

I looked back at Sumi. She held up her fractured snail shell shield with her left hand and her sword with her right.

The wyrm suddenly burst through the ground right in front of me. Dirt and stone exploded from the earth, and I was sent flying backward. The beast instantly turned its rage on me, and I curled up in a ball, hiding as much of my body as I could under my shield just as the wyrm unleashed a green fiery blast at me.

The snail shell held, but it got hot enough that it scorched my fingertips. I squeezed my eyes shut and buried my face in the dirt, and my skin felt sunburnt. All the hair stood up on my body, like I was consumed by static electricity, and my teeth ached.

"Hey!" Sumi shouted, and I peered out from under the shield to see her throwing broken elk antlers and bones at the wyrm.

The wyrm roared—right above me at earsplitting decibels—and then it slithered after Sumi. I crawled out from under the shell, and then I was on my feet, charging after the wyrm before it killed Sumi.

She held her own against it, dodging out of the way of its fiery attacks in the nick of time. I came up behind the giant beast, and in a quick motion, I slid my sword under the thick scales, stabbing at the tender flesh again.

The wyrm whirled around me, screeching and coiling itself up. I looked around to see Wendy holding her hands up palms out at the wyrm, and it abruptly took flight.

"Ulla's up in the tower," Noomi yelled at me from where she stood a few meters away from Wendy. Then she looked up at the dragon, circling above us. "It's time to send it back."

82

❦

shatter

ulla

My hip throbbed from the wyrm throwing me in the rubble, and the palms of my hands were in ribbons from gripping the spiky tail. The beast appeared reptilian with all its scales, but it felt more like a leather cactus. Hundreds of tiny spikes had left my hands a bloody mess.

My feet were torn up from being dragged all across the dirt, and I'd futilely been digging my heels in the ground to hold it. But there was no way I could overpower that thing.

The worst, though, really, was my hip, because it slowed me down. I ran as fast as I could, but it hurt like hell and tears formed in my eyes.

Dagny and Sunniva were waiting for me at the bottom of the steps of the tower, and when I reached them, Dagny asked, "Are you all right?"

"Yeah, yeah," I lied. "Let's go. I don't know how long they can hold it."

I ran up the stairs behind them, and I had managed to get almost halfway up the first set when my hip completely gave out. It was all too much for my body. All of my muscles ached and trembled from using all my strength to fight the wyrm, and the pain was so intense, tears and sweat were streaming down my face.

"*Jakla*," I cursed, and tried again, but it was an excruciating feeling, like a blinding white light that somehow surpassed everything I'd ever known about my pain. I collapsed on the steps and groaned through gritted teeth.

"Ulla!" Dagny stopped on the stairs and reached back to help me.

"No, go on ahead," I told her. "The wyrm could be over here any second."

Dagny hesitated a moment, then ran up the stairs. Sunniva stayed back and crouched beside me.

"Can you stand at all?" Sunniva asked.

I grimaced and tried again, but it instantly gave out and I let out an agonized moan.

"That's a 'no' then," Sunniva said. "Okay, I'm going to try something, and it might not work. And even if it does, it won't last long. My healing is not very effective outside of auras."

She pressed one hand against the soft flesh of my abdomen, and then she put the other hand on my injured hip. Gently, she kneaded the tender area, but it was enough to make me cry out in pain.

"This will hurt a bit," she said. "But it won't last long."

"It's fine," I said, and held my breath.

But slowly, the pain lessened, and a soothing warmth spread through me, radiating out from my hip and all through my body. I wasn't a hundred percent—not by any means—but I felt considerably better, and when I tried to bear weight on my leg again, I could do it with only minimal pain.

"Thanks," I said.

Sunniva only replied with, "Let's go."

As I ran up the stairs, I looked down and saw Noomi barely outrunning the wyrm. It threw its head back, like it was about to expel fire all over Noomi, but Wendy did something—the wyrm reacted like it had been slapped—and that gave Noomi enough time to find cover.

And that's when I noticed the bodies lying in the ruins. Indu Mattison impaled on a wooden post, and nearby, Jem-Kruk lying on stones. His long hair was splayed around him like a halo, and his arms and legs were askew. Somehow, he looked serene and beautiful, even in death.

"Jem," I whispered as fresh tears formed in my eyes, but I wiped them away and lunged up the stairs.

Jem-Kruk had been nothing but kind to me, and I would shed many a tear for him later, but right now, I couldn't.

I arrived on the landing just as the wyrm struck the tower with its tail. The tower quaked—and stones tumbled past us— but it remained standing. Sunniva stumbled backward, but she caught herself just before she tumbled over the edge. Dagny fell to the floor, landing on her knees. But the bottle of *sorgblomma* blood slipped from her hand, and it shattered as it hit the floor.

Dagny had begun dipping her arrow tips, but she'd only done one so far—I could see the shimmering arrow in her quiver.

"That was it," she said breathlessly. "That was all we had." She looked over at me with wide, terrified eyes. "How will we stop it now?"

83

Gutted

BRYN

From where I stood, I saw the wyrm crash into the tower, and I saw the bottle shatter. The wyrm was flying around the tower, and Dagny, Ulla, and Sunniva were scrambling on the landing.

They were going to be incinerated before they figured out what to do.

I had to buy them time.

"Hey!" I shouted, running toward the wyrm. "Hey, you smelly, slimy son of a bitch!"

The dragon tilted toward me but kept flying around the tower. It moved, bobbing up and down in the air, like a roller coaster cutting through the smog.

When it came lowest to the ground, I chucked my sword like a spear, aiming for the eye.

It missed—barely—and stuck into the exposed flesh just above the eye. The wyrm howled as it flew at me.

I dove behind a crumbling wall, and the beast sailed right through it. A rock wall fell on me, but I held the snail shield over me. It helped protect me, but when a large rock hit it, it shattered like glass.

I scrambled out from under the rocks and broken shield, and I was instantly up and running because the wyrm was on my heels. It was winding to the side, using its long body to block my escape toward cover.

I ran faster, my legs burning underneath me, but the wyrm was herding me to the cliff. If I tried to veer to one side or the other, it was there, pushing me away.

I ran up to the edge and stopped just as my toes skidded past it. I had nowhere else to go. I turned back around to face the monster head on.

"I'm sorry I couldn't be safe this time," I said breathlessly, and my voice was lost in the wind.

84

uncage

ulla

"What do we do? What do we do?" Dagny asked in a rapid whisper, and it sounded more like she was asking herself than me.

I tried to scoop up the tiny droplets of liquid that had pooled on the rough stone landing, but my hands were such a bloody mess, it was impossible, not to mention it burned like hell.

"My blood," I realized, staring down at my hands. "It was powerful enough to get the protection spell to work."

Dagny looked at me. "We need enough for your dagger."

Bryn was yelling, and I looked over to see the wyrm chasing her to the edge of the cliff.

I hurried to pull out my dagger, and I ran the blade across my bloody hand, coating it as much as I could.

I lifted my head to see the wyrm pinning Bryn against the cliff's edge. Wendy held her hands up in front of her, but she collapsed to the ground in exhaustion. Sumi was running at the wyrm, but she was still so far away.

Bryn stood her ground and faced the dragon defiantly, and I yelled her name. She closed her eyes, and the wyrm's breath engulfed her in green flames. Within seconds, she was nothing but ash and bones.

"Ulla!" Dagny shouted. She grabbed my hand and squeezed drops of blood onto her arrows.

"We should light it, right?" Sunniva asked. "Like the spell? And killing fire with fire?"

Dagny fumbled for a match. I tore off the bottom of my shirt and wrapped my hands with fabric.

"Ulla," Sunniva said as a match broke.

"I'm trying," Dagny muttered, striking another match. It finally took, and as soon as the flame touched the blood on my dagger, it went up in bright purple flames.

"Ulla!" Sunniva shouted.

I looked up to see the wyrm flying straight at us. I took a running start, and I leapt off the landing with all my might. My flaming dagger raised high over my head, I stared right into the primal emerald eyes of the beast.

I drove the dagger deep into one eye, then landed roughly on the head of the wyrm as hot blood spilled down my arm. The wyrm screamed and flew erratically. The dagger was stuck in the eye, so I held on to it with both hands until the wyrm crashed hard into the ground.

I was thrown from the monster, and I rolled and bounced to a painful stop, barely stopping before the edge of the cliff.

The wind was knocked from my chest, and I gulped down the air greedily, even though it still burned my lungs. I forced myself up until I was sitting and watched the wyrm give a few half-hearted thrashes of its tail.

Once it finally stopped moving, I lay back on the ground and stared up at the cloudless, starry indigo sky. The air still tasted of brimstone and chlorine, but the haze was starting to clear.

"Ulla!" Dagny shouted as she ran over and crouched beside me. "Are you okay?"

"I'm still breathing, so sure." I looked up at her. "Is it over?"

"Well, the wyrm's dead," she said flatly. "But the portal's still open, and all the Ögonen are crowding near the bridge."

"All what Ögonen?" I sat up and looked to where dozens of the sinewy beings had gathered, their skin seeming to glow a dark golden ochre. "Where'd they come from?"

"The Älvolk caged them on the mountain, but now they're free," Dagny said.

"They did this," I realized. "All of this . . ." My voice cracked as I thought of all the lives lost today.

I got to my feet and started to run as fast as my legs would carry me, racing toward the Ögonen.

85

odyssey

They all had their backs to me, but I could see their eyes through their semi-translucent heads. Still, it was startling when the Ögonen whipped around to look at me—dozens of them in unison—all of their golden-brown eyes zoning in right on me.

I froze in my tracks a few feet away from them, and I realized dismally that I'd left my dagger in the eye of the dragon. Not that it mattered, because I couldn't move at all.

The Ögonen stepped closer to me, and it was Ur, the Ögonen who had done memory recovery on me in Elof's lab. I didn't recognize them, but it was something I *knew* when I looked into their eyes.

"Why are you doing this?" I shouted.

It's best if we show you, an androgynous voice said inside my head.

And then—*I was flying through the air before I came crashing down in a soft green meadow. The sky above was grapefruit pink with a trio of suns lighting up a lush meadow of vibrant flowers and fluttering bugs.*

A group of Ögonen were lounging peacefully in the grass,

outside the mossy burrows. Nearby, in front of the opening of the cave, were a small group of trollian beings. Álfar. They wore tailored clothes made of spotted kuguar hides with jewelry of bones and gemstones.

The álfar were excited, and they called for the Ögonen to join them. They had found something in the cave.

I followed the Ögonen as they quietly crept by a sleeping pack of wyrms coiled up together.

And there, in the darkest part of the cave, was a window to another world.

Áibmoráigi—the sky passage.

The Ögonen stepped through, and I cautiously reached my fingertips out to touch it. It seemed to be a shimmery pane of glass, and through it, all the color seemed to bow and pull toward it.

All at once, it pulled me in, and I was thrust into swirling darkness. I couldn't breathe or scream, but it didn't hurt. Air was rushing around me, through me, in the tiny spaces between the smallest particles that made up my body.

And then I was tossed out the other side. I crashed through a cold waterfall and landed in the grass. When I looked up, I was on the mountain on the far side of the Lost Bridge, across the ravine from the ruins of Áibmoráigi. Only, the ruins and the bridge weren't there. Even the plateau that Áibmoráigi was built on wasn't there.

It was only a sheer mountain across from us, with a small ledge.

But the álfar and Ögonen were already building. Stones floated on by, and the Ögonen used their powers to stack them up.

It was safe here. No wyrms or etanadrak. The Ögonen kept the window closed, so no one else from Alfheim could get through.

The first winter was hard. The bridge wasn't finished when the heavy snow came. We all went underground together.

We lived like rodents, burrowing deep in the dirt and huddling together. The Ögonen hibernated, but spring came and the álfar started hunting and gathering before the Ögonen. They helped each other—the álfar kept the sleeping Ögonen safe, and the Ögonen shared their powers so the álfar could work more easily.

The summers were short, and the álfar ventured down from the mountains to find more to survive the harsh winters. They found human tribes—first the Sami, then Vikings. They traded them food for fur; for elk, rabbits, and fish; for gemstones—they even shared languages.

And the álfar did more than that. They communed, they started families, they brought humans back to their village in the mountains.

Áibmoráigi was growing, the plateau was expanding and was covered in homes of rock and wood. The álfar went out to settle new lands, and they built villages with humans, living and growing with them until they were all one tribe.

The Ögonen stayed underground all the time, slumbering in warm caves, while the álfar and humans only grew stronger. They called themselves trolls, and they called their ruler King. The crown sat first on Waudin before passing to his son.

And this is how things were done. The son of the King ruled, unless overthrown by a younger, stronger troll. There was peace, and all the Ögonen slept, the way the trolls suggested.

Until King Egil, who reigned over the Longest Winter. He no longer believed that here was better than where the troll ancestors had come from. Egil woke the Ögonen and asked them to open the window home.

The Ögonen did as they were asked, and a pair of wyrms

came through. I watched in horror as the Grændöden happened—the wyrms leveled Áibmoráigi in a green fire.

An álfar *named Frey came through the window, and he defeated the wyrms using a sword dipped in his flaming blood. He closed the window to Alfheim, using his blood to seal it, but since he might want to return home in the future, he left it open only to those with* álfar *blood.*

We rebuilt the city, but we moved it underground, in case a wyrm ever came through again. The trolls warned that someone might open the window again, so they asked the Ögonen to stay awake and help to guard and protect Áibmoráigi.

This is when the bridge was lost, when the Ögonen cloaked the city.

By then, King Asa the Cold had grown tired of living underground. The trolls that had moved to southern villages were plagued by conflict with humans, so Asa the Cold ventured west, across the sea.

In the new lands, the trolls thrived, and soon they all but forgot about Áibmoráigi. Over time, the kingdom grew larger, and it splintered. One tribe became two: the Kanin in the north, and the Vittra in the south.

But the Vittra Queen Bera, she remembered the stories of the First City and its powerful guardians. She worried about enemies—the Kanin, the humans, those she had yet to know.

She brought her stronger troops across an angry sea and through the mountains to pound on the doors of Áibmoráigi. The trolls refused to give up the Ögonen, and a bloody fight ensued.

In a truce, Bera agreed to take only the Ögonen and all of their sorgblomma, *and they left the rest with the Áibmoráigi trolls, now calling themselves Älvolk.*

The Älvolk became fearful that others would come for

the Ögonen and the window to Alfheim would be left unguarded.

So they built cages in the mountainside, made of iron and stone, and they locked the Ögonen up. They told themselves it was to keep them safe, to keep everyone safe, as they sapped power and magic from the Ögonen.

The Ögonen the Vittra took fared only slightly better. The Vittra built the Mimirin Talo institution, and the Ögonen had shifted to standing guard in towers and sleeping in dirt. From the top of the Mimirin, I watched as the tides went in and out, the citadel sprawling around dust.

Two tribes became five, and the Ögonen protected the Mimirin from the Kanin to the north, the Trylle to the east, and the Omte to the south.

The Ögonen watched as the world moved on, and they stayed frozen, trapped in glass like fireflies in a jar. The Vittra would slaughter them if they left, so they stayed, and listened to the cries of the Ögonen left in Áibmoráigi.

In Áibmoráigi, they never left their cages. They'd stretch their long arms through the bars, reaching for one another, but never touching. All of their work for trollkind left them weakened, unable to fight back.

And from the mountain walls, they watched as the Älvolk rose to power, and they watched as a brash Omte King fell in love with a brave álfar woman. I saw them—Thor and Senka, hiding behind a stable as they exchanged words of love and stolen kisses.

And as Senka's belly began to grow, the Ögonen watched and knew that their freedom might finally be within reach.

My birth brought my blood into this world. I had preternatural resilience and strength that came from my mother, and I had the álfar blood the Älvolk needed to open the bridge. For the first time in centuries, someone had the motivation—

the Älvolk's misguided belief that Alfheim was a kingdom paradise being denied from them—and the means—with me; I deciphered the recipe, gave them my blood, and brought them to the elk heart.

I was suddenly whisked ahead to when I first arrived in Merellä, and for the first time, I could see the subtle touches of the Ögonen pushing me where they wanted me to go, closer to Áibmoráigi so I could open the bridge.

I saw myself lying on the roof of the Mimirin beside Pan, and then I was pulled upward faster and faster, into the sky, into the stars.

86

away

I was left in darkness, and when I opened my eyes, it was Pan's worried face in front of me. But for one surreal moment, I had no idea where or when I might be. Ur had taken me through the whole breadth of our history, and when I blinked I was afraid I'd wake up caged on the mountain with the Ögonen.

But I was still here, in Pan's arms, and he brushed the hair back from my face. He smiled down at me, tears in his eyes.

"Good morning, Ulla."

"It's morning?" I strained to see but the sky was dark above us.

"No, but I have no idea what time it is." He glanced around. "It's night, I guess."

"What happened?" I asked him.

"I don't know." His brow knotted. "I came up, and you were unconscious on the ground. Dagny was chasing after the Ögonen, but they're all crossing the bridge."

"The Ögonen." I sat up so I could see them strolling single file across the ravine. "They're going home and they're going to shut the door behind them."

"What?" Sumi asked.

I looked over to see her. She'd been crouched, but she stood up, her dark eyes intense.

"They told me," I explained. "Or showed me, really. They're going back to Alfheim, and they want to ensure that no one will ever cross again."

"We have to go," she said quietly.

"What?" I asked. "Why do you have to go?"

"Eliana can't stay here," Sumi said. "She's only gotten sicker since she's been here. I promised Senka I'd watch over her, and I promised Jem-Kruk I'd take her home."

"*Jem,*" I echoed, feeling a sharp pang in my chest. Tears filled my eyes when I looked to her. "Did you see . . ."

Sumi swallowed hard and nodded once. "I saw that he's gone."

"I'm sorry," I said thickly. "I know he was a good friend to you."

"I'm sorry for us all." She stared off for a moment, her lips twitching slightly, and her gaze off at some distant point.

"Jem thought of himself as an adventurer above all else," she said finally. "But he was a knight. He wanted to save every injured foundling he met on his travels, and I am forever grateful that he met me.

"I loved him," she went on after a pause. "Not as a lover, but as a brother." Then she looked at me, a strange smile forming and her eyes glistening. "Which was good, because he was still in love with your mother."

"I knew he was very fond of her," I replied uncertainly.

"You have a strong heart like Senka." She breathed in through her nose. "And like Jem. Strong hearts are drawn to one another."

"That explains how you ended up hanging out with us all the time," I said, and she laughed as a tear rolled down her cheek.

She blinked several times, then looked around. "And now I need to be a good friend to Eliana. Have you seen her?"

"I think she's still down underground," Pan said.

Sumi started jogging back toward the stables. "Eliana? El-lie!"

I stood up slowly, and my hip was starting to ache again. Sunniva had warned me that her healing effects wouldn't last long, and it felt like they were starting to wear off.

"Are you okay?" Pan got up and put his arm around my waist—I wasn't sure if it was to steady me or comfort me, but I needed it either way.

"I think so." I nodded. "How about you?"

"I'm alive and you're alive, so I'm not gonna complain right now," he said.

We walked toward the bridge, but the growing pain meant it was slow going, and almost all the Ögonen had made it completely across the bridge. Sumi came running, half dragging Eliana behind her.

"Ulla!" Eliana shouted when she saw me, and she wriggled free from Sumi's grip and ran at me.

"Eliana!" Sumi shouted. "We can't get left behind!"

"I have to say goodbye!" Eliana yelled, and she was crying as she lunged at me. She threw her arms around me, and I hugged her tightly, lifting her off the ground with the last strength that I had.

"I'm sorry I didn't get to know you better," I said.

"I'm happy that I got to know you at all," she sniffled. "Do you think I'll ever see you again?"

"I don't know," I admitted. "But I'll always remember you."

She let go and looked up at me, her bottom lip trembling. "I'll never forget you, Ulla. I promise."

"Eliana!" Sumi yelled, sounding more panicked. "They're going through the waterfall! We have to go *now*!"

"Go," I told her, and Eliana sobbed as she took a step back. "I love you, Eliana."

"I love you, Ulla." And then she turned around and ran to Sumi.

Sumi grabbed her hand and they ran across the bridge. Pan and I stood at the edge watching them go, and when they made it halfway across, the bridge started to collapse. It was a slow rumble, with stones plummeting down into the epic cavern. Sumi and Eliana ran faster, and they barely made it across in time.

Once they made it over, Eliana waved at me once more, and then she and Sumi disappeared into the waterfall.

epilogue

In the weeks that followed the wyrm's devastation of Áib-moráigi, change rippled slowly through the kingdoms. All of the five tribes had suffered severe casualties, and the Älvolk were almost entirely wiped out, with only a handful of children and thrimavolk left to pick up the pieces.

All of the Ögonen had made an exodus back to Alfheim. Even the ones that had been in Merellä. Nobody saw them go—they were there the morning before the wyrm came crashing through, and gone the next.

Underneath the mourning and sadness was a feeling of restlessness and reevaluation. Trolls for so long had thought of ourselves as higher beings, something inherently superior to humans because of the possibilities of our blood. But the Ögonen had used a vision to show the truth to me, and their absence showed the truth to everybody else.

Once, trolls had descended from the *álfar* and humans, but we were now so far removed that we were basically humans ourselves. Only, we had been siphoning magic from the Ögonen, who truly were the powerful beings we only pretended to be.

The issues that the tribes had been facing—the infertility, the weakening of powers, even the deleterious effects that the psychokinetic powers left on us (like Tove's and Wendy's premature aging)—were because we were not meant to have the powers we had. Our bodies were those of humans, but the abilities were stolen from the more powerful Ögonen.

After I told my friends about the vision, Wendy launched an investigation to make sense of what was happening. A long time ago, Frey had helped the Älvolk—he'd had to siphon the Ögonen's power to create such a powerful spell to keep the door to Alfheim closed. But they learned to twist the spell, to drain the power and push it into their children.

The incantation that drained the power and magic from the Ögonen was built on the back of Frey's bridge closure spells. It went on long after anyone even remembered it; even after all trolls moved across the earth, the children of the Älvolk carried the incantation with them. Their blood was tied to a promise that was never theirs.

Now all of the kingdoms were uniting, holding meeting after meeting to discuss what to do, how to handle the impending changes that our world was undergoing. There were talks of destroying the monarchy, since it was based on a faulty premise that certain trolls had been given higher priority than others.

As for me and Pan, we understood even less than ever where we fit into this world. We'd been treated as half-bloods only to learn there was no such thing as a pureblood.

After the battle in Áibmoráigi, I went back to Merellä, to my apartment with Dagny. Although I did spend far more time at Pan's place than I did at hers, and we talked about what we wanted to do and where we wanted to go from here. None of us really felt a calling for the Inhemsk Project, which seemed like a moot point in the face of everything we'd learned.

Dagny decided to stay on at the Mimirin. Regardless of where trollkind goes in the future, she believes it's important to understand our past and our present. She wants to continue working with the Mästares to add to and maintain the knowledge and the history.

Mästare Amalie became the Korva of the Mimirin in the wake of Ragnall's abrupt demise. From what we gathered, she'd been completely in the dark about Ragnall's true allegiance and intentions, and she vowed to put the Mimirin back on course in its pursuit of knowledge.

Elof, meanwhile, didn't follow us back from Áibmoráigi. He was alive and well—thriving, really—helping the survivors, like Noomi, that wanted to stay on to rebuild the First City. He saw it as a chance to restart the city on a better, less cultish track, and he now had unfettered access to all the history he'd been dying to read about all these years.

Finn went back to Förening to be with his family. During our phone calls, Hanna assures me that he's working less now, but that he still advises Wendy and Loki on how to run the Trylle kingdom. Hanna is a huge gossip, and she always gives me an update on how *everybody* in the whole city is doing, but it's good to hear that Tove and Sunniva seem to be happy and doing well, although rumor has it that Sunniva is thinking of traveling with her partner.

Meanwhile, Pan and I spent weeks trying to figure out what we wanted to do with the rest of our lives. Merellä didn't feel like home to me, and Förening was too small with too few options. Pan suggested Ottawa, but I'd never lived with humans before. He said it casually, but that night, when we went to bed, I lay awake thinking about what he said.

"I've just never lived with humans before," I said finally. He was lying on his side, facing me, and he was half asleep, but he blinked and looked at me.

"What are you talking about?"

"Moving to Ottawa," I explained. "I just don't know how I'll feel being around humans all the time."

"You realize that I'm human, right?" he asked. "And you're basically human too?"

"No, it's not that." I rolled over to face him. "I mean I've never lived in the human *world*. It seems more fast-paced and aggressive."

"Sometimes it is," Pan allowed. "But most of the time, it's neither of those things. Unless you live in New York or something."

"Then we should cross those places off our list," I said.

"Wait." He sat up a bit, propping himself up on his elbow. "Are you saying you want to move to a human city?"

"I'm saying that I'm up for it if you are." I smiled at him as nervous butterflies filled my stomach.

"Yes." Pan kissed me. "Let's go for it."

A few days later, I was at the apartment packing things up. Dagny was moving into staff housing at the Mimirin, and Pan and I were getting ready to go out on our own into the world, so we didn't need it anymore.

While I packed up all the misshapen clay mugs the kids had made me, Dagny and Pan were patching the nail holes in the wall and reminiscing about all the delicious food that Hanna had made at the beginning of the summer.

"That feels like a lifetime ago," I said.

"That's what happens when you live several lifetimes in a few months," Dagny replied matter-of-factly.

Someone knocked at the door, and Brueger—who had tagged along to watch us pack—let out a surprised bark.

"It's okay, buddy. I got it." I scratched his head as I went to answer the door.

And there was Ridley Dresden—Bryn's longtime boyfriend—on my front steps. He was pale and a little scruffy, but otherwise he looked about as good as he had the last time I'd seen him. But still, there was a dimness in his eyes that hadn't been there before.

He gave me an uncertain smile, and I pulled him into a hug. I hadn't seen him since . . . Bryn was still alive. As soon as I had my arms around him, he started to cry, and then I did too.

Dagny made us tea, and Pan sat on a steamer trunk and pet Brueger. Ridley and I sat on the lumpy sofa and slowly composed ourselves. It didn't last long, though. We managed some pleasantries about how Ridley's trip down here had been, and then I blurted out, "I'm sorry that I didn't bring her back alive."

He laughed then, even as tears slid down his cheeks. "If she couldn't get herself back alive, then there's nobody else on earth that could've done it. I know she . . ." He paused. "She did what she thought was the right thing to do, and nothing could move her from that course.

"And I know that she'd be happy that she died the way she lived—protecting those she loved," Ridley went on, and his dark eyes rested warmly on me. "She loved you, you know. She was so upset when she found out that Indu might be her father, but she was . . . she was so excited about gaining you as a sister."

"We weren't really," I said. "Indu wasn't my father, so we weren't sisters."

He reached over and put his hand on mine. "Yes, you were."

"Thank you for saying that," I sniffled.

"Actually, that's why I'm here." He let go of my hand and reached into the messenger bag he'd carried with him, and he pulled out papers. "Bryn really did consider you family, and you know she always wanted to take care of her family. One of the benefits of being a guard to the King is that the palace awards your family a large insurance payout if you die."

"What?" I glanced over at Dagny, but she only shrugged. "What are you saying?"

He held a paper out to me. "Bryn named you and me as her primary beneficiaries. You can see for yourself."

"What?" I repeated even as I took the paper with trembling hands. It was a short letter with the Kanin seal at the top and the King's signature at the bottom. After a paragraph of condolences about Bryn's bravery and all the honors she'd been awarded in her service to the kingdom—in service to others—the benefits were explained.

"A million dollars?" I asked quietly, disbelieving. "This can't be right." I looked up at Ridley with fresh guilty tears springing into my eyes. "No, I can't. I can't take this. I don't deserve it."

"Ulla, you haven't done anything wrong," Ridley assured me. "This is a gift for you, from Bryn. That's your share, and that's what she wanted you to have."

"But . . ." My heart was racing, and I felt too light for my body, like I might just float away in the sky. Somehow I stayed on the couch, gaping at Ridley. "What do I do with it?"

"You do what Bryn would want you to do." He smiled at me. "You *live*."

New tenants would be moving into the apartment over the weekend, so we worked our butts off and managed to have the place ready by Thursday afternoon. "It's so weird," I said as I surveyed the empty apartment above the carriage house. "It looks so much bigger without the furniture."

"So does my place," Pan reminded me.

We'd mostly emptied his apartment—either giving away or selling most of the furniture, and we'd put some stuff in a storage space above his friend Hugo's garage. All that we had left was an air mattress and the things we were taking on the road with us. There were a few more things we needed to get in order, but if all went well, we'd be leaving Monday morning and heading out across the world to see where we wanted to live. We'd start with North America, since it was easier traveling with an active dog like Brueger by car than by plane.

But we didn't know where we'd end up, and that filled me with such wonderful excitement. I had spent so much of my childhood reading Mr. Tulin's nature magazines, imagining all the places I could visit and all the lives I could lead.

And now Pan and I were about to actually go off and lead the lives we'd only hoped for.

"Are you ready for all of this?" I asked him.

"Yeah." He came over and looped an arm around my shoulders. "Aren't you?"

"Yeah." I surveyed the apartment one last time, the high open ceilings and the beams I had seen Eliana do acrobatics on, the loft where I had talked to Jem about my mother, the living room where Dagny had become my best friend, where I spent my last happy memories with Bryn.

And then from the ceiling beam, I spotted a big fat spider hanging from a long thread.

"There's a giant spider up there." I pointed to it.

"Oh yeah," Pan said. "Looks like the new tenants are moving in early. That probably means we should head out."

"You're right," I agreed. "It's time to move on."

He kissed me. "On to our new chapter."

"On to our happily ever after."

GLOSSARY

Adlrivellir—the name of a legendary land.

Áibmoráigi—the oldest troll establishment on earth. It is located somewhere in Scandinavia, but its exact location has been lost since before 1000 CE. Frequently referred to as the "First City."

akutaq—a traditional Inuit food often referred to as "Eskimo ice cream." It is not creamy ice cream as we know it, but a concoction made from reindeer fat or tallow, seal oil, freshly fallen snow or water, fresh berries, and sometimes ground fish. It is whipped together by hand so that it slowly cools into foam.

álfar—name given to the trolls from the legendary kingdom of Alfheim.

Alfheim—a mythological realm. To humans, the legend is that it is one of the Nine Worlds and home of the Light Elves in Norse mythology. To trolls, the legend is that it is a utopian kingdom hidden across the Lost Bridge of Dimma.

Älvolk—a legendary group of monk-like trolls, who guard the Lost Bridge of Dimma, along with many troll secrets and artifacts.

angakkuq—an Inuit word that roughly translates to "shaman" or "witch."

ärtsoppa—a Scandinavian soup made of yellow peas, carrots, and onions. Traditional versions have ham, but vegetarian trolls skip that.

aster—a flower in the daisy family, usually purple or pink.

attack on Oslinna—a surprise military attack by the Vittra on the small Trylle village of Oslinna, Wyoming, during the War for the Princess. It left the city destroyed since January 2010.

attempted assassination of Chancellor Iver—the attempt on the life of the Kanin Chancellor Iver Aven by the Queen's guard Konstantin Black in January 2010. It was an attack unrelated to the War for the Princess. It was eventually tied to Viktor Dålig and his coup against the Kanin monarchy that lasted over a decade and ended in the Invasion of Doldastam.

aura—a field of subtle luminous radiation surrounding a person or object. Different colors of auras denote different emotional qualities as well as physical or psychokinetic ailments.

Aurenian Ballroom—a grand ballroom in the Mimirin named after the old Vittra King Auren.

bardiche—a pole weapon common in medieval Europe. It has a long, cleaver-like blade attached to a pole, making it something like a cross between an axe and a spear.

Battle for the Bridge—a legendary battle over the Lost Bridge of Dimma that took place in Áibmoráigi over a thousand years ago. In old myths, it is known as the Vígríðabifröst.

Bay of Bothnia—the northernmost part of the Gulf of Bothnia, which is in turn the northern part of the Baltic Sea. The bay today is fed by several large rivers and is relatively unaffected by tides, so it has low salinity. It freezes each year for up to six months.

beetroot salad—a common Scandinavian dish. It is traditionally made with diced beetroots, apples, vinegar, herbs, olive oil, red onions, yogurt, and lemon zest.

binrassi—a word in Irytakki meaning "small flower."

blodseider magick—a type of taboo occult practice in extremist troll sects. The practice of *seiðr* is believed to be a form of magic relating to both the telling and shaping of the future.

Candida viridi—a fungal infection that afflicts trolls, similar to *Candida auris* in humans. The differences are that *C. viridi* is hearty enough to thrive in cold temperatures and that it leaves a greenish tint to the skin of the affected individuals. The fungus causes invasive candidiasis infections in the bloodstream, the central nervous system, and internal organs. With modern medicine it is easily curable, but without proper treatment it is often deadly. Troll historians believe that *C. viridi* is what caused the Green Death (Grændöden) in the thirteenth century, which wiped out most of the trolls that remained in Scandinavia.

Catacombs of Fables—a mazelike vault in the basement of the Mimirin that houses many of the fictional stories of the past, so as not to confuse fact with fiction.

changeling—a child secretly exchanged for another. For trolls, it's an ancient practice, with elite royal families leaving their babies in place of wealthy human babies. The humans unknowingly raise the troll baby, ensuring that the troll will have the best chance of success, with fine education, top health care, and rights to tremendous wealth. When they are of age, they are retrieved by trolls known as trackers, and the changelings are brought back to live with their tribes in their kingdom. The Trylle and the Kanin are the only two tribes that still widely practice changelings.

Churchill, Manitoba—a small human town in Canada. One must stop in Churchill if venturing to either Doldastam, Manitoba, or Iqaluit, Nunavut, and it may be the easiest way to get to Iskyla, Nunavut, as well.

cloudberry—an herb native to alpine and arctic regions, producing amber-colored edible fruit similar to the raspberry or blackberry. It is commonly used in Scandinavian pies and jams.

Dålig Revolt—the uprising that took place after the unmarried Kanin King Elliot Strinne died unexpectedly in 1999 without a clear heir. The Chancellor appointed Elliot's cousin

Evert Strinne to the throne, overlooking Elliot's sister Sybilla and her three daughters. Sybilla and her husband, Viktor Dålig, contested Evert's appointment, and they staged a revolt that left four men dead. The Dålig family was exiled.

docent—a member of the teaching staff immediately below professorial rank. In the U.S., it is often a volunteer position, but it can be paid or done in exchange for room and board. At the Mimirin, docents are paid a minimal stipend in addition to room and board.

dödstämpel—a form of martial arts practiced by trolls. The name means "death punch" in Swedish.

Doldastam, Manitoba—the capital and largest city of the Kanin kingdom, located in Manitoba, Canada, near Hudson Bay. The Kanin royal family lives in the palace there, and the city is surrounded by a stone wall. The population is a little over twelve thousand as of 2019.

dragon—a mythical monster like a giant reptile. It has a total of six limbs—two wings and four legs. It often breathes fire. "Dragon" is sometimes used as a general broad term for other mythical reptiles, including wyrms, wyverns, drakes, and amphipteres.

Eftershom, Montana—a small Trylle village located in the mountains near Missoula. It is nestled in the convergence of several mountain ranges in western Montana. The terrain is notoriously rough and the winters are brutal. When it was originally settled by the Trylle, a Markis asked "Why do we stop here?" And the leader answered, *"Eftersom vi har gått* *tillräckligt långt,"* which roughly translates to "Because we have gone far enough."

ekkálfar—an old term used for "troll."

eldvatten—a very strong alcohol made by the Omte. The name literally translates to "firewater." It is also known as Omte moonshine, and it is used in Omte sangria.

ex nihilo nihil fit—a Latin phrase meaning "nothing comes from nothing." It is the motto of the Mimirin.

First City, the—See *Áibmoráigi.*

fluorspar—a crystal that comes in many colors, including purple, blue, and green; more commonly known as "fluorite" outside of the troll communities. It is believed to help with memory when used in crystal healing.

Förening, Minnesota—the capital and largest city of the Trylle kingdom. It is a compound in the bluffs along the Mississippi River in Minnesota where the palace is located.

Förening Tertiary Educational Center—a post-secondary institution in Förening that specializes in trades and apprenticeships, aimed at non-changeling Trylle and *mänsklig*. It offers licensures in nursing, woodworking, culinary arts, veterinary medicine, and teaching, among many others.

Forsa River—the river that runs through Merellä. It is a wide stream that slices the city in half and meets the ocean. The name means "rushing stream."

Frey—a mythological figure. To humans, he is known as the legendary Norse deity of virility and fair weather. To trolls, he is a troll from Alfheim who stayed behind to help rebuild their kingdom after the Battle for the Bridge. He is a prominent figure in the Älvolk cult known as the Freyarian Älvolk.

Freyarian Älvolk—the followers of the Älvolk who began following the more extreme teachings of Frey. See *Frey*.

fúinn muitit—an incantation used by the Älvolk to cause slow memory decay over time. It is a phrase from Irytakki meaning "rotting memory."

Fulaträsk, Louisiana—the capital city of the Omte, spread out in the trees and swamps of the Atchafalaya Basin in Louisiana.

gädda—the Swedish name for pike. See *northern pike*.

geitvaktmann—a goat watchman, similar to a shepherd or a peurojen.

giant woolly elk—a name that trolls have given the line of Irish elk they breed. See *Irish elk*.

girjastu—the Älvolk word for "library."

gräddtårta—a Swedish cream-layer cake. Common during Midsommar.

Grændöden—a plague. See *Green Death*.

Green Death, The—a mass death in the thirteenth-century of Scandinavian trolls. Troll historians believe that it was an outbreak of *C. viridi*.

häxdoktor—a medicine man for the Älvolk.

hnefatafl—a family of ancient Nordic and Celtic strategy games played on a checkered or latticed game board with two armies of uneven numbers.

hobgoblin—an ugly troll that stands no more than three feet tall, known only to the Vittra tribes. They are distinct from Vittra trolls with more humanoid features and attractive appearance who have dwarfism. Hobgoblins are slow-witted, possess a supernatural strength, and have slimy skin with a pimply complexion.

host family—the family that a changeling is left with. They are chosen based on their ranking in human society, with their wealth being the primary consideration. The higher-ranked the member of troll society, the more powerful and affluent the host family their changeling is left with.

hrudda—a word in Irytakki meaning "hurry."

Hudson Bay—a large bay in Canada. Doldastam is located on the Manitoba side, with Iqaluit across the bay on the Nunavut side.

Information Styrelse—a committee in charge of information (similar to a board of education) in the Mimirin. These boards are subordinate only to their members and the Korva, and they preside over the Mästares and the teaching staff (including docents). The name comes from the Swedish word *styrelse,* meaning "board of directors." The word *information* is the same in both Swedish and English. Each of these boards has thirteen members.

Inhemsk Project—an effort undertaken by the Mimirin in Merellä to help trolls of mixed blood find their place in the troll world. Though it is primarily run by the Vittra, it is open to trolls from any of the five tribes. The main purpose is to combat the dwindling populations of the trolls (due both to issues like infertility among the Vittra and Skojare, as well as changelings choosing to live among the humans or being exiled because of their mixed race). The effort also seeks to reconnect trolls with their heritage and pass along history and culture.

inovotto muitit—an incantation meaning "never remember." The Älvolk use it to erase memories.

Invasion of Doldastam—the final battle in the Kanin Civil War that ended the war in May 2014. The Dålig supporters were led by Viktor and Karmin Dålig allied with the Kanin guards and the Omte, and the Strinne supporters were led by Bryn Aven and Mikko Biâelse allied with the Skojare, Trylle, Vittra, and many of the Kanin townsfolk. The Strinne supporters were victorious in the Invasion of Doldastam, and the invasion ended with the traitors being executed and Linus Berling coronated as the King of the Kanin.

Iqaluit, Nunavut—the capital city of Canada's northernmost province. It has a large Inuit population, but most residents can speak English. Despite being the largest city in Nunavut, it has a population of only around seven thousand. Nunavut has no roads connecting the towns to one another, and it is only accessible by plane, usually by flying in from Winnipeg or Churchill in Manitoba.

Irish elk—a species of deer believed to be extinct; also known as the giant deer. It is believed to be one of the largest species of deer, but humans hunted them to extinction in the wild thousands of years ago. The Vittra have been secretly breeding and raising them, and they are known as "giant woolly elk" or "woollies." They stand about 2.1 meters tall at the shoulders, carrying the largest antlers of any known cervid, and they can weigh over fifteen hundred pounds.

Irytakki—a language spoken only by *álfar* and the Älvolk. It is a blend of the native Alfheim language and Nordic languages.

Isarna, Sweden—an island and village in the Kalix archipelago in the Bay of Bothnia in Sweden. It is a Trylle/Skojare co-op, and the largest—and essentially only—troll settlement in Scandinavia, and is accessible only by ferry or boat. The name means "islands of ice." The nearest human settlement is Nikkala, on mainland Sweden.

Iskyla, Nunavut—a small Kanin village, it is one of the northernmost troll communities in the world. Some Inuit humans also live there. It has become a dumping ground for unwanted babies. The name translates to "ice." In 2014, Iskyla had a population of 878.

Jakob W. Rells University of Parapsychology and Medicine—a university in Seattle, Washington. Rells University is renowned for paranormal and scientific studies, and is sometimes referred to as the Harvard of parapsychology.

It was established by renowned telekinetic expert and medical doctor Jakob W. Rells in 1889. Rells presented as human, but he is suspected to have been from the Trylle kingdom.

jallaki—a word in Irytakki meaning "foolish."

Juni's Jubilant Confectionery—a bakery in Doldastam, owned and operated by Juni Sköld.

Kalix Skärgård—a group of 792 Swedish islands in the north part of the Bay of Bothnia. *Skärgård* literally means "archipelago" or "string of islands" in Swedish. A few of the islands have small permanent populations, but most are used only for recreation in the summer months. They are icebound during the winter.

Kanin—one of the most powerful of the five troll tribes. They are considered quiet and dogmatic. They are known for their ability to blend in, and, like chameleons, their skin can change color to help them blend in to their surroundings. Like the Trylle, they still practice changelings, but not nearly as frequently. Only one in ten of their offspring are left as changelings. The Kanin are also the oldest tribe of trolls, having been the original troll tribe before the brothers Norund the Younger and Jorund the Elder fought about moving south in circa 1200 CE. Norund stayed in the north, strengthening the Kanin in Doldastam, while his brother went south and established the Vittra in Ondarike.

Karelian Piiraka—a Finnish rye pastry. Rye-crusted, handheld pies with rice porridge as the most common filling, but a mix of root vegetables as filling is a frequent variation.

kasteren axe—a small hatchet with curved blades, similar to an ulu knife, with a long, slender handle. Used in the game of *økkspill*. The name means "thrower."

Kebnekaise—the highest mountain in Sweden. The Kebnekaise massif, which is part of the Scandinavian Mountains, has two main peaks, of which the southern, glaciated one is highest at 2,097.5 meters (6,882 feet) above sea level as of August 2014. The mountain is in Swedish Lapland, about 150 kilometers (93 miles) north of the Arctic Circle.

klampiveleska—an *álfar* term for spouse or life partner; the literal translation is "the one you fondly choose to be joined with."

Korva—a title for the Mimirin dean. The name means "crown." The Korva is the highest position in the Mimirin.

Lake Sodalen—an elongated mountain lake in the valley of the Kiruna municipality in the Swedish Lapland. In summer, boat traffic runs on the lake. The name means "valley lake."

leat fámus—an incantation meaning "to be open" in Irytakki.

Lost Bridge of Dimma—a legendary bridge in troll mythology—akin to the city of Atlantis or the Hanging Gardens of Babylon—that is watched over by the Älvolk. The bridge was alleged to have connected the ancient troll city Áibmoráigi to the utopian kingdom of Alfheim, and it was believed to have collapsed before the end of the Viking Age (circa 1000 CE). The bridge was lost and the First City of Áibmoráigi was destroyed during the Battle for the Bridge, also known as Vígríðabifröst.

lysa—a telekinetic ability related to astral projection that allows one troll to psychically enter another troll's thoughts through a vision, usually a dream.

mänsklig—often shortened to *mänks*. The literal translation for the word *mänsklig* is "human," but it has come to describe the human child that is taken when the Trylle offspring is left behind.

Markis—a title of male royalty in troll society. Similar to the title of Duke, it's given to trolls with superior bloodlines and their correlating telekinetic abilities. Markis have a higher ranking than the average troll, but are beneath the King and Queen. The hierarchy of troll society is as follows: King/Queen; Prince/Princess; Markis/Marksinna; Högdragen; troll citizens; trackers; *mänsklig*; host families; humans (not raised in troll society).

Markis and the Shadow, The—a troll reinterpretation of the Danish fairy tale *Skyggen* (in English, *The Shadow*).

Markis Ansvarig—a position of authority in troll communities, similar to a mayor or chieftain. Literal translation is "Markis-in-charge." It is a position used in cities without any major royals, like King/Queen or Prince/Princess. The female equivalent would be Marksinna Ansvariga.

Marksinna—a title of female royalty in troll society. The female equivalent of the Markis.

Mästare—the title given to prestigious department heads at the Mimirin.

Merellä, Oregon—a large, affluent citadel in Oregon. It is technically under the Vittra rule, but many trolls from tribes all over live there. It is virtually a metropolis compared to most troll towns and villages, and it is essentially a college town built around the Mimirin Talo institution and library. The name means "by the sea." It is one of the oldest cities in North America, having been colonized after the trolls came over with the Vikings. Trolls first arrived in North America in early 1000 CE, and the trolls began moving west to get away from the violence of the Vikings. They settled Merellä around 1400 CE. It remains hidden with powerful cloaking spells by the Ögonen.

Midsommar—a trollized version of the festival "Midsommarafton" or "Midsummer's Eve." It is a summer festival, celebrating the end of the long winter, with flowers, greenery, and maypoles.

Mimirin, the—the great institution and library that holds much of the history of the trolls, located in the city of Merellä. The full official name is "Mimirin Talo," which means "House of Mimir," a reference to Mimir, the Norse god of knowledge and remembering. The Vittra were inspired by the Museum in Alexandria to build the Mimirin hundreds of years ago.

Mörkaston, Nevada—a Vittra city located near Ruby Dome in northeastern Nevada. The name is an anglicized version of *mörkaste höjden,* which means "darkest point."

mourning flower—See *sorgblomma.*

nettle—a stinging herbaceous plant common in Scandinavia. Nettles lose their sting when cooked and can be used in lieu of spinach or any other leafy green. Nettles can also be used dried and brewed as a tea.

Ningrava, Newfoundland—a Kanin village located in Newfoundland, Canada. The name is a shortened version of *kanin grava*, meaning "rabbit burrow."

Norra av Nord—a restaurant on Lake Sodalen in Sweden. The name means "Norra of the North" in Swedish, after its owner Norra.

northern pike—a species of carnivorous fish common in the brackish and fresh waters of the Northern Hemisphere, including the U.S. and Sweden. Pike can grow to a relatively large size, with European versions being the largest. Known as northerns and pike in Minnesota, and *gädda* in Sweden.

Ögonen—the trollian guardians who use their powerful psychokinesis to hide the city of Merellä from humans. They are not considered to be part of any tribe and are almost considered to be something of another species. Their name means "eyes." They are described as sinewy and nearly seven feet tall. They are covered in leathery, ochre skin, but it's so thin it's slightly transparent. They are androgynous, with very humanoid dark brown eyes.

ogre—ogres are similar to hobgoblins, except they are giant, most standing over seven feet tall, with superior strength. They are dim-witted and aggressive, and they are known only to the Omte tribes.

Öhaus—the proper name given to the town hall of Isarna. The name means "island house."

økkspill—a game similar to darts. The name literally means "axe games." It involves a board with three bull's-eyes—in white, black, and gold, respectively—and five kasteren axes.

Omte—one of the smaller troll kingdoms, only slightly more populous than the Skojare. Omte trolls are known to be rude and somewhat ill-tempered. They still practice changelings but pick lower class families than the Trylle and Kanin. Unlike the other tribes, Omte tend to be less attractive in appearance. The Omte split off from the Vittra tribe in circa 1280 CE, when Dag felt like the Vittra favored the smaller hobgoblins and more conventionally attractive "humanoid" trolls. He took the ogres and established the tribe in Fulaträsk. Since 1280 CE, they have had forty monarchs—much more than any other tribe. The high turnover rate among Omte monarchs is due to their violent lifestyle, compromised immune systems, and lower intelligence. They are currently in the Torian Dynasty, with the widowed Queen Regent Bodil Elak ruling until her son Crown Prince Furston Elak comes of age in 2028.

Ondarike, Colorado—the capital city of the Vittra. The Queen and the majority of the powerful Vittra live within the palace there. It is located in northern Colorado, near Walden in the mountains.

Oslinna, Wyoming—a Trylle village that was decimated by the Vittra in 2010, but it has been slowly rebuilding. It is near Gillette, Wyoming.

Ottawa, Ontario—the capital city of Canada, located in eastern Ontario. It is the second most populous city in Ontario.

Överste—a position in the Kanin military. In times of war, the Överste is the officer in charge of commanding the soldiers. The Överste does not decide any battle plans, but instead receives orders from the King or the Chancellor.

persuasion—a mild form of psychokinesis that enables weak mind control. The ability to cause another person to act a certain way based on thoughts.

peurojen—the one in charge of the giant woolly elk, similar to a shepherd.

precognition—a form of psychokinesis that is knowledge of something before its occurrence, especially by extrasensory perception.

psionic—referring to the practical use of psychic powers or paranormal phenomena.

psionic stun gun (PSG)—a weapon similar to a Taser or stun gun, but instead of electricity, it runs on psionic power.

psychokinesis—a blanket term for the production or control of motion, especially in inanimate and remote objects, purportedly by the exercise of psychic powers. This can include mind control, precognition, telekinesis, biological healing, teleportation, and transmutation.

Rektor—the Kanin in charge of trackers. The Rektor works with new recruits, helps with placement, and generally keeps the trackers organized and functioning.

rose hip soup—a soup common in Sweden, with a deep rosy color and sweet-tart tang. Rose hips, which ripen long after the rose blooms have faded, can be dried to enjoy all year and serve as an important source of vitamin C in northern countries.

sage—an aromatic herb with lavender flowers. It is often used in herbalism and believed to have benefits relating to memory.

Sámi—the indigenous peoples of the Arctic Circle in Scandinavia. They have lived in arctic and subarctic regions for over 3,500 years. Also known as Sami, Saami, Fenni, Laplanders, or Lapps. They have historically had an appearance similar to Inuit and other First Nation peoples.

semla—a Scandinavian sweet roll made of wheat bread, whipped cream, and almond paste. It is similar to a cream puff.

Sintvann, North Carolina—an Omte city located in the Great Dismal Swamp in North Carolina. The name means "angry waters."

Skojare—the aquatic tribe of trolls that is nearly extinct. They require large amounts of fresh water to survive, and one-third of their population possess gills and are able to breathe underwater. Once plentiful, only about five thousand Skojare are left on the entire planet. In circa 1300 CE, Aun the Blue broke off from the Kanin tribe, heading south from Doldastam for a warmer water source. He took all the gilled trolls with him and established the Skojare in Storvatten. They have had twenty-four monarchs since 1300 CE, and they are currently in the Rolfian Dynasty, with King Mikko Rune. His daughter, the Crown Princess Lisbet "Libby" Biâelse, is next in line for the throne.

Sommar plum—a vibrant fleshy fruit in the rose family. The skin is deep violet with white speckles, giving it a cosmic appearance similar to a black diamond apple, and the fruit itself is especially sweet and juicy.

sorgblomma—a flower similar to the *smörboll*, with bold golden petals that are bloodred near the stem. The plant "bleeds" a reddish viscous liquid (similar to aloe in texture and taste) and has thorns. It is also known as the mourning flower and *trollius funus*.

sounding horn—a sound device that is usually made of or shaped like an animal horn.

Storvatten, Ontario—the capital and largest city of the Skojare, it is home to the palace and the Skojare royal family. It is situated on Lake Superior, not too far from Thunder Bay, Ontario, with a population of just over fifteen hundred in 2019.

Sverige—the name for Sweden in Swedish.

thrimavolk (or Þrimavolk)—a secret group of female warriors belonging to the Älvolk. The thrimavolk are theoretically the female counterpart to the Älvolk, and they are all the daughters of Älvolk.

Tonåren—in the Skojare society, a time when teenagers seek to explore the human world and escape the isolation of Storvatten. Most teens return home within a few weeks. Similar to Rumspringa.

Tower of Avanor—the tower in the Mimirin where the lineage and ancestry records are stored.

tracker—a member of troll society who is specifically trained to track down changelings and bring them home. Trackers have no paranormal abilities, other than the affinity to tune in to their particular changeling. They are able to sense danger to their charge and can determine the distance between them. The lowest form of troll society, other than *mänsklig*.

Tralla horse—a powerful draft horse, larger than a Shire horse or a Clydesdale, originating in Scandinavia and only known to be bred amongst the Kanin. Once used as a workhorse because they could handle the cold and snow, now they are usually used for show, such as in parades or during celebrations.

triskelion—a symbol consisting of three lines radiating from a center.

troglecology—a branch of biology in the Mimirin devoted to studying the relationships between trolls and the environment around them and with each other. It is derived from the words *troglodyte* (Latin for "troll") and *ecology* (branch of biology dealing with the relationships of organisms with their environment and with each other).

trollius funus—genus name of *sorgblomma*. See *sorgblomma*.

troll of mixed blood (TOMB)—any troll that has parents that are not of the same tribe. This includes both full-TOMBs (both parents are trolls) and half-TOMBs (one parent is a troll, one parent is human). By using People First Language, it is more inclusive and socially acceptable compared to *half-breed*, *half-blood*, or *halvblud*. There are fifteen distinct types of TOMBs (ten full-TOMBs, five half-TOMBs). They are as follows:

KanHu (Kanin & Human)

KanOm (Kanin & Omte)

OmHu (Omte & Human)

OmTry (Omte & Trylle)

Omttra (Omte & Vittra)

SkoHu (Skojare & Human)

Skomte (Skojare & Omte)

Skonin (Skojare & Kanin)

SkoTry (Skojare & Trylle)

TryHu (Trylle & Human)

Trynin (Trylle & Kanin)

VittHu (Vittra & Human)

Vittjare (Vittra & Skojare)

VittKa (Vittra & Kanin)

Vittrylle (Vittra & Trylle)

Trylle—the beautiful trolls with powers of psychokinesis for whom the practice of changelings is a cornerstone of their society. Like all trolls, they are ill-tempered and cunning, and often selfish. They were once plentiful, but their numbers and abilities are fading, though they are still one of the largest tribes of trolls. They are considered peaceful. The Trylle became a tribe in 1510 CE, when Aldaril became fed up with the inept Kanin King Harald. He went south, taking many wealthy nobles with him, and established the Trylle in Förening along the Mississippi River. They have had twenty-one monarchs since 1510 CE, and they are currently in the Mógilian Dynasty, with Queen Wendy Staad. Her son, Crown Prince Oliver Staad, is next in line for the throne.

Trylle Toy Shoppe—a store in Förening that sells handcrafted toys for children.

tupilaq—an Inuit word meaning "witch" or "shaman."

Ugly Vulture, the—a roughneck Omte bar in their capital city, Fulaträsk.

ullaakuut—an Inuit word that means "good morning."

ungblod—a term referring to the generation of Älvolk that came of age in the 1960s, under the rise of the Freyarian Älvolk. The children of *ungblod* are called *ungbaba* (singular) and *ungbabar* (plural).

valknut—a symbol sometimes known as the "warrior knot." It consists of three interlocked triangles, and it's frequently seen on Norse artifacts.

varrarassi—a name used for the *sorgblomma* by the Sami people. See *sorgblomma*.

veloma—an *álfar* term for boy-/girlfriend or significant other; the literal translation is "the one you fondly choose to be with."

Viliätten—House of Vili, the oldest troll dynasty. See *Vilings Dynasty*.

Vilinga Saga—the document that explains the lineage of the troll monarchy that Ulla is archiving. The opening lines of the saga are as follows: *One war-king called Vili; with his House of Vilings, went to the Western Lands, to conquer all that they would find.*

Vilings Dynasty—the oldest dynasty in troll history. It is the only dynasty of the united kingdom of trolls. It ran from circa 770 CE with Vili in Áibmoráigi, Scandinavia, and ended with the feuding brothers Jorund the Elder of the Vittra in North America and Norund the Younger of the Kanin in the already established Doldastam, in circa 1200 CE. In circa 1040 CE, Asa the Cold and many of the trolls fled from Scandinavia out of fear of the war on paganism. They sailed with Vikings over to North America and relocated the troll capital from Áibmoráigi to Doldastam.

Vittra—a more violent faction of trolls whose powers lie in physical strength and longevity, although some mild psychokinesis is not unheard-of. They also suffer from idiopathic infertility, with increased frequency in the past century. While Vittra are generally beautiful in appearance, more than fifty percent of their offspring are born as hobgoblins, and a quarter of their attractive populations are born with dwarfism. The Vittra are one of the oldest tribes, having been the first one to split off from the Kanin in circa 1200 CE, when feuding brothers Norund the Younger and Jorund the Elder disagreed about staying in the north. Jorund went south, establishing the Vittra in Ondarike. He took all of the strong, less attractive trolls with him, leading to the eventual creation of ogres and hobgoblins. In circa 1280 CE, Dag broke off from the Vittra, fearing they were favoring the hobgoblins and more attractive "humanoid" trolls. He led the ogres down to Fulaträsk and established the Omte. Despite being the second oldest tribe, the Vittra have had the fewest monarchs, in large part due to their supernatural longevity. They have had twenty-one monarchs since their establishment in circa 1200 CE, and they are currently in the Sarafina Dynasty with Queen Sara Elsing.

War for the Princess—a 2009–2010 violent conflict between the Vittra and the Trylle over their shared heir, then Crown Princess Wendy Luella Dahl. Wendy chose to be with the Trylle, and after her coronation as Queen, the Trylle attacked the Vittra and defeated them with the execution of their King, Oren Elsing.

Wisteria & Whimsy Bed & Breakfast—an inn in Trylle, owned and operated by Birdie Vinstock.

withania root—a root in the nightshade family; more commonly known as ashwagandha. It is believed to help with memory.

wolfram—a silvery-white heavy metal with a very high melting point; more commonly known as *tungsten* outside of the troll communities.

woollies—another name for the "giant woolly elk." See *Irish elk*.

wyrm—a mythical limbless and wingless dragon or dragonlike creature. It often flies and/or breathes fire.

wyvern—a mythical winged dragon or dragonlike creature. It has a total of four limbs—two wings and two legs. It often breathes fire.

Yggammi Tree Inn—a treetop hotel in Fulaträsk, Louisiana, built on a trio of Southern live oaks.